Leaves of Fortune

LINDA BARLOW

LEAVES OF FORTUNE

Doubleday

NEW YORK LONDON TORONTO SYDNEY AUCKLAND

Excerpt from "The Choice" reprinted with permission of Macmillan Publishing Company from *Collected Poems* by William Butler Yeats. Copyright 1933 by Macmillan Publishing Company, renewed 1961 by Bertha Georgie Yeats.

Excerpt from "Spring and Fall: To a Young Child" reprinted with permission of Oxford University Press from *The Poems of Gerard Manley Hopkins,* Fourth Edition, edited by W. H. Gardner and N. H. Mackenzie.

Excerpt from "The Love Song of J. Alfred Prufrock" reprinted with permission of Harcourt Brace Jovanovich, Inc., from *Collected Poems 1909–1962* by T. S. Eliot.

Published by Doubleday, a division of
Bantam Doubleday Dell Publishing Group, Inc.,
666 Fifth Avenue, New York, New York 10103

Doubleday and the portrayal of an anchor with a dolphin
are trademarks of Doubleday, a division of
Bantam Doubleday Dell Publishing Group, Inc.

Library of Congress Cataloging-in-Publication Data

Barlow, Linda.
Leaves of fortune.

I. Title.
PS3552.A67255L43 1988 813'.54 87-30506
ISBN 0-385-23385-X

PRINTED IN THE UNITED STATES OF AMERICA
FIRST EDITION
SEPTEMBER 1988

BG

To my parents, Babs and Bob Barlow, for sharing with me their love of tea and of India.

And to my husband, Halûk, and our daughter, Dilek, for everything . . .

PART ONE

Thank God for tea! What would the world do without tea? —how did it exist? I am glad I was not born before tea.

—Sydney Smith

PROLOGUE

THE CHINA TEA HOUSE TAVERN

BOSTON, 1730

Helen Templeton lifted the China porcelain cup to her lips and sipped. Slightly smoky, the tea ran hot over her tongue and warmed her throat as it went down. Souchong from China. Bitter and strong, the drink would give her clarity of mind and fortify her will.

All was in readiness—the altar, the herbs and ointments, the white robes, the black-handled dagger, the caldron, and the ivory chalice. Through the small window opposite her narrow bed, Helen could see the moon riding the night sky. It seemed an auspicious sign that the full moon should fall this year upon May Day Eve, the ancient festival of Beltane.

Downstairs in the tavern, all was still. Even the rowdiest patrons had left off drinking and sought their beds. Outside in the busy commercial district that had mushroomed around her once-isolated hillside house, there was no sound but the distant chiming of a solitary clock. The racket from the boatyards ceased at night, the otherwise endless hammering of the shipwrights who had made Boston one of the primary shipbuilding centers of the New World. By day Helen could look from her hill—Mt. Whoredom, as it was sometimes known—upon the masts and spires of merchantmen that came to the city from Europe, the West Indies, even as far away as China. There had been a time when she'd invested heavily in the China traders who imported the tea she needed for her business, a time when their fate at the hands of the fierce gods of wind and of sea had kept her awake nights, fretting. But that was over now. There was naught left for Helen to do but drink the stuff.

She stooped to sketch the chalk circle. Nine feet in diameter, it had to be; Helen had paced it off earlier. There was just enough room, with the bed and the handwoven rugs pushed back against the walls, for the ring to fit.

The work was slow, for her slender, long-fingered hands, once the objects of such vanity, were gnarled and stiffened now. Her muscles were stringy and uncooperative, her neck and shoulders ached from bending over, and her thighs screamed with the strain of bearing her weight, slight though it was. She coughed as her heart rose to her throat in that now familiar pattern of rapid, arrhythmic pulses. There was pain sometimes, too. A burning pressure radiating from beneath her breastbone, often accompanied by an aching in her jaw and a glimmer of light behind her eyelids, as if a door were opening somewhere, then slowly closing.

It was possible that she would die this night. Times without number, she had seen herself dying in this manner, in this room. But the visions might be in error. Nothing, the Wisdom taught, was fixed. The material world was a place of probability, uncertainty.

Helen took one final sip of tea and began to change her garments. Some said it was necessary to perform the rituals skyclad, but Helen smiled at the notion of her naked body finding favor with the Goddess. Years ago, perhaps.

"Look at yourself, Mistress Templeton—a silly old woman in your sixty-ninth year with aching bones and a weakened heart still practicing the ancient arts that nearly got you hanged forty years ago. This blasted sense of adventure is going to kill you yet!"

The smile became a laugh, and her laughter still had the power to transform her aged face and make her young again. She donned the white linen robe she'd embroidered herself, cinching it around her waist with the scarlet cingulum, painstakingly plaited of purest China silk. Then she assembled her various articles and implements inside the chalk circle.

Her altar was a sturdy tea chest. Upon it she set two white candles and, between them, bowls of salt and water to represent the elements. Her caldron, a brass teakettle, contained the herbal drug; her chalice, an ivory drinking horn, held enough watered wine to ease the bitter mixture down.

She took a handful of salt from the bowl and sprinkled it on the floor. Barefoot, she stood upon the salt and lit the votive candles. She dipped her fingers in the bowl of water and anointed her forehead, eyelids, mouth, breasts, thighs, knees, and ankles, asking, as she touched each spot, for the Goddess's protection. Over and over she chanted, "Blessed be."

Taking the chalice, she dipped it into the kettle and filled it with the herbal brew. Raising both hands high, she gallantly toasted the moon, then put the chalice to her lips. There was death in the brew. Death and power. For one she might pay with the other. A fair exchange, if the power worked.

She drank, then waited, uncertain what to expect. Never before had she taken so strong a dose. Almost immediately her heart began to palpitate, her blood roared through her veins, and before her eyes, colors proliferated. Clutching her athame, the ancient black-handled knife, she touched its tip to the candle flame, then glided it around the perimeters marked by the chalk on the floor. The candles flickered as she cast the magic circle. And it seemed to her, as she slowly revolved, that a stream of fire was passing down her fingers, through the knife, and out into the air, wreathing her in a faerie ring of flame.

The divine force had entered—pure and golden, it flowed through her in molten waves, raising her spirit to ecstasy. Words issued from her lips, incantations she scarcely knew the meaning of, although she felt their strong creative impetus. There was a buzzing in her ears, growing ever louder. A surge as her powers flared. A feeling of suspension as she arched to form a bridge between the heavens and the earth. Then light burst upon her and the door opened.

Dizziness for a moment, followed by the realization that she still lingered in the master bedchamber of the China Tea House Tavern. She was floating near the ceiling, flying, as witches do. The entire chamber had changed, from the color of its paint to the number and styling of its furnishings. It was her old bedchamber, yes, but it was filled with shadowy folk whom Helen did not recognize.

She saw as through a veil, bodies and faces indistinct, dancing slightly as if they were not entirely fixed in space or time. Helen strained, summoning more of the power, until a corner of the veil shifted and she could make out a small, elderly woman sitting hunched upon a bed. Her hair was white, pulled severely back from her finely lined, patrician face, but her eyes were dark, vivid, and young. The woman's arms were clenched about her midriff, and she was leaning slightly forward as if frightened or in pain.

Who is she? Why do I feel a kinship with this woman?

The answer came readily, sent to her, perhaps, by the same power that fed upon the drug. This was her future, her family's future. This was one of the Templetons, whom Helen had striven for years to reach, using the Wisdom recklessly, without the proper rituals or precautions. Until this moment, she had despaired of her success.

Helen reached out toward the woman on the bed, but could not draw closer. The air between them shimmered, and she sensed an open channel, but even so, there seemed no way to touch the vision, to heal her, or to make her see.

At that moment the bedroom door flew open and another person rushed into the room. The newcomer was young, healthy, crackling with energy. Crowned with a rash of wild black hair, she wore a frock that would have scandalized Puritan Boston, falling no lower than the knee and displaying long, well-shaped legs sheathed in the sheerest hose. Running to the bed, she flung herself down on her knees and seized the elderly woman's frail hands. She held them hard, then brought the small, twisted fingers to her lips.

As Helen struggled to hear their voices, the angle of her vision widened, revealing the presence of others—men, two of them—one golden-haired and devious, the other dark and full of fears. They seemed familiar to her, yet she could not place them. Were they Templetons, too? For they shall have prosperity, but neither joy nor peace, *boomed the Reverend Matthew Broadhurst's prophecy for Helen's descendants. Her descendants . . . and his.*

Her hands rose, palms outward. They had no awareness of her as yet, these creatures of another time. They knew nothing of the curse that was upon them, the result of her sin, her silence, her pride. They suffered, yes; she could read it in their faces. But they did not understand why.

Called up by her own guilt, something black and heavy descended upon the room, threatening to engulf Helen and suck her into the tableau beneath. The faces below flickered and changed. No longer were they faces of the future, but her own dear children, Charles, and poor Lucy, his wife. "No, no," Helen whispered, trying to pull herself out of the scene. She cried a warning, but they did not hear. Charles, his face contorted, raised the pistol in his hand, which turned to living flame. Lucy fell back, blood streaming from her breasts. Her husband fired again, then reversed the pistol and put it to his own temple. "Abomination," he said, and pulled the trigger.

Around him the entire room burst into flame—one of those devastating Boston fires that had so often plagued the town. The fire spread, consuming the China Tea House Tavern, burning it—and its secrets—to the ground.

"But that never happened," Helen whispered. "The Tavern stands. It didn't happen that way at all."

Then she noticed that Charles and Lucy were not Charles and Lucy at all, but two entirely different people. Which meant what? That what had happened once would happen again? Repetition. It seemed her descendants would share the suffering, be visited with it again and again, until they learned for themselves how to avert it.

She could see nothing more. Her power seemed inadequate to bridge the gulf. Exhausted, Helen sank to her knees in the magic circle. Her heart was an anvil; she heard the hammering, felt the flame. "There must be a way to reach them. I know the Wisdom; I can find the way."

There was a burning through the center of her chest. It mattered not; she gathered herself and reached for the power, feeling it pour through her, a golden bolt of vision and grace. The images coalesced again, nearer this time, and the dark-haired woman cocked her head and searched the room with her witchy green eyes. My eyes.

"You are in danger, daughter of my daughters. The next time it happens, that bullet's target will be your breast."

The woman, who was laughing now and in love, did not hear. Around the China Tea House Tavern, the sky darkened. Helen gathered herself to try, and try again.

Boston, 1986

1

"I ought to kill you off this time, Drake," Nick Templeton said. "Do something that dumb and you deserve to die."

He stared for another ten seconds at the screen of his IBM PC, then pressed a key to store the chapter. Removing his glasses, he rubbed the back of his hand across his eyes. VDT fatigue. He'd read somewhere that heavy users of computer display terminals were supposed to take a ten-minute break every hour. Impossible. When the story was flowing and he was on a burn, the hours passed without his noticing.

He wasn't going to get any more work done today, though. Drake, his ex-CIA hero, had just stumbled into a KGB double cross, and Nick had no idea how to extricate him.

He shut down the machine and stretched. A glance at his watch told him he'd been at it for five hours. Must be lunchtime. His stomach sent up a confirming rumble. Drake never got hungry, of course. He never had to answer the call of nature, either, and if there was a beautiful woman in the story, he bedded her. She usually got shot in the end, though; if not by the bad guys, then by Drake himself. So much for romance.

Nick moved his chair on its squeaking casters away from the computer table to the rolltop mahogany desk where he kept his files and correspondence. The desk was up against a large window, a bad location on the days when the story wasn't flowing. Once the bedroom he'd shared with his brother, Travis, Nick's second-floor office looked out over the back gardens of the Concord estate that had been in the family for generations. Some of his friends thought it odd that he should choose to live in the same place where he'd grown up, but Nick relished such connections to the past.

He began a search through the pile on his desk. His office was messy, as it always tended to be while he was in the middle of a book. Rejected manuscript pages were dumped on the floor near the printer, and notes to himself about his plot and characters were crookedly tacked to the walls. Diskettes and letters—including a stack of as yet unanswered fan mail—were strewn across the desk top. The only spot that remained inviolable was the left top corner of the desk, where Nick kept an eleven-by-fourteen portrait of his daughter, Kelsey, taken a few months ago on her seventh birthday.

"I look yucky in this picture," Kelsey had told him on one of her recent weekend visits.

"You look beautiful to me."

"Wait'll you see my new picture, Daddy. I'm going to dye my hair orange like Cyndi Lauper's."

"Seven-year-olds don't dye their hair."

"I'm getting my ears pierced, too, in three places so I can wear all these earrings. You'll see. I'm sure I can talk Mummy into letting me."

Not if I have anything to say about it, he thought. Jesus. She was growing up so fast.

He often contemplated the picture when he was stuck on a scene, scrutinizing those impish hazel eyes as if he could find in her his muse. Since Janet had taken the job in Chicago, he only got to see Kelsey one weekend a month. A common situation for divorced fathers nowadays, but wrenching nevertheless.

Nick brushed a finger across the image of his daughter's curly dark hair before resuming his search through the mess. From the bottom of a stack of manuscript pages, he located a thick manila folder marked HELEN TEMPLETON. He spread out the contents: two rough chapters, an outline, and a stack of voluminous research notes on seventeenth-century Boston, including customs, religious factions, laws, commerce, maps, and parish registries. Your basic preliminary material for the biography he hoped to write. The *serious* work that was going to remind those pompous book reviewers at the New York *Times* that he was a talented writer, by God, not just a popular hack. Maybe he'd even collect a Pulitzer or a National Book Award.

Nick caught himself and grinned. "That's why you're a fiction writer, man. You're an old pro at weaving dreams."

The telephone rang. His answering machine started to pick up, but since he wasn't working, he flicked it off and lifted the receiver.

"Nick?" His grandmother's cultured voice still retained something of an English accent despite her many years in this country.

"Hi, Gran." He leaned back in his chair and put one long leg up on the corner of the desk. "You weren't supposed to call me today. It's up to me to call you on this very special occasion. Happy birthday."

"Thank you, but turning eighty is hardly a matter for celebration. I have more important things to worry about. Which is why I'm calling. I need your help. If you're not right in the middle of a crucial scene?"

He came alert. Minerva Templeton didn't ask his help often. Wealthy, powerful, and fiercely independent, she rarely asked anybody's help. "I'm about finished for today. What do you need?"

"I'd like you to go to the airport and meet a plane. I'd go myself, but I have the semiannual board meeting at five, and quite a bit of preparing left to do before then."

Logan Airport was about an hour's drive from his Concord home, but Nick didn't hesitate, even though it would mean scrapping his plans to work on the Helen Templeton biography. "No problem. Who am I meeting?"

"Delilah."

The name reverberated. For a second he was certain he must have misheard.

"Your cousin Delilah," Gran repeated into the silence on the line.

"That's what I thought you said. I'm surprised, that's all." *Delilah.* The name called up a wealth of images: green eyes, vulnerable, frank. A mobile, never silent mouth. Black hair, forever escaping from its rope-thick plaits. A husky voice that in childhood had sounded far too sophisticated. And a wonderful, life-engaging laugh.

"She's on her way home."

"What for?"

"I doubt if it's to wish me a happy birthday."

"No, I suppose not." Nick hadn't seen his cousin Delilah since 1970. Beautiful, passionate, heart-on-her-sleeve Delilah, whom he'd adored ever since the age of seven, when she'd brained Eddie Haggarty with a baseball bat because that sadistic bastard had been beating him up on the baseball diamond. "If you ever attack Nick again, I'll slam you into right field," Delilah had declared, and Eddie must have been convinced, because he'd never tried it again; at least, not while she was around.

There were other things he remembered about her. Aches and laughter, erotic images, feelings he'd repressed for years. An apple tree, a hotel room, an agonizing wait in a hospital corridor . . . Delilah. But it had been his brother she'd wanted, his brother she'd loved. In that, as in so many other arenas of their lives, Travis had been the favored one.

"What does she want?" he asked his grandmother even as his mind swiftly considered the various possibilities. Reconciliation? A happy ending to a long-standing family feud? Surely not. Delilah didn't need the Templetons anymore. She was a successful businesswoman, a savvy celebrity entrepreneur who'd been written up in *Business Week, The Wall Street Journal, Time, People.* She'd cashed in on the health foods craze, building an empire on herbal tea. What was left that she didn't have?

He no sooner formulated the question than he knew the answer. "She wants Templeton Tea, doesn't she?"

"I imagine so."

His breath whistled out through his teeth. "What are you going to do?"

"I expect I'll rise to the occasion," his grandmother said dryly.

"No doubt," Nick said with a smile. "You always do." But in truth he was worried. The tea company was her life. Ever since the death of her husband during World War II, Minerva Templeton had devoted herself almost exclusively to the family business. A number of years ago she had declared that she would retire from her position as Chairman of the Board and Director of Templeton Tea at the age of eighty. Now that day had come, and Nick wondered if she meant to confirm those intentions. According to his brother, Travis, her heir apparent, their grandmother was in no hurry to assuage anyone's curiosity.

Nick couldn't imagine her retiring. She was one of those people who would sooner go into the ground than give up her job.

"Will you meet her, Nick?"

This time he thought he could detect a hint of uneasiness in her tone. He closed his folder on Helen Templeton and dropped it back onto the paper mountain on his desk. "Of course. Give me the flight information."

Half an hour later, speeding down Route 2 toward Boston in the BMW he'd bought with last fall's royalty check, Nick pictured his grandmother, small, slender, and frail. She'd endured more trials and tragedies than anybody should have to face, and it was Nick's hope—indeed, his mission—that the time she had left would be spent in relative security and peace.

" 'Night, Mr. Templeton. Mrs. Templeton said we could all go home an hour early to get ready for the party."

"Sure, Susan," said Travis Templeton, Vice President and Director of Operations for Templeton Tea. He glanced at his watch. "That's fine. I'll look forward to seeing you later on tonight. Are you going to wear that knockout black dress?"

"The one I wore to the Christmas party? I don't know. Maybe. How on earth do you remember that?"

"Great dresses like that I remember."

Preening herself a bit, Susan slid into her coat right there on the threshold of his office. Travis grinned, studying the effect of the three open buttons on her blouse. The breasts weren't bad, not bad at all. But she had thick ankles. He hated thick ankles.

The hallway was busy with the sounds of employees gossiping as they locked up their offices. Everybody was hurrying home to dress for the bash at the new Four Seasons Hotel. All the notables of Boston were coming to celebrate his grandmother's eightieth birthday.

Several other feminine faces peeked in to say a flirtatious farewell. Travis treated each of them to the full power of the Templeton smile. He knew all their names, their birthdays, the colors that suited them best. He made a point of showing a personal interest in everybody who worked for him, and because they knew it wasn't just flash—he really did care about them—they loved him for it.

When the place was finally quiet, Travis rose from his desk and strolled over to the full-length window of the Georgian mansion that housed the corporate offices of Templeton Tea. Across the street the trees were budding on the Common. A pale carpet of green was asserting itself. Springtime in Boston. Life was being renewed, but not for him.

He could see a wavery reflection of himself in the hundred-year-old glass. Wheat-tinted hair, stylishly cut. Strong features, so finely sculpted that some people went so far as to call his face beautiful. Beautiful Travis Templeton, the crown prince. Heir to a monarch whose reign went on and on forever. Eighty years old. Wasn't the old terror ever going to die?

Louse, he said to himself. She's your grandmother, and you love her. Don't tell me you're getting impatient. Next you're going to be wondering if this is really what you want to do with your life, and that wouldn't be like you at all.

Travis got an unpleasant flash of the elevator—its reality as well as all it symbolized for him. Moving less steadily than usual, he crossed to the discreet bar he kept in the corner and poured a splash of Chivas into a Baccarat tumbler. He'd nearly been killed yesterday. Things like that linger for a while, no matter how clever you are at repression.

His insides cramped as he slipped back, seeing once again the interminable elevator shaft, its depth, its darkness. He had been checking things out at his latest investment property, a newly constructed harborside condominium complex. He'd left the penthouse on the twenty-third floor and walked down the hallway to the elevator. He pressed the button. The elevator door opened, and he stepped forward, only to realize that the doors had malfunctioned and the elevator wasn't there. Nothing was there, nothing but an empty shaft, falling twenty-three floors to the ground.

Off balance, he pitched himself to the side and fell on his face in the corridor, somehow managing to avoid what had seemed like an almost certain dive into the abyss. All at once he was not in a high-rise condominium building at all, but in the cramped wooden structure where his ancestors had lived for generations. He was not in an elevator shaft, but tumbling down a steep staircase, his head cracking against the walls, his heavy body splintering the banister. At the bottom waited an oblong shadow that would become an oblong box.

In the hallway of the condominium, Travis lurched to his knees and vomited.

Last night he hadn't slept. Every time he closed his eyes he saw images of the fall, the impact, his poor broken body being screwed into a coffin and left to rot for eternity underground. Even today he kept falling. Sometimes it felt as if he'd been falling for years.

Knock it off, asshole. What the hell's the matter with you?

Travis glanced at the calendar hanging over his desk. April thirtieth, the day he'd been waiting for. This evening his grandmother would preside over the small gathering that was far more important than the gala tonight. This evening—presumably—she would announce her choice of a successor. Confirm his fate as the next Director of Templeton Tea.

He needed the appointment. For years he'd been planning his future around it. The sooner he was in sole command of the tea company, the sooner he could move on to accomplish all his other ambitions and goals. The corporation, and all that went with it—100 percent of the stock in Templeton Tea and all its subsidiaries—was worth a fortune. The assets were enormous, and he already had a number of ideas about how he was going to invest them. Minerva Templeton wouldn't be pleased to know that most of his plans had little to do with tea.

Tea, for God's sake. He'd never even liked the stuff.

Travis's office telephone rang and, with no secretaries to answer it, kept on ringing. He turned away from the window to watch the light dance on the console. He made no move to answer. The ringing finally stopped, but a couple of minutes later, he heard his grandmother's footsteps in the corridor. She rapped on his door and entered.

"Still here, huh, Gran?" he said, going over to give her a hug. "You sure look great for eighty years old, lady."

She pulled away. "I want to talk to you, Travis. There's something you ought to know." His grandmother paused, plumbing his depths—or trying to—in that imperious manner that always made him uneasy. She made him feel he could hide nothing, but this was an illusion. He'd been hiding things for years.

"Your cousin Delilah is back."

The elevator doors opened again, and this time Travis fell into the shaft.

2

I'm not nervous, Delilah Scofield said to herself as she stared out the window of the descending DC-10. I'm too *old* to be nervous. Too mature, too confident, too successful . . . Dammit! I think I have to go to the bathroom again.

"Hey, aren't you on TV?"

Delilah turned to meet the curious stare of the kinky-haired girl who'd been raising hell ever since she'd boarded the flight in Chicago. The child, who was perhaps twelve years old, had been up and down through the flight, asking questions, making demands, annoying the other passengers. The two female flight attendants serving the first-class section were no longer attempting to be nice to her. They were undoubtedly fantasizing about how it would feel to throttle the brat.

Delilah, who remembered similar antics of her own at the same age, smiled. The child immediately continued, "You're on TV; I know you are. You're the lady on the herbal tea ads. I hate that stuff. My mom drinks gallons of it, to like make herself look younger. As if it would. She's such a dingdong."

"I'm Delilah Scofield, yes, from Merlin's Magical Brews. What's your name?"

The flight attendant collared the girl. "I told you not to bother the other passengers, Amy. Now, get back where you belong and fasten your seat belt. Didn't you hear the captain? We're descending."

Delilah patted the empty seat beside her. Why not? Anything

was better than sitting here trying to convince herself she wasn't nervous. "She can stay for the landing if she wants. I don't mind."

Both Amy and the flight attendant blinked at her in disbelief. "No shit?" the girl said.

"No shit," Delilah returned solemnly.

Amy dropped down beside her, leaned back in the wide seat, and put her feet up against the locked-in tray table. "I hate to fly. It's boring."

"I love it."

"Jeez. Why?"

"It's exhilarating. Look. It's beautiful down there." She put up the armrest so the girl could lean over and see out. "Of course, it's a lot more fun if you're sitting next to the window."

It was a perfect day to fly into Boston. A brisk wind had swept away the city's air pollution, and they had a magnificent view of the late afternoon sunlight glinting off the glass and steel structures that marked Boston's redeveloped skyline. The jet banked in over the harbor; several thousand feet below, the whitecaps danced. Delilah could see, set in from the shoreline, glimpses of red brick and brownstone, so stately and serene compared to L.A.'s tacky urban sprawl.

"Big deal," said Amy. "I hate Boston."

"You're a negative kid, aren't you? Do you live here?"

"Nah. I live in Denver. Denver's awesome. It's got cowboys and mountains and stuff."

Divorce, Delilah figured. A lot of children were traveling alone these days. "Who's down there waiting for you, Amy? One of your parents?"

"Nah. They left for the People's Republic of China this morning. My dad's a brain surgeon, like real well-known. He was invited to give a paper or something, and my mom decided to go, too. They'd have taken me along, but I didn't want to go. I mean, who cares about the Great Wall and acupuncture and all that crap? They asked me if I wanted to visit my grandma in Boston instead, and I said sure, that's cool."

Busy parents, a child shuttled off to the grandparents . . . no wonder she'd been drawn to Amy. Delilah recognized that hard, bright face, the big eyes, the shadows. The smart mouth she used as a weapon to keep people from zeroing in on her loneliness, her fear. I was like that for a while after my mother died, Delilah remembered. Impulsively, she took Amy's hand and gave it a squeeze. "My grandmother used to take care of me a lot when I was about your age."

Amy looked at her as if she had trouble imagining a grown-up with a grandmother. "Bet she's dead now, huh?"

For some reason this casual assumption shocked Delilah. She couldn't imagine Grendam dead. "No. She's alive. And just like your grandmother, she's down there somewhere waiting for me."

"Awesome."

When the big jet landed and the passengers started to deplane, Delilah and Amy walked up the jetwalk together. Delilah's nervousness had returned. The entrance to the terminal loomed ahead of her like a gateway to another dimension. She was crossing the Rubicon, smashing through the looking glass to emerge into a far different world from the one she'd left behind a few hours ago at LAX.

There was a bottleneck at the terminal entrance. Their fellow travelers were being pounced upon by waiting relatives. As Delilah shouldered her way through the crowd, shepherding Amy, she said to herself over and over, hey, *hey,* it's going to be okay.

"Grammy!" Amy yelled and catapulted into the arms of a heavy matron clad in an off-the-rack wool coat that was too tight under the arms. The woman's face was lined and innocent of make-up, her chin double, her eyes warm. She hugged Amy and patted her hair. "Hi, baby," she said, and kissed her.

As she was led away, Amy turned back for a moment and waved to Delilah. She was smiling now, that hard look gone.

Oh, sweetheart. I hope you don't ever end up doing to your grandmother what I'm planning to do to mine.

Delilah felt a light touch on her arm. As she half turned, her bulky garment bag collided with the tall man beside her, who winced and said in a familiar voice, "I know you hate the bunch of us, but Christ, you needn't castrate me."

"Nick?" It took her a second, because he looked so different—bigger and stronger and more masculine somehow. She remembered her youngest cousin as a skinny kid in a Peace Now headband and tattered jeans, but he had gained a few pounds, and he must have had a late growth spurt, too, because he was well over six feet. That angular face was the same—high forehead and hollows beneath his cheekbones, which, unlike the rest of him, hadn't filled out at all. Thin lips that ought to have grown severe with age but instead looked softer and more inclined to smile.

He was smiling now. He still had that crooked front tooth that crossed slightly over the one beside it. His body was fit and hard, his hair black and curly. His eyes were his best feature—arching brows, mascara-thick lashes, and gunmetal-green irises. She couldn't remember noticing Nick's eyes before; they'd always been hidden by his glasses. He must be wearing contact lenses these days.

"Who's the kid?" he asked.

"Just a little girl I was talking to on the plane." Delilah flung her arms around him. "She was traveling alone and we adopted each other for a while. How are you, Nick?" Without waiting for an answer, she pulled his head down and kissed him lustily on the mouth.

He laughed and pushed her back so he could see her. "Look at you. You're even sexier than you appear on TV."

"You're not so bad yourself, Mr. Famous Writer." She had a sharp memory of Nick, the shy one, the intellectual, hiding from a scary world behind a pair of thick-lensed glasses. When his first thriller had come out a few years ago, she'd been stunned by the fast-paced action, the sex, the give-'em-hell violence. Nicholas the Fainthearted had written *this?*

She hugged him again. He'd changed, and so had she. You see? Of course it's going to be all right. "Jesus, Nick. I've missed you."

His arms tightened around her. "Me, too."

"I didn't expect anybody to be here to meet me. Thanks for coming; I was scared to death," she added, which was the last thing she had ever thought she'd admit to any of the Templetons. Nick was okay, though; she could be honest with Nick.

"Got a suitcase?" he asked.

"Three of them."

"You must be planning to stay awhile."

"I am." She stepped back and spread her arms wide, feeling elated all of a sudden. She wanted to embrace the entire city of Boston. "I've come home."

"She's not there this afternoon, is she?" she asked as they drove through the refurbished Quincy market section, past Faneuil Hall, across Cambridge Street, and up the north slope of Beacon Hill. Delilah was looking out the window, enjoying that unique blend of colonial and modern, prim and sophisticated, tasteful and sleazy, that characterized Boston. Before her eyes flashed the red brick, the cobblestone streets, the antique lampposts she remembered from her childhood. Delilah had always loved this neighborhood, which seemed to her to have much more vitality than the clipped green elegance of Beverly Hills.

"She?" said Nick.

"Grendam." It was her own personal name for Minerva Templeton. She'd come up with it during her turbulent days at one of her many prep schools, where everybody had affected names for their relatives, like Pater and Tante and Mumsy. She'd been proud of Grendam, which everyone thought was short for Grande Dame. It was actually short for Grendel's Dam, which to Delilah's mind was a far more appropriate sobriquet for her grandmother.

"She's at the office, as usual. Not even for such an occasion as the eightieth anniversary of her birth would Minerva Templeton take the day off."

He glided to a stop in front of the China Tea House Tavern. Delilah had asked him to drive by and let her have a look at the old place. "I see it's still painted shit-brown," she said. "I used to take great delight as a teenager in referring to the color that way. When they repainted the place in the sixties, the paint even smelled like manure, remember?"

"That's because it was a special milk protein-based paint that's only used on antique buildings."

"Grendam suggested I cultivate a less delicate nose and a more delicate mouth."

Nick laughed. They got out of the car for a better look at the building that had been the Templeton family home for 250 years. Delilah slipped her hands into the pockets of her silver fox jacket and leaned back against the car. She'd seen the Tavern so many times in her dreams during the past sixteen years. In some strange way it seemed to represent both her past and her future.

"If it belonged to me, I'd paint it red."

"But it doesn't belong to you."

No, she thought. Not yet.

The Tavern confronted her, squat and narrow, its leaden glass eyes regarding the street in the same implacable manner they'd affected for decades. Located just below the crest of the Hill, on the less fashionable side away from the Boston Common, the Tavern was a woodframe building whose central portion had been constructed in the early eighteenth century. It was one of the oldest houses on Beacon Hill, and indeed, in Boston. A modest building, the Tavern was out of step with its neighbors, which were constructed of stately Georgian brick. But Delilah thought it more noble than they, for the Tavern had stood undaunted through nearly three centuries of fire and flood, revolution and urban decay.

"It's reassuring to see something that lasts, isn't it?" she said. "Too bad the people who live here have never proved to be as stalwart and dependable as the timbers that have housed them."

Nick picked up immediately on the bitterness underlying her words. "You left us, Delilah. You maintained the estrangement that several of us, on various occasions, attempted to break."

She stared at the Tavern. Its very stolidity seemed to mock her.

Nick said, "I don't want our grandmother hurt."

Delilah could see her, petite and fire iron-straight—Minerva the redoubtable, Minerva the invincible, who had sprung full grown and fully armed from the god's head with no less militance than her ancient Roman namesake. Minerva the bitch, whom she had once vowed to destroy.

"Lock horns with Travis, if you must. But have a little pity, if it's in you, for her."

"Pity? Dear God, it would be an insult to her to offer Minerva Templeton pity."

"She's eighty years old."

"And in full command of her faculties, from everything I've heard. She may well be the worthiest opponent I've ever had."

"She needn't be your opponent anymore. I wish you would stop thinking of her as such."

Delilah shrugged. It was difficult to think of Grendam in any other terms.

"Is that why you've come back? To do battle with her?"

"There are several reasons why I've come back." She was aware that she sounded defensive. How strange that he could do that to her. "I've done everything I wanted to accomplish at Merlin's. I was born here. My roots are here. Minerva Templeton is my grandmother, and there was a time when she wanted me to succeed her."

"You want revenge. You're planning to nail her, and Travis, too."

Delilah tossed her head. She could feel her thick hair heavy on her shoulders and the slight pull of her earlobes as her earrings spun. "And I thought I was the melodramatic one."

A delivery van honked loudly just behind them. "Let's go," Nick said. "The street is narrow and we're causing a traffic jam."

Inside the BMW, Nick reached over and gave her hand a squeeze. "I don't want to quarrel with you. But I'm concerned about Gran."

Why? she thought; I should ask him why. But she wasn't going to, dammit. She didn't want anything to interfere with the resolutions she'd made.

Nick dropped her hand and started the engine. "Shall I take you directly to the tea company, or would you like to stop at your hotel first?"

"The hotel, please. I want to shower and change before the business meeting."

As he turned onto Beacon Street and drove down toward the Ritz-Carlton, Nick was more aware than he'd been before of the scent of her perfume permeating the air. It was a perfect signature for her—sexy, exotic, aggressive.

He knew she wasn't as obdurate as she appeared. He suspected she was determined not to let her softer side show. He remembered the way she'd watched out for that kid from the plane, staying by her side, paying no attention to her surroundings until she was certain the little girl had found her relatives. Maybe he was sensitive because his own daughter had to fly alone so often, but he was a sucker for gestures like that.

It was unfortunate that Delilah and Gran seemed destined to be at odds with each other. If it ever came down to a choice between them, his first loyalty was to his grandmother.

After dropping Delilah off at the Ritz, Nick drove to the headquarters of Templeton Tea, a graceful Georgian mansion on Beacon Street opposite the Common. He pulled up on the sidewalk beside the building and unlocked a wrought-iron gate leading to a tiny parking area in front of the brick annex that had once been a stable. Parking was scarce in the city; he saw several passing drivers regarding his maneuver with envy.

He didn't leave the car immediately. On the radio Bruce Springsteen's raspy "Born in the U.S.A." deplored the loss of the American dream. Nick's stomach felt queasy; was he coming down with something? He smiled wryly. He'd been a closet hypochondriac for years.

In the lobby of the Ritz Delilah had hugged him again. He'd put her back from him, his fingers brushed by the mixture of silky dark hair and soft silver fox on her shoulders. There was still an attraction; no doubt about it. All the drama and flair that had characterized her as a young woman had burst into fruition—that glossy mane of black hair, that wide, sexy mouth that was so often stretched in laughter, those elegant dance hall legs.

Forget it. Just forget it. You're too smart, too mature to fall into that trap again.

And his brother Travis? Just how smart and mature was *he?*

Nick found his grandmother in her office on the second floor of Templeton House, bent over a sheaf of figures at her desk. He would have thought her deeply involved in her work if it weren't for the quick bob of her head when she saw him on her threshold.

"Did she come? Did you meet her?"

"Yes." Nick went to her side, bent down, and kissed her forehead just below the hairline. She smelled good, as always. She'd worn the same perfume, Chanel No. 5, for as many years as he could remember. In the current era of hot new fragrances with designer labels, his grandmother's scent remained reliably immutable. "She wanted to go freshen up at her hotel; she'll be here for the business meeting."

"How did she look?" Minerva Templeton's voice was low, insistent, and for just an instant, all her hopes were clear. Nick's hands tightened on her shoulders. Once again he kissed his grandmother's papery skin. She wasn't as robust as she used to be, and sometimes her voice had an odd, breathless quality. She was eighty, after all. She wasn't going to live forever.

"She's changed, Gran. Oh, not in basics. But on the surface, she's quite different. She's chic, for one thing, and very dramatic. And she's got confidence—she bristles with that. She's—" He paused, forced to censor the rest: sexy, dynamic, probably great in bed. He pursed his lips, both startled and amused at the images his subconscious mind insisted on flinging up.

He thought of something his cousin had said in the car about Max, her husband, who had died last year. When Nick had apologized for not coming out to L.A. for the funeral, Delilah explained that Max had hated funerals. "He told me to toss his ashes off the end of the Santa Monica pier."

"Did you?"

"No, I rented a sailboat and went out about five miles to a place where the sea is a luminous green when the sunlight strikes it. I scattered them there. It was beautiful, Nick. His ashes sparkled as they sank into the water, winking like a thousand tiny stars. Max would have liked that. He would have laughed."

Nick had wanted to cry. With her passion for life, Delilah deserved more, he thought, than sun-struck ashes.

"Is she happy, Nick?" his grandmother asked.

That wasn't difficult to answer. "No. I don't think she is."

In the understated elegance of her hotel room overlooking the Boston Public Garden, Delilah kicked off her shoes, slipped out of her suit, shed her silk underthings, and went into the bathroom for a quick shower. A few minutes later, wrapped in one of the luxuriously thick bathsheets provided by the hotel, she sat down at the dressing table to fix her hair and renew her make-up. Thanks to nature—which had given her thick, ageless hair that still, at thirty-eight, showed no trace of gray, Delilah achieved without too much effort a look of carefree elegance.

Her skin, too, was good—translucent and oily enough to discourage the formation of lines and wrinkles. Minerva had once informed her that her features were "an amusing combination of the well-bred and the coarse."

It was a good face, or so she'd convinced herself over the years. Strong, dramatic, and full of that indefinable essence people call character. The straight nose and high cheekbones were Templeton legacies, as were her deepset green eyes. It was the witch-black hair, she supposed, that Grendam accounted coarse. That, or her lush and sensual mouth.

For an instant her reflection seemed to shift and change into the pale, drawn visage of the broken girl who'd fled Boston to take refuge in one of the seedier sections of Los Angeles. The Fendi fox had been an ancient tweed jacket then, the silks and fine leathers ragged blue denim.

That girl leapt out of the mirror at her, and Delilah had to close her eyes for a moment. She was still inside somewhere, that lonely, defiant child. As was the foolish young woman who'd loved so recklessly and been so deeply scarred.

She remembered the family motto, which was actually more of a curse: *For they shall have prosperity, but neither joy nor peace.* Several of Delilah's ancestors had committed suicide. Brothers frequently hated brothers, parents and children resented each other's mistakes. Death at an early age was common. Delilah's mother had died of an aneurysm at the age of thirty-two; her father had succumbed to a heart attack at fifty-six. Nick's mother had died of anorexia nervosa when he and his brother, Travis, were very young. Tragedy seemed to stalk the family; people sometimes compared them to the Kennedys.

What a legacy: tea and anger, tea and tears. No wonder I fled, she thought. So what the *hell* am I returning for?

But she knew. For years she'd been a successful, independent woman, but the past still haunted her. She had to come to terms with it. With her grandmother, who had been such a formidable influence in her life. And with Travis.

As for tragedy, you couldn't avoid that by running away. She thought of Max, who had urged her to come back to Boston and take up what he considered to be her heritage. She was doing this for herself, yes, but to some degree she was also doing it for him.

Delilah rose and dressed quickly in her latest Sonia Rykiel—a maroon cashmere cardigan and matching skirt. As a finishing touch she cinched the outfit with a wide, slightly kinky Hermès belt, then assumed a jaunty pose in front of the dressing table mirror. The well-bred and the coarse. She placed one hand on her hip and sucked at her lower lip, deliberately making it coarser, redder, more sensual. "Eat your proper Bostonian heart out, Grendam," she said.

Ten minutes later, after a brisk walk through the Public Garden, Delilah arrived outside the Beacon Street entrance to Templeton House. She was a little late, but she'd planned it that way. She wanted to be sure the tea was served and the meeting was in progress when she made her appearance.

She looked up at the graceful stone and brick facade of the old building which housed the corporate offices of Templeton Tea. The tall windows on the second floor were perhaps its most striking feature, along with the Ionic columns at the front entrance, and the hand-turned balustrade around the roof line. Designed in the Federalist style of Charles Bullfinch, the house had once stood free on Beacon Hill, but was now flush with the dwelling on its left. On its right was a cobbled driveway guarded by a wrought-iron gate.

Nick's BMW, she noted, was behind that gate.

She was admitted to the downstairs foyer by a butler. She appreciated the touch. There had always been something very old-world and privileged about Templeton Tea. Delilah noted with satisfaction the way the fellow's eyes widened when she identified herself. "You needn't show me up. I know the way."

Nothing had changed. She swiftly climbed the graceful winding staircase that led up to the main floor of the house, trying to ignore the static of her heartbeat, the faint dampness of her palms. Damn, she was nervous. She held her briefcase with her financial documents in her right hand, while clutching the smooth mahogany banister with her left.

At the top of the stairs she turned left down the short hallway that opened into two drawing rooms, each looking out over the Boston Common. A line of mammoth portraits of her ancestors dominated the hallway wall. Delilah had been ten years old when Minerva had made her memorize their faces and recite a litany of their exploits. Grendam had taught her to venerate her forebears as quasi-gods, but as she grew older she realized they were very human figures indeed.

She recognized Josiah, a merchant, who had imported tea from

China in such huge quantities in the eighteenth century that he'd made the family rich. Josiah had the misfortune to be on the wrong side during the American Revolution. A hefty portion of the tea dumped into Boston Harbor on that memorable night in 1773 had belonged to the Templetons. "They weren't patriots," Minerva had always said of the participants in the Boston Tea Party. "They were hoodlums."

Then there was Jake, Josiah's son, who'd turned pirate after the Revolution. With the powerful East India Company holding a worldwide monopoly on the tea trade, Jake Templeton's successful attacks on their ships made him a hero to the British-hating Americans.

Looking to the next portrait, Delilah recognized Stephen Templeton, who had piloted one of his sleek clipper ships to Canton in the mid-1800s. Beside him were his grandsons Earnest and Harrison Templeton. The latter had been Delilah's great-grandfather, and she remembered him vaguely from her childhood. Harrison Templeton had enjoyed himself hugely with too much alcohol and too many women while running a tea plantation in Darjeeling. He'd returned to Boston after the partition of India and fallen to his death down the steep staircase of the China Tea House Tavern.

Lastly there was Edward, Grendam's husband, whom Delilah had never known. He'd died in the war, somewhere in Nazi-occupied France, and Grendam had run the company ever since.

A colorful bunch of rascals. They looked so serious and proper, but these dour portraits were nothing more than pale shadows of the actual men. Many of them had spent their youth riding the decks of a sailing vessel, clad in boots and open-throated shirts, tan and merry and ruthless as the pirates they had imitated. She would have liked to know them, Stephen Templeton in particular. Or maybe Jake. She would have loved to sail beside them through the great heaving waves of the ocean, carrying chest upon chest of coppery-black gold in the cargo bay and laughing her triumph into the wind.

But most of all she would have liked to know Helen Templeton, whose portrait occupied the place of honor at the end of the hall. Helen had founded the tea company in the early eighteenth century. Her portrait had been restored in the 1950s, and although she had sat for it late in her life, she looked surprisingly vibrant and young. Her hair was auburn, and there was something about her expression that suggested to Delilah a full-blooded enjoyment of life.

Delilah stopped to beg her ancestor's blessing. She'd always relished the idea that a woman had started the business, that a woman was Director now, and that a third woman—Delilah herself—had every intention of taking the reins in the future.

At the door to the oval ballroom, where the meeting was in session, Delilah paused for an instant to marshal her courage. The door, made of gently curving cherrywood that melded flush into the oval walls of the room, was shut; behind it Delilah could hear the rise and fall of voices. She had a moment of utter panic during which she envisioned herself fleeing down the stairs and into the street. No fleeing for you, she thought, with a glance at her narrow skirt and high heels. You can barely walk!

Snap out of it, duchess, Max would have said. Chin up and give 'em hell.

She knocked once, loudly, then thrust open the door and stepped into the gilded room. Her grandmother and several other people were seated at an enormous horseshoe-shaped table. Delilah couldn't number or identify them yet; her gaze went directly to the elegant white-haired woman in the center of the table.

She was small, not over five foot two, and as straight and slim as a girl. Her face was wrinkled, yet ageless somehow, its patrician bones more prominent than ever. Her eyes, which were dark, almost black, radiated confidence and power. Delilah had always thought of them as man's eyes, for there was nothing feminine about the iron-willed authority that burned behind those long, pretty lashes. She was exquisitely dressed, as always, in a classic dove-gray Chanel suit.

How alone she looks. And how magnificent, in spite of her age.

"Hello, Grendam."

Minerva rose, one hand briefly touching her throat. When she spoke, her voice was firm and clear. "Delilah. Come in. You're just in time for tea."

"Happy birthday, Grendam." She moved into the middle of the horseshoe, leaned down, and kissed Minerva sedately on the cheek. Those skinny eighty-year-old arms closed around her, hugging fiercely. Delilah yielded for an instant, then pulled away. Oh no, she said silently. It can't be solved with something as fleeting as a hug. It's going to take a lot more than that.

"My turn," said the light, charming voice she'd heard so many times in her dreams. "Welcome home, Delilah."

She turned to greet her cousin Travis. She'd hoped to find him graying and fat, but no such luck. His hair was still the color of newly minted gold, his body was lean—well worked out, obviously; he could have been a Californian, damn him—and his eyes still blue enough to dazzle everyone within a ten-foot radius.

"Travis." She tried to give him her hand, but he was too quick for her. He pulled her into his arms and kissed her. It was just as she remembered; she wanted to cry.

"You look terrific," he said, and she knew he meant it. Travis's compliments were always sincere.

Delilah smiled an acknowledgment. Her fingernails were chewing into her palms, but Travis couldn't see that. Nick saluted her. He was lounging in his French Provincial chair, tipping it back on the highly fragile rear legs and rocking. There were four other men present, none of whom Delilah recognized, who comprised the remainder of the board of directors of Templeton Tea.

"You must be wondering why I've come," she said. Get on with it, she was thinking. Say it now, before you lose your nerve. "I wish to pay my respects on our grandmother's birthday, of course. But that's not the only reason."

She glanced at Travis, then, defiantly, at Nick. "I'm here because Grendam is eighty years old and about to retire. It is my intention to succeed her as Director of the corporation and Chairman of the Board."

There was a brief silence, then her grandmother said, "Sit down, my dear." Grendam's hands were steady as she reached for the blue and white hand-painted Limoges porcelain cup that was poised at her elbow on the table. One extra service, Delilah noted. They had been expecting her.

"Refresh my memory," her grandmother said. "Do you prefer Earl Grey or Lapsang souchong?"

Delilah grinned. She could tell by the look in those hard man's eyes that her grandmother had been anticipating this confrontation with a certain amount of pleasure. The old contest of wills that had raged between them years ago was about to begin again.

She was astonished to find herself looking forward to it.

3

"It's true, is it not, Grendam, that you plan to retire?"

Minerva Templeton took her time before responding to her prodigal granddaughter's question. She was savoring the moment —Delilah back at her side, back in Boston, back in the boardroom of Templeton Tea, where she had always meant her to be. The girl would never know—Minerva couldn't possibly allow her to know —how much she had missed her. The estrangement between them had gone on long enough.

"I plan to retire eventually, yes."

"Eventually?" Travis repeated, coming to attention. "We've all been expecting you to announce your retirement today, Gran. Although I must admit, I can't imagine the company operating without you."

Can't you indeed? But you've been waiting for just that, Minerva said to herself. Oh yes, and Delilah's been waiting, too. Minerva had an image of India: a trip to the south near Bombay where the Towers of Silence loomed over the dry plains—the tall, squat towers where the Parsees exposed their dead. Overhead, she saw the huge birds of prey circling, silent, ominous, waiting to begin the feast.

No. Deliberately, she softened the image until her imagination was filled instead with the sight of the clouded purple mountains that soared to heaven above Darjeeling, her childhood home. Mt. Kanchenjunga, the third highest peak in the world. And far in the distance, Everest. She could see them as if she were standing there among the dark green tea bushes, not yet the wealthy Director of a major company, but a humble tea picker, her nimble fingers rapidly plucking the tender leaves that would be packed into wooden chests to be shipped to the great tea auctions in Calcutta 450 miles to the south.

"Gran?" The concerned voice was Nick's. "Are you all right?"

"Of course I'm all right." She managed a smile for Nick, who was here today only because she'd requested it. Nick had made his lack of interest in the affairs of Templeton Tea clear twenty years ago and, unlike Delilah, had never wavered. "I've been giving a great deal of thought to the problem of a successor."

"What is there to think about?" Travis asked. "I've been preparing myself for the job for years."

Minerva heard the unaccustomed sharpness in his voice and felt some satisfaction in the shedding of masks that was already going on around the table. It was at high-pressure meetings like these that one could truly take a person's measure.

To Delilah she said, "You've been away for years and have never worked for Templeton Tea. No doubt Travis is wondering—as am I—why you consider yourself more qualified than he to take over my job."

"No doubt," Delilah said with a hint of her old irrepressible grin. She had put down her things on the end of one horseshoe of the table, and her fingers were drumming the leather of her briefcase. Still impatient. Still grabbing life by the throat. Minerva knew herself to be cooler, more calculating. Their styles were as different as a politician's and a showgirl's.

"The question's simple enough to answer," Delilah said. "The fact is, you and Travis have made a hash of things lately. According to everything I've learned about the current financial status of the corporation, you've really screwed up."

She paused, and Minerva had to admire her audacity. She certainly had everyone's attention. And yet, how rigid she was. Her arms, her shoulders, the elevation of her chin. She's nervous, Minerva realized. Most people reveal it in the voice, the hands, perhaps in an unconscious blinking of the eyes. Delilah was not so obvious. There had never been any doubt in the old days about what Delilah was feeling, but now she had learned control.

Her granddaughter had matured considerably while living in California. Minerva had hoped this would be true, but she had not necessarily expected it. She knew a number of people, several of them her own age, who had never matured at all. She appraised Delilah's well-cut, colorful clothes, her costly accessories, her skillfully applied cosmetics. That witchy dark hair that brushed her shoulders. Her look was dramatic and almost blatantly sensual, but she carried it off well. The girl had presence, and a style that was distinctly her own. What a change from the breezily defiant ragamuffin she remembered so well.

And yet, Minerva missed that ragamuffin, that too tall hellion with the huge, solemn eyes. Always in trouble, her Delilah with the wise mouth and the soft, sloppy heart. Loving too much and losing too often. I hurt her so badly. I'm surprised she's come back at all.

"What the hell are you talking about?" Travis asked. His genial smile made a mockery of his cousin's assertions. "We're selling more tea than ever before. The corporation is solid. We've had a steadily rising curve of increasing sales over the past several years."

"There's more to the financial success of a corporation than increasing sales and steady profits," Delilah said. "How long has it been since you've taken a look at market share? Despite the increased demand for tea in this country, Templeton has a smaller share of the total tea market than ever before. If this trend continues, your increased sales and profits will be eroded in short order."

She paused for a moment, then continued, "You've lost a significant market share largely because your recent marketing strategy—if you can dignify it with that term—has been an across-the-boards failure. Templeton Tea has always had a stodgy image, and you've done nothing in recent years to change that. You've been forced to put out your own line of herbal and decaffeinated teas to compete with mine, but are they competing? No. Templeton Tea is in trouble."

"Bullshit," Travis said.

Minerva said to Delilah, "I presume you have the figures to back this up?"

"Yes, of course." As Delilah's eyes locked with hers, Minerva felt a ripple of unease. Have I made a terrible mistake in allowing her back? I am old. Is it wrong to want forgiveness, reconciliation? Is it arrogant of me still to be playing with other people's lives?

"I have the documentation right here."

"Fine. You have the floor, Delilah. Please present your case."

She did have figures. On just about everything from the recent fluctuations of the price of tea on international commodities markets to the projected expenses of a rigorous new advertising campaign. While Minerva listened in silence, the other board members interrupted now and then with questions. Delilah answered them all, cogently and convincingly. She was articulate, well prepared. When she hit them with her well-documented financial analyses, there was little anyone could say to contest her claims.

Minerva herself was already aware of most of what Delilah was saying. The girl was quite right; the company was in some difficulty. Nothing dire—their investments were too broadly based and conservative for the corporation to be in disastrous straits. But there had been some setbacks recently, yes. Travis knew it, too, despite his disclaimers. Minerva had been waiting to see what, if anything, he would do about it.

Delilah's presentation took about thirty minutes. Toward the end she said, "I am confident that our grandmother will wish the company to be run by the best-qualified person. I've started my own business, built it up from nothing into what was at first a modest, and in the last couple of years, a spectacular, success. I'm particularly known for my exciting and effective marketing strategies, which is precisely what Templeton Tea needs. But I'm also good at finance and operations, and I work well with the people I have to manage.

"Although it's true I haven't worked for Templeton Tea, the problems you face here are not dissimilar to the ones I've solved in the past for Merlin's. Plus, I would bring all the energy and excitement of a fresh, new approach."

She paused, allowing that vibrant green gaze to touch upon each of them in turn. Minerva felt her power. The others, surely, must feel it, too.

"When Grendam retires, I want complete control," she said in a quiet voice. "If you care about the future of this company, you will give it to me."

Travis, who rarely displayed emotion, tugged at his tie. Nick rocked his chair back and forth. Nobody spoke.

"You've heard my qualifications," Delilah continued. "Now, what about my cousin's?" She turned to Travis. "You've worked here since you got out of college, and by all reports, you've done a competent job. Yet you have never once come up with a creative marketing strategy, nor have you ever developed a new product. You have experience, yes, but do you have drive or vision?" Her eyes hardened. "You're lazy, Trav. We all know that."

Travis smiled, his golden charm intact. "And you're entertaining as hell, Delilah. I've missed you."

For an instant there was such a terrible look on Delilah's face that Minerva blinked her eyes. The girl had returned in spite of Travis, she reminded herself. And it had been years ago, that nonsense. Long over, long dead. She had crushed it out of them forever, surely. It would not rear its head again.

Delilah controlled herself and addressed Minerva: "You're very quiet, Grendam. Don't you have anything to say?"

Minerva took a tea cake and bit into it, an indulgence in sweets that she usually didn't permit herself. At eighty, one had to work harder than ever to keep one's figure. *Keep it for what?*

Look at them, so angry, so ambitious, and, compared to her, so young. Once again she saw the Towers of Silence. She imagined the descent of the vultures, the feasting, the sun-blanched bones.

Lifting her delicate china cup, Minerva sipped her tea. It had gone cold. "Travis, ring for Joseph, please. We need a new pot."

They were silent, waiting. She felt her powers focus, sharpen; new energy flowed through her eighty-year-old frame. She could still command them; she would not underestimate her ability to manipulate their lives. Shrewd, canny, and worldly-wise, she had done it without compunction for years. Stubborn or not, ambitious or not, they would continue to do her bidding until she was ready to let them go.

Minerva lifted the folder at her elbow and rummaged through it for the papers she'd had her attorney prepare. She removed her reading glasses from their leather case as she spread the documents out in front of her. "As you've all known for several years, I set this day, my eightieth birthday, as the time when I would retire. I have not entirely changed my mind about that—I still wish to retire. But there are problems, as Delilah has pointed out. And the truth is, I am gravely concerned over what's going to happen to the company when I step down."

Joseph, the butler, appeared with a fresh pot of tea. Steam emerged from the gleaming blue and white porcelain spout as he silently refilled their cups.

"I am taking several steps to deal with these problems. I have before me a document that makes reference to the section of my will dealing with the disposition of my stock—and thus, my power—in Templeton Tea."

Minerva felt the enormity of their waiting. Her will. How they must have longed for a glimpse into that.

"My current will, written some years ago, leaves the common stock—of which I own one hundred percent—to Travis. He seemed the right person to take over as my successor; he was the oldest, and he was the only one of my grandchildren who worked for the company."

She paused to meet the eyes of each of them in turn. Eye contact was important. She knew that; Delilah did, too. None of the others were quite so willing to face her direct and naked gaze.

"As you know, by tradition, all voting stock in the company is left to one person in each generation. Others—all of you included—own equal proportions of the preferred stock, as a check upon the power of this particular individual. This system has worked well in the past, and I see no reason to amend it. I do not mean to imply that Travis is no longer my choice. Circumstances demand, however, that I do not ignore the ambitions of my other grandchildren—Delilah in particular."

"Delilah has no claim on you," Travis interrupted. "She turned her back on the family twenty years ago."

"Sixteen," Delilah corrected. She rapped her scarlet nails on the surface of the table as she added, "And it's a matter of some debate as to who actually turned their backs on whom."

Minerva continued speaking as if there had been no interruption. "The fact is, even before I knew that Delilah was returning, I had already decided upon my course of action. I am going to postpone my plans for retirement until this time next year. Delilah will begin working for us immediately in a top management position. Travis will continue in his usual capacity. I will maintain my position as Director and ultimate decision maker, but many of my actual day-to-day responsibilities will be divided between the two of you. At the end of one year, I shall sign a new will, leaving the stock to whichever one of you I judge to be the most effective leader. My decision, at that point, will be irrevocable.

"The will is a technicality, of course, necessary because of my advanced age. The stock will be legally transferred to my successor before my actual death, at the time I officially step down." She glanced from Travis to Delilah. "At the end of one year, one of you will control Templeton Tea. You have questions, I am sure. But such details can be dealt with later. It is my birthday, and I am weary of business."

She replaced her papers in the folder and rose from her seat. "Now, if you'll excuse me, I have a number of things to do before the gala tonight. This meeting is adjourned."

If she'd seriously thought she could escape without protest, Minerva was wrong. Travis followed her from the room, slamming the cherry door behind him. He cornered her in her office, where she had gone to fetch her coat, saying, "This is intolerable. You can't do this, Gran."

"I can and I will."

"You gave me no warning. You told me she was back, but you never even hinted you intended to alter your plans for the company's future."

"I am not obliged to explain myself to you," she said in a tone that once would have quelled him instantly.

But although Travis's normal strategy was to avoid arguments and confrontations, nothing had been normal since his grandmother had announced Delilah's return. He felt as if the past had opened a maw that would swallow him up, that would make him confront what he had been . . . and what he had become.

"I can't believe this. You expect me to work with her, *compete* with her, just as if nothing ever happened between us? She still hates me—couldn't you see it? She's never forgiven me. Or you, either, for that matter."

His grandmother's stiff face betrayed nothing of what she might be feeling. What an icy bitch she's always been, he thought.

"You are a sophisticated forty-year-old man," she said. "Your cousin"—she laid faint stress on the word—"is a mature widow who has suffered tragedies far more painful, I'm sure, than the breakup of a youthful love affair. Her sudden return is a shock to everyone, naturally, but I suggest you get hold of yourself and put things in perspective. What happened in the past has no bearing on the situation now."

"How can you say that when you know as well as I do—"

"That's enough. Delilah is my granddaughter, and equally entitled to share in the family heritage. I don't wish to discuss the matter further."

He might have continued to argue—or even to threaten—if Nick hadn't entered the office behind him, bearing a pot of tea in his fist like a weapon. "You didn't have your second cup after all," he said to their grandmother. "Want it now?"

"Get the fuck out, Nick."

"What's this—passion from Mr. Cool? I'm amazed, Travis."

Travis controlled himself fast. At repression, he was an expert. "We'll discuss it later," he said to his grandmother, and left the room.

"Are you all right, Gran?" Nick asked.

"Yes. But I will have that tea, I think. Thank you."

"I didn't think old Trav was capable of that much emotion."

"You don't like him much, do you?"

Nick shrugged. In many ways he was a chronic improver, but his relationship with his brother was one of the few things in his life he had never been able to rectify. Sometimes he thought there must be bad karma between them. He wondered how many lifetimes he and Travis had lived without resolving the subtle problems between them.

It was nothing he could get a fix upon. He and Travis didn't hate each other—they were too different for that. He didn't envy Travis, and he was reasonably sure Travis didn't envy him. But there had always been a cloud between them, something that had separated them even in childhood. Every now and then it touched him, a coldness, a malice almost, that made him shiver.

As children, Travis, the elder brother, had bullied him mercilessly, and Nick had been intimidated and resentful. But that was no longer a problem, at least, not as far as he was concerned. As Eleanor Roosevelt had said, "No one can make you feel inferior without your consent." Nick had withdrawn his consent, although he wasn't certain Travis had noticed.

His grandmother said, "You're perceptive about people, but you don't understand your brother. Life hasn't been as easy for him as you think."

"What's that supposed to mean?"

Minerva shook her head, not answering. With hands that were only a little unsteady, she poured herself another cup of tea.

4

At nine o'clock that evening Delilah ascended the grand staircase to the ballroom of the new Four Seasons Hotel stunningly attired in a silver fox by Karl Lagerfeld, and a full-length anthracite-black silk crepe gown by Ungaro. She knew she would need all her confidence tonight, so she'd dressed even more dramatically than usual. The dress left her left shoulder bare, draped softly but tightly over her waist and hips, and dipped daringly low in the back. Her sling-back silver pumps shone with the season's metallic silver, and her jewelry, too, was silver—flashing, curving, and just a touch barbaric.

She paused under the mammoth chandelier outside the ballroom, one hand on her hip, the other hanging loosely at her side. Through the archway leading into the humming, sparkling ballroom she could see the waiters with the tea trays on their shoulders, complete with squat china pots, petal-thin bone china cups, and gleaming silver sugars and creamers. There was champagne circulating, too, she noted, but the tea waiters were being stopped far more frequently. It was as if all the glitterati of Boston wished to do homage to Minerva Templeton on her eightieth birthday by saluting her with her own drink.

Delilah could discern the fine aromas of Darjeeling, Earl Grey, Jasmine, and Lapsang souchong. Possibly some Irish Breakfast, too. But no herbal teas; certainly not Merlin's Magical Brews, and none of Templeton's inept imitations, either, not one whiff of those. Grendam had always told her she had a fine nose for tea.

She looked in vain for somebody else she recognized. The Hollywood parties she'd attended with Max had always been rife with familiar faces, some of the legendary figures of stage and screen, but this was a different sort of crowd. More old-money, more conservative. The ballroom was milling with proper Bostonians. The men looked as if they'd just emerged from the pages of *Town and Country.* Among the women, classicism reigned. Dior, Saint Laurent, Chanel. One young woman moved among the crowd in a body-molding above-knee-length sheath that had to be an Assedine Alaïa, but she was the exception.

The air stirred beside her. "If you walk in on my arm, no one'll realize we're deadly adversaries."

She turned, slowly. Travis made her a mock bow, looking mouth-wateringly handsome in a crisp black tux.

"Is that what we are, Trav?"

"I hope not, Delilah." He paused, adding more lightly, "If you're looking for the dragon lady, she's over there, chatting with Mayor Flynn."

Delilah glanced in the direction he pointed. "Thanks. I believe I'll get a drink first."

"Good idea. I could use one, too." He took her elbow and steered her toward the bartender, cutting a swath through the crowd by dint of his height and charm and presence. Delilah did not object, although his hand on her bare arm was disconcerting. She was amused by her reaction to him. The physical chemistry between them had once been strong, but considering all the years and experiences that divided them, she hadn't expected any of those old feelings to persist.

Travis left her long enough to secure two glasses of Scotch on the rocks and a plate of hors d'oeuvres. "Oysters Rockefeller," he said with a grin. "Miniature quiches Lorraine and Cajun blackened shrimp. There's also a salmon mousse the size of Chicago, some very nice Beluga, and, on the far side of the room, a sushi bar. I hope you're hungry."

"I'm starved." She helped herself to an oyster. "Let's go back and pile up the plate."

"It's refreshing to see a woman with a healthy appetite. Most of the ones I know are on a perpetual diet. When they come to an affair like this, they eat the food, but apologize constantly in the process."

She sipped her drink. "Does it bother you?"

"Does what bother me?"

"That I'm back. And that you're not automatically getting the dragon lady's job."

To lie would be foolish; she would know. Travis had himself well back under control now; he regretted the lapse that had occurred in his grandmother's office. He was accustomed to being on good terms with everybody. Life was so much simpler that way.

Anyway, there was no reason to panic. Delilah had not yet accepted their grandmother's proposition, and even if she did, it was absurd to think that she would ultimately emerge on top. He knew the company inside and out. In his capacity of Director of Operations he was in charge of everything from purchasing to blending to packing to distribution. Delilah was reputedly a whiz at the marketing end of things, but even if she came in with some slick advertising campaign, he was the one who ensured that supply kept up with demand, and that the product made it onto the supermarket shelves. His work was substance, Delilah's nothing more than flash. Minerva Templeton was experienced enough to know the difference.

He would prevail. If his grandmother thought differently, there were ways in which he could dissuade her. He'd found it useful during the past few years to make sure he had something on everybody, and Minerva Templeton was no exception.

"It bothers me, yes," he admitted, shrugging his shoulders carelessly to show that it didn't bother him *very much.* "Am I to assume that you're going to take her up on her less than glorious offer? A one-year trial with both our futures on the line?"

She made him a mock toast. "You bet I'm going to take her up on it."

Travis looked into her eyes, trying to see that old honesty of hers, that old frankness. But she had the curtains firmly drawn. "You've never forgiven me, have you?"

She twisted the stem of her glass. Her scarlet fingernails against the fine crystal were stunningly erotic. "We were kids. It seems like another lifetime, that mess."

"Not to me. To me it seems as if it happened yesterday." As soon as he said it, Travis regretted the comment. Too much emotion, too openly displayed. Christ. What was wrong with him today? "I treated you badly, and I've always been sorry for that."

"Forget it," she said tightly. "I have."

Sure, Delilah. Sure.

"If you'll excuse me," she said. "I really ought to mingle."

Travis watched her as she presented her back to him and moved away. He didn't want to deprive himself of a first-class view of her bare spine in that incredible dress. What a glorious woman she'd become. Still sylph-slender, all legs and eyes and wild, sexy hair. He relived the moment she'd walked into the meeting today, looking both mischievous and arrogant, the black sheep proud of her defiance, yet ready, even eager, to join the fold again.

The past was swirling around him, pictures, memories, snatches of conversation. Feelings. All the things he usually buried. Or tried to. Doors were opening inside him faster than he could slam them shut again.

To him Delilah was a symbol of life fully lived. Stormy, shining Technicolor Delilah. It seemed incredible to him that he had once been her lover, that she had lain with him and loved him, giving freely of her fire, asking only his love in return. And he'd given it to her. He'd given it as he'd never given it to any other woman. And she didn't know . . . must never know . . . why he had had to leave her.

An elderly matron whom he vaguely recognized as a friend of his grandmother's came up beside him and said something he didn't hear. Travis responded with the dazzling smile that women of all ages seemed to find irresistible. But it was not an old lady he saw. It was the forbidden image of Delilah, bare-limbed and laughing, in his bed again.

Delilah located her grandmother at one end of the room surrounded by a venerable group of Boston's Doric Dames. Grendam was holding forth on her favorite subject, tea, while standing behind an elegant tea table, waving the waiters away and doing the honors herself. She was pouring from a family heirloom Delilah recognized, a magnificent rose, cream, and gold leaf china tea urn that had reputedly been presented to one of her ancestors by Queen Victoria.

"Originally teacups were made without a handle," she was saying. "The handle wasn't added until late in the eighteenth century when the ladies complained about the difficulty of manipulating the hot cups. It was considered mannerly to pour one's tea from one's cup into one's saucer, where it could cool more rapidly, and sip it from that."

She spoke on about several other items of tea equipage that were present on the table—a jewel-encrusted India tea caddy lined with sandlewood, tiny sterling teaspoons that had been a present to the family from George Washington. She knew all the details of their history, and Delilah enjoyed the impromptu lecture every bit as well as Grendam's friends seemed to.

"You were very clever this afternoon, Grendam," she said when she finally got her alone. "My compliments. What would you have done, I wonder, if I hadn't called to warn you that I was on my way home?"

"Probably very much the same thing."

"You could have shown me the door. I half expected you would. After all these years, there's no reason for you to feel any obligation to me."

"You're my granddaughter, and blood is thicker than water. It's time you returned, Delilah. Boston is your home, and the tea company is your heritage."

"If you're going to acknowledge me at all, why not put me at the helm, where I belong? I haven't decided yet whether I'll accept the yearlong compromise you're offering."

Her grandmother's expression was serene as she said, "When you make that decision, please let me know."

Grendam really knew how to work on her, she thought, amused. "You know I'll accept. You know how competitive I am, how loath to resist a challenge. You know altogether too much about me."

Minerva Templeton flicked an invisible speck of dust from the sleeve of her gown. "When will you be able to start?"

"I'll have to find a place to live first, and have some of my things shipped out here, but otherwise I'm ready. I'd like to begin as soon as possible. How about Monday?"

"Excellent."

"You don't look eighty, you know." Impulsively, she took her grandmother's hands between her own and pressed. "I'm glad to see you looking so well, Grendam. Happy birthday."

Her radiant smile left Delilah feeling absurdly pleased.

Because of the increasing popularity of his novels, which were set in the Boston area, Nick was besieged by fans, critics, and would-be writers for most of the evening. He didn't have a chance to seek out Delilah until his grandmother had cut her birthday cake and the party was breaking up.

He'd been admiring her from a distance, however. He'd seen her on TV, where she invariably came across as an appealing, fun-loving personality. The same was true here, without the cameras, without the lights. People gravitated to her, and she drew them into her circle with that brilliant smile, that low, husky laugh.

Nick signed an autograph and mocked himself for his new obsession. It was a good thing Karin Harvey, the corporate attorney he'd been seeing lately, wasn't here to catch him mooning after Delilah. Not that things were serious with Karin; if they had been, maybe she'd have made more of an effort to be with him tonight. Sorry, she'd said, trying to lighten her refusal with a kiss. She had an important meeting on the West Coast.

Kelsey wasn't here either. "I'm not going to pull her out of school for a party she's too young to attend anyway," Janet had said.

"It's not just any party. Gran is eighty years old. I know she'd like to have her great-granddaughter present for her eightieth birthday."

"I'm sorry, Nick. You can have her next weekend, as we agreed. If you have any objections, get in touch with my lawyer."

Bitch.

Feeling lonely and having nothing better to do than talk about Drake, who bored him, Nick said goodnight to his grandmother when Delilah retired to the cloakroom in search of her fur. He followed her out of the hotel. She was walking down Boylston Street toward the Ritz when he overtook her. She stopped suddenly, apparently seeing his shadow bearing down on her.

"It's okay," he said quickly. "It's only me."

"Nick? What's this, an ambush?"

"Protection against same. I figured you needed a tough-guy mystery writer to walk you back to your hotel."

"Thanks, gallant sir, but I was thinking of hailing a cab. My gown's too tight and my feet hurt."

"It's only a few hundred yards. Want a piggyback?"

She laughed. "I'd split my dress for sure." She bent down and took off her shoes. "There. Now I can walk."

She grinned at him and his breath caught. There she was, her hair like black silk falling over the shoulders of the silver fox coat, her dress so tight underneath that no normal male could help wanting to wrestle her out of it, her legs long and beautiful, and her feet bare.

Watch it, man. This is getting out of hand.

Delilah, thank God, misread his expression. "You're not going to lecture me again, I hope. I've had enough tension for one day."

"Fair enough. No more lectures."

"I saw the reception you got in there from your readers," she said as they walked down Boylston Street alongside the iron fence that enclosed the Public Garden. "You're quite a celebrity."

"So are you. Everybody knows you from the Merlin's ads."

"It's a little strange, isn't it? I didn't set out to become any kind of public figure."

He grinned. "You were always an exhibitionist at heart."

"Do you like your work?"

"For the most part, yes. I can work at home, set my own hours, and there's no one leaning over my shoulder, checking up on me. On the other hand, there's a lot of pressure from editors, booksellers, fans. Expectations to live up to, bestseller lists to hit. And writing a series about the same central character is a drag."

"Yes, I guess it would be, after a while."

"I was tempted to kill Drake off two books ago, but when I suggested it to my editor, she nearly went into cardiac arrest." He chuckled. "As a result, I told my agent to hold out for twice as much money when they went to contract on the next novel in the series."

They had reached the corner, where they stopped and waited for the light to change. Streams of frenzied late night drivers poured along Arlington Street. Across and to the right, Nick could see tiny white lights winking on the trees in front of the entrance to the Ritz. "I miss university life more than I ever thought I would. I miss teaching, I miss my students, I even miss writing those arcane little monographs on subjects that are of no interest to anybody but a few Ph.D.'s."

"In that case, why not go back to your old job in academe?"

Nick had a brief vision of eight A.M. classes, piles of illiterate term papers, endless committee meetings. "I don't miss it *that* much. Anyway, I'm working on an idea that might enable me to combine the best of two worlds."

He gave her a brief sketch of his plan for the Helen Templeton biography as they crossed the street and walked the block to the hotel. "She was quite a woman. She survived both the Black Plague and the Fire of London in her childhood, grew up to run her father's apothecary shop. She started a school for both boys and girls with her husband, then emigrated to Boston after his untimely death. Here she ran one of the first apothecary shops, growing all her own herbs for the remedies she concocted. She was a rebel. She refused to remarry, even though every available man in Boston at the time was after her, and because she was a more competent physician than the quacks who were practicing in the colonies at the time, she eventually got herself accused of witchcraft."

"I knew about the witchcraft trial, but I didn't know it had anything to do with her practicing medicine."

"She started variolating her patients with smallpox virus to induce a mild case of the disease and save their lives. Smallpox killed hundreds of people in colonial Boston. Before cowpox inoculation was attempted, variolation was the only way to save lives, but traditionally trained doctors didn't recognize it. It wasn't one hundred percent safe, but it was a helluva lot more successful than any other remedy. Helen was unlucky: one of her patients died, and bingo, she was a witch."

"But she was acquitted."

"Yes. It wasn't as easy to be convicted of witchcraft in colonial Massachusetts as people think. Lots of people were acquitted. The scandal ruined her life for a while, nonetheless."

"So she was into herbal remedies and such," Delilah mused. "So am I. She went from that into tea, *Camellia sinensis.* Maybe I have more in common with my ancestor than I'd realized."

"Maybe." The thought stirred something inside him far below the level of normal consciousness. A memory came to him—a game he'd played years ago with Delilah and Travis. It must have been the summer she lived with them, the summer after her mother's death. He, the imaginative one, had created a scenario in which they'd all taken roles—he was the minister, Travis the judge, and Delilah the accused. She was guilty of witchcraft, they proclaimed. They'd sentenced her to be burned at the stake.

The apple tree in their back yard had served as the place of execution. Nick found a length of rope, while Travis collected kindling. They'd bound their cousin to the trunk of the tree, and Travis produced a soggy old pack of matches. He struck a couple and waved them in the air, then carelessly dropped one, and Delilah had stopped giggling when the leaves and sticks unexpectedly caught.

For a second they all froze as a burst of yellow flame erupted near Delilah's feet. She screamed. Travis dug out his jackknife and began sawing at the ropes that bound her. Nick just stood there, his heart racing painfully, terrified that Delilah was going to die.

"Stamp on it," his brother ordered, tearing futilely at the thick ropes. You've got shoes on, Nick. Do it." Travis's own feet were bare.

They're only sneakers; they'll melt, Nick remembered thinking, but he didn't hesitate. He kicked at the pile of kindling and scattered it, then he jumped on the flames as his brother sliced through the ropes and pulled Delilah free.

They were all punished afterward. By some miracle none of them was burned—Nick's sneakers had been scorched, but they'd protected his feet, and the fire hadn't quite reached Delilah's bare legs. Delilah had accepted her spanking along with theirs—"It was only a game; they weren't picking on me," she loyally told their grandmother. Nick wasn't sure he'd have been so forgiving.

They had arrived in the foyer of the Ritz. Delilah gestured toward the bar, but Nick shook his head. There in the light of the lobby he could see the slightest traces of strain around her eyes. "You're tired," he said gently. "Better go upstairs and get some sleep."

"You're right," she admitted. "Thanks."

For an instant as he looked down at her, Delilah's form seemed superimposed on that of a beautiful Puritan woman with auburn hair. Nick shook his head and she came back into normal focus again.

He had no intention of kissing her. It was she who put her arms around him and lightly touched her mouth to his. She had always been physically demonstrative, he reminded himself. Unlike Gran, who found it difficult to express her love, Delilah's nature was affectionate and warm. It didn't mean anything. The embrace wasn't sexual, for chrissake.

Nevertheless, as Nick closed his arms around his dramatic black-haired cousin, resplendent in silver fox and silk, as he inhaled the exotic scent of fine cosmetics and felt the supple grace of her body, he muttered a single, inaudible word against her lips. The word was, *shit.*

When all her guests finally bade her their final good wishes and she was free to leave, Minerva had her driver take her directly home to the China Tea House Tavern. As she entered, she was greeted by Mary Mango, her housekeeper, whom she had hired in part because the name reminded her of the hot days in India when she'd greedily sucked the rich, orangy fruit and felt the juices trickle down her dry throat. She'd never returned to the green foothills of the Himalayas, where she'd been born. One day she really must go back.

"You look exhausted, Mrs. Templeton," the housekeeper said. " 'Tisn't right to work all day on your birthday, and then be out partying so late at night."

"Please, Mary, don't fuss."

"I've laid out your night things. You go straight on up and get a decent sleep."

Minerva was too weary to object. Within fifteen minutes she was in bed.

Sleep did not come easily to her; it never had. She relived all the events of the day, which inevitably led to recollections of the past. At first Travis and Delilah were foremost in her mind, then her guilty conscience began to reconstruct other, earlier disasters. Elizabeth and Jonathan, her two children, one dead, the other a rootless wanderer. Edward, her husband. Harrison Templeton, that monster, Edward's father.

"Don't let me dream of *him,*" she whispered. "I'd rather lie awake all night than dream of him."

To block out the persistent images, she tried instead of focus on externals: the wallpaper, the furniture. Although the lower floor of the house had been extensively renovated, its interiors redone every few years, Minerva had kept a stark colonial simplicity here in the master bedchamber. The walls were painted ivory, but the original walnut paneling had been carefully preserved.

The floor, too, was original—wide planks of rough oak covered with two Turkish kilims and a colorful antique hooked rug. A New England Carver chair stood against the rear wall beside a maple drop-front desk, and a Queen Anne chair in the opposite corner. The chest of drawers was early eighteenth century and had been refinished by an expert on colonial antiques. Minerva's pencil-post bedstead with a honey-gold canopy and a two-hundred-year-old hand-sewn quilt occupied its rather odd position right in the center of the room.

The location of the bed always startled people, and indeed, it was difficult to explain. One night several months ago, Minerva had awoken with a strange compulsion. She rose from bed and, still half-asleep, squatted down on her hands and knees to roll back the rug. It was hard work, for the rug was heavy and her bones were ridden with arthritis, but eventually the floor with its scorched black circle was revealed. Something niggled at her—voices overheard in the dream, perhaps? The circle was important. She did not know why.

Nine feet in circumference, the circle was so regular, it might have been drawn with a compass. It had apparently been burned into the wood, although none of the experts she'd consulted several years before when she was having restoration work done could tell her how. It reminded Minerva of a faerie ring. Nick had told her she might feel stronger sitting inside it, just as some people claim they can focus their physical and mental powers by sitting within the structure of a pyramid.

Minerva had laughed. Nick was interested in strange phenomena, but she was a child of reason. She had no superstition in her soul, not even the conventional religious variety. Although she belonged to a church, she rarely attended, and the only time she thought about God was in the middle of the night sometimes, when she had the dreams that threatened her soul with childhood visions of hell.

On this particular night, however, moved by the same irrational impulse that had propelled her out of bed, Minerva had proceeded to drag and shove the small four-poster until it stood entirely within the confines of the circle. Only then did she feel comfortable enough to climb back under the covers and continue her sleep.

In the morning, embarrassed, she'd pushed the bed back to its original position. But after several successive restless nights, she'd had the servants rearrange all the furniture in her room so that she now slept within the ring.

Silly, of course. Childish. How Edward would have laughed at her. Nick had looked so like him this afternoon. This evening, too. Sometimes she almost thought Nick *was* Edward, come back again. But that was impossible, surely. She didn't believe in reincarnation, although, admittedly, it was a more appealing philosophy than the Christian notion of reward and punishment.

She closed her eyes, and saw reflected in her mind the magnificent green hills of Darjeeling.

PART TWO

She was as immutable as the hills. But not quite so green.

—Rudyard Kipling

British India, 1916

5

"I am the resurrection and the life: he that believeth in me, though he were dead, yet shall he live; And whosoever liveth and believeth in me shall never die."

The minister intoning the words sounded like the voice of God himself, even though Minerva Carstairs knew it was only Father Jacobs, an ordinary-looking man with longish hair and a skinny face. She couldn't quite see him, for the Easter service was crowded, and a lady with a huge straw hat decorated with lilacs was sitting in the pew in front of her, blocking her view of the altar. It was always crowded on Easter; tea planters from the hills all around Darjeeling emerged from their bungalows once a year to acknowledge that they were Christians. Minerva's father said they weren't really Christians at all, but hypocrites who, like some ancient pagans, felt the need to rush out and celebrate the fertility rites of spring.

Despite her father's pronouncements on the subject, Minerva loved church. She liked the Bible lessons and the hymns and even some of the prayers, except on Holy Communion Sundays, when you had to stay on your knees for what seemed like hours while the grown-ups prepared to approach the communion rail and the minister read on and on about how Jesus had taken the bread, broken it, and said, "This is my body which is given for thee." All the stories about Jesus fascinated her. She was sorry, though, that there was never any mention of the other wonderful stories she'd grown up with, the tales of Rama and Krishna and Hanumant, the monkey god, which her *ayah* had regaled her with since she'd been a babe in the cradle. The British, she'd learned long ago, were very condescending about the colorful gods of India.

Sometimes, while Father Jacobs talked about hell, Minerva thought of Ayah's declaration that there was no such place. "When the spirit passes out of the body, it is born again. Here on the earth is all the evil that exists, Missy baba. Round and round we go on the wheel of life, coming back into this world of suffering until we become enlightened and are freed."

Minerva liked this much more than the picture in her children's illustrated Bible of little angels sprouting wings in heaven and tossing golden balls to one another through the clouds.

Her father shared her doubts about the Christian version of the afterlife. "I've no intention of subjecting myself to the castigation of some ridiculous minister raving about a hotter clime than this," he said. So he sent his daughter off to church in a tonga with her governess, Miss Grainger, who had recently come out from England to take over her education.

Miss Pamela Grainger was sitting beside her now, her head tilted slightly as she listened to the comforting words of Christ. Minerva liked Miss Grainger, who was not a formidable sort of governess, but very nice and very pretty. She wasn't strict at all. Only a few days before she had set aside Minerva's Latin grammar and taken her outside instead to the garden. "You can learn much more from nature than from some stuffy Roman author," she had said.

It was cool and dark in the church, although there were many more candles alight today than usual, in celebration of the joyous feast. Minerva had sat quietly, hands folded in her lap, staring into the chancel. She wondered what it was like to be an acolyte, to wear white robes and be allowed the momentous task of lighting the tall yellow candles. Or to sing in the choir and be seated close to the altar, surrounded by the power of God. The bronze candlesticks looked like gold to her, as did the great bronze cross that hung in the sanctuary. The altar was draped in white and decked with Easter lilies, and Father Jacobs wore a pure white cassock finely embroidered with threads of silver and gold.

The music, too, was beautiful. They sang all the Easter hymns—the ones everybody in the congregation knew since they were the same ones, year after year—"Jesus Christ Is Ris'n Today," "The Strife Is O'er," "Welcome Happy Morning."

The Communion Hymn was sung—"Hail Thee Festival Day"—with the men and women in the congregation alternating verses, then the ushers moved slowly backward through the church, pew by pew, as the adults went up to partake of the bread and the wine. At ten, Minerva was still too young to receive, but Miss Grainger always took her up anyway, to be blessed by the priest.

The church was not large, but it was full, and Minerva and her governess were seated toward the back. The procession of communicants toward the altar rail seemed particularly slow, and around them, several members of the congregation began whispering, which Minerva found shocking. You were supposed to keep your mind and heart pure while waiting to receive God's blessing.

"That's the Carstairs girl," someone in the pew behind her said. "Her mother was a whore, you know."

Minerva's breath rushed out of her, and for a moment she couldn't seem to get it back. The woman was whispering, but the sound carried.

"You don't say so!"

"Honestly. Shocking business. Very hard on her poor husband, of course. And *such* an example to set for the child. The mother came to a bad end."

"Indeed?" The clipped British voice managed to be both disapproving and encouraging. Minerva kept her face averted so they wouldn't see how hot she had become.

"She finally ran off with one of *them,*" the first harpy was saying.

"You don't mean—"

"Precisely. An Indian, as black as they come. They disappeared into the stews of Calcutta six or seven years ago and haven't been heard from since. The family put it about that she was dead, of course."

"How positively dreadful!"

"Poor Carstairs was a fool to marry her. Isabella was a wild one. Carried on even before she was married, or so everyone says."

"How old did you say the daughter was?"

"Nine or ten, I suppose. She's small for her age." Minerva could feel them scrutinizing her. "Those dark eyes of hers remind me of her mother's. Witch's eyes, and much more sly than they should be."

"But she's a pretty child. Striking."

"So much the worse for her. She'll take after the mother; you mark my words."

Horrid old monsters! Minerva didn't dare move or breathe or turn her head. She didn't dare let them know she'd heard what they'd said. But she pressed a little nearer to Miss Grainger, and slipped her hand into hers. Miss Grainger's fingers tightened fiercely, and Minerva knew she'd heard it, too.

"It's not true, it's not true," she wept all the way home to the tea plantation, while Miss Grainger hugged her and stroked her hair. "My mother was beautiful and good! She didn't run away; she died of cholera when I was three years old."

"I'm sure she did, love. Your father is right about those hypocrites. Did you see the way they marched right up and received communion afterwards just as if they considered themselves entirely without sin?"

"I wish I'd turned around and thrown my prayer book in their faces!"

"No, my dear, you did just right. You must hide your feelings. Don't give them the satisfaction. Don't ever give anybody the satisfaction of knowing they've hurt you. You were very brave and strong, and I'm so proud of you."

"It's not true what they said, is it?"

"Of course not, lovey. Of course it's not true."

But it was, and Minerva's father confirmed it himself later that same day. "Is Mama really dead, Papa?" she asked. Minerva could barely remember her mother. She'd had blond hair like her own, she thought, and she'd always smelled wonderful, like wildflowers. "Is it true she ran away to Calcutta?"

"Where did you hear that?" His voice went all harsh and tight, the sort of voice that might have discouraged her from pursuing the subject, had she not been so distressed.

"I want to know about my mother. She wasn't really a whore, was she?"

"Who the devil has been telling you such tales? Miss Grainger!" he bellowed, demanding an explanation. Upon hearing it, he cursed long and loud. "Goddamn their gossiping souls! Dear

Christ!" He put his head into his clasped hands. "Reputation, reputation, reputation! I have lost my reputation."

Minerva had heard him declaim these words before. They were from a play by Shakespeare. Her father loved Shakespeare and would often come into her room at night to read to her from his thick book of plays. There were certain phrases, like the one about reputation, that he seemed to find particularly fine. He often spoke wistfully of England, of his home in the west country of Devon, where the rich red earth formed sculpted cliffs that ran to the sea, of Dartmoor, where the wild ponies ran free over the scrubby land. There was some reason—something to do with his family, she believed—why he couldn't return to England. "Banished," he would mutter sometimes when he'd had a drop of two of whiskey. He would always accent the last syllable when he said it: "Ban-i-shed." Then he would go on with such words as, "Ah, the pity of it, the pity of it. Nevermore to see this scepter'd isle, this precious stone set in the silver sea, this blessed plot, this earth, this realm, this England."

"I want to know about my mother," she insisted now. "You told me she was dead."

"Ah, lassie, there's every reason to believe she is. But 'tis true, it wasn't the cholera that brought her down. 'Twas a fever of another sort."

Her mother, he explained, had never been content with life here on the large tea plantation in the high, hilly country of Darjeeling near the border of Nepal. "She pined for England, angel. She didn't grow to love this land the way you and I do. She dreamed instead of the great cities, London, Paris, New York. I guess she wanted a man who would take her away from this wild land. In the end she found one. But it wasn't London or Paris he took her to. It was that stinkhole, Calcutta."

"So it's true, then? She ran away with an Indian?" Even at ten, Minerva was enough a child of the Raj to find this shocking.

"Yes. But he was a good man, for all that." Unlike most Britishers, Douglas Carstairs was uneasy with the white supremacy of life in India. He saw no reason to suppose that the good Lord had made the people of one nation inherently any better than the people of another. "Ravi was smart, ambitious. I'd made him overseer of the tea-processing factory when the chap who had the job before him went sickly on me and had to be shipped back to Sussex. Ravi was good-looking, too—taller than most, and a smooth-tongued fellow. I should have seen what was coming, I suppose, but I've never had a jealous or possessive nature. I prided myself on that, but sometimes you can overdo virtues, little one, just as you can overdo faults."

Minerva was silent, watching and listening, her big, dark eyes fixed upon his face. Carstairs wondered if she understood exactly what he was saying. She had always seemed clever to him in many ways, but still, she was only ten.

"You were still a baby, Min, and maybe it was hard for her, trying to be a mother to you. I'd always thought a child would settle her down, but it didn't turn out that way. Some women just don't make natural mothers. I know that now, angel. To my shame, I didn't know it then.

"They fell in love, you see." Did she see? He had no idea. "She ran off one morning with Ravi, who claimed, poor sod, to have had a glorious future awaiting him in Calcutta."

He remembered the morning—it had been one of those misty days so common in Darjeeling when you couldn't see the mountains but only sensed they were there, huge, lurking shapes behind the clouds. Isabella had been last seen by the sweeper early in the morning as the fellow was dusting the veranda. The sweeper reported later that the young memsahib had been running down the road in the direction of the narrow-gauge railway. She must have caught the first train down the mountains to Siliguri, leaving behind her a three-year-old daughter and a too loving, too trusting husband.

"We searched for her, of course. 'Twas months before I gave up hope of tracing her. But you've seen the city, Min, and you must be able to imagine the difficulty of the task."

Minerva had indeed seen the horrible wonder that was Calcutta, where she had now and then accompanied her father to attend to the final disposition of their tea. She vividly remembered the tour her father had given her of great Kidderpore warehouse on the banks of the Hooghly River. They had stood in an archway inside the long, narrow brick building where tea from the hills was housed prior to sale. Row upon row of tea chests were stacked in the room, and tea brokers were boring holes in the sides of these chests, to take samples for the auctions. Her father had explained the process to her, declaring that he liked to check up on his agents now and then, to make sure they were getting the best price for his fine Darjeeling tea.

She had been frightened, because the inside of the warehouse was so dark, and in the corners behind the tea chests she heard scurryings that sounded like rats. "Rats? Nonsense!" her father boomed. "Even if they had 'em, the cobras would keep 'em in control."

The city itself was a great metropolis, both frightening and exhilarating. Long known as the Empire's Second City, Calcutta was a great center of trade and British culture. But the same city that was graced with the munificence of the Victoria Memorial was also a teeming slum with filth belching from numberless factories and uncollected refuse spilling over into its serpentine streets. Its merciless wet, hot weather incubated cholera, smallpox, typhoid, and malaria, and every time there was a famine in the surrounding countryside, thousands of refugees poured into Calcutta and set up housekeeping on the street, living, dying, and giving birth without privacy, without hope.

"It's been seven years since she disappeared," her father said. "I know in my heart we'll never see her again. Calcutta devours its refugees, and spits out their bones. Your mother abandoned her heritage, Min. She sacrificed all for love. You'll soon be a young lady, child. Hard though it is, I want you to remember this story, and grow up wiser than she."

Minerva listened to his words, but was by no means certain that she would profit from his advice. She had always imagined her mother as some sort of fairy princess, and she was determined to hold on to that dream, despite the harpies in the church. Now she imagined Ravi as well—handsome and strong with dusky hollow cheekbones and that sonorous way of talking that she loved to listen to among the tea laborers. She felt sorry for her father because his voice had been so sad, but in her secret heart she thought the story of the lovers very romantic, and dreamed that one day she, too, would throw away all for love.

"I am the resurrection and the life: he that believeth in me, though he were dead, yet shall he live . . ." Father Jacobs was murmuring the words again, three years later, in the fragrant little churchyard where the wildflowers blossomed around the gravestones. Minerva could barely hear the words now, so distraught was she. She and Miss Grainger, now Mrs. Carstairs, were burying her father, who had sickened and died of a heart seizure three days before.

It had come on without warning. He had been sitting on the veranda at dawn, having his morning tea and talking to his wife and daughter about his problems with this season's tea crop, when he'd suddenly put a hand to his chest and looked off into the distance with an odd expression on his face. "The pain," he'd said, sounding puzzled. "Good Christ, the pain!"

Pamela—for so Minerva now called her stepmother—screamed for the bearer, who forgot his usual dignity and came running when he saw the sahib toppling out of his wicker chair to the floor. Somehow they got Douglas Carstairs to bed and sent for the English doctor from Darjeeling, but by the time the doctor arrived, Carstairs was unconscious and there was little the physician could do.

Minerva and Pamela had huddled all day by his side, waiting for the end. Minerva had a strange, dislocated sensation. She seemed to see herself lying upon her own deathbed. She thought: one day, I, too, will lie like this, barely breathing, about to die. In a blink of the eye, I will lie here. My life, which seems to stretch before me like a dream, will fly by before I know it, and I, too, will come to this.

Why? she wondered. What is it all *for?*

"Ashes to ashes, dust to dust," said the priest. And later, after the burial, he told the widow and her stepdaughter, "God will assuage your grief."

"I hate God," Minerva said, and fled from the churchyard, vowing never, never to return.

Pamela Grainger had married Douglas Carstairs not long after that distressing Easter Sunday when Minerva had found out about her mother. "The girl needs a mother," Douglas had said gruffly. "And God knows, I need a wife."

The marriage had been successful, bringing warmth and laughter to the plantation. With her new stepmother's encouragement,

Minerva had laughed and dreamed and made elaborate plans for her life there in the shadow of the magnificent Himalayas, surrounded by the deep green bushes that produce the finest tea in the world.

Pamela's widowhood was less successful. She was no businesswoman. She was left to run the tea plantation on her own, and the managers she hired cheated her. There followed in rapid succession a drought, falling tea prices, and an acquisitive American tycoon named Harrison Templeton.

Templeton was the latest in a family of entrepreneurs noted for turning up an innovative teaman in every generation. Although he was the younger son—his brother Earnest had inherited all the voting stock in the family-run company—Harrison was fascinated with the tea business and had devised what seemed to be a highly practical plan to reduce prices: instead of buying tea at auction in Calcutta or London, he would grow his own. He told his brother that he was going to find a way to "control this blasted operation from plant to cup."

Templeton had come to India looking to invest in a tea plantation. Someone had put him onto Pamela, hinting that she was in trouble and ready to sell. Templeton took one look at her long chestnut hair, generous mouth, and slim figure, and knew at once he wanted more than just her land.

He was a big, black-bearded man, a Teddy Roosevelt adventurer, given to hunting, shooting, hard drinking, and a rakehell pursuit of women. "There's just something about me they can't seem to resist," he was fond of boasting to his friends. "Young ones, old ones, well favored and plain, they can't wait to fit me between their pretty white thighs."

"It sure looks like you could use a man around here, ma'am," he said to Pamela when first they met. He stared out across the courtyard at several female tea pickers who were sitting in the shade, eating their meager noontime meal. "Need someone to get those layabouts working again."

Pamela explained that life was slower in India, but that eventually things got done. Her real problems, she admitted, were with her finances. She wasn't the best manager in the world.

"As to that, ma'am, I come from a long line of successful financiers. I'd be glad to look your books over in a friendly sort of way and give you some advice."

Pamela was grateful, and Templeton was elated. He figured he could manage her right into the bedroom.

Pamela was still relatively young—twenty-six—and not a good judge of duplicitous people. Although she was less restless and more sweet-natured than the unfortunate Isabella Carstairs, she was equally foolish when it came to breaking society's rules for the sake of love.

Harrison Templeton excited her. He made the other men she knew—Britishers, most of them—seem washed-out and ineffectual in comparison. When he took her into his arms and roughly kissed her, he aroused in her a wicked heat of passion that was far beyond anything in her experience. She tried to hold him off until he married her, but this proved impossible. She surrendered one lush evening in the privacy of the bedroom she'd shared with Douglas, delighting as much in the pleasure he brought her as in his avowals of everlasting love.

Templeton wisely made no mention of his twenty-year-old marriage, nor did he admit that he had already sent for his wife and son to join him. India, he'd decided, was the spot where he was going to make his mark.

Upon hearing that Pamela intended to keep the plantation for Minerva, Templeton slowly worked his lover around to entrusting him with all her business and legal affairs. She was not even aware until it was done that among the many papers she signed on his instructions were the deeds transferring ownership of the plantation to him.

And so began a new regime. Servants who had been with the family for decades were dismissed, more labor was hired to pick the tea faster, and Pamela went from being mistress of the household to mistress of a ruthless man. As for Minerva, she was treated as little more than a servant.

Pamela had just begun to realize—and to regret—her folly when the final blow fell. Slightly less than a year after Douglas Carstairs's death, Harrison Templeton's wife and son arrived from the United States.

"I'm disgraced, Min," Pamela said to her stepdaughter. "I've done something very wrong, and now it looks as if I'm to be punished for it. Take heed, my dear, and learn from my fate. It happened to your mother; now it's happening to me."

"What rot," said the girl. She was by nature optimistic, but it frightened her to see how much Pamela had changed, going from the cheerful, laughing girl who had married her father to this shamed, frightened woman who, in trusting a man, had made a terrible mistake. "We'll think of something. Maybe he'll get a divorce."

But Pamela shook her head. "A man doesn't bring his wife and son halfway around the world if he has any intention of divorcing her. No, sweet. I'll have to leave, of course. I'll go south to my relatives in Bombay. But you must stay. The plantation should have been yours, Min. Oh God, how will you ever forgive me? You're too young to understand what I've done!"

Minerva hugged Pamela, saying firmly, "I'm not too young. And I do understand. He may have tricked you into selling, but it's not over yet." At fourteen she already had the spirit and determination she would retain at the age of eighty. Her path was clear. Harrison Templeton had shamed Pamela and cheated her out of her inheritance. For that he was going to pay.

Minerva regarded the tea plantation as her birthright and the Templetons as lying, thieving interlopers. She loved the high green slopes of Darjeeling; she loved the mountain winds, the faint smell of fermented tea that wafted from the factories to mix with the natural scents of wildflowers and grass. The crass Americans had no appreciation for the savage beauty of the land, and she was determined to banish them to the far-off country from which they had come.

"Someday I'll get back everything he's stolen. Someday I'll own the plantation again, and run it, too, as my father intended I should."

Pamela held her close and cried. She doesn't think I'll be able to do it, Minerva realized. But I will. She'll see; I will.

She had decided how it was to be done. Three years had passed, and Minerva was a mature seventeen. She had inherited both her father's steady tenaciousness and her mother's unconcern for petty rules of social behavior. And she had something else that neither of them had possessed in so great a measure—a determination to control her own destiny.

Minerva's plan was to marry one of the wealthy tea planters in Darjeeling. Templeton's rough manners and his constant philandering with other men's wives had already made him several enemies. She would wed one of them, and together they would put Templeton out of business.

She felt no moral qualms. Living close to the land as she did, she had always been in touch with the relentless march of nature. One of her tasks had been to transplant the nursling tea bushes that were grown up from their tender shoots in the greenhouse; every season she would watch the hardy plants survive and the peaked ones die. She knew from her visits to Calcutta that India was a land where this lesson was repeated every day a dozen times over. Death was all around—in the fields, where the deadly vipers lurked, in the city streets, where thugs slit throats without mercy and the cholera raged, in the sectarian fighting that erupted without warning between Hindu and Muslim. India was the land of the weak and the strong. Templeton was one of the latter, as was she. When the time came, she would deal with him on his own terms.

For three years she had watched and waited. She knew Templeton gambled excessively. She knew he was lavish in the amount of money he spent on his mistresses. She also knew that the plantation was not turning a profit, and that his planned innovations for his American tea company were not having the desired results. Soon, she thought, soon.

In the meantime, she concentrated on making herself attractive to the men from among whom she intended to choose her husband. Mrs. Templeton, into whose graces Minerva had insinuated herself in order to avoid being sent away from the plantation, had given her several old gowns that she no longer required for her own use. Minerva had altered them, making them short and slinky. She had gleaned the latest fashions by spying upon the English garden parties in Darjeeling to which she was no longer invited and memorizing the details of the young women's clothes.

One of the servants bobbed her hair so she looked like the American girls in the magazines that occasionally arrived, rolled up in brown paper from the States, for Mrs. Templeton. She practiced making up her face with lipstick and rouge and light matte powder. She applied nail varnish. She tinted her eyebrows with kohl to accent her dark eyes. Her hair remained blond, a striking contrast, and her body had blossomed into the early voluptuousness that had also been her mother's.

She went visiting with Mrs. Templeton, whom she flattered outrageously whenever she could. Privately she despised both Mrs. Templeton and Edward, her shy twenty-one-year-old son who was always malingering with some illness or other. Edward did have several friends, however, who were older than he was and eligible. When they came to see him, Minerva made sure she was around, looking her most attractive.

In her determination to carry out her plan, Minerva made one crucial mistake. She failed to notice the effect her growing beauty and seductiveness was having upon Harrison Templeton. So she was surprised when one evening at sunset he waylaid her a few hundred yards from the plantation's factory, where the fresh leaves were withered, rolled, fermented, and fired in the four-step process that made them into tea.

"Come, little pigeon," Templeton said. He took her arm roughly and led her up the terraced hillsides to the north tea garden, where the women had labored all day gathering the precious second flush in their baskets, their saris making bright flashes of vibrant color against a background of green.

"Where are you taking me?" She was beginning to be alarmed. He rarely paid any attention to her, and she did all she could to avoid him. His touch revolted her.

He led her into the shadows and tossed her down under a tea bush, dirtying her frock. When she cried out, he covered her mouth with one big hand and tore at her bodice with the other. "No fuss now. You've been signaling your willingness quite frantically, little miss. All the men have noticed it. I know a few who'd like to have you for themselves, but you're here, aren't you, under my roof. You're a bit young for it, but who am I to question such avidity?"

Truly frightened now, Minerva struggled, but this only incited Templeton to greater passion. "Like it rough, do you? I'll be happy to oblige." Pinning her arms to the ground, he covered her slender body with his and pushed her carefully altered dress up around her thighs. He favored her with no tender caresses, not even so much as a kiss. Grunting with his own arousal and without care or consideration for hers, he tore away her panties, spread her legs, and relieved her of her virginity with a single powerful thrust.

Minerva screamed. Templeton grunted and drove into her even harder, again and again until his lust reached a climax. Minerva lay whimpering beneath him, her cheeks streaked with bitter tears.

He rolled off her, disgusted with her lack of the most elementary knowledge of how to please him. "I've no taste for amateurs," he said as he rose up from the dirt and buttoned his trousers. "You'd better learn to deliver what you offer, or you're likely to have an abbreviated career."

He left her bruised and bleeding under a tea bush, watching the night stars turn slowly overhead. Her spirit shriveled within her; for the first time in her young life, she thought about dying. To make it worse, every whisper she'd ever heard about sex had been idyllic; she had not imagined it would hurt so much.

"Bastard," she whispered. "Someday I'll get even with you; I swear it."

Minerva might have lain there under the tea bushes all night, seeing her plans—and her future—dissolve before her eyes, had it not been for Templeton's milksop son, Edward. He was out in the gardens hunting butterflies when he came upon her. Minerva heard him approaching and scrambled to her feet, adjusting her dress to cover the evidence of her shame. Her father's words suddenly came back to her: "Reputation, reputation, reputation!" So much for her fantasies of marriage. Now she would be the one who was whispered about in church.

"Miss Carstairs! What on earth has happened to you? Are you hurt?"

Minerva was furiously casting about for an explanation. "I slipped and fell, I'm afraid. The slope is so steep hereabouts. I've twisted my ankle, I think."

"Well, you mustn't put any weight on it, then. Here, lean on me. That's it; hold tight. I'll get you back to the bungalow."

These were more words than she'd ever heard him utter, particularly in conversation with a female. Edward Templeton had the habit of avoiding everybody's direct gaze, and seemed afraid even of the most lowly Untouchable servant. She was certain he never would have ventured to address her if he hadn't found her in such dire straits.

His hands were gentle, so different from his father's. He took her home and filled her with tea and biscuits, looking at her with such adoration in his gray eyes that it occurred to Minerva she might still be able to triumph after all.

6

"Please, Min. I love you so much. Please let me."

"Edward, no." Her voice was a mere whisper and her resolution was fading. She and Edward were together on the veranda of a deserted bungalow. The mountain behind them was wearing the full moon like a crown. The evening was warmer than usual and humid, and the promise of the coming monsoon had brought with it a heat, an urgency, of quite another variety.

He had his hands on her breasts. The buttons of her blouse were still closed, and Minerva had no intention of allowing him to open it. It was all he wanted—just to touch his palms to her bare breasts. He felt good to her; his strong young body, which had always seemed so awkward, lost its clumsiness when he was sexually aroused. But he was gentle, respectful, and although he pleaded sometimes, he never pushed. It seemed ridiculous to her to deny him, and yet she knew she must. What had happened with his father was not going to happen again.

"Edward, we mustn't."

"Min, I love you. You know I love you. I want to marry you, Min."

"It's wrong," she whispered. "My darling, it's so very wrong."

"I don't believe you. Nothing so good, so beautiful, could possibly be wrong."

Ah, but you don't know the truth about me, my love. You would cringe away from me in disgust if you knew the truth.

"Please say you'll marry me, Min. Say no to everything else if you must, but don't say no to that. I love you. I can't live without you."

He was saying all the words she'd longed to hear. And he was sincere. But instead of rejoicing in the means of her salvation, Minerva wanted to weep.

When he'd first come to her on that dreadful evening in the tea gardens, Minerva's first thought had been to use Edward as her instrument of revenge against his father. She gave up the plan of marrying one of Harrison Templeton's rivals; instead she would marry his son and heir. That way she would reclaim the tea plantation—and everything else that belonged to the Templeton family—sometime in the future when the older man died. And she would force him to recognize the young girl he had so callously raped as his daughter-in-law.

Minerva had been determined not to make the mistake her mother and Pamela had made: instead of surrendering her body to the boy, she would tease him mercilessly all the way to the altar.

But nothing was working out the way she'd planned. In the first place, Edward had proved to be remarkably sensual. His caresses inspired passions in her that Minerva hadn't expected to feel. When he pressed her against his skinny body and kissed her, she burned with a need for real closeness, true love. He was gentle with her and kind, and it had been so long since she had known affection from anyone.

She felt justified in her plotting against Harrison Templeton, but she was increasingly guilty about using Edward as the means to her revenge. He was nothing like his father. Why should he suffer for the old man's sins? He didn't know she'd been ravaged by his father. He had no idea that her head was full of schemes and plans. He thought her an innocent young woman with no more notion of the harsh realities of life than he himself possessed.

He wanted to marry her, but how could she agree? She'd had sex forced on her by his father—that was bad enough. But something even worse had been the issue of that short, brutal interlude in the tea garden, something that made this intimacy between them even more sinful: Minerva was pregnant with Harrison Templeton's child.

Edward kissed her shyly, and she shivered. Lying here like this with him . . . was it incest? If she married him, she would bear to her husband his own half brother or sister. If anyone ever found out, they would say she was a whore like her mother. They would say she was unnatural, an evil, immoral slut.

Edward's mouth sucked at her lips, inspiring sweet urgings in the pit of her belly. It was a desperate, hot yearning that tempted her to forget her qualms, forget her very self. In a few months, when her pregnancy became obvious, Mrs. Templeton would turn her out to fend for herself. She had no money, no friends. She would end up on the streets of Calcutta, living out every nightmare she'd ever had about her mother's fate.

"Min?" Edward's hand was gentle as he stroked her golden hair. He was always so careful with her, hardly daring to touch her in the beginning, but becoming bolder when he discovered that she would allow small intimacies . . . light kisses, gentlemanly caresses. "Is something wrong? What's the matter? Please talk to me. I want to share your troubles."

Not this one, she thought. This is one trouble you must never share. Instead she let him unbutton her blouse and caress her naked breasts.

The following morning Minerva was walking in the tea gardens, watching the women gathering the two leaves and a bud that represented the new flush, when she was seized with a terrible urge to vomit. Crouching in the shrubbery, she surrendered to the spasms that continued even after there was nothing left in her stomach to expel. She heard a footfall, then she felt a cool hand upon her head. She looked up into the ancient face of Sita, her old ayah, who had been reduced by Harrison Templeton to the less exalted status of a tea picker. It was hard work, but the old woman seemed none the worse for it.

"This is the third time I have watched you be sick in the mornings, Missy baba," she said in the Hindustani dialect that Minerva had spoken since childhood. "Come to me this night in the servants' quarters and I will help you."

Minerva grasped the small brown hands that her old nurse held out to her. She was very close to tears. It was two weeks since she had missed her monthly courses, and there was no sign—none—that her bleeding was about to begin.

"Oh, Ayah, I've been such a fool."

"Come to me, daughter. You are young and strong; there might be a way."

That night when the sun had burned its way down the purple mountains, Minerva put a knitted shawl over the gold hair and crept out of the family bungalow to the outhouses where servants lived. The servants' quarters consisted of a low row of attached two-roomed dwellings, one allotted to each servant, whether or not he had a family. Most did. Sita shared one with her son, his wife, and their five children. The eldest of these children, Mohini, a sultry girl who was just coming into her womanhood, was perhaps three years younger than Minerva. Sita and her son were worried, Minerva knew, about arranging a marriage for her. They had no money for her dowry.

Once Minerva might have felt sorry for Mohini, but now she thought, she still has her hopes, her innocence. She is better off than I.

Minerva knew that for years her ayah had been the healer on the tea plantation. She gathered herbs and seeds both for cookery and for medicinal purposes. When Minerva was a child, Sita's herbal syrups had eased many a nasty cough. For serious illness, however, her father had preferred to consult the English doctor from Darjeeling, for he had no faith in medicine practiced by the Indians, so many of whom he had seen dying in the streets of Calcutta and Bombay.

"The Indians are too fond of leaving everything up to fate," he often said. "If you take ill and die, you will simply come back in another body, so why fuss too much over your current one? Medicine can hardly be expected to prosper in such a climate."

Sita welcomed Minerva into her home; her son, daughter-in-law, and all the children were shy and respectful. The daughter-in-law brought tea in a chipped china cup, and Minerva was invited to partake of their evening meal. When she saw how little food was available to feed the entire family—just a few spicy vegetable *samosas,* some unleavened *chapatis,* and a little rice—and what a large portion of it they were dishing out into a cracked bowl for her, she felt ashamed. But she ate it all, for she knew they would be insulted if she refused.

"But I am not Missy baba anymore," she whispered to Sita,

after hearing a short speech from the son about his pleasure in welcoming her to their humble home.

"In our eyes you will always be Missy baba."

Sitting there on the dirt floor among this poor but contented Indian family, Minerva felt their love and wanted to cry. If only she were one of them. If only she could remain here always, never having to face the consequences of what had happened to her. What peace it would be simply to rise with the sun, gather tea, eat a simple supper with one's beloved family, and go to sleep.

Their lives were not so simple or so free of care, she knew. Yet she enjoyed the illusion, the *maya,* and she drank it in.

Somewhere in another part of the servants' quarters a woman's voice was singing in the high-pitched, wavery manner of the Hindus. Sita closed her eyes and swayed slightly with the music, as if gathering strength from its mysterious patterns. Then she touched Minerva's shoulder and said softly, "Come."

There was a small sleeping area separated from the main room by a coarse curtain. Sita led her into this relative privacy, accompanied by Mohini. "She will learn my ways. If she can stop thinking about strong young men long enough to listen."

The girl flushed and looked away. Minerva had felt her eyes upon her several times during supper, taking in the details of Minerva's drop-waisted dress, her bobbed hair. Mohini had large brown eyes, shiny as beetles. She made Minerva uneasy. Although she could not fathom the reason, she sensed a wave of hostility coming from the girl.

"How will you help me?" she asked Sita.

"I must examine you first, then we shall see. When did you last bleed in the manner of women?"

"It was six weeks ago, I think."

"And you were with the man, when?"

"Perhaps a fortnight after that."

Sita nodded. "It is as I thought."

Minerva added, a little desperately, "It was only once."

"The power of the gods comes when it comes."

Sita ordered her granddaughter-apprentice to unroll a sleeping pallet on the beaten dirt floor. When this was done, she covered it with a diaphanous cloth, shot with saffron threads. The material was rich and would have made a lovely sari. Minerva was reluctant to lie upon it.

"The cloth is dedicated to the gods," Sita explained. "You must remove your English drawers and lie down."

Minerva glanced at Mohini, wishing she could ask her to leave. The girl stared back at her, seeming to challenge her. I will not let her intimidate me, Minerva decided. She raised her skirts and pulled at her underthings until she was naked from the waist down.

"Have no fear; I will be gentle."

The brief examination was unpleasant, chiefly because it brought back the memory of Templeton's rough penetration. When it was finished, Sita said, "The signs are there, but it is early still, which is good. I will give you a remedy. It will bring on your bleeding, but it will bring pain also. There is some danger. The life force of the gods is powerful and sometimes will not be expelled. In other cases, the expulsion is so harsh and violent that the woman's own life bleeds away with her child's."

Minerva sat up and clasped her knees with her arms. "Danger or no, if there is a way to be rid of it, I must try."

"You cannot marry the father?"

She shook her head violently. "I hate him."

Sita touched her hair. "My child, my child. You were forced?"

"Yes. By Harrison Templeton," she said through clenched teeth. "He raped me, he hurt me, and then he cast me aside. He stole my father's land and my stepmother's honor. He will have no child of me."

Sita nodded. "He is an evil man and will come to evil in the end."

Over the old woman's shoulders Minerva saw the dark face of the granddaughter. Those beetle eyes were gleaming with something akin to triumph. Minerva felt frightened. She had promised herself never to speak the name of the child's father, and already she had done so. She would have to be more careful in the future. Harrison Templeton must never find out that she had aborted his child.

Minerva took the drug the following evening, inserting the strong-smelling packet of tightly woven leaves into her vagina, near the mouth of her womb. She felt nothing for nearly an hour, then she was taken by a strong cramping in her vitals. It grew steadily worse. Groaning, she crouched on the wooden commode in the bathroom of her room, waiting for the promised bleeding to begin. In the end, wracked with pain and sweating from her scalp to the soles of her feet, she stuffed her fists into her mouth to keep herself from screaming.

There was some bleeding at last, but very little. It was not enough, she knew. The cramping continued throughout the night, but no further bleeding ensued. By dawn Minerva was exhausted, her belly so tender from the violent muscle contractions that she was forced to plead illness and remain under her sheets and mosquito netting, curled up in bed.

In the evening she summoned the *hamal* with hot water for her bath and washed herself carefully to remove the stains and the sweat. When it got dark she slipped out and stumbled again to Sita's room in the servants' quarters. When she described what had happened, the old woman shook her head. She examined her quickly, drawing back when Minerva cried out, so tender was her body still.

"We have failed, child. The growing life inside you is strong and insists upon being born. Perhaps it is a soul who has long yearned to reincarnate and has chosen your womb as its means of reentering this world."

"Can't you give me anything stronger?" Minerva asked, even though she quaked at the thought of going through such torture again.

Sita shook her head. "No, Missy baba. It must be your karma to give birth to this child."

That night Minerva wandered up to the tea gardens where Templeton had violated her and climbed higher and higher onto the steep hillside of dark green tea. She climbed until her weary legs gave out. Her stomach was queasy again; there was no doubt about it, the pregnancy continued to cling. There was no outward sign of it now, of course, but in three or four months, her belly would swell and everybody would know.

Her mother, you know, was a whore.

She would have to leave the plantation, leave Darjeeling. She would have to go to Calcutta like her mother, and be devoured there.

She seemed to hear her father thundering, Reputation, reputation, reputation! I have lost my reputation! "Oh, Papa, I've failed you," she whispered to the night wind. "I'll not have you ending up like your mother," he'd said to her so many times. "You must never give those vultures reason to revile you."

For the first time ever, Minerva was glad her father was no longer alive to see the wreckage she'd made of her life.

"Minerva?"

She jumped at the sound of the voice that called her name in the dark. Edward. She'd been avoiding him for two days while struggling to rid herself of the babe in her womb, but there was no avoiding him now. She was huddled on an exposed hillside, fully visible as he rounded a curve in the track.

"Thank God, Min! I've been frantic. What in blazes are you doing, rushing up here into the hills at this time of the night?"

There in the darkness, Edward looked taller than usual. He stopped before her, legs braced slightly apart, his stance demonstrating the possessiveness that he didn't dare proclaim aloud.

She had believed him weak, but there in the night Minerva understood that in some ways he was stronger than she. He was a male, the preferred sex. His body could never betray him the way a woman's could.

It was not right! If only she had been a man. Harrison Templeton would not have dared to abuse her. Never before had she felt fragile or dependent. It was not until now, confronted by the fundamental facts of her biology, that she understood the necessity of having someone to protect her. She was not a man, and she must use what weapons she possessed.

She shivered as the wind from the mountains raked her. She was unaccountably afraid.

"Min?" Edward knelt beside her and took her cold hands in his. "What's the matter? You look frightened. You're not, surely, frightened of me?" Tenderly, he lifted one palm to her forehead and stroked back her finespun blond hair. "I love you, Min. I'd never, ever, do anything to hurt you. You know that, don't you?"

He thought she was a nervous virgin, distressed by the intimacies she'd allowed him the other night. A sob rose in her throat. Edward held her closer. Frantically, she pressed her body to his.

His head came down and his lips caressed her. She sighed as the yearning began.

Edward kissed her more insistently, sliding his tongue deep into her mouth. Her limbs ran with fire. She arched her back as he laid her back on the ground and covered her body with his own.

"We'll be married," he whispered. "Don't be afraid. I love you so much, Min, my sweetheart, my angel. Please let me show you, please."

Her father had called her angel. As she'd loved Papa, she loved this man. Their love could not be wrong. Surely something that felt so wondrous could not be a crime.

He undressed her slowly, adoring each ivory inch of flesh that his hands exposed. He praised her and promised that he would be hers forever. They would be married. Their souls were mated, and they would be together eternally.

When Edward, awkward but tender, entered her body, Minerva's muscles convulsed with the pain lingering from the attempted abortion. She cried out, and Edward soothed her. She realized that he must have thought he was rupturing her hymen. Although she had not set out to deceive him, her lover clearly believed she had come to him a virgin, a notion she would not contradict.

He was patient, waiting until she was more relaxed before continuing. She could tell what the delay cost him by the sweat that blossomed on his skin. Unlike his brutal father, he put her pleasure before his own, and that in itself was enough to make her love him more.

She did not enjoy it the first time, but her lover was tireless, and as he applied himself to discovering what pleased her, the pleasure began to come in waves. He made love to her several times in succession, and before the interlude was over, he had succeeded in bringing her to climax. She was touched, dazzled, physically obsessed. Now at last she understood the power passion could wield.

"I love you, I love you," she whispered, spreading kisses all over his naked chest.

Edward's voice was full of boyish delight and he reverently touched her golden hair. "Min, my sweetest angel, this is just the beginning. We'll have fifty years together, darling, at least. Fifty years in which I can continue to show you how wonderful love can be. Will you marry me, darling? Will you marry me, please?"

She hardly recognized as herself the woman who closed her arms around him and whispered, "Yes."

They were married quietly a week later. No one from the family was present. Indeed, as Minerva had expected, when he'd heard of his son's marriage plans, Harrison Templeton had been enraged.

"Are you mad?" he'd shouted.

Minerva was summoned to quiver before him while he brutally told his son his version of what had happened a month before in the tea garden. "I've had her myself—she's a trollop, a whore. Have some sport with her if you want; there's nothing wrong with that. It's high time you took to women, but don't play such a fool as to offer her marriage. By God, Edward, the slut is a fortune hunter; can't you see? Ask her what happened between us. Ask her about the night she offered up her body to me."

Minerva had been terrified of this moment. She knew that Edward did not get on with his father. Infuriated with the boy's lack of what he considered rough-and-tumble manly vigor, Templeton had beaten him frequently over the years, and Edward hated him for that. He also hated him for the shabby way he treated his mother.

Even so, when Templeton began his verbal attack on her right there in the presence of his wife, Minerva had little real hope that Edward would take her word against that of his terrible, puissant father. But he surprised her. He surprised everybody. He didn't ask her for her side of the story; he didn't consider for so much as a moment that Harrison might be speaking the truth. He had made love to a virgin, after all. A virgin, an angel, whom he loved.

He defied his father openly for the first time in his life.

"Where are you going?" Harrison bellowed as Edward took Minerva's hand tightly in his and walked away.

"To church."

"I forbid it!"

"I am fully of age. You cannot stop me, Father."

"If you marry that slut, I'll not permit you to set foot on this plantation ever again."

"Good-bye, then," Edward said calmly. "You've never been a real father to me, and I want nothing more from you."

Minerva half expected her lover to weaken, but he did not. They left Darjeeling that same afternoon on the small railway train that inched its way down the hills amidst steep terraces of deepest green tea. "I'm taking you home," Edward promised her, and only for a moment did the thought flicker inside her: But this *is* my home.

They traveled south to Calcutta and were married in a pretty English church there, sheltered by the tall Gothic windows and stained glass that provided an oasis of cool silence in the merciless summer heat. Minerva tried not to think of her mother—the beautiful, reckless Isabella, who had followed this same course before her. She had stayed in Calcutta, but Minerva was to travel on to America, that uncouth promised land of gangsters and motion pictures and jazz.

They crossed the Indian subcontinent by train, slowly wending their way southwest to Bombay, where in late August of that year, 1923, they boarded a P&O steamer bound for England. From Southampton they journeyed onward immediately to Boston, passing their traveling days in a sensual dream. Although their cabin accommodations were Spartan, they needed little more than a bed and an occasional meal to keep them content as they reveled in the ecstatic pleasures of new love.

A month after leaving Darjeeling, Minerva and Edward arrived in Boston. "I have my own house on Beacon Hill," her husband explained. "It was left to me by my paternal grandfather. My father refused to consider living in the place, so Granddad willed it to me. It's called the China Tea House Tavern, and it's over two hundred years old."

This was the first Minerva ever heard of the building that was for so many years to be her home.

7

"Let me see my baby."

Minerva was almost afraid to look upon the face of the son she bore in March of 1924. Her guilty conscience suggested to her that the child would be the image of his father, Harrison Templeton, and that Edward would take one look into the babe's face and know the truth.

According to Minerva's calculations, the boy was about a week overdue. She had lied about the dates, of course, telling everyone her labor was beginning early. "A hefty young brat he is, and he a month before his time, too," the nursemaid said with apparent guilelessness.

Augustus Cox, the Boston physician who attended her lying-in, undoubtedly knew the truth, but he was far too tactful to hint that he might be aware of any discrepancy in the dates. No doubt he believed that she and Edward had anticipated their wedding night by several weeks.

Throughout her pregnancy Minerva had experienced periods of almost agonizing guilt. Never, never, she thought, should she have married Edward. She loved him dearly, so dearly that the child in her womb seemed an abomination. If he ever found out that she was carrying his father's child, the knowledge would surely blister his soul.

In the beginning she had hoped for a miscarriage. But at five months, when the babe had begun to kick and roll about in her belly, she softened a little. The child was innocent, and not responsible for the unpleasant circumstances of its conception.

After a relatively easy labor and delivery, when Gus Cox laid the baby in her arms and she looked into alert blue eyes and saw the little mouth that sucked fiercely on the knuckle she put to its lips, Minerva felt a rush of maternal pride and love so strong she began to cry. When the boy rooted about and fixed upon her breast, digging his tiny fingers into her flesh, she cuddled him close and trembled at the thought that she might have lost him. If the drug her ayah had given her had worked, she *would* have lost him. In retrospect it seemed unthinkable that she had not always loved this child.

"Look, Edward, isn't he beautiful? Look at the lusty way he sucks. He's going to grab life and enjoy it. Isn't he a darling?"

"He's a miracle," her husband agreed. "And his mother is an angel."

They named him Jonathan. His hair was fair, like hers, and his eyes that pale clear blue that promised to hold their color. He did not resemble Harrison Templeton in the least.

Minerva loved Boston, and she loved her new role as a mother. She was only eighteen, and childhood was not so far behind her. She spent many happy hours that spring walking Jonathan along the steep streets of Beacon Hill, pushing the shiny new perambulator past venerable brick buildings and down onto the Boston Common. Once when they were trundling past the State House, Jonathan gurgled loudly and seemed to point up at its magnificent golden dome.

Although the land lacked the wild, raucous beauty of India, there was no savagery in it. The winters were fiercer than anything she was used to, but the misty, rainy springs reminded her of the temperate climate of Darjeeling, and in the fall of that year, when she first experienced Massachusetts's long, warm autumns and saw the trees on the Common burst into flames of scarlet and orange and gold, she thought the sight more beautiful than anything she had ever known.

The city itself, built mostly of red brick and gray stone, seemed to her very elegant and civilized. The drama of India was missing, but the fine edge of fear that comes with it was mercifully lacking, too. In Boston one had no real fears about survival; one could not only grow, but thrive.

Edward insisted upon entering Harvard to complete his education as soon as they settled, something generations of Templetons had done before him. He was a little old for it, but his bookish days in Darjeeling paid off, for his professors quickly agreed that he was a superior student, already well versed in most of the subjects they taught. Long a student of French literature and history, he majored in romance languages and was able to complete his courses and graduate in only two and a half years.

Finances were not a problem. While Edward studied and Minerva enjoyed her new role as devoted wife and mother, their living expenses were met, and indeed, far exceeded, by the income from several trust funds. Harrison Templeton had followed through on his threats to cut Edward off, but this made little difference since his father had no control over the money that had been invested for Edward by his grandfather. Her husband, Minerva knew by now, was quite extraordinarily rich.

The wealth made possible what was to Minerva a new way of life consisting of luxury motor cars (they had a chauffeur-driven Daimler and a Rolls for Minerva's own use), fashion from top Paris couturiers like Chanel and Schiaparelli, jewels from Cartier. Minerva enjoyed these advantages, but she was not dazzled by them. More important to her was her marriage, and her growing family.

Minerva's second child, a daughter, Elizabeth, was born in early 1926. Although the children had a nursemaid, Minerva spent most of her day taking care of them herself. She delighted in giving them all the material comforts that she herself had been deprived of. She was determined that Jonathan and Elizabeth would have everything they ever wanted or needed. She would see to it: they would grow up privileged, wealthy, and adored.

The year was 1929, and Minerva was bored. She sat in the dining room of the China Tea House Tavern sipping Darjeeling tea from a blue and white Chinese porcelain cup and reading the newspaper that had become her favorite morning amusement, *The Wall Street Journal.* When she finished her first cup of tea, Paulings, the butler, who was hovering, poured her another from the eighteenth-century silver tea service designed by the silversmith Paul Revere.

She was reading an article about tea prices on the world commodities market. Crops had been excellent, and production was at an all-time high. There was even some talk of forced reductions in planting and production because supply was exceeding demand, resulting in lower prices.

Lately the paper had been full of articles about the booming stock market, along with an occasional hint that business was not actually as good as it looked. In Europe, one analyst said, money was tight all over, consumption had leveled off, inventories were rising, production dropping.

Over the last few months Minerva had discovered that she possessed an almost instinctive understanding of such dry concepts as credit expansion and capital investment. "I ought to have been a man," she'd said to Edward several nights before. "I could have come into the business with you and your Uncle Earnest if I had been a man."

A little amused, her husband had pointed out that they couldn't have been married if she had been a man. No, she thought. Man to man, I'd have ousted Harrison Templeton in a more direct manner, and I'd be there, at home in Darjeeling, running my own tea plantation and beholden to nobody.

The vehemence of the fantasy made her feel ashamed. She loved Boston, she loved her husband, so why should she wish for such a thing?

Thoughtfully sipping her tea, she admitted to herself that she was discontent. The children were still a source of delight, even if Jonathan, five, and Lizzy, three, spent more and more time with their tutor these days. They were too young for studies, she'd protested, but Edward insisted that it was never too early to have fine literature read to them, fine music played for them on the phonograph. This was good for the children, she supposed, but it left her with nothing to do all day.

She had undertaken several projects in recent months, including the renovation of the China Tea House Tavern. She had called in the best colonial designers to work on the two big common rooms downstairs and the four bedrooms on the second floor which comprised the core of the house. Constructed in the early eighteenth century, these six rooms had served as the parlor, taproom, and three guests bedrooms of the colonial inn. The fourth bedroom, larger than the others and equipped with a mammoth central fireplace, had been the innkeeper's quarters, and it was here that Minerva and Edward slept.

The twentieth-century Tavern was more than three times the size of the original. Additions had been built both along the left side and the rear of the building, providing the family with a formal dining room, a gigantic kitchen, a butler's pantry, and a sewing room on the first floor, and a library and several extra bedrooms, each equipped with a private bath, upstairs. A third story had been added, complete with a nursery and servants' quarters. But most of this construction dated from the mid nineteenth century, and renovation was necessary throughout the house.

Minerva enjoyed discussing the work with the decorators, and it had been fun to assemble the eclectic mix of styles and period furnishings that fit into the various segments of the house. There was a certain pleasure in having the money to spend on Picasso and Chagall paintings for the library, Sèvres and Meissen china for the dining room, a Daum crystal stained glass panel for the skylight in one of the bathrooms, and the newfangled refrigerator for the kitchen. But the work was done now, and so far Minerva had been unable to come up with a similar project to occupy her time.

Her friends urged her to join various charitable institutions, but she lacked the patience and commitment necessary for such work. She donated money, of course, but she dreamed of an occupation that would enable her to develop her own skills and knowledge. She wanted—why not admit it?—some sort of recognition for her talents and achievements. She wanted to be something more than Edward Templeton's wife.

There was no reason, she decided, why she couldn't be. The world had changed since the Great War—women had finally been recognized as equal partners with men, given the right to vote, to hold political office, even, if she listened to the exploits of some of her more daring friends, to indulge in love affairs with the same impunity that men had always enjoyed. While some people predicted a bashlash of new conservatism in the country, she refused to worry about this possibility.

She finished her third cup of tea and rose from the dining table. Walking over to the windows, she looked out into the enclosed private garden at the back of their property. The morning was warm. The trees were beginning to shows signs of the dramatic explosion of color to come.

"Will you require the automobile this morning, madam?" Paulings asked.

She'd shopped yesterday and the day before, and if she spent one more morning enduring a fitting for a new gown, she would scream. "No, thank you, Paulings. I believe I'll collect the children and take them for a walk."

Mrs. Cummings, the children's tutor, protested, but Minerva smiled graciously and ignored her. She and Jonathan and little Lizzy strolled through the Boston Common and the Public Garden, and along the wide avenues of Back Bay, which had been reclaimed only a few decades ago from the sea when the three peaks that had crowned Beacon Hill had been lopped off and used for landfill. On the way home, they paused outside the Georgian mansion on Beacon Street that housed the corporate offices of Templeton Tea. She explained to the children that this elegant building was where Daddy worked.

"May we go inside and see him, Mummy, may we?"

"Oh, please!"

"Well, I suppose so. Why not?"

They entered through the portico and climbed the graceful stairway to the second floor, where their father's office was. There in the hallway was the picture gallery of the children's Templeton ancestors. It was Jonathan, with his questions about the somber figures there on the wall, who inspired his mother to embark upon the venture that was to change her life. "Who's this woman, Mummy?" he demanded. "Why is her picture up here on the wall with all these men?"

Minerva looked at the very old painting of a stately woman with auburn hair. She was embarrassed to admit that she had no idea who the woman was.

She proved to be Helen Templeton, the founder of Templeton Tea.

"You mean it was a woman who started the business?" Minerva asked Edward that evening.

"Yes indeed."

"Back in the eighteenth century, when women didn't do such things? But that's extraordinary."

"Helen Templeton was an extraordinary woman. She was tried for witchcraft early in her life and, fortunately for us, acquitted. I don't suppose there ever would have been a Templeton Tea if she'd been hanged as a witch on the Boston Common."

Minerva was intrigued. She invaded the company archives and found a wealth of material about the family history and genealogy. Edward's grandmother, Clara (who also probably had had nothing to do all day), had prepared an unpublished pamphlet on the Templetons. This, along with several trips to the Boston Public Library and the Massachusetts Historical Society, soon put Minerva in possession of many of the facts.

The business had been started by Helen Templeton in 1710 when she, a woman of fifty with a grown mariner-trader son, began selling tea in the China Tea House Tavern. A former Londoner, Helen ran the tavern in the style of a fashionable English coffeehouse. It soon became the chic place to go and drink a dish of this fine herbal brew from China, which was said to cure all manner of illness, strengthen the constitution, and refresh the mind.

Helen's son, Charles, imported tea from England for her in ever-increasing quantities. She marketed it in two ways—serving it as a hot drink in the Tavern, and selling the dry leaf in bulk over the counter in a shop next door. Within a couple of years, Helen began making a hefty profit selling such varieties as congou, hyson, and gunpowder tea from China.

Charles Templeton rose quickly among the powerful Boston merchants on the strength of his mother's tea trade. He married Lucy Broadhurst, the niece of a successful Boston trader and shipbuilder, thereby gaining access to the Broadhursts' shipping agents in London. He was able to work out a deal with the British by which he was, for a while at least, the sole American agent for the increasingly lucrative trade. Charles's son James solidified the family fortunes, increasing the China trade to include silks and spices.

The history of the Templetons in the mid to late eighteenth century, Minerva learned, largely paralleled the history of the British East India Company. During this period the Templetons acquired most of their tea from the East India Company, which had become increasingly powerful as the world's greatest tea broker. The Company had set up a trading base at Canton in 1700, which they maintained until 1836. They essentially held a monopoly on tea, for they were the only foreign agents with whom the Chinese would officially deal. But tea was taxed heavily and prices were high, so a network of smugglers soon set up its own commerce in the commodity.

The Templetons prided themselves on buying only through official channels and never dealing with these smugglers, some of whom sold vile and even poisonous mixtures of adulterated tea. But when the Parliament finally cut the domestic tea tax, they refused to rescind the three-pence-per-pound duty on tea exported to the colonies. The increasingly independent Americans protested by raiding the tea-laden East Indiamen that lay at anchor in Boston and dumping 342 cases of tea into the harbor.

Minerva's British education had not taken much notice of the American War of Independence, and this was the first she had heard of the Boston Tea Party. In fact, she realized, although she'd grown up in Darjeeling, where the finest tea in the world is grown, she knew very little about what happened to the commodity after it left the producing countries.

"I want to learn everything there is to know about the industry," she told Edward. The story of Helen Templeton had inspired her. "It's part of my own heritage, after all."

"You don't need to know the details, Min. That's my job."

"Don't treat me like a child! What else do you propose I do all day?"

Somewhat tentatively he said, "Why don't we have another baby?"

But Minerva did not want another child, and in fact, she'd been insisting lately that Edward use rubber sheaths when they made love to prevent conception. Much as she loved the two children she had, she did not want to start all over again with another. There should be something more to life for women than the constant drudgery of giving birth. Certainly there had been more for Helen Templeton.

Tea had been known and drunk for nearly five thousand years, Minerva learned, after its legendary discovery in China by the emperor and herbalist Shen Nung in 2750 B.C. The use of the invigorating herbal drink slowly spread through China and Japan, where teaism became a spiritual cult, and even more slowly into the western world. In the sixteenth century, Dutch traders in the East introduced the herb into Europe, where it became popular in the Netherlands. But tea did not become the rage in England until after 1662, when Catherine of Braganza, a princess of Portugal, married Charles II and brought a chest of her favorite drink to the English court as part of her dowry.

The fashionable coffeehouses became the place to go and sip tea in London during the late seventeenth century, and by the eighteenth century, the custom was well entrenched. Loose tea, considered an herb with certain medicinal properties, was typically sold at apothecary shops. Its proponents promoted it as a curative, capable of fending off dropsy and scurvy, and preventing consumption.

It wasn't until the mid eighteenth century, Minerva learned, that the English began taking "afternoon tea." Anna, the Duchess of Bedford, supposedly started the custom of serving tea and light snacks in the late afternoon to hold her over until the traditionally late evening dinner at nine o'clock.

Minerva had grown up with the custom of afternoon tea in India, and insisted upon its being served at four o'clock every day to herself and the children. Without her two cups of tea in the morning, and another two in the afternoon, she felt lethargic and dispirited.

Minerva studied a botanist's account of how tea is propagated and grown, adding that to what she knew from her own experience in India. She read about the processing, blending, and the different varieties of the herb, which depended so much on soil, climate, altitude. Then she returned to her study of the Templetons and dutifully committed to memory page after page of information about the decline in the popularity of tea during the War of Independence, the nasty business of the opium trade (during which British and American merchants traded opium to the Chinese in exchange for tea), and the romantic heyday of the swift China clippers, which were capable of delivering their cargo in record time and carrying more than a million pounds of tea.

The clipper ship era came to an end in the late 1860s with the advent of steamships, and the Templetons, ever adaptable, had shifted to the new technology. By this time the family not only traded in tea, but had also become a power in American shipping, and the glory of the Templetons was at a peak.

But the company was plagued by problems during the late nineteenth century. A brother-brother feud ended with the shipping and other mercantile interests being split off and separated from the tea corporation, and for a while it had looked as if the entire empire was crumbling.

Matters were not helped when Harrison Templeton rushed off to India with the plan of growing his own tea. He was still out there (thank God) and had apparently lost all interest in the company. It was his brother, Earnest, the current Director, who owned 100 percent of the company stock and controlled the entire enterprise. Earnest had no children. Edward was his heir.

It would be up to Edward, Minerva realized, to bring Templeton Tea to glory during its third century.

Because of her fascination with business and financial news, Minerva was less bewildered than other American wives when her husband came to her shamefacedly a few days after Black Tuesday, October 29, 1929, saying, "I'm afraid we've lost some money, Min. Quite a lot of it, actually."

His announcement prompted a major marital battle. It came as a shock to her to discover that Edward had caught investment fever along with so many other people in the late twenties and made a number of unwise decisions about his personal fortune. "It's not the money," she told him. "I'm angry because you made so many substantial investments without consulting me."

"It never occurred to me, Min. I never dreamed you'd be interested."

"I'm interested in all aspects of our lives together, even those that have traditionally been left up to the males of this world," she said scathingly. "I'm not some twit without a brain in my head. In future I demand that you consult me on the major decisions that are going to affect not only our lives, but those of our children. We will have a complete and equal partnership, or none at all!"

Her husband was disconcerted, and perhaps even a little frightened, by her anger. He apologized, and promised it would never happen again.

The rest of 1929 was a dark period not only for Templeton Tea, but also for banks and businesses all over the country. Worse news to follow. Uncle Earnest had made a series of investments that were even more catastrophic than Edward's, not only of his personal funds, but of corporate profits. The company faced a growing crisis.

"We have money, you understand," Edward explained to Minerva. "It's our ready cash that's restricted. Earnest was in the process of expanding, and our capital investments on new stock, blending machines, and a new processing and packing plant have been exorbitant. We've had to borrow from several banks, and although our credit is still good, the banks are having troubles of their own and are threatening to call in the loans."

"If they do that, can we make the necessary repayments?"

"I'm not sure. The situation's grim. The worst is, Earnest is feeling pretty low about the whole thing. He gets depressed, you see. Terrible black moods of despair. He's had them on and off for most of his life. His mother had them, too; depression seems to run in our family."

Feeling waspish at what she was beginning to suspect was some very inefficient management on the part of Edward's uncle, Minerva felt no great sympathy for Earnest's mental state. "Exactly how much money does the company owe the banks?"

"I'll have to look into it. I hate to interfere in matters that are officially Uncle Earnest's concern, but—"

"Damn Uncle Earnest. You are the heir to a business that is over two hundred years old—do you realize how unusual that is? If your uncle is too despondent to work, you must assume the responsibility. There must be a way to weather this crisis. Maybe I can help. I'm good with figures, and I know quite a bit about tea. Tomorrow I'll come to the office with you, and together we'll sort this mess out."

But she did not go to the office with him the next day, for the office was closed, and Minerva spent the day berating herself for her insensitivity to poor Uncle Earnest. While she and Edward had been planning company strategy, Earnest Templeton had been tidying up his affairs and loading his pistol. At midnight, while Minerva and Edward were passionately making love, Earnest put a bullet through his head.

The situation was even worse than Minerva had feared. At the age of twenty-seven, with only four years of experience with the family business, her husband had become the Director of Templeton Tea. The money the company owed was staggering. Minerva and Edward sat down with the chief company accountant to calculate if there was any possible way to meet their creditors' schedule of payments. "We'll have to hold off on the new packing plant," Minerva said. "The money just isn't there."

"The foundation's already been dug," Edward protested. They looked at the plans for the new blending and packaging plant that was about to be constructed in East Boston. Nestled into a steep hillside, it was to have housed all the most modern equipment, and revolutionized several aspects of their business.

Minerva paused to admire once again the design for the building, which utilized a highly efficient gravity system whereby tea was delivered by truck to the top-floor entrance at the crest of the hill, tested for quality on the fifth floor, dropped through mechanical sifters to be blended on the fourth floor, and then delivered by ceiling chute to the third floor, where the tea would be packed in half-pound, quarter-pound, and ten-cent paper packages. The packages would then pass by mechanical conveyor through sealing machines on the second floor and be dumped into wooden crates on the ground floor, where another road gave the distributors' trucks access to the shipping dock.

"We can't afford it," she said regretfully. "Construction will have to stop. Can we sell the site?"

"Nobody's buying. The entire economy is falling into a slump. Besides, it's an excellent location; we've been trying for years to acquire that land."

"We'll keep the site then, and continue building when business looks a little better. Next year, perhaps. In the meantime, we'll just have to make do with the packaging system we already have."

This was a commonsense decision, but there were other matters that she couldn't give an opinion on until she learned more about the business. There were endless things, it seemed, that she still didn't know about Templeton Tea.

But this only made it more of a challenge. Every morning Minerva dressed in a elegant tailored suit (waistlines were beginning to make a comeback, which she was glad of; despite childbearing, she had a trim waist) and a small cloche hat pulled down over her forehead and walked to the office with her husband. In the afternoon she came home in time to have tea with the children and play a few games with them before suppertime. When Jonathan and Elizabeth were in bed and she and Edward had dined, Minerva would retire to the library with a stack of books and papers, charts and graphs, and cram until her eyes crossed and her body slumped in the chair.

She learned. Unlike many American tea concerns, Templeton Tea was not simply an importer, or a blender, or a wholesaler and distributor of packaged tea. The company did all these things. The only thing they did not do was actually grow the commodity in the tea gardens. They employed purchasing agents and tasters in the tea-producing capitals of the world (chiefly India, Ceylon, Java, Sumatra, Japan, and China), but their major buying occurred at the great tea auctions in Mincing Lane in London.

Once purchased, the tea was packed in crates and shipped via the Suez Canal to New York, or sometimes Boston, where, after being subjected to inspection to make certain it was unadulterated and fit for human consumption, it was delivered to the plant to be blended and packaged.

"Actually, we don't blend all the tea we import," Edward explained to her. "Some of it we sell to other blending concerns, who may then wholesale it themselves or broker it off to other wholesalers and retailers. We import a great deal more tea than we actually end up selling under the Templeton name."

"Why?" she asked.

"Because we have always been known for quality teas. And not all the tea we import meets our standards. We want the tea we sell under the Templeton name to be the best. I think we ought to continue that policy, don't you?"

"Absolutely. Continue it we shall."

Edward worked hard, too, trying to acquire the knowledge that his short experience under his uncle's tutelage had not yet enabled him to learn. They made a good team. Minerva's quick brain was complemented by Edward's solid analytical ability. She had the new ideas, and he offered the means of initiating them.

It was clear from the start that the only way to save the company would be to divert to it everything from Edward's personal fortune that was not tied up in complicated family trust funds. Since Edward had lost some of these monies in the Crash, they would be reduced to a standard of living that would be significantly more austere.

"Even then we might not manage to rescue the company," Edward said one evening several weeks after they had embarked on their research. "Even if we invest everything we have, there's a chance we'll go under anyway."

"And end up poor, you mean?"

"Not exactly poor, perhaps, since we'll still get interest on some money that I can never touch, money that's already slated to come down to our children and our children's children. We won't have to live in a hovel, but we'll have to sell the Rolls. I won't be able to restock the wine cellar, and you'll have to give up jewels and evening gowns from Paris."

"To hell with jewels and gowns. What about the heirloom china and silver and antiques? And this house?"

"Those are safe, even if we go bankrupt. They're part of the Templeton Trust."

"In that case, I think we ought to take the risk, Edward. I can't bear to stand back and watch the company die."

Edward made love to her very tenderly that night. He adored her, he said, for her willingness to put the company ahead of her personal security and comfort. He told her how proud he was of her unselfish courage and how touched he was that she should love him enough to devote so much of her energy to the heritage that was only hers by marriage.

Minerva listened to his words with guilt in her heart. She knew she wasn't doing it out of selfless devotion. She was doing it because there was nothing more thrilling than to pit her considerable talents against such odds. And because working for the tea company made her feel intellectually fulfilled for the first time in her marriage . . . fulfilled and achingly alive.

8

"Tea bags," Minerva said one morning in 1933. "The future is in tea bags, Edward. Imagine: the husband goes off to work, the children go off to school, and the housewife wants a quick cup of tea to get her started in the morning. Instead of having to brew an entire pot, most of which will go to waste, she drops a tea bag into a cup, pours boiling water over it, adds a little milk and a little sugar, and drinks. Think of the ease, the convenience."

"What I'm thinking of is the taste. It sounds terrible."

"Frankly, I'm beginning to wonder just how discriminating the general public is about the taste of tea. Seems to me that most of the time all they want is something hot, something that will keep them alert, and something they can afford, particularly nowadays when everybody's so strapped for funds. Most of the people I know can't tell one tea from another."

"It does take some practice, as we both know," Edward said, smiling.

"We've been successful in the past dealing with that discriminating portion of the American public who desire quality teas," Minerva went on. "But if we're going to grow, we must go after a larger market. By that I mean ordinary people who will prefer the convenience of a tea bag to the finer taste of a pot of brewed tea."

"You may have a point," her husband conceded.

Minerva told him that tea bags had been invented accidentally around the turn of the century when a wholesaler named Thomas Sullivan packed small samples of his tea in hand-sewn silk bags as part of an attempt to interest retailers in his product. Some of the samples ended up in people's cups, and Sullivan began getting requests for more of the bagged tea. He substituted gauze for silk, and the tea bag was a reality.

"Tea bags have been accepted by the trade since about 1920," she said. "At first they were used mostly in restaurants, but now more and more people are demanding them in the home." She had collected a sampling of the various kinds of tea bags. One was an unsewn piece of circular gauze gathered together at the top and tied with a thread. Another was made by stitching the gauze on two sides to form a pouch. Others were small squares of gauze, stitched all around after the tea was inserted. Each had a little string attached to the top of the bag, with a tag indicating the blend and the distributor.

"This is the latest thing," she said, showing him a transparent bag of perforated cellophane. "The idea is that in the long run it may prove cheaper to use paper instead of gauze. However, gauze works better because the water flows evenly through it. Also, the cellophane gives the tea an odd taste. If we could find some sort of sturdy, yet water-permeable paper, we might be able to create a better tea bag and get a jump on our competitors. It's the wave of the future, I'm convinced."

Edward smiled at her. "If it's not, you'll make sure it *becomes* the wave of the future, won't you?"

"Well, we'll certainly have to put a great deal of thought into our marketing. We ought to hire someone to work specifically selling this project."

"That shouldn't be too difficult. There are qualified people all over the city, hungering for a good job."

This was all too true. Unemployment in the United States was approaching an all-time high. Americans were being evicted for nonpayment of rent, and every day one heard of more mortgage foreclosings. New skyscrapers stood empty, and the market for new cars had collapsed. Minerva's working career no longer seemed so extraordinary—wives of unemployed men were taking jobs (if they could find them) as secretaries and stenographers.

Minerva knew how lucky she and Edward had been so far to come through what people were beginning to call the Great Depression relatively unscathed. Their emergency investments in Templeton Tea had succeeded in buying them enough time to pay off their loans. They had even been able to resume construction on the new blending and packaging plant.

Franklin Roosevelt, the new president, had promised to deal with the country's severe economic problems, and Minerva hoped he would have some success. But as long as Templeton Tea continued to do well, she vowed to be satisfied.

One rainy weekend in 1935 when the Templeton children were cooped up in the house on a long summer afternoon, nine-year-old Elizabeth emerged from her brother's room clutching Jonathan's leather-bound journal.

" 'I love him, I love him,' " she shrieked, running down the hallway on the second floor of the house holding the journal open to a blotted page. " 'He is so beautiful and wise, and I'd do anything to please him. I will love him till I die.' "

Minerva's attention was caught immediately. Normally she did not concern herself with the children's squabbles, but the scene that was erupting here touched a nerve.

"Give that back!" Jonathan was shouting.

"Jonathan loves Matthews, Jonathan loves Matthews," his sister chanted, giggling as she continued to flee. Elizabeth was not usually a tease or a snoop, but she was high-spirited and capable of mischief. " 'My glorious Christopher, I'm going to love you forever,' " she read.

"That's private, you horrid little monster! Give it back to me right now!"

"Elizabeth," Minerva said. "Return the journal to your brother at once."

"But, oh, Mother, don't you see? Jonathan's in love with his tutor, who's a man. Isn't that the funniest thing? Everyone knows that boys can't be in love with men."

"He's not in love with his tutor," Minerva said calmly. "That is merely a figure of speech, isn't it, Jonathan?"

Her son was close to tears, so Minerva decided not to pursue the subject. She reprimanded Elizabeth for reading her brother's private journal, then suggested to Jonathan that he keep his personal items out of his little sister's reach. The matter was closed, she declared, but in fact she worried about it for the rest of the day.

It had not escaped her notice that Jonathan had been making sheep's eyes at Christopher Matthews, the tutor she hired to give him extra instruction in history, English, Latin, and French. When Matthews had taken the position about a year before, Minerva had noted immediately that the somewhat lackadaisical Jonathan had begun to apply himself. Pleasing Christopher Matthews was clearly important to him. If his tutor was satisfied with his progress, Jonathan was happy for hours. If not, he moped, refused to eat supper, and retired to his room to study even harder.

The more she thought about it, the more Minerva realized that Jonathan seemed subtly different from other boys his age. It was nothing overt, nothing she could objectify in any way. Although he had never been rough-and-tumble athletic, he didn't display sissified behavior, either. He wasn't interested in his sister's toys or his mother's clothes. None of what Minerva understood to be the telltale signs of effeminacy were there.

Yet there was *something.* Tall and slender with golden hair and the most charming smile, at eleven her son was already beginning to be noticed by the opposite sex, but as far as his mother could tell, he wasn't responding at all.

She related the journal incident that evening to Edward, expressing some concern. "Nonsense," her husband assured her. "I had crushes on any number of tutors when I was his age. On the older lads at school, too. It's perfectly normal, nothing to worry about."

When Matthews announced a few months later that he was quitting the job to take a part-time teaching position at Yale, Jonathan was inconsolable. He lost weight, his blue eyes grew huge in his face. Very slowly, he adjusted to life with a new tutor—a much older man this time, and married—but his mother sensed the depth of his grief and was frightened by it.

She began to insist that Jonathan take more interest in pursuits that she considered masculine—sports like rugby and soccer and boxing, for example, none of which he was good at, although he tried. He had a passion for classical music, Mozart in particular, and he adored opera. *Die Zauberflöte* was his favorite. When he expressed a desire to study the flute in imitation of Papageno, she encouraged him to try the trumpet instead.

It became a pattern between them—Jonathan would try in some

small way to assert his identity, and Minerva would stifle him, for his own good, of course. When he turned twelve and started boarding school at Loomis, he had more freedom, but whenever he was home on vacation she watched anxiously for some sign that he was beginning to exhibit a normal, healthy interest in the opposite sex.

There was none.

"Don't worry," Edward continued to say. "I started rather late myself, if you'll recall."

Certainly she would rather her son take after Edward than after his biological father, who, according to the occasional peevish letter they received from Edward's mother, was still continuing his boozing and whoring in Darjeeling. Jonathan was a bright, well-mannered, and affectionate boy, who filled his mother's heart with love and pride. But she continued to fret about him all the same.

In 1937 Minerva put aside her concerns about Jonathan to worry about Edward instead. The Great Depression seemed to have entered his soul.

He had never been as lively or as enthusiastic a personality as she was. But lately he had grown increasingly dispirited. Minerva was the one making all the major decisions, both at the office and in their home. Although she reveled in this, for her mania for controlling her destiny seemed to grow stronger with each passing year, she worried sometimes that her husband might resent her. When she tried to discuss the subject with him, he pooh-poohed it, saying, "Don't be nonsensical, my dear. I love you *because* you're strong. You know what you want from life, and you're perfectly willing to leap into the fray and strive until you get it. I admire that very much. I wish I had your determination."

"Edward, I don't understand. If it's not me, then what's wrong? You have a world-weariness that worries me."

"There's so much misery, and for what? No work, no food, no hope. People all over the world have suffered so during the past few years. And I don't see much evidence that economic conditions are improving."

"I don't agree, Edward. Look at our own prosperity with Templeton Tea."

"We're doing well because tea is cheap and hot and perhaps it even buoys people's spirits a little bit. We're essentially taking advantage of other people's misery, capitalizing on their weaknesses, and profiting from their desperation."

Minerva didn't see it this way at all, but Edward's politics were growing increasingly left-wing. There were a great many strikes that year, and her husband tended to sympathize with labor rather than with management. He encouraged his own employees to join the IWW, and as more and more reports came in of the ravages of the civil war in Spain, he even talked of sending money to help the republican forces fight the fascists.

"You're starting to sound like a socialist," she said.

"Well, I'm not one. But I do think that the world economic crisis has been brought on by the excesses of capitalism. And I feel quite strongly that American business ought to spend less time worrying about the Reds erupting from Russia and more time figuring out what to do about that maniac Hitler."

There was conviction in his voice, but it was coupled with a hopelessness, as if he didn't really think anything could or would be done. It frightened her. Her husband didn't trust or believe in himself, and this was a state of mind that she found difficult to imagine. "I don't know what's happened to you lately. You're not the man I married anymore."

"You're still the woman I married," he said in a more conciliatory tone. He took her stiff body into his arms. "I love you, Min. Be patient with me." He kissed her tenderly and took her to bed, where Minerva slowly relaxed. When they were together, body to body, flesh to flesh, everything was as wonderful as it had always been. Edward continued to be as generous a lover as any woman could ever wish for.

He was a good man, a sensitive man. He cared about others—her, their children, their employees, even the faceless, suffering masses of humanity. He was an idealist, yes, but deep in his heart he recognized that life was too complicated to be explained by simplistic ideologies. Like many sensitive people, he was looking for explanations, ways to make sense out of the hopes and dreams, angers and frustrations, ambitions and passions that were central to human existence.

She herself had long ago decided that life *had* no sense. She remembered her lost Eden—the small church in Darjeeling in which her communion with divinity and mystery had been so ruthlessly destroyed by two harpies calling her mother a whore. Nothing had ever been quite the same for her since then.

"We can't change the world," she whispered now. "We're only two people; there's a limit to what we can do."

"I know. And it's our very impotence that depresses me."

"These up-and-down moods of yours frighten me. Sometimes I worry so much about you, Edward."

"Don't fret, angel. I promise you I'm not planning to shoot myself, the way Earnest did."

The possibility had occurred to her. She knew from her research into the Templeton family history that there had been an unusual number of suicides down through the years, as well as a rash of premature deaths from other causes. From somewhere in the past a saying had attached itself to the family: "For they shall have prosperity, but neither joy nor peace." Hateful words! Several of Edward's ancestors had spoken uneasily in their private papers about a family curse.

It all went back, apparently, to Helen Templeton. Her son Charles had come home one evening to the China Tea House Tavern and shot both his wife and himself. It was rumored that he also tried to set the house on fire, which would have resulted in the deaths of his children as well if alert servants had not doused the blaze before it did much damage.

No one knew exactly what had driven Charles to such an act of madness, but legend had it that he had died cursing his mother's name.

Helen Templeton, who was still alive at the time of her son's demise, died a few years afterward, also under somewhat mysterious circumstances. The great lady had been found dead in her bedroom wearing a strangely embroidered robe and surrounded by pagan objects. The physician who examined her body declared she had died of a weak heart, but others said she had swallowed a poisonous potion, the dregs of which were found in her room. Although she had been acquitted of witchcraft, some had whispered that Helen might have been a practitioner of the black arts after all.

Nonsense, thought Minerva. Witches didn't exist. Neither did curses. She certainly wasn't going to waste her energy worrying about such supernatural claptrap.

All the same, the next time she was in the portrait hall of Templeton House, Minerva paused for a few moments in front of Helen's likeness. The artist had captured something enigmatic in his subject's expression. She had a generous mouth, but her smile was thin, a little caustic perhaps. And there was something both sad and defiant about the large green eyes.

For they shall have prosperity, but neither joy nor peace. Minerva had the eerie feeling that the long-dead Helen Templeton knew something that she didn't. If she hadn't been determined not to give in to superstition, she would have ordered the portrait removed and donated to a museum.

9

Minerva awoke one night in early September 1940 screaming that the house was on fire. She had seen it so clearly—whistles and explosions in the distance, an eerie silence, then all around her falling beams and an angry crimson glow. Even when she realized that there was no fire, that she was awake and safe in her bed in the China Tea House Tavern, her limbs would not stop shaking.

Elizabeth, awakened by her mother's screams, came running. She was fourteen now, a pretty girl with tawny hair and the excited sparkle of young womanhood. She had her father's sensitivity combined with her mother's energy and will. "Mummy, what on earth's the matter?" She dropped to the bed and put her arms around Minerva. In a more grown-up tone than her mother had ever heard from her, she instructed the frightened housekeeper, who was hovering outside in the hallway, to go down to the kitchen and make a pot of tea.

"It's your father. I'm so worried about him."

"He'll be all right. Please be calm, Mum. He'll be coming home soon."

Edward was in London, meeting with other brokers and wholesalers to consider the ramifications of the war on the price and supply of tea. Templeton Tea had always bought some of its goods at auction in London. But with the war spreading in the Far East, and England itself being in such a precarious situation, tea was becoming increasingly difficult to acquire. "Tea is more important for our soldiers than ammunition," Churchill had reportedly said, for in Britain the drink was regarded as a necessary tonic, essential to bucking up one's flagging spirits. The war could not be won without tea, and the supply routes from the East must be kept open.

"Don't worry, darling," Edward had said to her before leaving. "The British have been holding the Germans at bay for weeks since the fall of Paris, and I doubt very much if they're suddenly going to be invaded during the short period I'll be there."

"I suppose you're right," she'd said, but her nervousness, which was unusual, had persisted. She'd been having a number of restless nights lately, although nothing quite so dramatic as this.

With the help of the tea and her daughter's determined cheerfulness, Minerva managed to relax and go back to sleep, but when she heard on the radio the next morning that London had been bombed and a number of civilians killed, the panic rose up to choke her again.

Every evening Minerva would retire early to her room, aware that three thousand miles away in England the clocks were five hours ahead and the devastation and death was already being wrought. She tried to pray for Edward's safety, but she seemed to have forgotten how. Except to be married, to bury her father, and to christen her children, she had not been in church since the age of ten.

She knew the chances of Edward's being killed or injured were small. But she had a premonition—she had no idea where it came from—that something terrible was going to happen, that her peaceful life with her husband was drawing to a close.

On the third night after the blitz began, Edward Templeton was leaning against a wall in the elegant bedroom of a London townhouse gasping while the exotic woman kneeling before him took his penis into her mouth. Even as she suckled him, even as his limbs melted in pleasure and he spurted forth his seed, he hated himself. Vile adulterer. Rutting swine. He felt as if his wife could see him, as if she knew.

Except for the light of one thin candle, the room they were in was almost totally black. The drapes had been drawn around the windows and secured with thick electrical tape to prevent the slimmest blade of light from escaping.

In the distance they could hear the air raid sirens, the whistling passage of the bombs. Everyone else in the house had fled to the shelter in the cellar, and although Edward was terrified of the bombing, there was a part of him that believed he deserved nothing better than the hellfire of a direct hit. He'd never dreamed he'd betray Minerva, but he was weak, weak. This woman—this subtle, clever, infinitely sensual witch—was a temptation he could not resist.

They had fallen to the carpet—a crimson and gold Aubusson—and were wrestling with each other now. Edward pressed her down on her back and held her there while he licked her breasts, her stomach, her thighs. In between her legs, where she was hot and purple and moist. Her dusky skin breathed fragrance, and the wild animal cries she gave when he sucked at the hungry little nether-mouth made him rise up hard again, ready to fuck and fuck and fuck all night.

"Yes," she whispered. "Ah, the pleasure, ah, Edward." Her voice had a familiar singsong quality, one he remembered so well from those years out in India. He spread her thighs wide and settled himself atop her, spearing into her, driving hard. He pressed up on his elbows and wrapped her thick black hair around his arms, his wrists, his fingers. He touched his lips to her pointed chin, her high-arching cheekbones, her sable lashes, the faded red caste-mark in the center of her forehead.

"My princess. My sweet, hot, exotic princess," he said as he drew out and teased her opening with the very tip of his shaft. Her hips thrust up, but he eluded her, at least until she reached down and curved her crimson nails into his buttocks and demanded his lust, his force, his power.

As Edward lost control and hammered into her, he felt as if he were dying. "Christ, Mohini," he whispered. "Christ."

Her eyes were huge and wide, shiny like black opals. Her lips parted, and she smiled.

She was beautiful, well educated, and she had a good job as an administrative functionary of the Tea Council of India. He had met her at the beginning of the conference, noticed her beauty, but did not think of her as a threat to his marriage vows, which he had never betrayed.

It was on the first night of the bombing that he fell. Try as he might to imitate the British stiff upper lip, he couldn't seem to manage his fear. A building just down the street from the house where the tea conference guests were staying was razed and all the occupants killed. In the face of this carnage, which many people thought was the first wave of the Nazi invasion that had been feared for so long, Edward went a little crazy, just like everybody else.

She, too, was scared. She, too, felt the irony of being in the wrong place at the wrong time. They did not live in England, either of them, but far away where no German bombers could fly. Yet they'd been fool enough to journey to London in wartime, and now they might be killed.

No one knew where the bombs would fall—they could destroy your house and leave your neighbors' houses standing unscathed. One night Buckingham Palace was hit, proving that not even the royal family was safe. The docks were bombed, starting a blaze that destroyed several warehouses full of imports, including crate upon crate of tea. Edward was taken to the still-smoldering site in the morning. There was an overpowering odor of burnt tea in the air, the smell of waste, the smell of destruction.

Often the smell was even worse—the odor that rose from the bombed-out buildings was the odor of burning human flesh. Death seemed all-powerful, inexorable during those early days of the blitz. If the fates decreed it, a German bomb would find you, so why not revel in existence, seize the day, the night, the hour? Why not do whatever you could to spit in mortality's face?

On that first night, when Edward and Mohini took refuge in the bomb shelter in the basement, they huddled there together until the skies were silent. Afterward, wordlessly, they sought the comfort of a single room, a single bed. They did not sleep. What began as the need for fellowship and comfort turned to a fever of lust. Mohini's body became his food, his wine, his peace.

He did not recollect that he had seen her years ago on his father's tea plantation; nor, in the beginning, did she. Or so she claimed, and he believed her. Later, when they talked more about those early days, the days when they had both been young, Edward thought perhaps he remembered her, a slim, dark girl with big eyes who always looked as if she wanted more than she could grasp. She'd had dreams, she told him. The gods had smiled upon her, and she'd fulfilled them.

He did not ask how. The thought that his hated father might have had something to do with it was one he didn't care to pursue.

Mohini didn't mention the secret she knew about Edward's wife, whom she remembered far more clearly than she had remembered Edward. She had been jealous of the blond Missy baba when she was a girl, but those days were long over. She would not shatter Edward's illusions by informing him that his firstborn son —whom he talked about so often and obviously missed—was not the fruit of his own loins.

If there had been a future with Edward, she might have made a different choice. To keep him, she would have used whatever weapons she could find. But her life was back in India. Edward was sweet and she loved him dearly, but she had a lover waiting for her at home.

Still, Harrison Templeton might be interested to learn of his child. All men value sons. He had given her the education that had enabled her to change her life. Such opportunities rarely came to poor women in India. She was grateful. Edward was a passing fancy, less substantial than a dream. His father was real, and she sometimes had business in Darjeeling.

At the end of the conference, Mohini boarded a steamer for Calcutta, Edward for Boston. Despite the lust that still lingered in his blood, he was not sorry to see her go. With every day that passed, his guilt increased. Minerva would know, he was sure of it. She would sniff it on him, sniff the fire, the destruction, the betrayal.

In early October Minerva received a short letter from Edward informing her that he was on his way home. On the day his ship was due to dock in Boston, she dressed with care, making use of all her best cosmetics and taking extra trouble with her hair. She had the chauffeur drive her down to the pier so she could be there to welcome him when he stepped ashore.

As soon as she saw her husband, Minerva knew something was wrong. He was alive and safe, but he was looking at her as if she were a stranger instead of the wife he had lived with and loved for almost twenty years.

"What's the matter?" she asked, but he insisted it was nothing. The bombing was frightful, he explained. So many civilians dead.

"I've been so worried about you." She told him about her dreams, her fears. The more she told him, the more he seemed to withdraw. Even in bed that night he was not his usual affectionate self.

He was, in fact, sick with remorse. And, paradoxically, he was angry with her. From the moment he arrived back in Boston, it seemed, his wife besieged him with details about the tea company, asking his opinion, his advice. It was all a sham. She didn't need his advice. She'd made several major decisions while he'd been gone, and they were all excellent ones. He didn't run the company, even though he was its titular head. She did.

The truth was, his wife as a far more effective person than he was. She had a certain energy that was missing in him. He might be better at theory, but she was better at practice, and it was practice, he'd decided, that determined how well respected one was in this world.

He felt worthless. He *was* worthless. He was an adulterous bastard, and somehow, he was sure, she was going to find out.

The only place where he seemed to control things with his wife was in the bedroom. Yet even there, he felt ill at ease. Mohini had shown him aspects of sex and sensuality of which he had never even dreamed. He didn't dare show them to Minerva. She would know.

One night about two weeks after his return, Edward had too much to drink at dinner. Whiskey always loosened his tongue. It also made him lusty. Minerva's surprise turned quickly to arousal when he dismissed Paulings for the night and whispered to her, "Come on. Let's go upstairs."

In their bedroom he kissed and caressed her fiercely, tearing at her clothes until she protested that he was ripping them. "I don't care," he said, and flung her onto the bed.

"Edward, please—"

"Shut up," he said, and fell upon her.

But then humiliation came. He couldn't continue. He couldn't stay hard unless he thought of Mohini, and thinking of Mohini made him feel utterly abased with guilt.

"It doesn't matter," Minerva reassured him. "Remember what

Shakespeare says about strong drink: it provokes the desire but takes away the performance."

"To hell with Shakespeare."

"Edward, what's the matter with you? You haven't been yourself ever since you returned from London. Edward, please." She sounded frightened. "Won't you tell me what's wrong?"

And suddenly the urge to confess became irresistible. He had fought back the words night after night, but he couldn't suppress them anymore. Yes, she's going to find out. She'll find out because you're going to tell her. "I met a woman. A beautiful Indian woman associated with the Tea Council of India. She and I spent some time together in London; her name is Mohini."

Minerva went very still. She wasn't sure what she had expected, but it wasn't this. A woman? Edward was telling her he was having an affair with an *Indian* woman?

"It turns out that Mohini grew up on a tea plantation," he continued. "My father's tea plantation."

"My father's tea plantation." Minerva heard the snappishness in her own voice and was startled by it.

"She was the daughter of one of the tea laborers. She was a bright girl who wanted to get a good education. I take it that she acquired it partly through the agency of my father."

A little frightened, and not sure where this was leading, Minerva said, "And you've fallen in love with this woman? Is that why you've been so—" She broke off. *Mohini?* Fear swept her. Sita's granddaughter, Mohini? The girl who'd watched her that evening in the servants' quarters when Sita had examined her and confirmed her pregnancy? The same girl who had heard her confess that Harrison Templeton was the baby's father?

Within a heartbeat she was back under the brooding hills of Darjeeling, the mountains that were the province of the gods. The gods whose eyes are all-seeing, whose power can crush. She had sinned. And now her evil was revealed. She should never have married him. She loved him, yes, but love was not enough to redeem the fundamental wrongness of her action.

"Edward?" she whispered. For the first time ever she was afraid of her husband. He must know now that Jonathan was not his son. That Jonathan was his *father's* son. Dear God. Would he cast her off, demand a divorce?

Briefly she thought of the scandal that would ensue. She had come to value her good name. She was well respected, a leader, a successful businesswoman. Now all her accomplishments were to be trampled in the dust.

She pushed the vision away. No, Papa, she thought fiercely. To lose one's reputation is not so painful as to lose one's love.

She lay stiff, her nightgown sticking to her thighs, her heart a hollow drum; she waited for him to accuse her. It didn't occur to her that he was waiting just as wretchedly for her to accuse him.

"I love you, Edward." She raised her slippery fingers to his face and lightly touched the corners of his mouth. He winced and pulled away, and she could not contain a tiny cry of grief. "Don't turn away from me. I love you so."

Edward seemed to sag. He buried his face in his hands. "I love you, too. But I slept with her. I'm so sorry, Min. I couldn't help myself. Forgive me, my darling. I've betrayed you."

He was crying. His shoulders convulsed as he wept into the pillow. He was guilty, she realized. He wasn't angry with her, but with himself.

Was it possible that Mohini had kept her secret after all?

When she tentatively touched the back of his head, Edward rolled over, making no attempt to hide his tears. "I've been in hell since this happened. I was so afraid you'd find out. It didn't mean anything, I swear to you. It was a sort of lechery, bred of fear and darkness . . . It wasn't love. I think perhaps she was familiar to me, that I remembered her from the tea plantation. She also remembered me."

"And me?" Minerva forced herself to ask the question. "Did she say anything about me?"

"Of course not." He sounded outraged at the idea. "Certainly I would not discuss my wife with my—my mistress. Can you ever forgive me? I'm so sorry, Min. If you forgive me and take me back, I give you my most solemn promise that it will never happen again."

Minerva felt hysteria rising. She was supposed to be angry. She was supposed to throw him out of the house, screaming about divorce. Wasn't that how the betrayed wife typically behaved? Tears . . . or even a rolling pin?

Instead she pressed close, clinging to him and thanking God for his answering caresses. Who was she to judge him? All she felt was relief, and an overpowering guilt of her own.

"Yes, I forgive you. Of course I forgive you. I'm told that these things happen, particularly in wartime. I love you, Edward." She opened her arms for him. "Make love to me."

"You're so good," he told her. He was crying even harder now. "I don't deserve you, Min. I was afraid you'd leave me. I don't deserve a wife like you."

Minerva lay awake that night long after her husband slept. She felt jealous of his sleep, which was deep and peaceful. He was free of his guilt. Hers, however, was more burdensome than ever.

But Edward was not at peace. As the weeks and months went by, he began to understand that his adulterous affair was symptomatic of a larger malaise. He loved Minerva very much. Yet, even so, things were changing inside him. The rapidity of these changes had turned his mind into an emotional battlefield.

It had been coming on, he realized, for some time. He was almost forty years old, but he had never proved himself. Edward had never thought of himself as a particularly strong or brave man. Smart, yes; he had always been confident of his intellectual abilities. But he felt that he'd lacked the will, the force to translate thought and words into deeds.

Meeting Mohini, learning her connection with Darjeeling and his father, had somehow taken him back in time to the days when he'd done little more than grovel at the old man's feet. His marriage had removed him from the shadow of his father and given him confidence. In a very literal sense, his wife's love had been the foundation of his adult identity, and as a result, he was completely dependent upon her. This frightened him. It was not right, not healthy, for a man to be so dependent on a woman.

Somehow the terms of their relationship had to be altered. If their marriage was to survive, if *he* was to survive, he must become a different man, a more active man, a man who was her equal.

But how was he to do it?

At the end of the following year, when Pearl Harbor was bombed and the Americans finally entered the war, Edward shocked everyone by announcing that he was going to enlist.

"They won't take you," Minerva said, hoping to God she was right. "You're forty. That's too old."

But they did take him, although not as a soldier. Because of his excellent French, and some minor intelligence work he'd been doing at his desk during the past year, they were sending him to Paris as a spy.

"You don't have to do this," she said to him on the night before he left. "Please don't go, Edward. Please tell them you've changed your mind."

"No, sweetheart. It's something I have to do."

"I'm afraid for you. I'm afraid they'll kill you and I'll never see you again."

"Not if I can help it," he said with the most incredibly cocky grin.

And he *felt* cocky, although part of him knew how foolish that attitude was. At the age of forty he was going to France, to prove himself at war the way men had done from time immemorial. Although he had no illusions about the glory of war, he had believed for years that Hitler had to be stopped. Now, finally, he was going to take a small but active role in bringing the megalomaniac down.

If he survived, he would come home infused with new confidence and authority. He would be Minerva's true partner at last.

If he died, it would be with the knowledge that he had finally shown some courage, some gumption. That when it was important for him to do so, he had risen above mere theory to suit the word to the action, the action to the word.

"I love you very much," he told his wife. "Forgive me, my angel. Forgive me for all the times I've hurt you, made you sad." He gave himself to her in the manner she treasured, gentle and loving and exquisitely tender. "Don't worry about me. I'll be careful. I'll be fine."

But she wept in his arms. "Edward, please listen to me. Don't go. I have a premonition. Don't leave me."

"Nonsense. I'll be back and we'll love again. Better, more unselfishly, more honestly. I promise, Minerva. In a few months I'll be home."

She didn't believe him, but when he caressed her deeply and merged his body with hers, she could think of nothing but the beauty and pleasure of their mutual love, which had made their life together a sacrament.

PART THREE

Love and scandal are the best sweeteners of tea.

—Henry Fielding

Boston, 1943

10

Naked, Jonathan Templeton pushed up onto the examining table for his Army induction physical. He was nineteen years old and midway through his sophomore year at Harvard. He had learned three weeks ago that his father was dead, killed by the Nazis. In the grips of a grief that felt like explosions inside his head, he'd gone down to the army recruiting office and signed himself up to kill a few Nazis in return.

It was chilly in the examining room, and Jonathan began to tremble just a little. Try not to start crying, okay? They don't like crybabies in the Army. They like men, real men. He'd been crying a lot lately, especially at night. But his tears were a tribute to a man he'd adored, a good man, a kind man, an affectionate and understanding father, and Jonathan was not ashamed of them.

The doctor, a hefty, white-haired fellow with deep laugh lines around his eyes, came into the tiny cubicle. He was wearing a white jacket over a pair of gray wool trousers. Under the trousers he was wearing hand-tooled western boots, and around his neck a stethoscope dangled from its rubber tubing.

"Hello, son," he said, giving Jonathan a thorough once-over. "You old enough to be here?"

"I'm nineteen, sir."

"Parents know you're enlisting?" The doctor had a southern, or perhaps a southwestern, accent. Texas or someplace. He sounded like a cowboy—or was that just the impression given by the boots?

"I haven't told my mother. My father's dead. The Germans killed him."

"I'm sorry to hear that, boy. When?"

"Three weeks ago, sir."

The physician pursed his lips and said nothing for several seconds. He commenced his examination of Jonathan's eyes, ears, and throat. He tested his reflexes, then checked his body all over while asking a number of questions about his various bodily functions.

"In general, would you call yourself healthy?"

"Yes, sir."

"You still in school?"

"College, yes. I'll finish when I get out."

"Humph," said the doctor, as if he didn't believe it.

"I want to be a doctor."

"You'll have to lick right down and cram for that."

"I know. I'm a good student. I'm in the top ten percent of my class at Harvard."

"Are you now?"

Jonathan flushed. It had sounded like bragging, and he hadn't intended to brag. It was just that the doctor made him feel nervous, as if he had to justify himself.

"Harvard, huh?" The doctor tugged at his stethoscope. "Wanted to go to Harvard myself, but I didn't have the grades. Or the dough." He stuck the shiny metal ends in his ears. "Take some deep breaths."

Jonathan obeyed. The doctor moved the cold head of his instrument around several times, first on his chest, then on his back. Frowning, he moved it around again on Jonathan's chest, listening intently. He shook his head. Jonathan felt a thread of anxiety. Was something wrong with him?

The physician jerked the stethoscope out of his ears and picked up a clipboard from the end of the examining table. "Sorry, boy. You're rejected."

"What do you mean? Why?"

"Heart murmur. We can't have our young recruits going into battle with heart murmurs, can we?"

Jonathan ran a hand through his blond hair. He could feel his heart beating. It seemed to have speeded up. "Are you saying I have some kind of heart disease?"

"No. You're perfectly healthy, as far as I can tell. Probably just a functional murmur of no real consequence to your health."

"Then why are you rejecting me?"

"Technicality. It's not much, but it's enough to keep you out until we start getting desperate. If Hitler and the Japs are still at it in a couple of years, come back and you'll probably pass."

"I suspect I could pass now if I went to some other doctor."

The physician, whose name was Tom Hamilton, late of Dallas, Texas, put down the chart and regarded him with eyes that had seen many sorrowful things. He was thinking he could get in trouble with some kiss-ass army official for this. If he wanted to save some kid's skinny butt, he ought to have chosen one of the slum types whose miserable job building bombs in some war factory was putting bread on his mama's table, not this toady rich bastard from Hahvahd Yahd. The boy wasn't even grateful. Wanted to go over there and kill a few Huns for revenge, as if revenge ever solved anything in this rotten world.

And yet, there was something about his manner that made Hamilton want to do something for this boy whose daddy had bought the farm. "Listen," he said. "You're young. You're upset about your father, and you're hot to get those cocksuckers where it hurts."

Jonathan blinked, never having heard a physician use such language.

"I can understand that, not that I necessarily think it's right. But look at it this way: you're still in school, you're obviously smart. You want to follow my own esteemed profession, a profession that claims, somewhat self-righteously, to believe in healing, not killing. Your country needs you right here. In school. If we allow Hitler and the boys to wipe out all the best young minds in the United States, we won't have much left to fight for, will we?"

"No, sir. I guess not."

"Go back to Harvard. Getting yourself killed isn't going to help your pa, is it? I've got a feeling in my gut that he wouldn't be too pleased to find you joining him on the other side of the pearly gates."

This was true. Before leaving for Europe, his father had told him to stay in school and take care of his mother. He'd added he was counting on him as he was the man of the family now and all that typical father-son sort of cant. Except suddenly it didn't seem like cant at all.

Jonathan almost broke down. He managed to contain his tears until he left the doctor's office and could melt into the cold anonymity of the icy Boston streets.

Minerva was lying in her bed—the bed she had shared with Edward—when Jonathan came home that afternoon and confessed to her that he'd tried to enlist. Terrified, she sat up. Her head ached as she moved, and she felt dizzy. She wasn't sure how long she'd been lying there; since breakfast, perhaps. Or had she skipped breakfast this morning?

"Are you insane?" she screamed at him. "You're only nineteen!"

"Nineteen is old enough, Mum. But they rejected me."

"They'd damn well better reject you! I've lost one man to the war effort. I refuse to sacrifice another."

"I wanted to get the bastards who murdered my father."

Minerva grabbed a metallic-gray silk dressing gown from the foot of the bed and wrapped it around her. She rose from bed, ignoring the weakness in her legs. What day was this? Since Edward's death, she'd lost track. It must be January something. Edward had died at the end of the year.

Eleven months after Edward left, Minerva received a cable from the War Department. She knew right away what it meant. She held it flat on the palm of her hand for several seconds as if, like a conjurer, she could make it disappear. She'd always prided herself on her ability to face and deal with reality, but when that cable arrived she wanted magic, illusion, and a chance to relive the past.

"Coward," she said out loud, and forced herself to open the envelope and read the heavy blocked letters that seemed to whirl in a *danse macabre* before her eyes.

Some official she'd never heard of regretted to inform her that her husband had been captured by the Germans and shot as a spy. He had died with honor, serving his country, the cable went on, and she had their very deepest sympathy.

After that (when was it? A month ago? More?) she'd lost track of everything. Certainly it had never occurred to her that her sweet, sensitive Jonathan might be entertaining the same crazy thoughts as his father.

(Oh, Edward, Edward. Why did you do it? Was there something wrong with me, with us? Why did you have that affair in London? What did I fail to give you? If you weren't happy, couldn't we have searched for some other way to solve the problem, something that didn't involved your *getting killed?)*

They hadn't even returned his body for burial. No one seemed to know exactly what had happened to his body—or what the Germans had done to him before they'd shot him. (Her worst nightmares were about that.) For a few days after she had heard the news, Minerva had been obsessed with Edward's body . . . his *dead* body, wanting it as much as she'd ever wanted it when he was alive, wanting to see him one final time, no matter what they had done to him. Wanting to kiss him and tell him good-bye before they put him into the cold, cold ground. It wasn't right that she had no corpse to grieve over. How could she accept his death without seeing him, touching him, feeling the warmth and breath gone out of him, the spirit withdrawn from the clay?

What had they done to him?

"I want to get them," Jonathan repeated. "I couldn't think of any other way to get them except that."

"Come here." Minerva put her arms around him and held him hard. "I know how you feel. Believe me, I feel it, too. But it's war, Jonathan. To my way of thinking, war itself is the real enemy here. It's a pointless horror, a senseless waste of human lives. Your father could have lived many more years. When we were married, he promised me fifty years. We only had twenty. It wasn't enough."

She stopped a moment to control the crack in her voice. "But twenty is better than nothing. At least Edward had a chance to live and love and see his children grow up. Your life is just beginning, and I'm not going to let you throw it away. Promise me you won't try to join up again."

Jonathan didn't want to promise, but he was moved by his mother's plea, by the haunted look of fear in her eyes. She looked so frail. She never got dressed, she wore no makeup, and her blond hair was unbrushed and limp. Since she'd heard the news from the

War Department, she'd rarely left her room. There were calls from the tea company asking when she was going to return to work. She wouldn't take them, which was in itself disturbing. The tea company had always meant so much to her.

Since both Jonathan and his sister Lizzy were attending college in the Boston area, they took turns coming over to the Tavern in the evenings to be with her. Jonathan had learned from Paulings, the only one of the old staff still in residence, that his mother didn't sleep much at night, that she wandered through the house in her nightgown, looking like a ghostly inhabitant of the Tavern from an earlier century.

Her doctor, Augustus Cox, assured them that her reaction, though severe, was not unusual. She refused to take sedatives, which Gus said was not a bad thing. "She's strong, your mother. She'll work it through. You be as supportive of her as you can be, all right? She needs you."

Remembering this, Jonathan gave her his promise.

"You're the only male left of the Templeton line," she said. "The tea company and its entire rich legacy will come to you one day. You, in turn, will pass it on to your children and your children's children." She pressed one hand to her head and added, "My God, I must go into the office. How could they possibly be managing without me?"

She crossed to her dressing table and sank down on the stool. Touching a finger to the dark circles under her eyes, she reached for a cake of rouge and daubed a little on her pale cheeks. "Dear God, how I've let myself go." She picked up the sterling silver-backed hairbrush that had been Edward's gift to her on their tenth anniversary and began vigorously to brush her lank gold hair.

"Don't you have classes today? You must return to school immediately and apply yourself, Jonathan. You'll have to work hard to develop the skills you'll need to run Templeton Tea. Perhaps we can send you to the Harvard Business School for your M.B.A. Your grades are excellent, I know, but just to be sure, I'll send them a handsome donation in Edward's name."

Jonathan didn't want to argue when they were both so emotionally fragile, so he didn't correct her misconceptions about his future. But he wasn't going to business school. He certainly wasn't going to work for the tea company. And as for the legacy of the

Templetons being passed on to his children, that could never happen.

"Good-bye, Mum," he said a little while later, giving her a hug. She had gotten dressed and done something with her hair, and her makeup had brought the color back into her face. "Love you."

"I love you, too, my son."

Jonathan wasn't sure exactly when he'd realized that he was that horrible thing, that ugly word, queer. Even in childhood he'd had sexy feelings about boys, men. He hadn't known there was anything wrong with it then. It was just one of the myriad sensations of being alive.

When he was old enough to understand, he denied it. He was late reaching puberty, that's all, he told himself. So what if looking at the girly magazines the other boys swiped from their dads didn't make him hard? So what if his wet dreams contained more images of biceps than breasts? It didn't mean anything, did it?

Next came alternating periods of panic and rage. What if it was true? What was wrong with him? Was it a punishment for some horrible sin? Did God hate him? Why him?

It wasn't until he was sixteen and the pressures inside him had begun to grow intolerable that he started considering the practical aspects of his problem. How? Who? Where? And what if he got caught?

The first time it happened was during his junior year at Loomis. He'd been drinking. So had the other boy, Jimmy Kelly, who was a senior from the same dorm. Jimmy had initiated it; he had experience, he made it good. "How did you know I was like you?" Jonathan asked afterward.

"It's instinctive," Jimmy told him. "After a while you just know."

"I feel so guilty."

"Don't. It's your nature. You can't change it."

Jonathan didn't want to believe that. He yearned for love, for romance, even for the perfect marriage to his eternal soulmate. He couldn't accept that all this could be lost to him because of some freakish twist of his sexual nature.

So he tried it that summer with a girl. Annie Lindsey, his partner, was a bright girl from Miss Porter's School who characterized herself as a sexually free spirit. She was pretty, lively, and very likable. He could easily fall in love with her, he decided, maybe even forever.

But their lovemaking was a disaster. He managed to get into her, despite his fears that he wouldn't be able to, but there was no pleasure for him, no joy. Her body was too soft, too delicate, and her perfumed scent too cloying. There was no fine edge of danger or excitement in their coupling. While she was writhing and moaning and otherwise enjoying herself, Jonathan was thinking, so what?

His disappointment was severe. If Annie couldn't cure him, who could?

As he grew older and more accepting of his feelings, the sexual appeal of women became more and more incomprehensible to him. With his own sex, everything was different—here was the passion, here was the excitement. Another hard male body, tough and strong; no need to be gentle, to worry about causing pain. How could anyone not prefer the rough, driving power of another male?

It was never easy to find partners, but neither was it impossible. He hadn't been long at Harvard before hearing rumors about the existence of a discreet homosexual underground consisting of students and even a few faculty members. Chasing down the rumors proved difficult, but once you were known and accepted, life became much simpler. You might not find true love and everlasting passion, but at least you weren't alone anymore.

Now, in his second year at Harvard, Jonathan's instincts had become as finely honed as Jimmy Kelly's had been in prep school. He knew how to identify others like himself. It was a gut thing, and until he met David Scofield, he was never wrong.

David was a discovery of his sister's. Elizabeth was in her first year at Wellesley College (although she was two years younger than her brother, she had skipped a year in primary school), where she was already making her mark as something of a social butterfly. Slender, tawny-haired, and lightheartedly playful, Lizzy attracted hordes of escorts, most of whom she saw only a few times before flitting off to someone else. David Scofield was Lizzy's date for the spring formal in April. She invited David home for a late supper that evening after the dance, and Jonathan was there too.

David was in Jonathan's class at Harvard, but they'd never met. Elizabeth laughingly told her brother she was in love with him, but when Jonathan asked if they were lovers, she winked and said, "Not yet." Jonathan noted at supper that David was polite, yet restrained—almost cold—with her, unusual behavior for one of Lizzy's men. At one point during the meal, he caught David's eye, and their gaze held long enough for Jonathan to amend her statement to "Not ever."

David had the body type that Jonathan found most appealing—tall, elegant, and graceful. Although he was not effeminate, neither was he muscle-bound or coarse in any way. His face was aristocratic, his hair dark, and his eyes seemed to burn with inner passion. Byronic, Jonathan thought, already beginning to entertain elaborate fantasies.

David's passion proved to be politics—he was a socialist. He made it subtly clear that he disapproved of the Templetons and everything they stood for, which did not endear him, naturally, to Mother. But Jonathan knew that his own father had been sympathetic toward the socialists, and made a point of saying so, which earned him a caustic look from his mother.

Jonathan had recently bought a spiffy new Chevy convertible with a rumble seat and custom-made leather upholstery, so he offered to drive Elizabeth and David back to their respective colleges after supper. They drove Lizzy out to Wellesley, where Jonathan watched as David escorted her to the door of her dormitory and gave her a perfunctory kiss on the cheek. When he returned to the car, Jonathan said, "Want to go somewhere and get a beer? If we can find one, of course." The war had made alcoholic beverages difficult to come by.

David seemed to consider for a moment before saying, "No need to go out. I've got a bottle of whiskey in my room."

Jonathan's stomach turned over. This is it, he thought.

They lay on the floor in David's room, drinking and talking endlessly and listening to Benny Goodman records, and the rapport was terrific, and Jonathan thought, oh God, I'm in love. They discovered a shared admiration for T. S. Eliot (Let us go then, you and I/When the evening is spread out against the sky), but Jonathan did not receive the subtle signal he was waiting for. And he began to wonder. Was he wrong about David? (So how should I presume?) Should he make a physical advance and risk the crushing rejection that would surely come if his new friend did not share his desire? (Should I, after tea and cakes and ices,/Have the strength to force the moment to its crisis?)

"Your sister's beautiful," David said. "Are you twins? You look very much alike."

Jonathan took this as an encouraging remark. But even so, he sensed a coldness that continued to make him wary. (Do I dare/Disturb the universe?) Maybe David was inexperienced. Maybe he knew what he wanted but didn't know how to go about it. "We're not twins. She's two years younger than I." He inched closer.

"Do you suppose she's a virgin? I think she's a little in love with me, but I wouldn't want to despoil a virgin."

Jonathan froze. He felt something unravel inside. "I don't know if she's a virgin."

David smiled, and for the first time Jonathan noticed how wintery his eyes were. "I guess it's not something I ought to discuss with her brother, huh? You might come after me with a shotgun."

For an instant Jonathan hated his sister, a sweeping feeling that was almost instantly replaced with guilt. "Do you want her?"

"Christ, I want someone. It's been weeks since I had to break things off with Cynthia, my last girlfriend. She wanted to get married. Why do women always want to get married? Why can't they just enjoy a good fuck?"

"I've no idea." Now he felt sick, and rather puzzled. The intensity of his attraction to David was so strong that he couldn't believe it was one-sided. Mutual currents were there; he was sure of it.

"I'm afraid I don't know very much about women," Jonathan said to David. "I don't know how they feel about sex, and I don't particularly care."

David leaned up on one elbow. "Why not? How do you expect to make it if you don't figure them out a bit? Don't you date? You're not shy, and you're certainly good-looking. I know lots of girls who would kill to go out with you."

"I don't date."

David slowly sat up. Benny was blowing his clarinet rather morosely, Jonathan thought. Imbecile, he said to himself. What the hell is the matter with you? He waited to see David's expression change from curious to disgusted. Remarkably, it didn't. He remained curious.

"Are you telling me you don't *like* women? You're, uh, you . . ." He stopped.

"Yes." He had no idea why he was acting as if he were in a confessional. He'd never been so reckless before. He'd been struck with the *coup de foudre* by this slender young Byron, and it was futile, wasted. It would never happen. To hell with everything. "I do it with men."

"Jesus." David ran a quick, nervous survey of Jonathan's body. "I wouldn't have thought you were the type. I mean, we think of homosexuals as effeminate, don't we? That is, the cultural stereotype is so—" Once again he stopped. "I'm sorry. I'm being insulting, aren't I? I don't know what to say." David glanced around the room, as if noticing for the first time their casual posture, the near-empty bottle on the floor. "Did you think I was the same? Did you come here hoping that I would—we would—"

"Yes."

The record on the phonograph had come to an end, and the truth sounded bald in the quiet room. David eyed the door, as if wondering how long it would take to make his escape. Then he shook his head, obviously remembering this was his room.

"Take it easy," Jonathan said. "I'm not going to attack you. I made a mistake. If you need to run to the john and vomit in disgust, don't let me stop you." Jonathan knew he sounded bitter, and probably whiney as well, which made him even more embarrassed. Nothing quite this mortifying had ever happened to him.

"I'm not disgusted," David said quickly. "I'm, uh, surprised, that's all. I mean, our mores are so hypocritical, so bourgeois. People should be free to do what they want without being chastised by anyone for their private sexual feelings."

It sounded a little like a political tract. Jonathan wasn't convinced that David actually believed what he was saying, but at least he wasn't doing anything melodramatic, like fleeing the room. "It's very late. I'd better go."

"I'd like us to be friends," David said. "I've never known a—that is, it doesn't matter to me what you do in bed, Jonathan, or with whom. Really. I don't think you're perverse or anything like that."

David obviously fancied himself to be tolerant and liberal, but Jonathan suspected he was horrified all the same. It didn't matter. He didn't plan to see David Scofield again anyway. He knew better than to make himself wretched yearning after something he could never have.

But in the weeks that followed, he and David did indeed become friends. It was not his own doing; David went out of his way to facilitate it. He dropped by Jonathan's dorm to visit him. He talked him into joining the debating society. He invited him to political rallies and introduced him to his radical friends.

Jonathan endured it all through a veil of misery. On his side, the attraction remained, but he was baffled as to what David saw in him. In the beginning he wondered cynically if it had something to do with the Templeton fortune and name. David came from a poor family in Chicago. His Harvard education was being financed by scholarships. He had espoused socialism, yes, but at Harvard he'd made friends with young men whose family names represented decades of wealth, tradition, and political clout. He might rant on and on about the problems of the disenfranchised poor, but his time was spent in the circles of the elite.

But as they got to know each other better, Jonathan realized that David was sincere about his beliefs. Money really didn't matter to him, and it was the intellectual qualities of his blue-blooded friends that attracted him. The intellect was his god. Reason above passion. He was by no means as emotional as he had seemed. No Byron, after all, despite that dark and wicked physical grace. David's passions, if he felt them, were devoted toward his studies.

With his friends, he could be cold. There was a touch of arrogance about him that annoyed people, but David countered it by his constant efforts to be high-minded and fair in all his dealings. If he was at times too much of a blind-alley idealist, Jonathan could forgive that. In some ways, David reminded him of his father.

In short, he loved him.

David's flirtation with Elizabeth did not continue, fortunately. (Jonathan didn't think he could have borne that.) Lizzy complained that David had dropped her, a rare state of affairs that obviously left her intrigued. "I never heard from him again after that night you drove him back to school. What did you do, tell him all my faults?"

As a means of burning off his frustration with what looked as if it would forever be an unconsummated, unrequited love, Jonathan flung himself into a liaison with a fellow student whose sexual proclivities bordered on the degenerate. Barky Bennett, scion of another old Bostonian family, thrived on risk taking. He insisted on a tour of the China Tea House Tavern one afternoon that summer, and Jonathan realized when they reached his bedroom that a tour was not all Barky intended.

"This is reckless," he protested when Barky pushed him down across the bed and rifled open his fly.

"You love it. Shut up."

He didn't love it, though. For the first time in his life, his desires thoroughly disgusted him; he was ashamed of what he was.

His mother, returning home early from work with a rare indisposition, caught them at it. White-faced, she fled to her own room without saying a word. Jonathan dressed, got rid of Barky, and with more courage than he'd known he possessed, went down the hallway to knock at his mother's door.

Surprisingly, she was calm and controlled, as Jonathan also intended to be. "She was going to have to know sooner or later, old chap," Barky had said callously. "Might as well get the big dramatic scene over with now so you can have some freedom."

But Jonathan could think only that his mother had lost her husband less than six months ago, and that coming now, this was too heavy a blow.

"I'm sorry, Mother. I can imagine how shocked you must feel."

In fact, Minerva was not shocked. She'd suspected the truth for years. She was, however, afraid. She loved her son. Since Edward had died, her feeling for the children seemed to have grown even more passionate. She knew now how fragile life could be, and she wanted to protect them from anything that had the potential to hurt them.

She had been plotting furiously, trying to find a solution to Jonathan's problem. A solution was absolutely necessary. For all its supposed sophistication, American society was not tolerant of people who deviated from the accepted sexual pathways. In Europe—the old Europe before the Germans had made the new rules—

Jonathan's nature might have found expression, but here in Boston such behavior simply would not do.

"Sit down, Jonathan. I believe we should talk about the subject of your future marriage."

Jonathan had been prepared for a number of things she might say, but this had not been one of them.

"I'm aware, of course, that you're still young. But I was married young and I have no complaints. I think it is a useful practice, one that forces a person to mature early and begin to make adult decisions."

"Mother, you can't be serious."

"Don't interrupt. You're aware, I'm sure, that because of your position in life, you can't marry just anybody. I intend to make some inquiries among my friends to find out where we might begin to look for a suitable young woman. Naturally, I expect you to do the same."

"I am not going to marry," he said with dignity. "Not now, not ever."

He looks like Edward, she was thinking. But he was not her husband's son. How ironic that the man who was the natural son of the hard-drinking, womanizing Harrison Templeton should grow up with a distaste for the opposite sex.

"Indeed you are, Jonathan. You will either marry or be disinherited."

Whatever color was left in his face slowly drained. Minerva felt sorry for her son, sorry for herself. More guilt, she thought helplessly, to carry around with her. But she had to stand firm. Other people would *not* feel sorry. They would brutalize his feelings—perhaps even his person—without care, without consideration.

She continued, "Understand me, please. I don't condemn you. I understand that some men have these desires. I will ask you once, because I feel it ought to be asked: are you committed to this way of life, or is there any possibility that it is simply the result of the desire for experimentation that is so common among the young?"

Jonathan swallowed hard and shook his head. His mother was pacing the room now, and he could not help but admire her composure. She was clad in a form-fitting navy wool suit with squared shoulders that was almost militaristic in its tailoring. Her blond hair was cut short and smart, and she looked younger than her thirty-seven years. The severe headache that had driven her from her desk at Templeton House had obviously been forgotten.

"Then I repeat, you must marry. The sooner the better. We are not living in ancient Greece, Jonathan. Liaisons of the sort you desire are not tolerated. You will seek them anyway, I know; people always do. But at least if you are married, you will have that as a cover, a mask, for whatever secret life you choose to lead."

"That's vile, Mother. Am I supposed to spend the next fifty years living a lie?"

"If necessary, yes."

"Well, I won't. I'll go somewhere else to live, somewhere where people like me are tolerated."

"There is no such place. Not now. Not in today's world."

"That can't be true."

"It is true. Where would you go? Berlin? Yes, that city's always had a reputation for decadence, as has Paris, where everything is tolerated. Obviously, Berlin is out of the question now, and there may be no Paris left when the Nazis get through with it. London? Everyone hints there's a segment of the British upper classes who make a sybaritic cult of homosexuality, but it's certainly not out in the open. What else do you expect besides a life of hypocrisy? You're a fool if you think things are going to be easy for you.

"The world is changing, Jonathan. There are many people who believe that the excesses of the twenties—the freedoms that everybody started to feel—have led to global disaster. We're entering an age of repression, and it's your misfortune, your tragedy, perhaps, to be growing up during such a time."

There was truth in what she was saying; he knew that. "What must I do, then? How can I live?"

"The same way others who share your feelings have lived for generations. You must be one man on the surface and someone else underneath. I see no other solution."

Something in her voice clued him in to the fear she was feeling . . . and the love. Jonathan's own head was aching. This was hurting her. He wished he could be everything that she wanted him to be. "You're being very decent about this, Mum."

"I love you, Jonathan. I want you to be happy."

"I can't marry. I tried it once, with a girl. To see, to make sure."

He made a wry face. "I don't want to do that again. I'm not even sure I *could* do it again."

"You're still young," she said gently. "Even if your natural inclinations were toward women, you would have a few disasters at this age. Give yourself time. From what I understand, it's quite common for men who love men to have relationships with women also. You're my only son, the last Templeton. My fondest wish is that you will marry and give me grandchildren."

"Oh Christ, Mother. That's very unlikely, I'm afraid."

"At least consider it. That's all I ask. Can't you do that for me?"

Of course he could. It would be rotten of him not to. She loved him; she wanted the best for him. And all his life nothing had made him happier than to see her smile.

That night Minerva lay awake until the sky began to lighten with the dawn. When she finally dropped into unconsciousness, she dreamed Jonathan was sitting at a sidewalk cafe in Paris, cradling a baby in his arms. The Nazis snatched it away from him and trampled it to death beneath their jackboots. The child, they shouted, was a spy.

In the morning she rose with the determination to find her son a wife.

11

"You'll be glad to hear, Mum, that Sarah Manchester and I are engaged," Jonathan said to his mother in December 1944.

"Oh, my dear, thank God." Minerva closed her arms around him. "She's a lovely girl. You'll make a go of it, I know you will."

Jonathan wished he could be more certain of that, but he was going to try. David Scofield, who agreed with Minerva Templeton that Jonathan had no choice but to marry, had introduced him to Sarah. She and David had gone out together a few times. "She wants to get married," he said ruefully to Jonathan. "I figured better you than me."

Sarah was a blessed relief from the half dozen eligible young ladies whom his mother had bullied him into escorting to one damnable social function after another. He'd agreed to do it partly to demonstrate to her that he was attempting to cooperate with her wishes for him and partly to find out whether the double life she urged him to lead was at all possible.

From one responsibility, at least, he'd been freed. His mother had given in on his career when Elizabeth had announced a desire to learn the tea business in his stead. "It's perfectly obvious that a woman can handle the job," she'd said to their mother. "You've been doing it for years, so why shouldn't I?"

But his mother would not relent on the subject of marriage, and Jonathan had come to realize she was probably right. He'd applied to and been accepted at Harvard Medical School. Physicians were generally a conservative group, and he could hardly parade before them the fact that he was homosexual. In order to achieve the goals he'd set for his life, he had to be socially acceptable, that is, married.

He had been impressed with Sarah Manchester from the moment they met. She was a quiet young woman, with an otherworldly air about her that intrigued him. Her hair was fair, not unlike his own, and she was tall and exquisitely made. Her bones were delicate, and she moved with the grace of a dancer. In fact, she had studied ballet seriously for a number of years and given it up only because, as she quite brutally put it, "I wanted to be the best, and I realized I never would be."

She was an excellent ballroom dancer, too, which had been one of the first things Jonathan admired about her. He loved to dance. He could put up with dating, he decided, because it gave him the chance to take a girl to a club and swing for hours to the tireless beat of the horns, the drums, the clarinets. Dancing slow with Sarah was pleasant, too. Her body was fit and strong and flower-stalk slender. No breasts to speak of, hardly any flare at her hips. In bed with the lights out, maybe he'd be able to pretend she was a boy.

This was despicable, he knew, but he told himself that marriage wasn't based on sex anyhow, especially among men and women of his class. He was fond of Sarah and he figured that as long as they suited each other in other ways, it wouldn't matter if their physical relationship wasn't entirely satisfactory.

They did suit in other ways. Sarah loved books, opera, and classical music. When they were together she was talkative and affectionate without ever being aggressive. (Much as he loved her, his mother tended to be a little overbearing, and this was something Jonathan wanted to avoid in a wife.) Sarah was also a perfectionist, which seemed an admirable trait to him. And she was fiercely honest.

He felt he ought to be honest in return.

"I'm going to tell her the truth," he said to David. "I'm not going to marry her under false pretenses. It would be wrong to do that to anyone."

"Don't be a fool. She won't marry you if you tell her. You'll have gone through all this agony for nothing."

But Jonathan insisted his future wife had a right to know what she was getting into.

Late one spring evening after they had been jitterbugging madly for hours at a private club, Jonathan pulled the car off on the side of a deserted road and turned to his fiancée, who seemed to stiffen a little in her seat. He took her hand in his. She was wearing the two-carat pear-shaped diamond he had given her at Christmas.

"What's the matter? Why are we stopping?"

He noticed that her palm was slightly damp. Was she frightened? He squeezed her hand reassuringly. "You must be wondering why I haven't urged you to make love with me."

Sarah looked down; he could see the flush rising on her throat. "I don't think we ought to. We're not married yet, Jonathan."

"I wasn't going to press for it. The fact is, I've only been with a woman once, and that was something of a disaster."

He sensed her relaxing; the tightness around her mouth loosened, and she smiled in her usual graceful manner. "We'll figure it out, I imagine. People do."

He was momentarily distracted, astonished at her conclusion that he was sexually unsophisticated. She looked pleased about it, too.

"Sarah, you don't understand. In some ways, I'm not like other men. I envision our marriage as more of a spiritual union than a physical one."

"Oh yes, so do I. I've always dreamed of that, Jonathan. It's one of the reasons I was drawn to you. The others I dated were always pawing at me, but you've been a perfect gentleman. Sex is so meaningless. Real love transcends the physical, don't you think?"

This was not going quite the way he had planned. He wondered briefly if David had "pawed at her," and decided, knowing David, that he probably had. It had not escaped his notice that when David was around, Sarah grew very thoughtful. He had wondered once or twice if she'd been genuinely in love with him, and if it had hurt her to be handed off to his best friend.

He pushed that subject aside. David was not the problem here; he was. "Sarah, you do know, don't you, that there are people who love each other regardless of their sex? Men who love men, women who love women?"

"Yes," she said, a little uncertainly. "I guess that's exactly what I mean. Sex is limiting, but spiritual love has no bounds."

It was difficult to believe that she could be so innocent. Was she deliberately misunderstanding him? Jonathan didn't think he was capable of explaining the anatomical details. "What I'm trying to tell you is that our marriage might not live up to your expectations with regard to what happens in the bedroom. Doesn't that bother you?"

She seemed anxious now. "Haven't we discussed this enough? It's—it's embarrassing, Jonathan."

He gave up. Maybe her sexual drives were not strong, which might turn out to be a mercy. Maybe she wouldn't expect too much from him.

He graduated from Harvard in June amidst jubilation over the winding down of the war in Europe. Two weeks after commencement he and Sarah were married in an elaborate ceremony, attended by nearly three hundred guests, at the Church of the Advent in Boston. His sister, Elizabeth, was one of Sarah's attendants, and David Scofield was his best man. David and Lizzy danced together often at the reception, and Jonathan was furious with himself over the brief spurt of agony he felt when he saw his sister kissing the handsome David under an archway.

David also danced with Sarah. Jonathan did not notice that after the one dance they shared, his new wife vanished briefly into the ladies' room, where she indulged in a short but violent cry.

At Christmas 1945, Jonathan invited David to spend a few days with him and Sarah in the Chestnut Hill home where they'd been living since they'd returned from their honeymoon. David was a graduate student now at Harvard, studying English, and as usual, he didn't have the extra funds to go home to his own family in Chicago.

Jonathan didn't think he could face Christmas with no one except Sarah for company. His mother was traveling in Europe—taking one of her rare vacations—and Elizabeth had driven down to Florida with her roommate to enjoy a little December sun.

David would be a good buffer. Sarah sparkled around him. David would start some sort of discussion, if not of politics, then about poetry or art or music, and they'd all get so intense about whatever it was they were discussing that they wouldn't have to think about anything more personal. That was one good thing about David—he never got personal unless you pushed him.

Sarah cooked a Christmas goose, a custom she'd learned from Minerva, who believed in observing English traditions even though she'd never lived in England in her life. The men stayed up late, drinking whiskey on top of a bellyful of rich food. Jonathan was drunk and could hear himself talking rather inanely to David long after Sarah had said goodnight and gone up to bed.

"Sarah seems happy," David said to Jonathan. "She's very elegant. She complements you. The two of you look great together."

"She's an angel." Jonathan gulped some more whiskey and added, "I'm thinking of asking her for a divorce."

David's expression darkened. "I thought things were going well between you."

"You know what they say about appearances being deceiving."

"She loves you." David sounded alarmed. He'd been nearly as insistent as Minerva that Jonathan get married. Jonathan suspected that his marriage made it easier for David to pretend his friend was normal. "Can't you see that?"

"I love her, too. That is, in an emotional way, I love her. I don't love her in an erotic way, but as we've agreed, eros isn't everything. I love her, dammit, but I'm destroying her."

David avoided his eyes, and Jonathan knew David didn't want to hear any of this. He'd always been a little uncomfortable with Jonathan's confidences. The fact was, Jonathan thought morosely, it was pretty damn difficult to get close to David.

Screw him. He was supposed to be his friend, wasn't he? He was one of the only heterosexuals to whom Jonathan had ever confided the secrets of his nature. If he *was* heterosexual, which Jonathan still wondered about. Oh sure, he slept with women—when he wasn't too busy ranting about imperialistic capitalists—but Jonathan had a niggling feeling that somewhere deep inside David lurked the same yearnings he felt.

But David would never admit it. He'd keep the impulse buried and sublimate his desires into other, less threatening channels.

"I never should have gotten married," Jonathan said.

"I don't think I want to hear this."

"I need to talk to someone. It's tormenting me, David."

"Shit." David put his head in his hands. A moment or two later he said, "All right, talk."

"The marriage isn't working. In bed, I mean; it isn't working in bed. Otherwise, it's okay—we get along, we enjoy each other's company. But sex is a mess." He took another gulp of whiskey. "Sarah was very nervous on our honeymoon, and more innocent than any woman her age I've ever known." He met David's eyes briefly. "The marriage hasn't been consummated."

"Jesus," David muttered, and looked away again.

"I guess she's afraid of sex. She's certainly disgusted by her own body. You've seen how thin she is . . . Well, she's not thin enough. She diets constantly. Some days she doesn't take anything but tea and a little fruit or cereal. She's obsessive about it, really.

"Because she has such low regard for her appearance, she insists on coming to bed with all the lights out. Then she lies there, stiff and silent, while I try to get her aroused. Is it any wonder I can't stay aroused myself long enough to do it? Even if I were attracted to women, I don't think I'd be able to perform under those circumstances."

"Nor would I," David said feelingly.

"She acts as if she's scared to death. I don't understand it. It's not as if I've ever hurt her. I've been nothing but gentle and understanding with her."

David said nothing. His head was in his hands.

Jonathan hesitated, then said, "You dated her for a while. I thought, I wondered . . . It would be helpful if you could tell me—"

"If we made love?" David broke in. "Is that what you're asking? Christ!"

"All I was asking is whether or not she seemed afraid." Jonathan was startled; he'd always presumed his wife was a virgin; she'd seemed too innocent to be anything but. Now it occurred to him that if she *had* slept with David, her reluctance might arise from the fear that he would find out. Or from something worse: a preference for David's lovemaking over his own.

Which would hardly be surprising, would it? What do you know about women, after all?

"She wasn't afraid," David said slowly. "Shy and inhibited, yes. With a little patience and persistence on your part, I would imagine she'd prove to be as sensual as any other woman. And stop looking at me like that. We didn't do it. She's a virgin as far as I'm concerned."

As Jonathan relaxed, another thought struck him. "In a way I wish you had slept with her. It would have made things easier for me." He drank more whiskey, pouring it down his burning throat. "The worst of it is, she may not want sex, but she longs for a baby. If she could get pregnant, she thinks everything would be all right. But how's she going to have a baby if she won't let me near her?"

"Jesus."

"The irony of it all is, I've been faithful to her. For six bloody months. I *do* like sex, but it's like sleeping beside a holy martyr. A *female* holy martyr. I want to hold her close and protect her. I want to save her from whatever demons are tormenting her. But I can't go on this way forever. Maybe you're right: she needs a man who's got more goddamn patience than I do."

"Or less," said David.

"What do you mean?"

"I mean she's your wife. Maybe you ought to insist."

Jonathan stared at him over the top of his crystal glass. "You're suggesting I force her?"

"I'm suggesting you say, okay, this is it, no more nonsense; like it or not, we're going to make love. You don't have to hurt her. Tell her how much you love her. Tell her she's beautiful and that her body drives you wild. Then go through with it. Don't back down."

Jonathan was silent, wondering if he could actually do such a thing. He doubted it. That was part of his thing about women—he'd always been afraid he'd hurt a woman somehow.

"Some women don't respond until you master them," David continued. "It's not surprising considering they're taught by their mothers that sex is sinful and only enjoyed by whores. They can't allow themselves to become aroused. But if they're forced—particularly by a man they know would never really hurt them—then it's okay. They're not responsible. They can tell Mommy, he made me do it, he made me feel these forbidden feelings, it's not my fault."

"The old sheik in the desert routine."

"If she responds, the problem's solved. If she doesn't, at least you won't be any worse off than you are now."

The image that came to Jonathan's mind was so vivid, he felt himself flush. He imagined taking his partner into a darkened room. He saw the bed, heard the tearing of clothes. "You know you want it," he heard himself saying. "You've wanted it for years."

There were protests, but he ignored them. And soon there was pleasure, deep, gut-wrenching pleasure . . . for both his partner and himself.

David. Not Sarah. David, David. Who knew so much about women, and so little about himself.

"I think you should get her drunk first," David was saying. "Get a bottle of the best champagne and pour it into her until her inhibitions are gone. Then do your husbandly duty, get her pregnant with the family heir, and if you still need to, satisfy your other desires discreetly on the side."

"She doesn't drink. Champagne has too many calories."

"Screw that. Look—it's New Year's Eve next week. Your sister's coming back from Florida and has agreed to be my date for the evening. We could all go out together. Go dancing. Sarah loves to dance, and let's face it: dancing's one of nature's more seductive activities. She'll be relaxed; we'll get a few glasses of champagne into her during the course of the evening, a little more as we ring in the New Year, then you can take her home, carry her off to bed, and break down that barrier once and for all."

"I suppose she'll have to drink champagne on New Year's Eve."

"It's certainly worth a try."

In his semidrunken state, Jonathan thought it was a brilliant idea. He raised his glass. "To a successful drunken orgy on New Year's Eve."

She'd had too much champagne. Far too much. But the most important of her New Year's resolutions was to be more accommodating to her husband, and he'd insisted she drink tonight. He kept refilling her glass. And it was fun to drink, fun to feel the bubbles in the back of her throat, and later, in her blood. They danced and danced. Jonathan was a divine dancer. And although David, her husband's best friend (she must not think of him as anything else but that), was not as technically adept with the steps, she adored being in his arms. Never never would she forget New Year's Eve 1945 and the thrill of being in David's arms.

When midnight struck and they cheered the advent of 1946, Jonathan kissed her while David kissed Elizabeth, and when Elizabeth—who was always so merry, so gay—kissed her brother and David turned to Sarah and drew her close and touched her lips, she thought, I love the way he kisses. So warm, so warm, so *hot.* I love his dark hair, his poet's eyes, his full, clever mouth. I want so much to be alone with him, in a darkened room, his flesh warm (hot) and bare against mine . . .

There her fantasies stopped. It was wrong. That was over; she was married. She was married to his closest friend. Anyway, David didn't love her. He never had.

Tomorrow she would have to start her diet again. She'd been bad tonight, terrible. She'd eaten too much, drunk too much. If she were more careful about her diet, she wouldn't be having these wicked thoughts. She would eat nothing tomorrow, not even a crust of bread.

"Sarah? Have another glass of champagne," her husband said, smiling as he put it into her hand. "To a wonderful New Year," he said, clicking glasses with her, and she was forced to drink.

Tomorrow. Only water. Only water for three days.

They danced some more, then drove home. They'd dropped off Lizzy at a friend's (David wasn't sleeping with her, Sarah thought in exultation), but when David, who had left his Model T in the driveway, said he ought to leave, Jonathan said he'd better have some coffee and sober up before attempting to drive back to Cambridge.

David agreed. Sarah put a Benny Goodman record on the phonograph and turned it up loud. While Helen Ward sang about someone taking the high road and someone else taking the low road, they danced again—she and David—and Jonathan opened another bottle of champagne.

David was still there when Sarah said she couldn't seem to stand up anymore and simply had to go to bed. She had trouble walking. "I can dance," she said, laughing. "But I can't walk!"

"I'll help," offered David as Jonathan swept her into his arms and headed for the stairs. Jonathan looked handsome tonight, too, in his dark tux and ruffled shirt. Piratelike, she thought dreamily.

How lovely to be dancing with two such handsome men. Around her the staircase seemed to whirl.

"Shit," said Jonathan, who never used such language. "I think I just wrenched my back." He set her down on the landing, groaning a little but also laughing. David took her up. He was thinner, slighter than Jonathan. But just as strong. He was darker, much darker. She loved his straight black hair. And his eyes. He was so handsome. Valentino-handsome. He had that sensual, sardonic mouth the romance novels always termed "cruel." Once again she remembered how it had felt to feel that mouth against her mouth, against her throat, against her trembling breasts.

That could never happen again, of course.

David carried her into the bedroom and laid her down across the huge white bed. The entire room was white—the carpet, the curtains. White and gold. The bed was brass, and the art deco dressing table, the bureaus, were all white trimmed with metallic gold.

Jonathan, just behind them, lurched into David, who fell onto the bed beside her. They all laughed. David's thigh was against her thigh. He'd ripped off his tie long ago, downstairs, and his starchy dress shirt was open at the collar. She could see black smudges of chest hair curling out from around his open buttons. Unthinkingly, she reached up and touched the place. The hair was springy, soft against her fingertip.

David's laughter died. His face went very still. Jonathan, somewhere above them, tall and golden and indifferent as a god (she knew he was indifferent. He pretended not to be, but it was something she could sense), said quietly, "Kiss him, Sarah."

He'd never given her an order like that. He sounded firm, inexorable. There was nothing to do but obey.

David tried to draw away, but she wrapped her strong ballerina's arms around his shoulders and arched up against that slim body, that hair-sprung chest.

"It's all right," she heard her husband say to David. "If you want to, I don't mind."

David gave a sigh and kissed her back. He'd always enjoyed kissing her. When they were dating and he kissed her, she went crazy. But she'd never let him do more than touch his mouth to her face, to her neck, and once or twice when she'd been really daring, to her breasts. It would have been wrong to let him do more, but several times he'd tried anyway and kept on and been angry when she'd insisted he stop. "You know you want it," he'd said to her, and it was true. Her husband had never made her want it the way David did.

His tongue slid deep into her mouth, exciting wicked little demons of sensation that bubbled with the champagne up and down her limbs. Then he drew back so just the tip of his tongue was sliding along the serrations of her teeth. She felt his teeth closing over her bottom lip and nipping her before his tongue plunged in rhythmically, deeper, deeper. So wicked, so good.

Sarah moaned. David lifted his head, as if wary, but she bent her fingers into that thick, dark hair and pulled him back down. Then, suddenly, he was touching her breasts. His fingers made small circles around her areolas, through the silky rose fabric of her evening gown. His hands were warm, so warm. He teased her, and her nipples turned hard as pebbles. He tweaked them between thumb and finger, then slipped his hand inside the low neckline and stroked her bare skin. She hadn't worn a brassiere—her breasts were too small, too firm, to require one.

She was on fire. Her head was spinning, and in the pit of her stomach was a fierce, insistent ache.

"Unbutton his shirt," Jonathan said. She'd forgotten he was there. She hesitated, frightened. *What are you doing? You're married.*

"It's all right, Sarah." Her husband's voice was sweet, understanding. "I love you and I want you to be happy. Touch him, Sarah. David wants you to touch him."

As her fingers flew to comply, David said, "Jonathan, you're drunk. We're all drunk. Are you sure—"

"Yes." Jonathan's hands were on Sarah's chest now, pushing the dress off her shoulders, down her arms. He had bared her upper body, and for a few moments she was entangled in the straps of the dress, unable to move her arms, their prisoner. "Look. She has very pretty breasts, doesn't she? Apple-breasts, peach-breasts. Small and pointed and firm. Kiss them, David."

David groaned, and Sarah felt triumphant. When he'd told her he wasn't going to date her anymore, she'd thought he didn't want her, but he did, he did.

His mouth was moist and hot as it settled over her left breast and sucked and nibbled and devoured her while his hands—or was it Jonathan's hands?—tore away what was left of her dress, her slip, her hose, her panties.

They left her lacy white garter belt on.

Someone dimmed the lights. Sarah's head tossed on the pillows. Someone—a woman—was making breathless little sounds, sounds of excitement, sounds of pleasure.

The mattress squeaked as Jonathan, who didn't seem to have on any clothes, lay down beside her. She felt his hands, big and gentle, stroking her hair. "I love you," he said again. "I love you, Sarah; it's all right."

Then he was kissing her mouth while David moved lower on her body, stroking his devilish tongue across her belly, her legs, her thighs, and even up into her secret place, which was as hot and moist and hungry as his mouth. She should have been embarrassed, but she wasn't. She should have been ashamed, but instead she thought, I love him, I love them both.

David drew back and Jonathan took over. They seemed perfectly coordinated, as if they did this all the time. Somewhere in the distance she heard a rustling of clothes, and then David was naked, too. He lay down beside her and turned her to face him. He caressed her all over with fingers that teased and probed and flew.

"Oh!" she gasped as something convulsed inside her. It almost burst, but didn't quite; it made her feel maddened, needing, needing . . . she wasn't sure what.

Jonathan's hands were on her, too, curving over her shoulders, stroking down her spine. He found and caressed her liquid heat. Something convulsed again. Against her cheek, where his face was, she felt him smile. "You're not afraid?" he asked.

"No, no."

"I love you, Sarah. David loves you, too. And I love David."

"We all love each other," David agreed in a voice that was breathless and slurred. His mouth was sucking at her breasts again, licking and nipping, making her writhe.

Jonathan took one of her hands and pressed it to his friend's belly. Then lower. She touched David's penis, which was large, larger even than her husband's. David jerked, breathing hard.

Sarah didn't know exactly what to do. Jonathan showed her, guiding her hand up and down, up and down.

David said, "I'm losing control," and Jonathan pushed Sarah flat. His gentle hands parted her thighs and caressed her deep inside. "She's ready."

"Do you really want—"

Jonathan gripped his friend's shoulder and forced him down upon her. He turned David's face toward him and kissed him full on the mouth. Sarah felt David's body vibrate. He sucked in his breath and turned his face back to her. He shifted his hips until he found her. He pressed. "Okay, Sarah. Hang on."

A blackness came down on her and she was suddenly very tense. This was wrong, *wrong.* But before she had a chance to panic, David thrust inside her, obliterating in one rough stroke her maidenhead. Sarah mewed once, then her husband's mouth covered hers and absorbed her cries. She heard him, no, both of them, murmuring praises, soothing words, encouragement. David's body moved on her, in her. Jonathan stroked her hair, her throat, the sensitive shells of her ears. Sometimes he stroked David's hair, his arms, his naked shoulders. There were hands and lips and tongues everywhere.

As the pain faded, the pleasure built. David rolled over onto his back, keeping himself inside her. Now she was riding him and Jonathan was massaging her back, her buttocks, in between her legs, in between her lover's legs. His lips moved down her spine. He patted her bottom, kneaded it. He slapped her there with the flat of his hand and she cried out in a sudden burst of almost agonizing pleasure that exploded and exploded again. Her cries were echoed by David as he arched violently one final time and spilled his seed.

That night, during the first few hours of the New Year, they made love to her again, many times. They both kissed her, they both caressed her. But it was only David who penetrated her body, David who came inside her again and again and again.

"Your husband needs you," he told her sometime during the long, haunted night, and it was true, for Jonathan had grown increasingly tense, almost frantic.

"What should I do?"

"Take him in your mouth. Kiss him intimately, as we have both kissed you. He's given you pleasure. You must return it."

"How?" she whispered.

"Show her," said Jonathan.

David hesitated, his eyes locked with Jonathan's. "What the hell," he said, and did.

Exhausted, Sarah watched, and learned, her eyelids heavy, her thoughts a blur. Seductive unconsciousness began to claim her. She didn't think they were even aware of her after that.

On a cold morning in mid-February, Jonathan stood on the pedestrian bridge overlooking the Charles River rubbing his hands together to try to get warm as he watched the scarfed and mittened figure moving slowly toward him. The landscape was hazed with newly fallen snow that had hardened in the bitter cold of night.

As David came up on the bridge, his feet made a crunching sound. He stopped walking before he got too close.

"This is a helluva chilly place to meet," Jonathan said. "What's so important that you had to get me out of bed at this hour?"

"I'm going to marry your sister," David said, his voice flat, colorless.

"I see. Does that mean you're going to stop sleeping with my wife?"

"I did it for you."

"The first time, maybe. For the past few weeks you've been doing it for yourself."

David turned away from him, leaning his elbows on the wall and looking seaward along the serpentine river toward the hills of downtown Boston. "Sarah loves you. She doesn't want me; she feels guilty. Surely you can take her now, for chrissake. She's not inhibited anymore."

"Oh, I can take her now, yes. Unfortunately, it's not Sarah I want."

David avoided his eyes. "I love Elizabeth. I'm going to marry her."

"Marry a woman, of course. One must do that, mustn't one? Marry a woman who looks enough like me to be my twin."

"Shut up, Jonathan! I know what you're implying, but you're

wrong. It was an experiment, that's all. I was curious. I wondered what it was like. I think people should try everything once."

"Sure. Okay. Take it easy."

"I'm not like you. Christ. Would I be sleeping with your wife as well as your sister if I were like you?"

Jonathan laughed sadly. "You want my mother as well? She's still quite young. Lots of men are after her, and she hasn't had any sex for years, as far as I know."

"Fuck you, Templeton."

Jonathan grabbed his arm as David was about to stalk away. But he couldn't really feel him through the heavy winter coat. Like armor, he thought. David had a multitude of ways to shield himself from other people. "I'm sorry. Wait, David. Wait."

David stopped, sullen, ill at ease. "It was all your doing, and you know it. You got what you wanted, both from her and from me. If you're sorry now, that's tough. I have no sympathy for you; it wasn't my fault."

"I'm not sorry," Jonathan said. He was thinking, you've never had any sympathy for me, for me or for anybody. You take what you can get, but you don't accept any responsibility. Sarah's guilty, yes, but she's also weeping over you. Because you're leaving. Because you're marrying Elizabeth. "Does my sister know about any of this?"

"Don't be an idiot. Of course she doesn't know. She'd probably throw up if she knew. Sometimes I feel like throwing up myself."

Jonathan's temper flared again. "I know you better than that. You're a lot cooler than you pretend to be." *You're a cold son of a bitch, as a matter of fact.* "Part of you is reveling in the way you've been screwing the old New England capitalists. You wouldn't be marrying Lizzy for her fortune, would you, Comrade Marx?"

David whitened. A personal attack he could tolerate, it seemed, but go after his precious ideals and he reeled. "You son of a bitch. I'll never touch a dime of her precious fortune, and I'll even sign an agreement to that effect. I love Elizabeth. I desire her. I want to be inside her in a manner that you, apparently, can't understand. Too bad for you, Jonathan. Too bad for Sarah."

He turned and walked away. Over his shoulder he called, "If you ever come near me again, I'll tell everybody you're a queer who pimps for his own wife. I've had it with you."

Jonathan stood in the cold, shivering. I've had it with you, too, he was thinking. And it was good. If it hadn't been so good, it would have been easier to forget.

For the first time in years, Jonathan hated himself. Hated what he was. A couple hurried by, a man and a woman, huddled together against the cold. Men and women, everywhere. What have I done to be excluded like this? Is there no place on this earth for me?

No self-pity, he ordered himself. Not now, not ever.

You have a wife. She loves you. If she loved David for a while, that's okay, that doesn't matter. The important thing is what you do for the rest of your life. You can make love to her now; you did last night. You have a marriage . . . now make it work.

Below him the icebound Charles River slowly crawled toward the sea.

In October 1946 Minerva welcomed her first grandson into the world. Travis Templeton, blond, blue-eyed, and beautiful, smiled his first smile about a month later. "Look at the glint in his eyes," his grandmother cooed. "He knows how dazzling he is. He'll be charming people with that smile for many years to come."

The proud parents were delighted with him, Minerva could tell. Sarah was more radiant than her mother-in-law had even seen her. Even Jonathan seemed content.

Minerva congratulated herself on the successful outcome of her plans for her son. Thank God she hadn't indulged his notions about remaining single and pursuing God only knew what sort of decadent life. The marriage was working, and here was a child to prove it. They were a well-matched couple, and as long as Jonathan continued to behave himself, they shouldn't be any worse off than many other husbands and wives. They might not have what she and Edward had had, but that was difficult to find.

Edward would have been pleased. Jonathan was decently married and the father of a son who would carry on the Templeton name. He was doing well at medical school despite a somewhat shaky start in his first semester. He would, no doubt, have a brilliant career ahead of him.

Other things, too, were going well. The postwar economy was beginning to boom, and Minerva's decision to go into paper tea bags had paid off. Under her administration, Templeton Tea had increased its annual profits by fully 10 percent. After so many generations of male rule, Minerva took pleasure in the idea of a woman's carrying on the traditions of Helen Templeton, who had started it all.

Her only concern these days was her daughter's recent elopement with David Scofield. Their marriage had come as a complete shock. Elizabeth had graduated with honors from Wellesley in the spring and begun working full-time for Templeton Tea, satisfying her mother about her potential ability to carry on for her after she was gone. Not that she intended to die for a good many years. After all, she was only forty, and in excellent health.

Elizabeth was as capricious with men as she was levelheaded where business was concerned, so Minerva had paid little attention to her infatuation with the handsome but penniless Scofield. She flattered herself that her daughter was too well brought up ever to make a disadvantageous match.

She had been wrong. They'd run off at the end of June and been married before a justice of the peace on Cape Cod. According to Jonathan, who was on less friendly terms with David than he'd once been, they had been planning to wed for some time. "I advised against it," he told her. "But they wouldn't listen to me."

Her daughter's new husband was a socialist. He wanted none of his wife's filthy capitalist fortune and, to Minerva's contemptuous surprise, had actually signed away any rights to it. They were going to live on his meager income as a part-time English teacher. He'd insisted that Elizabeth move into a dingy Cambridge flat with him while he completed graduate school.

Minerva had advised her daughter on reliable methods of birth control and sent the happy couple the newfangled television set they'd asked for as a wedding present instead of the fine china, crystal, and silver they obviously had no room for in their flat. Privately she was giving the marriage a year. Two if the dark-haired David was any good in bed. Meanwhile she started a file on attorneys who specialized in divorce.

12

April 7, 1948, was for Minerva Templeton a day of mixed delight and despair. It was then that her past and her future collided.

She was working in her office during the middle of the day waiting for Jonathan, who had invited her out to lunch. The building was quiet; most of her employees were on their noontime break. Minerva was surprised when she became aware of heavy footsteps in the hallway. These were combined with an odd scraping noise that she couldn't immediately identify. The shuffling stopped on the threshold of her office. She looked up.

"Ah, Mrs. Templeton," said a voice from out of her nightmares. "How delightful to see you again."

Minerva blinked at the man in the doorway. One hand went to her heart. She thought: my God, why didn't I have any warning? Then she realized that nothing could have prepared her for the shock of seeing his face again.

It was Harrison Templeton. The news of his wife's death several years ago had been the last she had heard of either of Edward's parents. Certainly she'd never expected him to return to Boston.

Fool, she said to herself. You've heard about all that's happened in India—the independence, the new Muslim nation of Pakistan being formed on the northwest frontier. Many foreigners were leaving now that the sun was finally setting on the British empire. She ought to have prepared herself for this possibility.

"You look a little pale, my dear. Think you're seeing a ghost? I am not dead, Mrs. Templeton, unlike my poor wife and your sniveling Edward. Oh no, not yet. I've a number of things I intend to do before I lay this body down."

There was hardly a trace of an American accent anymore in that voice—it was all British India, the Raj of her childhood. He'd been living there for twenty-eight years and sounded more British than she did.

Minerva put down her pencil as Harrison Templeton stepped into her office, into the light. The voice might be the same, but the body had aged. He was nearly seventy, she calculated quickly, and looked even older. The physical attractiveness that had been responsible for some of his success with women had long since vanished below layers of sagging muscle and fat. His dark eyes had sunken into his swollen face; the mustache that had once been rakish now hung limp and yellow-white, discolored, she was sure, by the cigar smoke that she could smell sticking to his shabby tweed suit. A sad case, she told herself. Pathetic.

She rose, more confident on her feet. "You've left India."

"Everybody's leaving India now. Leaving it to the natives, who don't know squat about running a country. Leaving them to kill each other—Hindu and Muslim—butchers, one and all."

He settled his bulk into the wingback chair in front of the window. "I sold your precious plantation. That was one victory over me you never had. It's part of a native-run operation now. Big, dark chappie running the place." He sighed. "It never turned a proper profit. All those years of backbreaking labor in that filthy country and I was never able to make it do as well as I had dreamed."

Backbreaking labor indeed! If he'd spent less time boozing and womanizing, he might have had more success.

"And so, here I am," he went on. He gave her a pathetic half smile. "Nowhere else to go, I'm afraid, but to the bosom of my family. You don't seem very pleased to see me, my dear."

"I can't imagine you would think I would be. You'll find no welcome here." But beneath her loathing, she was aware of a faint feeling of pity for the man. Compared to what she herself had accomplished, his was a wasted life. It was hard to believe, looking at the wreck of him, that this was the same man who had seduced her stepmother, stolen her land, raped her, and begotten a child upon her. She remembered how violently she'd hated him, how passionately she had longed for revenge.

A wicked life wreaks its own vengeance.

His eyes shifted around, taking in the fine furnishings of her office, which had been renovated since he had last seen the place. The oriental carpets on the floor. The Impressionist art on the walls. The leather-bound books in the solid walnut bookshelves. The Queen Anne chairs she so cavalierly used as office furniture. "You've done nicely for yourself, haven't you? Cleverest thing you ever did, wasn't it, seducing my son?"

Minerva kept her temper with some difficulty. She glanced at her watch. "I'm afraid I have a luncheon engagement. If you'll excuse me—"

"Not so fast. You forget who I am, my dear daughter-in-law. A Templeton. The only Templeton left of my esteemed generation. That entitles me to a little respect. I'll get it from the rest of my family, I'm sure, if not from you."

"I wouldn't count on that if I were you."

"Oh, but I am counting on it, and for a very good reason. I have no money. That vast fortune of mine is, I regret to say, spent. I have no friends and no means of support. Where does one turn in such straits if not to one's family? I was hoping that you, Minerva, would take care of your elderly father-in-law. Put a roof over my head and clothes on my back. Surely a good woman like you, known for her charity and her strong family feeling, could do no less."

"I am sorry. There's nothing I can do." Minerva might have felt more guilt if it were not for the wolfish cunning in his eyes. He ought to be pleading with her, but he was not. He was too arrogant. And yet she couldn't imagine why. Did he really believe that she would help him solely because he was a Templeton? Had he forgotten that he had once thrown her down in the dirt and raped her?

"Indeed, Minerva, there is a great deal you can and will do for me." He was clearly about to continue, but just at that moment there were footsteps in the hall again, a much healthier tread. Jonathan came in, smiling and new-penny bright. This was his third year of medical school, and he had already won high praise from all his advisors. His marriage was still working, as far as

Minerva could tell, and his eighteen-month-old son, Travis, was thriving.

"Hello, Mum. Sorry I'm a little late. Are you ready?"

She saw the way Harrison Templeton looked at her son, his mouth twisting, the gunmetal flash in his eyes.

"How do you do, sir?" Jonathan said affably, offering Templeton his hand. "I don't think we've met."

"This is Harrison Templeton. Your grandfather."

Templeton looked into Minerva's eyes and smiled. Then he nodded to the man who was in fact his son. "Jonathan, I believe? How do you do, my boy? I've been looking forward to meeting you for years. I've heard so much about you."

Not from me, Minerva thought. And suddenly she was deathly afraid.

Jonathan insisted that his grandfather join them for lunch at the Ritz, which proved to be an ordeal for Minerva, who could barely swallow her food. But Harrison succeeded in charming Jonathan as he related a variety of stories about India, which Minerva might have found entertaining had she not been overcome with dread. It wasn't until lunch was over and Jonathan was inviting his grandfather to come and stay with him and Sarah and the baby that Minerva summoned a wan smile and said, "No indeed, Jonathan, your grandfather will be staying at the Tavern with me. He is the patriarch of the Templeton family, after all."

"Thank you, my dear," said Harrison. "I accept your kind invitation."

Jonathan, whose intuitions had always been strong, asked his mother privately on the way out if there was anything wrong. "He's a quaint old chap, but harmless, I presume?"

"Quite harmless," Minerva said dryly.

It was after lunch that he mentioned Mohini. Jonathan had taken the trolley to the medical school, and she and Harrison were walking back to the office through the Public Garden. Minerva made a point of taking a brisk constitutional through the Common or the Public Garden every day, but Templeton, who used a cane to assist him in moving his great bulk, had some difficulty negotiating the short distance between the Ritz and Templeton House. Minerva couldn't find it in her to feel sorry for him.

"How pleasant to meet Jonathan after all these years," he said. "A very well-mannered young man, Minerva. I compliment you on his upbringing."

"Thank you." *He knew. She could tell by the way he'd continually stared at Jonathan during their luncheon that he knew.*

"You remember my friend Mohini. She was Edward's friend, too, or perhaps he never told you about that?"

She forced herself not to respond.

"She returned from a business trip to London during the war with a fascinating tale to tell. It seems she'd been swept away by a wartime passion." His expression was indulgent, as if he more than understood the lengths to which human passion can drive someone. "She and I had long since ended our more private relationship, but she often came to me with tidbits of various sorts that she thought I might find useful. I had been her benefactor, you see, sending her to England back in the early thirties so she could get the education she required to rise above her station in life. A rare woman, Mohini—smart and capable and, at the same time, a hellcat in bed."

He paused. "She's dead now, poor thing. Didn't believe in marriage—said it was the bane of woman's existence—but she had a jealous lover who lost his temper when she stepped out once too often with another man. A damned shame, really," he added, and he actually sounded sad.

Minerva felt a brief spurt of sympathy for the woman who had slept with her husband. She remembered lying on a Darjeeling hillside realizing for the first time the limitations of being born a female. She had succeeded despite these limitations; so had Mohini. But Mohini had been brought down by a man. If Templeton had his way, the same thing would happen to her.

No. Not by this man. Never.

"Imagine my surprise when Mohini returned from London in 1940 with the news that the little blonde who had married my milquetoast son had given birth to a baby a scant eight months after the wedding. She then told me about the failed abortion she'd witnessed years before. From that day onward, my dear, I have been very curious about my second son."

They were walking over the bridge that arched the pond in the center of the Public Garden. Minerva had a brief fantasy of pushing him over the stone wall and watching him sink.

"You are mistaken," she said coldly. "Jonathan is Edward's son."

His smile grew wider. "Well, my dear, I'm sure it's difficult to prove one way or the other after all these years. Still, I think the boy should know the possibilities, don't you? I assume, of course, that you haven't told him? It wouldn't be the thing at all, would it, for people to know that you slept with both the father and the son?"

"You raped me, you swine!"

"That's not the way I remember it. Seems to me you were more than willing. Why would I need to rape you when I had dozens of women at my beck and call?"

Minerva clapped the lid on her emotions. It was pointless to argue. No woman could charge a man with rape and escape with her reputation intact, anyway.

Reputation. Only her iron discipline prevented her from fleeing to the shelter of her home. But there was no shelter now.

He twisted the knife: "No doubt your friends and associates here in Boston would be quite shocked if they heard the tale. To marry a man and bear a child to that man's father is incest, my dear."

"You have no proof. If you ever betray any of this to my son—or to anyone else—I'll deny every word."

"A scandal requires no documentation, Minerva. A scandal is a fire that feeds on innuendo alone."

They had reached Charles Street. Once again she had fantasies of destruction as they slowly threaded through the busy traffic to the Common.

She said nothing further until they reached the privacy of her office on the second floor of Templeton House. She was searching for an escape of some sort. She could find none. "What do you want?"

"Ah. I thought you would begin to see it my way." He sat down heavily just opposite her. His bulk made the delicate Queen Anne chair creak. "You know what I want. Not your job; I'm too damn lazy for that. Nor your precious son, either—he's nothing to me. What I want is some comfort in my old age. I want to be pampered. I want a cozy place to live, and not just on a temporary basis. The China Tea House Tavern would do nicely for that, I think. You'll take me in, just as you told Jonathan you would, and you'll provide me with the funds I need to live a comfortable life. What charitable Boston matron would refuse to care for her husband's aging father?"

She stared at him, feeling her hatred rise.

"There is one other thing. An absolute requirement if I'm to maintain my discretion about your colorful past." He was looking her over, her figure still so firm and trim, her golden hair only just slightly tinged with silver threads. Minerva was a little vain about her appearance; she had no lines on her face and looked younger, her mirror told her, than forty-two. Since Edward had died, there had been several men who begged her to marry them. She'd put them off, devoting herself to the business, having no time, nor any particular interest, in taking on the responsibility of caring for another man. She missed lovemaking, of course, but she was not entirely without it. There had been several lovers, none of whom had made her feel a fraction of what she had felt for Edward.

Now, absorbing his leer, Minerva wished the years had been as ruinous to her as they had been to him.

"I want an elegant, compliant woman in my bed. Not often . . . I'm no hot young stallion anymore, I regret to say. But now and then, when the flesh becomes demanding, I'd like to be spared the trouble and expense of hunting up a whore."

She had become immune to shock. She sat there, stony-faced, as he reached out with one finger and stroked her brow just beneath the hairline. "I scarcely even remember the interlude that resulted in Jonathan. I'll be sure to pay a good deal more attention to you now."

A gun, she thought. If only I had a gun . . . and the courage to use it.

What could she do? Tell Jonathan herself? Brazen it out with whomever else he spread the story to? No, it was too lurid. Rape. Attempted abortion. Incest. She was in church again in Darjeeling, feeling the hot shame flood her as the harpies said, "Her mother was a whore, you know."

If the truth came out, Boston society would devour her. There would be a witch-hunt, not all that much different from what had happened to Helen Templeton 250 years ago. She would lose the tea company, of course. And Lizzy wasn't ready yet to take control; Lizzy wouldn't be ready for years.

Damn him. He had her.

"I will arrive at the Tavern with my things this evening. "You'll take me in. Into your house, Minerva. And when I wish it, into your bed."

"No," she whispered. "No."

"Yes. You will. You will because you're an intelligent woman, an imaginative one. You're quite well able to envision the unpleasantness that will result if you don't."

He was right, of course. I married Edward knowing I was pregnant with his father's child. All actions have consequences. Now it seems that I must live with mine.

She would take him in.

Minerva received word a few hours later that Elizabeth had been admitted to the maternity ward and, after a protracted labor, given birth to an eight-pound baby girl. She left work at five o'clock and hurried to the Richardson House wing of the Boston Hospital for Women to see her daughter and the new baby. Her first granddaughter.

Elizabeth was sleeping, so Minerva went directly to the nursery. The nurse on duty held the child up to the glass for her grandmother to see. Unlike the other newborns in the nursery, Delilah Templeton Scofield was not asleep. She was wide awake, alert, and seemingly curious about her new surroundings, so different from the moist, dark cavern of her mother's womb.

Minerva tapped on the glass and Delilah's round blue eyes peered directly into hers. For an instant it seemed as if there were already a mature intelligence residing in that tiny, black-frizzed head.

Minerva made up her mind. She left the viewing window and rapped on the nursery door. "That's my granddaughter," she said in her most imperious voice. "I wish to hold her, if you please."

The nurse protested that this was not allowed, but Minerva insisted, and got her way, of course. She sat down in a metal rocker in one corner and rocked the baby, who was squirming now and beginning to squall, clenching her tiny fingers in frustration and making sucking motions with her lips.

"Give me some formula."

"Excuse me, ma'am, but it's not her feeding time. It's only been two hours since her last feeding, and we like them to go at least three hours, and preferably four."

"Nonsense. The child is hungry. Give me a bottle at once."

When the girl hesitated, Minerva applied a little pressure. "Do you know who I am?"

"No, ma'am."

"I am Minerva Templeton, Director of Templeton Tea. I am currently on the board of trustees of this institution. If you wish to keep your job, you will give me the formula at once."

The baby was shrieking now. The nurse cast one last uncertain glance around her, looking for help. When none appeared, she rushed to do as she'd been told.

Delilah quietened as soon as the sterilized nipple was put to her mouth. She sucked greedily and moved her tiny fingers in obvious satisfaction and pleasure. While feeding, her intelligent eyes looked up at the woman who was holding her, as if to fix the visage in her mind.

Don't be absurd, Minerva told herself. She's only a few hours old and quite incapable of any such feats.

She felt a bond form and grow. More so even than with her own son and daughter it seemed to her that this child was the flesh of her flesh, the bone of her bone. How miraculous it was that something of herself had actually descended to a third generation. No matter what happened to her in the months and years ahead, a few sparks of her fire would continue to burn.

"You are very special," she said to Delilah, whose eyes were closed now as she communed intensely with the nipple. "And you shall do so many marvelous things!"

The baby stirred and kicked her tiny legs. She seemed to curl a little closer to her grandmother's breasts.

"I *will* go on," Minerva said. "Templeton Tea will go on. No one and nothing will stop me. I'll do what I must to keep Edward's legacy alive and my reputation—his reputation—intact. And one day, my darling, I'll pass it along to your generation of Templetons, as great—no, greater—than it was when it came into my keeping.

"And that, by God, I do most solemnly swear."

PART FOUR

For of those to whom much is given, much is required.

—John Fitzgerald Kennedy

Boston, 1958

13

On April 7, 1958, Delilah's tenth birthday, her mother baked her a cake in the shape of a clipper ship. She stood on tiptoe beside the kitchen counter while Elizabeth Scofield frosted it, dreaming of her grandmother's stories about the sleek clippers that carried tea from China in the old days. Sometimes on holidays Minerva Templeton would gather her grandchildren at her feet on the blue and gold China carpet in the parlor of the China Tea House Tavern and tell them of the great Templeton teamen who raced their yachts to China and back. Delilah would lean back, squeezed between the elegant chair leg and her grandmother's perfumed hose, and picture her ancestors at the helm of the graceful clippers, the metal-gray water churning around them, the stacked sails humming like bees as they caught the wind.

"That looks funny," Delilah said as her mother poured dark chocolate trim over the pale swell of the clipper ship's sails. "It looks as if the rigging's streaked with mud."

"Seagull droppings," her mother said solemnly, inspiring a smile from her husband, David, who, aroused from his work by the luscious smells coming from the kitchen, had wandered out of his study. Delilah took a lick from the wooden spatula, then offered it to her father, who accepted it absently. It was good to see her father smile. Lately he'd been so busy with his research and teaching at Harvard that he'd had no time for play.

It was a beautiful cake, and Delilah loved her mother for taking the time to bake it; she knew how hard it was for her to snatch time away from her job at Templeton Tea. Gran was always berating her mother for the time she spent with her husband and daughter; she would never be able to take over the company one day if she didn't dedicate herself to learning the business. "You and I are different, Mum," Elizabeth Scofield would say. "The tea company's important, yes, but my priorities are different from yours."

Elizabeth always arranged her schedule so she could have extra time to spend with her daughter—she'd go in early in the morning, for example, so she could be home in time to meet Delilah after school. And the weekends were Delilah's entirely. Her mother would take her somewhere different every Saturday—to the playground, to the movies, to the zoo. They spent as much time together as possible, and their love for each other was strong.

On the morning of her tenth birthday party, Delilah helped her mother decorate the dining room of the small home on Walker Street in Cambridge, where they had always lived. They blew up balloons, giggling every time one escaped and deflated before they could get it tied off with string. They hung streamers. They set the table with their second-best (and slightly chipped) plates.

When the guests arrived—mostly Delilah's friends from her fourth-grade class and her cousins, Travis and Nick—Elizabeth superintended the party games of musical chairs and pin the tail on the donkey. Then she shepherded the children into the dining room, switched out all the lights, and carried in the cake, which she placed in front of Delilah in the center of the table. Delilah clapped, the children oohed and ahhed, and David snapped pictures with his new Polaroid Land camera.

As Delilah made her wish and blew out the candles, a strange look came over Elizabeth's face. She moaned and pressed her palm to the side of her head. Her arms folded around her like butterfly wings as she slid to the floor. David knocked over a chair in his haste to reach her, and several of the children began to whimper.

"Call an ambulance," her father barked at Delilah.

Delilah's hands had frozen into ice blocks. She dropped the knife into the clipper ship's hull, splitting it in two. She ran to the huge black telephone in the hall, but she didn't know how to call an ambulance. When she picked up the receiver, lifted it to her ear, and heard the shrill dial tone, Delilah began to cry. She didn't know the number. She didn't know what to do.

Someone took the phone out of her hands. It was Travis, her older cousin. Coolly, he dialed the operator, gave their address, and asked her to send an ambulance, quick.

On the way to the hospital, David crouched in the back, speaking frantically to his unconscious wife. "Lizzy," he kept saying, over and over. "Lizzy."

Delilah huddled in the front, too scared to cry. "She's not going to die, is she?" she asked the driver.

"Don't know, kid. Hard to say."

Two days after her mother's collapse, Delilah arrived at the hospital clutching a battered bunch of violets. Her father was coming, too, but she'd run on ahead while he parked the car.

She hated the hospital, which made her think of iron lungs and children sick with polio. It also made her think of Aunt Sarah, who had died in a hospital like this one several years ago. It had been a long time since she'd thought of Aunt Sarah, Travis and Nick's mother. She'd been sick for ages, getting thinner and thinner, until her death was no real surprise. But it frightened Delilah now to remember . . . It proved mothers could die.

When she reached her mother's room, she found the door closed tightly. She knocked, expecting the private nurse hired by her grandmother to open the door. But no one came. Delilah's hand had closed around the doorknob when she was grabbed from behind. "No, honey. You can't go in there."

Delilah twisted in the arms of a middle-aged woman with bushy eyebrows and gray hair. She recognized her as the brisk, no-nonsense nurse who headed up the duty roster on the floor. Delilah didn't like her. The woman had a rugged face and a body as strong and hard as a man's. "I want to see my mother."

"Where's your father? Didn't the doctor call him?"

"He's parking the car. No one called him." She struggled but could not get free. Her mother was petite and elegant; her arms never hurt like this when she held her. Her mother was gentle and fragrant with the scent of rose, but this woman smelled sharply of disinfectant. "I want my mother! Let me go!"

The nurse drew her closer, patting Delilah's hair in a gesture that was awkwardly tender. "My poor little darling. My poor little girl."

Delilah still fought, staring at that closed white door. Why wouldn't they let her go in? She wanted to hold her mother's hand and talk to her. She had been so still yesterday, her chest moving lightly up and down in the midst of all the tubes and bottles and heavy, humming machinery they said were necessary to sustain her, but Delilah had spoken to her anyway, determined that she should hear. Her doctor, that nice young man with the sad eyes, had promised her mother would hear, even if she didn't respond.

Delilah wanted to assure her mother that she was doing her best to take care of things at home. She was keeping her bed made and her room picked up, and last night she had cooked supper for her father. Only hamburgers, and it was true she'd turned up the gas too high so the outsides had blackened and stuck to the pan while the insides had remained a little too rare, but she'd know better next time. They'd had peas from a can and potato chips on the side, and her father had smiled vaguely at her and eaten every bit. She was trying to be brave. Her grandmother was always saying how important it was for a woman to be brave and strong. When her mother woke up, she was going to be so proud of her.

"I have to talk to my mother," she repeated. When the nurse wouldn't release her, she drew back her foot and kicked her in the shin.

"Jesus Christ!" The woman lost her hold on Delilah, who threw herself at the closed door. She wrenched it open, and looked, and saw.

Her mother was still lying motionless on the bed, but the humming machinery had been turned off, the IV bottles disconnected. Elizabeth's body was draped from head to toe by a stiff, unwrinkled sheet. It flapped a little at one corner where the breeze from the open window lifted the fabric off her mother's left foot, exposing her dainty toes. They had a bluish tinge to them; Delilah could see that clearly.

She screamed. The big nurse caught her and dragged her away. Somebody else helped her; there were nurses all around, but they couldn't stop the girl's screaming. Nobody could stop it, not even the warmth of her father's arms around her. Even as he held her, she could feel his body shaking.

In the nights that followed, Delilah dreamt often of that hospital room door. It was the first of many doors that closed against her. Every afternoon when she came home from school, she was confronted with the oaken door to her father's study.

At first she ignored it. She would go in, sit down in the easy chair beside his desk, and try to tell him about her day at school, just as she had always done with her mother. But her father never asked her questions; he never seemed to do much of anything except stare at the picture of Elizabeth that was propped in the middle of his rolltop desk. Sometimes he smelled funny, and Delilah slowly began to realize that this was because he was drinking glass after glass of whiskey.

Once she found him unconscious, slumped over his desk. From pure terror, Delilah shoved her fist into her mouth and sobbed. For a few minutes she thought he, too, was dead.

"Daddy, do you want anything? Some tea? A snack? What shall I make for supper tonight?"

"You have to eat, Daddy. Please, please stop drinking, and eat."

But he had no interest in food, and soon Delilah's own appetite waned. What was the point in struggling to cook if nobody wanted to eat? She got by on crackers and an occasional peanut butter sandwich; anything else was too much trouble to prepare, too much trouble even to chew and swallow.

"I need you, Daddy," she whispered into her pillow at night when the emptiness inside her expanded and turned into a gnawing ache. "You're all I have."

It wasn't entirely true, of course. She had her grandmother and her cousins and her Uncle Jonathan. But her grandmother didn't like her father, and Uncle Jonathan seemed so sad all the time, and as for her cousins, they lived out in Concord, so she couldn't see them every day.

David Scofield went on drinking. He abandoned himself to the bottle, and after a few weeks of indulgence, he ceased to have any comprehension of the increasingly desperate state of his young daughter's spirits. He was beginning to forget he had a daughter. Certainly he didn't want the responsibility of one. Elizabeth had always taken care of the child; he didn't know how to do it. Elizabeth had taken care of everything.

Although he knew rationally that his wife's aneurysm had been one of those tricks of fate, a time bomb, as the doctor had put it, waiting to go off in her brain, still he hated himself. He shouldn't have married her. He hadn't been a very good husband. They were so different—Lizzy so full of life and spirit, he himself so pessimistic, so cold. He'd expected some of her warmth to rub off on him, but he knew in his heart it had never happened. Just as he also knew, but would never admit, except when drunk out of his mind, that Jonathan had been right all those years ago when he'd questioned David's motives in marrying his sister.

"Love is of the soul," Jonathan had argued one night back at Harvard. "What difference, really, does the sex of the body make?"

But it had made a difference. Jonathan had accepted his own sexual nature while David had done nothing but run from the impulses that made both sexes attractive to him. Just as he'd run from Jonathan, his best (his only?) friend. Of course they had seen each other often over the years; his marriage to Elizabeth had made that inevitable. But since that drunken New Year's Eve—that sensual, forbidden night—nothing had ever been the same between them.

He thought of poor Sarah Templeton, who had essentially starved herself to death out of God only knew what demons of self-directed anger and neurotic guilt. David knew that Jonathan blamed himself—blamed that night—for her illness, even though his wife had been set on her course to destruction long before their rather bizarre marriage had begun. It was typical of Jonathan to blame himself for things he couldn't control.

As you're doing right now.

Now Lizzy was gone—bright, laughing Lizzy, whom everybody had loved. The women were dead, while he and Jonathan, the men—the shits—remained.

When Minerva visited the Scofield household one evening a few weeks after her daughter's funeral, she took one look at Delilah—skinny and too tall, her black hair witch-wild and badly in need of a cut, those violet circles under her eyes, that raw, red nose that betrayed that she'd been off by herself somewhere crying—and knew at once how wrong she'd been to seclude herself in her own grief.

The loss of her daughter had been a crueler blow than Minerva could ever remember sustaining, worse than Edward's death in many ways. You could accept the death of a spouse, particularly in wartime. But your children weren't supposed to die before you, and nothing could be sadder than to bury the body that you had brought forth from your own.

There had been moments during the past few weeks when Minerva had wondered if she had the strength of will to carry on. Until now she'd always thought that brutal though life could sometimes be, it had some structure to it, some order. The world might not be kind, but she had always believed in its inherent justice.

On the other hand, maybe this *was* justice. A rather perverse brand of it, certainly, but such things were not unknown. The sins of the fathers being visited upon the children. Maybe her children were being punished for the evil she had done.

She shuddered at the thought. If there were accounts she must balance, surely she alone should be responsible. If there was punishment due, the whip should crack on her own shoulders, not on those of her innocent children.

But Elizabeth was dead, and Jonathan, respected physician though he was, was deeply unhappy. Were it not for his sons, he'd told her often enough, he would leave the country and indulge his penchant to wander, doing whatever he could to atone for his inability to save Sarah.

For they shall have prosperity, but neither joy nor peace. The Templeton curse was upon them all. Edward had died at forty-one, Sarah at twenty-eight, Lizzy at thirty-two. Harrison Templeton, however, had lived to be seventy-five. But she would not think of him, nor of the way he had finally died, drunk, at the bottom of the steep staircase of the China Tea House Tavern.

Now Delilah was suffering. Minerva looked more closely at her. The child had lost weight. Her skin was pale and her bones prominent; she seemed to be wasting away. "When did you last have a decent meal?" she demanded, watching her granddaughter lethargically nibble a Saltine.

"I don't know. I tried to cook, but Daddy says he's not hungry. He just drinks."

In her mind's eye Minerva saw an image of Sarah on her deathbed, wan and shrunken, her eyes huge with a strange sort of guilty satisfaction. Sarah had *wanted* to die. She had not been a Templeton by blood, but somehow in marrying she had taken upon herself the Templeton curse.

Delilah was a Templeton. Suppose she had inherited that weakness, that inability to survive the buffetings of fate? Suppose she, too, was subject to those soul-killing fits of depression?

Minerva went directly to David Scofield. She found him locked in his study, writing one of his left-wing magazine articles. "This nonsense must stop," she said. She'd never liked her daughter's husband. In her opinion he was an amoral, egocentric bastard. "If you want to drink yourself to death, that's your affair, but I'm not going to let you destroy Delilah. She needs decent meals, fresh air, and exercise; she needs to be out of this mausoleum and away from you. I'm going to take her home with me."

"Fine," said David, hardly looking up from his work. "I feel helpless with her, to tell you the truth. She's underfoot so much."

You swine, Minerva thought. You didn't deserve my daughter; you don't deserve your own.

"I won't go," Delilah said when told of the plan. "I'm staying here with my father. He needs me."

"Don't be ridiculous. Your father is busy with his work and can't even take care of you properly. Get your things together, my dear. You're coming with me."

"I am not!"

"Indeed you are, Delilah." I must not be soft with her, Minerva told herself. Not now, not ever. Her father is weak. He has set her a poor example. I will show her that a woman can be—must be—strong. "You will come home with me, and you will learn to be more respectful from now on."

"You can't make me leave." Delilah ran to her father, throwing her arms so hard around him that she nearly overbalanced them both. "Please, Daddy. Make her go away. I want to stay here with you!"

"Don't talk back to your grandmother," David said.

Minerva heard the little catch in Delilah's throat; she saw the look in her eyes as she assimilated her father's rejection. Dear God. She wondered how much Delilah understood, how much she would be able to face. She wondered if she knew that her pain simply didn't touch her father. He hardly saw her; she wasn't there.

Poor child. Minerva felt an unfamiliar tightening in her chest. Be strong, she reminded herself. Be sympathetic, yes, but unyielding.

Delilah thrust her chin into the air in the stubborn gesture that her mother had usually managed to curb. To her grandmother she said, "Go to hell, you mean old witch."

Without an ounce of mercy, Minerva cracked her across the face. Then, quickly, she pulled Delilah into her arms. She struggled for several seconds before going limp. "Daddy, Daddy," she whimpered. Over Minerva's shoulder, she watched her father's slump-backed retreat and the closing of his office door.

Minerva held the child and hugged her. For the first time since she had buried her daughter, her eyes filled and nearly overflowed.

Alone that night in the back bedroom on the second floor of the China Tea House Tavern, Delilah cried herself to sleep, missing her mother so much, the ache was physical.

She dreamed restlessly, then woke to a dark and unfamiliar room. The bed was an antique four-poster, its oaken spires stabbing up toward the ceiling, which was low, far lower than the ceilings of her bedroom in Cambridge. As she lay there, peering around her in the dark, she remembered all the things Nick had told her about the Tavern's being haunted. "All our ancestors lived in that place. Died there, too," he'd added, rolling his eyes. Delilah wondered how many of them had died in this bed.

One day I will die, she thought. Before her mother's death, this hadn't meant much to her—it was too far in the future to be real. But if her mother could die, anybody could.

"People don't die until they're old," her mother had told her when they'd had to have the cat put to sleep last year. Skittle had been old and deaf and nearly blind. But Delilah's mother had been young, and Aunt Sarah had been even younger.

Delilah felt her own heart, thump, thump, thumping into the mattress. One day it would stop thumping and they would put her in a box and lower her into the ground. Looking up at the bedposts that surrounded her, she felt as if she were in the box already. The house was alive around her, full of people talking, laughing, breathing, and ceasing to breathe. The ceiling was closer now. It was moving, coming down on her. Her heart thumped harder as the lid of the box closed. She screamed. Just as she had on that morning in the hospital when she'd seen her mother's body, she screamed and screamed again.

She was still screaming when her grandmother rushed into the room and pulled her into her arms. "It's all right, Delilah, it's all right." Gran rocked her back and forth. "There, there, lovey, we've got each other now."

Her grandmother got in bed beside her, her silky nightgown feeling oh so soft under Delilah's cheek. Gran smelled of perfume, something stronger than the one her mother used to wear. It was a nice scent, breathing of the forest. Delilah felt the faintest greening in her heart, and closed her eyes, smelling those smells and hearing the even beating of her grandmother's pulse.

For the rest of the night, they held each other. They were nearly the same size, for Delilah was tall and Minerva was petite, but Delilah felt safe and protected, cuddled there in those slim, elegant arms. The house was quiet now, empty of anything but the present. She fell asleep, and this time she did not dream.

In the morning her grandmother insisted that they walk over Beacon Hill to the corporate headquarters of Templeton Tea. She shepherded Delilah through the portrait gallery, pointing out each of her ancestors and telling her anecdotes about them. "This is Helen, your greatest ancestor. It was she who first imported tea and sold it. She founded the company, a very rare and courageous thing for a woman of her day to do."

Delilah knew the story of Helen Templeton; all the children did. But because it was a story she loved, she pretended ignorance, saying, "Isn't she the one who was put to trial as a witch by the people of Boston?"

"Yes, but they came to their senses and acquitted her. Years later, when people had put such nonsense behind them, she opened her inn, served the new China drink, and did so well that she began importing it in bulk. It was from her little shop in the building right next to the Tavern that our great business has grown."

For perhaps the first time ever, Delilah was struck by an anomaly. "Everyone knows there's no such thing as witches. Why did the early people of Boston think she was one?"

"People believed in witchcraft in those days."

"Even grown-ups?"

"Yes, child. They believed in witches and Satan and the immanence of evil, and they punished it whenever they thought they found it in society. Helen Templeton was a strong and determined woman. Strong and determined women are often looked at askance, even in our modern world. Other people try their best to beat them down."

"Has anyone tried to beat you down, Gran?"

"Yes, they've tried." Her grandmother's voice was harsh, and her black eyes seemed to glitter like the velvet edges of a star. "But they haven't succeeded. Nor will they, ever."

She cupped Delilah's chin and raised her face, looking from the portrait of Helen to her granddaughter and back. "You resemble her, Delilah. You have the same bone structure, the same fine eyes. The mouth is all wrong, but that doesn't matter. You must make her your model. You must strive, as your mother did, to continue the great tradition of the Templeton women."

"But my mother didn't really want to run the tea company."

"Of course she did."

Delilah didn't argue, but she could hear her mother saying, "I'm sick of the tea business. Damn the tea business. I want to be home with my husband and daughter, living a normal life."

"Your mother would have been my successor. Now that she's gone, I must look to your generation, Delilah." Minerva smiled as she considered the idea. "Perhaps you will be the one to step into my shoes. More than any of your cousins, you have the temperament for it, I think."

Delilah screwed up her nose as she tried to imagine her own picture hanging in the portrait gallery. Delilah Templeton Scofield, Director of Templeton Tea. She rather liked the idea. "What about Travis?" She pictured her golden cousin, whom she'd always adored. "Travis can do anything. And his portrait would probably look a whole lot better up there than mine."

Minerva sniffed. It was true that Travis, at nearly twelve, already showed the poise and charm of a much older boy. But this girl had promise, too, and she was Elizabeth's daughter. Minerva could see

Elizabeth in her bones, her smile, her vibrant green eyes. She smiled and ruffled her hair, happy to see that the child looked brighter already. "Perhaps one day you and Travis will compete for the honor."

"He'd win," Delilah said without rancor. "He always does, you know."

"We'll see about that," her grandmother said.

14

"Hey," said Travis.

"Hey yourself."

"What're you doing?"

"Nothing." It was a humid morning during the summer after her mother had died. Delilah was curled in the apple tree in her cousins' back yard in Concord, where she was spending several weeks while her grandmother was in London, buying tea. Travis was leaning against the tree trunk and smiling at her. "Can I come up?"

"If you want."

He swung up beside her in one quick move. He'd grown tall, so it was easy for him now. In earlier summers she and Travis would have to hoist each other along the thick base of the apple tree, reaching high overhead for handholds and clawing with their feet until they made it to the first milestone: the hollow nook where the trunk divided into three sections. This Delilah called Heart, because sometimes when she crouched there, she could feel the tree's great pulse beating. They rested there now, protected from the August heat.

"Why aren't you in Six Branch Camp today?" he asked, looking up to a platform of tangled branches, all sheltered and private, where they could wedge their bodies and hide from anyone who happened to pass below.

"It's cooler here, I think." Delilah tilted back her head to see the V-shaped fork they called Victory. From there it swept on to the most mysterious regions of the unpruned apple tree, retreating beyond sight and almost beyond imagination, like Jack's beanstalk, into the clouds.

The apple tree was huge, old, and majestic, king of the garden and lord of all it looked upon. When she was high among its lacework branches, Delilah forgot her troubles and became Queen of the World. All summer long since Gran had brought her here, she'd sought refuge in the tree, sometimes alone, but more often with Travis. The tree was their secret hideout, where the two of them could be separate from the world. When memories of her mother and longing for her father grew too burdensome, she would come to the tree and climb it. Even in her dreams sometimes she heard the spirit of the apple tree crooning, relieving her of some of her pain.

What the tree couldn't do for her, Travis could. Blond and beautiful, with guileless blue eyes and the widest smile east of the Mississippi, her cousin had a pleasant, easygoing charm that made it almost impossible to dislike him. Best of all, there was a special sympathy between them, and Travis loved her every bit as much as she loved him.

"Are you going higher?" she asked.

"Want to?" He looked up into the thick boughs, which were heavy-laden with hard, round apples. "I'll race you up Beanstalk."

"Oh, Trav, it's so hot."

"Lazy. I feel like racing."

"You always feel like racing these days."

More and more lately, he no longer seemed content to sit quietly with her. Instead he wanted to climb fast and furiously, propelling himself into the highest regions, breaking off twigs and shaking new apples to the ground in an orgy of attack and conquer. He had to use the tree: swing from it, hang things upon it, carve his initials in its tough skin, fling unripened apples at anything that moved beneath. Even now, sitting close beside him, Delilah could sense that he was fiercely animated, in body and in mind.

"What's the matter?"

"I don't know. Nothing." He reached out and captured an apple, green, tinged with pink on one side. He bit into it, then spat it out. "These things are sour."

"They're not ripe yet."

"They're terrible." He heaved the apple at the ground, and they both watched it bounce and roll away. "Delilah? Remember that word?"

"What word?"

"Yesterday. After the game."

She fingered a long strand of her hair. Of course she remembered. She and Nick had gone to the Little League game to watch Travis pitch. The game had not gone well for Travis, and when he'd been forced to surrender the mound to a teammate, Delilah lost interest. She spent the rest of the game examining the graffiti on the bleachers where they were sitting. It was mostly hearts and arrows and people's names, but there was also a word scratched in harsh spiked letters that she'd never seen before.

"Nick, what does this mean?" Nick was a year younger than she, but he was generally acknowledged to be the brainy one. When Delilah and Travis were running wild around the yard, tossing a hard baseball that would slam your fingers if you didn't catch it right, Nick would lie on his stomach in the grass so deep in his daydreams, they'd have to shout to get his attention. "What're you doing?" Delilah would ask, flopping down beside him.

"Writing a book."

Travis would come along and tease him. "Where's your pencil and paper, then? Where's chapter one? What kind of book is it, an invisible one?"

Sensitive and too often a victim of this sort of taunting, Nick would retreat inside to continue making up stories in peace.

"F-U-C-K," Nick read, squinting at the word through his glasses. "I don't know. Never heard it before." He sounded puzzled. "Maybe it stands for something."

"Maybe."

On the way home, Delilah asked Travis if he knew what fuck meant. He blushed from his hairline to the collar of his baseball uniform and refused to answer. Since he was rarely embarrassed over anything, Delilah had found his behavior baffling.

"Do you still want to know what it means?" he asked now.

"Do you know?"

"Sure. I just didn't want to say it in front of Nick. He's such a baby."

"Is it a swear?"

"Yeah, I guess. It means something dirty."

Delilah knew some bad language, but she hadn't come in contact with this particular word before. When her father was angry, he sometimes muttered son of a bitch under his breath, but that was about as foulmouthed as he ever got. Her mother had never even said damn.

"Shall I tell you or not?"

"Yes."

"It means having sex." He paused. "Do you know what that is?"

Delilah shook her head. One of her braids caught for a moment on a rough spot on the tree trunk and hurt a little as she jerked it free.

"Well, having sex is what a man and a woman do when they get married. He puts his thing, you know, his penis, up inside her, and something comes out of it that makes her have a baby."

"What do you mean, something comes out? What sort of something?"

"Like you're going to get your period soon, you know? I'm going to have this stuff that brings babies."

Delilah had no idea what he was talking about. She was ten and showing no trace of blossoming adolescence. Her mother hadn't felt it was necessary yet to speak to her about such things, and it hadn't occurred to anybody else to do so.

She wasn't about to betray her total ignorance, though, not even to Travis. One of the few things that worried her about their friendship was that he was two years older and he might consider her too young and silly to pal around with. She went on the offensive: "How can he put it inside her? Penises are big."

"Babies are bigger. How do you suppose they get out into the world?"

How come Travis knew all this, and she didn't? Her mother should have told her. It wasn't fair that she no longer had a mother to tell her these things. "Are you making this up?"

"No, I'm not. Cross my heart and hope to die."

She thought it over. "Well, if it's true, it's disgusting. I'm never going to let my husband do that to me."

"Yes you will. You have to or you'll never get a baby. Besides, when people are in love, they want to do it."

She was positive that couldn't be true. Who could ever want to do such an icky thing? She filled her mouth with sour apple so she wouldn't have to say anything. She wasn't going to argue with Travis; he'd crossed his heart, after all, but that didn't mean she had to believe him, either.

"I think maybe I'd like to do it someday," Travis said dreamily.

"With who?"

Travis grinned at her. "Not with someone who thinks it's disgusting, that's for sure."

She felt a pang of jealousy. Other girls besides herself liked to watch Travis when he pitched his Little League games. There was a sixth grader down the street who followed him around, mooning. "I thought you were going to marry me when we grow up."

His grin turned devilish. "Naw. You're too bossy."

"And you're a creep!"

"Hey," said someone down below them. Delilah peered down through the branches and saw Nick standing at the bottom of the tree. He had a stick in his hands that he was absently whittling with his Boy Scout jackknife. "I've been looking all over for you, Delilah. Can I come up?"

Nick hardly ever climbed the apple tree. Because he was short and slight and somewhat uncoordinated, he got left out of a lot of the games she played with Travis. She liked Nick, though. He always had something interesting to talk about. He knew about birds and plants and constellations and card games, all gleaned from his endless reading, she supposed. Delilah liked to read, too, but not as much as Nick.

"Sure," she said.

"No," said Travis. "We're having a private conversation. Go away."

Nick looked hurt. He was easily intimidated and, with anybody outside the family, painfully shy. He was gentle and kind—the sort of boy who rescued baby rabbits from cats—and on the rare occasions when she joined his brother in teasing him, Delilah always felt guilty afterward. The only fights she had with Travis were over his callous treatment of the smaller boy.

"He's so easy to push around," Travis said on one occasion. "I know I shouldn't—I try not to be mean to him, you know—but he's such a crybaby most of the time."

"You shouldn't have private conversations," Nick said now. "It's not polite."

If there was anything her mother had tried to pound into her head over the years, it was that she really ought to be more polite. In silent tribute to her mother that summer, Delilah was trying to mend her ways. "Travis was just telling me what that word meant."

"Delilah," Travis said warningly.

"What word?" Nick asked.

"Remember—on the bleachers? The one you didn't know." Delilah was gloating just a tiny bit. Mrs. Simons, the housekeeper who'd been living with the boys and their father ever since their mother had died, was always bragging that Nick was so smart he could already read Shakespeare. It wasn't often she could one-up him on vocabulary.

"You mean fuck? I know what it means now. I looked it up."

"Liar," said Travis. "It's not even in the dictionary."

"I found it in a special slang dictionary."

"Well, what's it mean, then?" Delilah challenged.

She and Travis exchanged a look, both of them expecting Nick to falter. They were stymied when he came back with complete aplomb, "It's a vulgar way of referring to sexual intercourse."

A long pause. "Well, I bet you don't know what that is," Delilah said. The term sounded terribly intimidating. Sexual intercourse. She committed it to memory.

"I wasn't sure, so I asked Dad."

"You did *what?"* Travis shouted.

"He gave me this long lecture on biology," Nick said, sounding bored. "Why can't I come up? It's just as much my tree as it is yours."

Travis began laughing. "I can't believe you asked our father. Come on," he added, reaching down to give his brother a hand. "What did he say? Did he tell you about . . ." Travis whispered something in Nick's ear, and they both started giggling.

"What?" Delilah asked.

Travis adopted the superior older-brother air that she hated. "There are some things," he informed her, "that boys don't discuss with girls."

Delilah glared. All of a sudden she felt like pelting them with apples. While they whispered some more, she scurried up the tree trunk to the large, hollow V they called Victory. There wasn't room for all three of them to be comfortable down there in Heart.

It wasn't fair. Usually she and Travis were best friends and Nick was the odd one out. Why should they close ranks on her just because she was a girl?

"Want to climb up to Six Branch Camp?" Travis asked his brother.

"What's that?"

"It's our fort. We keep stuff there, like cookies, a canteen, my harmonica, some of Delilah's books. It's a neat place."

"Sure," said Nick, obviously pleased to be invited into the citadel.

Delilah snapped off a twig and tossed it at the ground. *Traitor,* she thought. Travis wasn't supposed to tell what they kept in Six Branch Camp. It was their secret place.

"He can't come up. Not until he does the rope trick."

"Oh, come on, Delilah—"

"That's right, Travis. Everyone has to, remember?"

"Not Nick. He's my brother."

"Even so," she insisted.

"What's the rope trick?" asked Nick.

Delilah explained. The rope trick had begun with one of Travis's assaults on the tree: he had dragged an old coil of rope into the tree and hung it high on Beanstalk, using it to climb and swing upon, whooping like a jungle creature. At first Delilah had hated it, and they'd had one of their rare fights when she'd discovered how it had chafed and wounded her tree. But Travis had ignored her demands to remove it, and the rope had remained, rotting there in the summer damp.

No matter how recklessly she climbed, Delilah trusted the apple tree, never fearing it would fling her to the ground, but she was not so confident about the rope. Sometimes when she looked at it she was certain it was not really hanging from the tree, but rather rising out of the earth like a snake, thrusting its ugly head into the living limbs of the tree. But when Travis invented the rope trick, her animosity faded.

You had to climb into Victory, grasp the rope firmly, and swing to the ground, clearing a wide patch of black raspberries before letting go. You had to push off vigorously, slide low on the rope, and pump your legs hard to clear the brambles. It was difficult, as Delilah's scratched legs could attest.

It began as a test of courage between them, but later it became a device to protect their retreat from invaders. It had been Travis's idea that anyone who wanted to play in the tree must first master the rope trick. As a result, several of the neighborhood children ran crying home that summer, and the raspberries were ruined. But the tree had remained inviolable.

Delilah didn't expect Nick to accept the challenge. She emphasized the dangers of the swing, and the painful consequences of a bad landing. Nick's face grew whiter and whiter, but when she finished explaining, he said he was ready to try.

Delilah had a swift attack of conscience. "Are you sure? Maybe you'd better not, Nick. You'll hurt yourself if you land in the brambles."

But Nick was determined.

"Show him how to do it," Travis said.

That seemed fair. While the boys climbed up into Victory, Delilah clutched the rope and flung her body into space. She flew over the black raspberry patch and landed successfully on the grass. The rope swung back to Travis, who showed his brother how to hold it and gave him some advice as to when to let go.

For several seconds Nick crouched in Victory, biting his lips and measuring the distance to the ground. He looked scared. Maybe he wouldn't have the nerve to do it after all. She hoped he wouldn't. She didn't want him to get hurt.

"Go on, Nick, hurry up," said Travis impatiently. "Either do it or don't do it; make up your mind."

Nick looked down at Delilah, who was standing there, arms akimbo, waiting. That seemed to decide him. He drew a deep breath and launched himself. He swung back and forth once, twice, three times, sliding as low on the rope as he dared, then, with his eyes foolishly closed, he unclasped his fingers and dropped.

"Oh no," Delilah cried as he landed right in the middle of the raspberries and let out a muffled cry. The brambles caught on his sleeves and tore at his bare legs as he tried to extricate himself.

Delilah waded into the bushes, paying no attention as she

scratched her own legs in the process. "You weren't supposed to let go *then.* That was really dumb!" Although she was yelling at him, it was herself she was mad at. He wouldn't have done it, she knew, if he hadn't been so desperate to impress her.

"Are you okay?" She took his arm and tried to drag him out. "I'm sorry, Nick. I fell all the time when I first tried it. It's a hard thing to learn and—"

"Don't touch me." Tears were threatening to escape his eyes. He sniffed as if trying to hold them back. "You knew that would happen, you creep. I hate you! Why don't you go back home to your father and leave my family alone?"

This attack was totally unexpected, and she backed away. "It's my family, too," she whispered.

"You stole my brother!" Nick raged at her. "He never plays with me anymore, only with you!"

The rope swung again, and Travis landed a few feet away. "Come on, Nick. Don't be such a baby. You're not that hurt."

"You go to hell," Nick retorted, and plunged deeper into the brambles to avoid both Travis and Delilah. He emerged on the far side, dried his eyes on his sleeve, and ran toward the house.

"I never used to play with him anyway," Travis said as he and Delilah exchanged a guilty look. "I don't even think he likes me. It's you he likes, Delilah. Last week he told me he was in love with you."

"He just said he hated me!"

"He's crazy," Travis agreed. "Never mind. He won't stay mad. He'll be following you around like a puppy again before the day is over."

While Travis went off to climb the nearby pine tree in which he had built himself a fort, Delilah, depressed and still vaguely uneasy, settled into the old swing that was hanging from one of the apple tree branches and scuffed her feet against the ground. She kept hearing Nick say, "You stole my brother," and "Why don't you go back home and leave my family alone?"

Daddy, Daddy. Why haven't you come to take me home?

"Hey."

She looked up. Travis was right—Nick was back. He came toward her, whittling again. He had a couple of Band-Aids on his legs.

I'm not going to speak to him, she decided, and started to swing.

Nick didn't press her. He climbed into Heart and stayed there for a while. Every so often Delilah heard a scratching sound. "What are you doing?" she finally asked.

"You'll see."

Delilah hesitated, then said, "Nick, I'm really sorry. Are you all right?"

"I'm okay. I'm sorry, too. I shouldn't have said what I said; it was mean. I don't really wish you'd go home."

She began to feel a lot better.

Nick jumped down from the tree, dropping his open jackknife on the ground as he stumbled a little. Delilah hid her smile. He was really clumsy sometimes.

"I was carving. Want to see?"

"Okay." She got off the swing and crossed to the trunk of the apple tree to look up into Heart. There in the thickest section of the trunk Nick had inscribed a heart around the carefully shaped letters, "N. loves D."

"I really do, you know," he said, and before she could respond, her bookish cousin grabbed her and kissed her shyly on the cheek.

She was so astonished, she didn't do a thing. Encouraged, Nick kissed her again and might have kissed her a third time if Travis hadn't appeared from nowhere and practically leapt upon the smaller boy's back, knocking him to the ground. "You sneaky little runt!" he cried, and began punching poor Nick, who threw up his hands in feeble defense.

"Travis!" Delilah yelled, trying to pull them apart. They didn't fight very often, but when they did, Nick invariably got the worst of it.

Travis clipped Nick hard on the chin. The smaller boy howled, but he managed to roll over and get in a few punches of his own.

"Stop it! You're both crazy! Stop it right now!"

Nick got a hand in Travis's hair and pulled. The older boy yelled and doubled up his fist. He smashed Nick right below his left eye, and his brother groaned and clutched his face. He went limp, all the fight gone out of him. "If you ever kiss her again, I'll kill you!" Travis said, and kicked him to make the point even clearer.

Nick got to his knees, then jerked to his feet. Delilah tried to help him, but he shook her off. For the second time in less than an hour, he was forced to make an ignominious retreat.

"Are you out of your mind?" Delilah was trembling. For a minute she'd thought they were really going to hurt each other.

"Why did you let him kiss you?"

"I didn't *let* him kiss me. He surprised me, that's all. Anyway, so what?"

"So it was disgusting, that's what!" Travis was breathing hard. He bent over and scooped up Nick's jackknife from the ground, and Delilah felt a crampy, crawly feeling in her stomach.

Travis never lost his temper—or hardly ever, anyway. She recalled an evening when he and Nick had been arguing about some silly thing—she wasn't even sure what—and their father had interrupted, telling Travis he was wrong and to stop being so pigheaded. Travis left the dinner table and disappeared up the narrow stairs to the attic. Curious and hoping to comfort him, Delilah had followed him. She found him ripping into an old punching bag that dangled from a beam in the low ceiling, with no finesse but enormous passion. The sight frightened her. He was out of control, violent. When she inadvertently made a sound, he turned on her, fists raised, breathing hard, and for a moment she'd thought he was going to attack her.

He was mad like that now. Without stopping to find out what he intended, Delilah flung herself into the apple tree and began to climb. Up and up she flew, higher than she had ever gone before, as if freed up from the forces of gravity. Ignoring the rough bark and twigs that were lacerating her arms and legs, she scurried toward the thin, lacy branches that touched the sky.

Straddling a flimsy limb, she forced her way along it, away from the main trunk of the tree. She was out over the black raspberry patch, but far, far above it.

From her lofty perch, Delilah parted the leaves, thick with unripe apples, and looked down. She could see the rope below her, thin as a snake, twisting idly in the breeze. And she could see Travis. He was standing wedged in Heart thrusting with one arm at the great trunk. A red gleam from the afternoon sun played on the blade of the jackknife as he drove it repeatedly into the wood, like Jack sawing at his beanstalk.

What was he doing? Trying to cut down the tree? Surely he couldn't cut it down with a jackknife.

The entire world rocked as the wind shook the slender web of branches that supported her. Delilah's heart fluttered and her skin turned slick. The ground tilted beneath her, brown and muddy. The branches hissed, and she heard the plop plop of apples shaking off and falling to earth, taking so long to hit, and smashing when they did. What if the branch breaks? she wondered. What if he *does* cut down the tree? For a few moments she was back in that silent hospital room where her mother lay covered with a flapping sheet. *What if I die, like my mother?*

It seemed forever that she remained frozen there, hardly daring to move or breathe. Eventually her heart stopped pounding and she was able to open her eyes and look down. Her cousin was gone. Beanstalk still stood. Slowly, with infinite care, she began to retrace her climb.

It was one of the hardest things she'd ever done—much harder than the rope trick—but she finally managed to get back down to the safety of Heart. Putting her arms around the trunk of the tree, she sought the comfort she had always found there.

At length, she noticed an unaccustomed roughness against her cheek. She tilted her head back to look. Her wet eyes blurred and distorted the knife marks in the bark. She wiped her eyes on her arm and stared at the spot.

Nick's heart was still there, with its inscription "N. loves D." But gouged across it in much harsher, deeper letters, Travis had carved the word FUCK.

15

"You are a disgrace."

"Yes, Grandmother."

"I'm ashamed of you."

"I'm ashamed of myself," Delilah said. She spoke meekly enough, but there was a gleam in her eyes. "It was horribly embarrassing."

Minerva frowned. She wasn't convinced that her granddaughter was the least bit sorry. The girl had no respect for authority, no sense of decorum, and it was beginning to look as if she had no morals, either. "Your teacher, Delilah. The man was your ancient history teacher!"

Delilah didn't reply, but her face reddened.

"Of course, I blame him. Young or not, he ought to have known better. He'll be fired at once, of course. And you'll be extremely lucky if you're allowed to stay on at St. Crispin's and graduate."

Her granddaughter's control broke. "Don't let them fire him, Gran! It wasn't his fault. I led him on; I'll swear it if I have to. Please don't let them fire him."

"Enough. It's about time you faced up to the unpleasant results of your outrageous behavior. This is the fourth school I've enrolled you in, Delilah. The fourth! Stubborn and spoiled, one headmistress said. Incorrigible, said another. A difficult case, say the school psychologists. If I didn't know you for a good-hearted, if totally reckless and irresponsible, young woman, I'd wash my hands of you."

"Please, Gran," Delilah said in a muted voice. "I didn't mean any harm."

"You never mean any harm. But you do harm, all the same. All actions have consequences, Delilah. Maybe next time you'll learn to think a little first."

The trouble was, she *did* think first. It was just that she thought about the wrong things. She longed for the wrong things. "Miss Scofield," they always said when she was summoned to the headmistress's office. "I'm afraid we've been forced to notify your father of your appalling behavior. We're asking him to drive down here and take you home."

"I'm sorry," she would say, staring at the floor with what they would usually interpret as a modicum of guilt and shame. But what she really felt was hope—the hope that maybe, this time, her father would take some notice of her. She would wait, imagining the way he'd sweep onto the campus, accuse her persecutors of being narrow-minded bigots, and inform them that they didn't need to expel her because he himself was withdrawing her from their conservative, outmoded establishment. He, a well-known Harvard educator, would take on the task of completing her education himself rather than leave her to the mercy of such a place. Together, they'd return to Cambridge, where Delilah would live year-round with him in the Walker Street house, cooking his meals and listening to him lecture his graduate students on the intricacies of Spenser's sonnets or Marlowe's plays.

It never happened. It was always Gran who came, her narrow mouth twisted into a disapproving frown. It was Gran who drove her back to Boston, lecturing her all the while. Gran who patiently arranged for her to attend the next school on the list. By the time she was seventeen and a senior at St. Crispin's, Delilah had given up expecting her father to take any interest in her. He had become involved with various anti-Vietnam war groups, and he was a busy man.

Delilah's exploits at St. Crispin's had been relatively tame—no spiking fruit with vodka at parents' weekend, no exam stealing for her friends. She'd made it through two whole years without getting into any trouble, and would have made it safely to graduation if it hadn't been for Eliot Randall's brandy-tinted eyes.

Eliot was the most gorgeous man she'd ever seen—the personification of all her romantic fantasies—tall and slender with dark, curly hair, a sulky-sensitive mouth, and those magnetic eyes. There was a tiny dimple in his chin and a crinkle in his forehead when he frowned. He looked just like her favorite Beatle, Paul McCartney, whose picture was plastered all over her dormitory room.

At seventeen, Delilah yearned to have a real love affair. Although she dated occasionally and had fumbled around with more than one panting teenager, she didn't feel the least bit tempted by boys her own age. "When I fall in love," she informed her best friend, Julie Barnaby, "it's not going to be with some pimply adolescent who doesn't know where to put what. I want someone experienced, sophisticated, and mature."

Twenty-two-year-old Eliot Randall fit the bill perfectly. The only trouble was, he wasn't interested in her.

Delilah did everything she could to attract his attention. She studied very hard and earned A's in his class, but although he seemed pleased with her scholarship, he didn't notice her as a woman, not even when she hemmed her shirts high enough to display the full expanse of her long, slim legs and sported as much make-up as she dared.

"I need to do something dramatic," she told Julie. "Something to shock him out of his complacency, something to make him really *see* me."

On the day they were discussing Cicero's orations, she appeared in class wearing a rented Roman toga, with bare legs and one shoulder daringly exposed. The other students howled at her antics, but Eliot seemed unmoved.

"You're already dramatic, Delilah," Julie told her. "Your hair's down to your waist and you wear weird clothes and white lipstick and all those bright-colored belts and scarves. Maybe you're too dramatic."

"Oh God, do you think so? Do you think he wants someone conservative and demure?" She began braiding her hair and wrapping it around her head; she switched to knee socks and oxfords, blazers, and the palest pink lip gloss. But it didn't work. Eliot took no more notice of her than her father ever had.

One evening in late February she found herself a desk in the basement stacks of the library, where she'd gone to get the book about Alexander the Great that Randall had put on the extra reading list. After a chapter or two, she lost interest, set the book aside, and sneaked out the beaten-up paperback copy of *Fanny Hill* that she'd borrowed from Julie. The book graphically and with great style depicted the sexual act in such a manner that for the first time in her life Delilah could envision exactly how it was done. She wanted to finish it in private because *Fanny Hill* made her so flushed and hot that she absolutely couldn't read it in the presence of another human being. Which is why she almost died when she heard a footstep behind her and felt a hand come down briefly on her shoulder.

"I'm impressed," said the pleasant voice of Eliot Randall. "It's nine o'clock at night and here you are, hard at work in the ancient history section. That's the kind of thing that warms a teacher's heart."

Delilah slammed the book closed and looked up at him with a face already red from sexual tension. "You scared me!" She leaned over the desk, folding her arms tightly over her paperback and praying for the first time ever that he would go away and leave her alone.

"Sorry." He glanced around the empty room. "It's quiet here, isn't it? What are you reading?"

She jerked her chin at the history text. "That."

"But what's that you're hiding? A book for another course? Surely you're not worried I'll take offense if I catch you studying your English or your French assignment?"

She leapt on this excuse. "That's it exactly. We're having an English quiz, you see, and oh no, is it really that late?" She made a show of looking at her watch. "I'd better run or I'll never get prepared."

She must have sounded even more flustered than she felt, because after holding her eyes for a moment, Randall reached under her arms for the book. She tried to stop him, but he was too fast. He got hold of *Fanny Hill,* jerked it away from her, and peered at the title. There was a long silence before he grinned and said, "An English quiz, huh? You're right—I'd better leave you alone so you can finish it. I don't think they put out Cliff Notes on this."

Delilah groaned and put her face down on her arms.

"It certainly is one of the minor classics of Victorian Age London. Did you get to the orgy in the whorehouse scene, yet? Great verbs."

Delilah couldn't answer. It was the worst moment of her entire school career.

"Hey. Delilah?" Randall tossed the book back on the desk. "Don't die of shame on me, okay?"

"I just might."

He tugged on her hair until her head came up. His mouth was curved with that cute, irresistible smile. "Don't worry, I'm not going to report you. I don't imagine you can afford to be tossed out of another school at this late date."

"I don't think reading pornography is a toss-outable offense," she said with a little more spirit. "I mean, you have to do something worse than that."

"Like what?"

His tone was strange, and Delilah shot him a look. Those brandy eyes were so big. They were dilated in the dim light of the basement, and there was something decidedly decadent about his mouth. She felt a spasm deep inside her at the realization that Eliot was finally looking at her the way a man looks at a woman. He was staring at her breasts, in fact, and his voice sounded choked up as he added, "It hardly seems like the most enjoyable way to learn about lovemaking. Don't you have a boyfriend?"

She shook her head. The dark solitude of the basement room was beginning to crowd them. "It's hard to meet boys at a girls' school."

"They have mixers and dances and various social events with the boys' schools in the area. I know because I've been asked to chaperone a couple of times."

"No one ever asks me to dance. I guess I'm too tall."

"I don't think you're too tall."

"You don't?" Her heartbeat was threatening to strangle her.

"No. Look, I'll show you. Stand up."

He gave her his hand and pulled her to her feet. Her legs were all rubbery and her breasts felt swollen. He pulled her close to his body, as if they were about to dance. He must have been about six foot three, a height that meshed perfectly with her five-foot-nine frame. "You're not too tall for me."

Delilah didn't move for several moments. Neither of them did.

Then, unable to stand it any longer, she tipped her head back to see what he was thinking. He shook his head as if to acknowledge the craziness of his actions. "Delilah," he said softly. "Christ, you've been tormenting me for months."

She was in heaven. "You mean you did notice?"

"I noticed, all right. God." He pulled her against him and kissed her mouth. Delilah's knees melted. She clung to him, responding with all the longing she'd been saving up all year. That mouth *was* decadent, and its firm pressure against hers caused all sorts of wickedly delicious sensations to race along her nerves. And that tongue. When it slipped into her mouth and gently touched her own, Delilah just about died. She opened herself completely to him, not the least bit ashamed or reluctant. In no time her ancient history teacher had her blouse and bra undone and was murmuring endearments as he fondled her naked breasts.

It was then that Marion Carpenter, otherwise known as the barbarian librarian, rounded the corner in search of a book. She took one look at the dark, erect nipple that had popped from between Eliot's fingers and shrieked for reinforcements.

"Please don't let them fire him," Delilah said once again to her grandmother as she went in to discuss the matter with St. Crispin's disciplinary board. "I don't care what happens to me. Anyway, I've already told them it was all my fault."

"Well, I care what happens to you. You've got a very good chance of being accepted to Radcliffe, and I'm damned if I'll see you throw that away because of a man. Besides, as I understand it, Randall has accepted full responsibility. I fully expect the headmistress to accept his version of the story."

Which was exactly what happened. The verdict came down within the hour. Delilah was suspended for a month, but allowed to graduate, a decision that may have been facilitated by the large donation Minerva made to the school's endowment. Randall was fired posthaste, Delilah's passionate pleas notwithstanding.

They wouldn't let her see him to say good-bye, but he left her a note. "Don't worry, Delilah," it read, and she could imagine him smiling wryly as he wrote the words. "It was worth it."

She kept Eliot's note in the old tea chest lined with silver paper where she secreted her various other treasures, and vowed to remember her first love forever.

"I suppose it's high time you and I had a woman-to-woman talk," Minerva said to her granddaughter when they got home after the Eliot fiasco. They were seated in the dining room of the China Tea House Tavern, and she at least had felt the need to restore herself with a nice hot cup of tea. Delilah was drinking Coke.

"I thought you were a more sensible girl, but perhaps I've been wrong. It's time you realized there's more to life than falling in love with some good-looking man."

"If you're finally going to tell me about sex, don't bother," Delilah said airily. "I already know the gory details."

Minerva found the girl's breeziness just a little too hard to bear. "I'm sure you do. The permissiveness in this country is appalling. When I was your age—" she began, then abruptly stopped. *I was making love with Edward and pregnant with his father's child.*

"Yes, yes, I know," said Delilah. "When you were my age you still thought babies were delivered by the stork. My God, Gran, sometimes I wonder how the human race ever survived!"

"I have neither the time nor the inclination to lecture you about sex," Minerva said stiffly. "Except insofar as it may affect your future. You're no longer a child, Delilah. You'll be eighteen shortly, and it's time you gave some serious consideration to what you intend to do with your life."

"I'm going to be an actress," Delilah declared. She had performed in several school plays at St. Crispin's, although not in any of the leading roles. "Miss Bradley, the drama coach, says I have real stage presence."

"Don't talk rot. You're going to go to college and acquire some elementary knowledge of economics, then you're going to come and work for me at Templeton Tea."

Delilah groaned.

The truth was that now that Elizabeth was dead, Minerva's hopes and dreams for the future were bound up with Delilah. Ever since that morning in the picture gallery when Minerva had seen the resemblance between Helen Templeton and Delilah, she'd felt that she had found her successor at last.

Delilah was perfect. She was highly intelligent—she never did a lick of work, yet she made steady, solid A's at the best prep schools in the nation. Her scores on her college entrance exams had been in the top 2 percent. She was clever at managing money—she got by on the meager allowance her father gave her far better than either of her cousins did on considerably more. She was personable and showed numerous leadership qualities. Indeed, were it not for the high-spiritedness that so frequently got her into trouble, Delilah would have been a source of constant delight.

Minerva loved her wholeheartedly. But the girl was undisciplined and must be controlled. Otherwise she would probably throw herself away on some wastral like her father and end up married, pregnant, and unable to work.

"It is essential that you maintain a serious attitude toward your future, Delilah. You know that I expect you to take my place one day at the helm of Templeton Tea."

"But, Gran, that's so far away!"

"The time will pass much faster than you imagine. Listen to me, child. You are at the age where you are drawn to a certain type of shaggy-haired young man. That is natural. But I must warn you not to forget yourself so far as to do anything rash."

"Fuck, you mean?" said Delilah, taking obvious relish in using the word. "Don't worry, Gran, I'm saving it for Paul McCartney."

"As far as I'm concerned, you may fuck anyone you please, as long as you don't get yourself pregnant and find yourself forced to marry in haste and repent at leisure."

Delilah was struck silent, unable to decide which was more shocking, her grandmother's repetition of an obscenity, or her liberal attitude toward sex.

"I want you to feel you can talk to me about these matters. I may be your grandmother, but I am certainly not a prude. Sex, believe it or not, was not invented by your generation. Your generation is fortunate, however, in having a foolproof way of avoiding the consequences of mankind's most persistent weakness. I have made an appointment for you with my gynecologist. Before you submit to the embraces of another Eliot Randall, I intend to make sure you're on the pill."

Minerva could see that she'd finally succeeded in startling the girl. Maybe some of Delilah's friends' mothers talked to them about birth control, but she doubted whether any of their *grandmothers* did.

"The pill makes you fat," Delilah retorted, after half a minute of silence.

"Pregnancy makes you fatter."

Delilah began to laugh. She flung herself into her grandmother's arms and hugged her hard. "You're really something. I love you, you know."

They kept the appointment, and Delilah came home with her first diaphragm. She packed the slim plastic case away in a drawer, where it lay unused for another four years.

16

Delilah sat on a hard bench in the women's lockup of the Cambridge City Jail, biting her nails and wondering if the other woman in the cell was a prostitute. Her platinum hair was teased high, her knee-high boots were of dirty white vinyl, and her purple skirt reached midthigh. The top three buttons of her blouse were undone, showing a voluptuous cleavage. Delilah stared at her breasts, thinking, are those real? They can't be. Maybe she'd had silicone implants.

"Hey, honey, whadya starin' at? You a dyke or somethin'?"

"I was wondering what kind of justice there is in a world where some women end up with hourglass figures, and others"—she patted her own relatively flat chest—"have to stuff wads of Kleenex in our bras."

"Guess you weren't around when the good Lord was passin' out the boobs. Listen, honey, be thankful. Ten years from now you'll have a couple of nice round apples, and I'll have two basketballs."

Delilah laughed. The woman seemed friendly, and she was desperate for a little good fellowship. She'd been arrested several hours before and had had no one to talk to all night. She was scared.

"What's your name, honey?"

"Delilah Scofield. What's yours?"

"Candy. Used to be Mary Catherine, but I changed it. Delilah, huh? That your real name?" Candy took in her peasant blouse, blue jeans, and sandals and added, "Delilah's a great name for a whore, but you don't look like you're in for solicitation. You one of them hippie types that are always gettin' nailed these days protesting the war or some dumb-ass thing?"

"Yes. I was arrested last night during a peace demonstration. They put my father in jail, too, after clubbing him with one of their nightsticks. I'm a little worried about him."

More than a little worried. For the first time in her life Delilah felt as if she was getting close to her father, and it had terrified her to see some hefty pig grabbing her thin, ascetic father by the collar and clubbing him to the ground.

David Scofield had emerged from his scholarly cocoon two or three years before to become a leading activist and lecturer on American involvement in Vietnam. College students all over the country idolized him, which made Delilah absurdly proud. She stole time away from her studies to work alongside him, answering his mail and writing letters to Congress on the people's behalf. At Radcliffe she had become one of the campus leaders of the peace movement. She'd marched on Washington countless times, paraded in front of the White House holding banners proclaiming Peace Now, fled the violence at the 1968 Democratic Convention, celebrated the ideals of love and peace at Woodstock, and passionately proclaimed the evils of Lyndon Johnson and Richard Nixon.

It was heady, exciting work, and very noble, of course. For the first time in her life she believed she was doing something important.

Her father had been in jail a number of times, but this was Delilah's first serious run-in with the law. Despite the friendly advice of Candy the hooker ("Don't let those pricks push you around, honey. You got your rights."), she found the experience humiliating.

She'd made her one phone call last night to her grandmother. But Minerva Templeton was away in some exploited third world country getting a firsthand report on the current status of tea production. Delilah had been forced to leave a message with her grandmother's housekeeper, asking that somebody in the family contact the Templetons' attorney.

In retrospect she wasn't sure she ought to have left the message. Her father still had no liking for the Templetons. His own phone call would probably have been to the Cambridge office of Students for a Democratic Society, who presumably had funds for such eventualities.

But it wasn't the SDS bail bondsman who was there to meet them when she and David were finally released from their cells. "Hey, babe," drawled a familiar voice that she hadn't heard in far too long a time. "I heard you were in deep shit."

"Travis!" She ran and flung her arms around him. "God, it's so good to see you. I thought you were still off on your Grand Tour of Europe, romancing countesses and jetting about with dispossessed Hapsburg princes."

"I just got home, as a matter of fact. Flew in a couple of days ago without a single countess in tow."

With his gilt hair, well-proportioned physique, and tan, handsome face, Travis looked a bit like a prince himself. He dressed like one, too, in a buff cashmere coat, a tailored herringbone suit, and a pair of alligator skin loafers, all from pricey designers. What a change from the denim-clad, greasy-haired hippies she usually associated with. He was less than two years older than she, but the gap between them seemed wider.

As he turned to greet her father, Delilah wondered what sort of reception he would receive. She watched them warily, the young man and the older one, both of them tall and lean, one so obviously well-to-do and the other with no more clothes sense than a factory worker. "It's good to see you again, sir," said Travis, holding out his hand.

To Delilah's relief, David nodded and clapped Travis on the shoulder. Then he said, to her astonishment, "Your contributions to the cause have been much appreciated, Travis. Are you going to help us out in person now that you're back?"

"Not if I have to dress in rags like Cinderella here."

"What contributions?" she asked.

"Your cousin has been making handsome donations to the Stop the War movement ever since his senior year at Yale," her father explained.

Delilah looked at Travis with new respect. Much as she'd always loved him, she'd thought lately that he was too much of a capitalist roader, particularly when he'd taken off on what she could only assume to have been a self-indulgent tour of the finer things in life in Europe.

"Come on, folks, my car's outside. I'll drive you both home."

"I'm late for a rally," David said. "Would you mind driving me over to Brandeis, if it's not too much trouble?"

"I'd be glad to, sir."

Delilah had planned to attend the Brandeis rally, too, but the temptation to spend more time with Travis proved too much for her. After leaving David, they drove back to Cambridge, parked the car in a garage, and took a walk around Harvard Square. "So you're a closet war protester. I never would have thought it. Does Grendam know?"

"It's not something I brag about, but yeah, I'm sure she knows."

"I always thought you were apolitical. I remember a Christmas dinner at the Tea House Tavern three or four years ago in which you suggested we put all the politicians in a ring and nuke 'em."

"I still think that's a pretty good idea." His expression sobered as he went on, "I've never been big on theory, on polemics. I don't buy most of the crap your father preaches, even though I've given him money. But I do think peace is worth preserving." He winked at her. "Besides, I don't want to be drafted. Fortunately, both Nick and I drew high numbers in last fall's draft lottery."

"Thank God for that!"

They walked all morning, chatting animatedly, not paying a whole lot of attention to where they were going. It had been several years since Delilah had spent any length of time with Travis, but it was remarkable how easily their old intimacy came back.

Everywhere they went, Delilah noticed women giving her handsome cousin the eye. "What is it with you?" she said, laughing. "I feel as if I'm out with Paul Newman. All the girls are panting after you."

"Let 'em pant. I'm with you."

His words sent a thrill right through her. She stopped, breathed deeply of the air hanging over the Cambridge Common. Thick though it was with auto fumes, it smelled like spring to her. For a moment, somehow, she seemed to catch a glimpse of what lay ahead. She saw—or perhaps she only imagined—her cousin Travis smiling that sexy come-on smile as he stripped off his clothes in a bedroom she didn't recognize.

"Hey. You okay?"

Flushing, she closed her eyes. The vision disappeared. You're just horny, she told herself. He's your cousin; it's probably illegal or something. She took his arm in what she hoped was a comradely fashion, and they walked on.

"Now that you're home, are you going to start working for the tea company?" she asked as they settled into a booth at the College Grill on Mass Ave and ordered a large mushroom and onion pizza.

"I suppose so. Unlike you, I haven't sworn never to have anything more to do with our rip-off capitalistic family corporation."

"Sounds like you've heard about some of my more violent disagreements with Grendam." Ever since she'd been involved in the protest movement, she and Minerva Templeton had not been getting along. They'd had a fight during which Delilah had accused her of being racially bigoted because she'd grown up in a country where the white British imperialists considered themselves better than the Hindus they governed. Her grandmother had slapped her, and for several weeks they had not spoken.

"Yup," said Travis. "It's okay with me. You don't want to run the company, so I guess I'll just have to grit my teeth and do it myself."

"You're the eldest of our generation. It should be you. She'll groom you to rise through the ranks until you reach the exalted position of Director and get your portrait on the wall."

He grimaced. "I don't find the idea wildly appealing. But what the hell else am I going to do with my life?"

"You shouldn't let yourself be pressured into the tea business if it's not what you want."

He smiled, and those huge eyes sparkled. They were as large as robin's eggs and just as blue. Big, expressive eyes are definitely my weakness, Delilah thought, remembering Eliot's sherry-colored eyes.

"What I'd really rather do is continue to lead the life of a wealthy, dissolute playboy. Fact is, I like being rich. And I miss sauntering around first class, sipping Château LaFite-Rothschild and eating beluga on the Côte d'Azur, or cruising on the Nile watching the moon rise over some luscious countess's milky shoulder. No shit," he added when she made a skeptical noise. "Am I supposed to relinquish all that for the dubious pleasures of tea?"

"Shame on you, Travis. Here I am demonstrating my ass off while you're romancing countesses and devouring caviar."

He grinned. "I don't feel guilty. I'm contributing to the cause. Anyway, where would you jailbirds be if I weren't around to bail you out?"

When they'd finished devouring the pizza, they walked some more, finally ending up outside Delilah's dorm as the sun was going down. "Are you going to invite me in? I need a place to crash."

"My dear man, it's a girls' school. Male guests aren't allowed overnight."

"So who's to know?"

She giggled. It had been a long time since she'd got up to any of her old pranks.

Male guests were allowed in for several hours a day, so Delilah simply signed Travis in, and later that evening, signed him out again. "You'll have to keep your voice down," she told him. "I doubt if most people'll care, but there's always a goody-goody on every floor. I don't know how you're going to go to the bathroom. You'll just have to wait until everyone else is asleep."

They sat on her bed under the Make Love Not War poster and played cards for a while, then Delilah put on the Jefferson Airplane while they smoked a couple of joints. Travis told her riotous stories about life in the jet set, and she gave him all the behind-the-scenes gossip on the peace movement. They smoked some more grass and were feeling pretty mellow when the conversation descended to the level of who was sleeping with whom in St. Tropez and what Travis had learned about the sexual proclivities of the extremely rich.

All of which Delilah found deliciously titillating. Ever since the Eliot fiasco, she'd stayed away from sexual involvement. She wouldn't dream of admitting it to any of her friends, but at twenty-one, she was still a virgin. Her energy at college had been so efficiently channeled into the peace movement that she hadn't felt the lack of romance. Anyway, her four years at Radcliffe had been marked by the same problem she'd known in prep school, a resounding lack of men who came anywhere near to fulfilling her fantasies.

While they talked, Grace Slick's rough silk voice was advising her at full volume from the stereo that she'd better find somebody to love.

Sometime around midnight, after she'd sneaked Travis to the bathroom and back, he stretched out on the sleeping bag she'd provided him with and said, "How come there's no lover in your bed tonight, Delilah? I thought you were such a hot ticket."

Everybody thought so, she knew. Ever since she'd nearly been kicked out of school for sexual misconduct with a teacher, she'd had quite a colorful reputation. She never sought to disabuse anybody of this. In fact, she played it up by wearing flamboyant dime store-chic clothes. She liked being thought of as a woman who exercised her sexual freedom. Which was exactly what she had done: instead of fooling around with every Tom, Dick, and Harry, she'd chosen to wait for that really super man. Her true and eternal lover. "I'm fussy."

"Mmm. So am I."

He looked into her eyes, and Delilah felt once again as if a window were opening somewhere. But it was dark, and she couldn't quite see through. It was not a comfortable feeling. Something awaited her, something that was both delicious and agonizing.

When she undressed and got into bed, Delilah was very conscious of the way her beautiful cousin was looking at her bare legs. He was lying less than a yard away. She shifted, unable to sleep. Women had always been attracted to his devil-may-care grin, his tall film-star physique. Delilah acknowledged wryly that she was no exception.

"Delilah?"

She jerked to attention at the sound of his husky voice. "What?"

Several seconds went by. "Nothing," he said.

She rolled over and pressed herself up on one elbow. "Can't you sleep?"

He laughed softly. "Can you?"

"I'm sure I'll be able to soon."

"Well, I won't." He was staring openly at the curve of her body under the blanket. "Shit."

"What do you mean, shit?"

"I mean I want to make love to you, but I have a gut feeling you're going to say no."

"Oh God."

"What do you mean, oh God?"

"You're my cousin."

"So what? It's not considered incest. Cousins are always getting married in nineteenth-century novels."

She pulled a wry face. "I can't, Travis. Let's drop the subject." She knew she didn't sound convincing. Worse, she didn't really want him to drop it, which made her dishonest, not to mention a tease. "Go to sleep."

"Have pity. I can't seem to think of a single one of my usual suave, irresistible come-ons. Why don't you just slide down here and let me kiss you for a while."

"No, Travis! We're friends, we're family, and having sex would probably ruin everything. Anyway, I refuse to be one of your easy conquests."

"Lady, you don't know what you're missing."

Now she laughed. "You're right—I *have* heard smoother lines than that. Maybe you're not really the hot-shit lover you make yourself out to be."

"One more crack, one more, and I'm up from this floor and into that bed with you, Delilah. My real forte is nonverbal communication."

Despite the teasing tone, he meant it, she knew. And she wasn't sure why she was holding him off since she couldn't think of any man she'd rather take to herself and love. But there was danger here; she didn't know how she knew it. Danger and something darker still.

"See you in the morning, Trav," she whispered, and turned her face to the wall.

He groaned but left her alone.

She half expected him to be short-tempered with her the next day, but he wasn't; he seemed just as warm and friendly as ever. But something had changed. He no longer touched her in his usual fraternal manner, and it was clear why not: sexual awareness existed between them for the first time ever. Delilah had awakened in a state of unrelenting lust, and she knew he felt the same.

If they touched, she didn't think they'd be able to prevent themselves from tearing off each other's clothes and making wild, passionate love.

He talked her into taking a drive up to New Hampshire. The snow was so plentiful and powdery in the mountains that they wondered why they hadn't thought to bring their skis. "We'll rent skis," Travis announced, driving to the nearest resort. "We'll rent everything."

It was a spur-of-the-moment adventure the likes of which she hadn't treated herself to in ages. They skied all afternoon, then stopped for dinner in a picturesque country inn nestled between two mountains and a frozen lake. Travis ordered a full bottle of California cabernet sauvignon, and Delilah was more than a little drunk by the time they were draining the last two glasses. Over the smoothest, creamiest *mousse au chocolat* she'd ever tasted, Travis reached across the table and captured her hand. "It's late. We could stay here tonight. I asked about a room, and the owner tells me there's a nice one available, with a fireplace and a view of the lake."

"And a four-poster bed, no doubt?" Her voice was quick and high, for she was nervous. It was going to happen. As much as she wanted it, she was afraid.

"No doubt. I'll bet it even has a hand-quilted counterpane," he said huskily. "Very romantic. We'll build a roaring fire, order a bottle of the best champagne, and make love all night."

She gulped some coffee to wet her throat. After a day on the ski slopes, Travis's face was unshaven. He looked mussed and wild, not his usual well-groomed self at all. There was an unholy light of mischief gleaming in those blue-blue eyes. "I want you, Delilah. I ache for you. Please say you feel the same."

His voice was low and liquid, exactly the way a man's voice ought to be on such an occasion. The words repeated themselves endlessly in her head. *I want you, I ache for you.* God!

Travis's fingers were caressing the palm of her hand, which made it impossible for her to think up any excuses. "Finish your wine," he urged, smiling that thousand-watt smile. "And come upstairs with me."

By the time they entered their room, Delilah was a jangle of nerves. But she was determined that Travis shouldn't know it. He believed her to be experienced, and she was too embarrassed to admit that she wasn't. Maybe he wouldn't notice.

"You can use the bathroom first," he said matter-of-factly. "I'll build a fire."

"Okay."

In the bathroom she was too nervous to go. She washed her face, brushed her teeth as best she could with her finger, and took down her long, thick hair. She wondered if she ought to remove her clothes. If she'd planned this a little better, she'd have had a sexy negligee packed away somewhere, but since she didn't, she was damned if she was going to walk back out into the room stark naked, no matter how sophisticated that might be. She did take off her boots and socks, though, as well as her sweater. After a moment's thought, she pulled off her blouse, removed her bra, then put on the blouse again, leaving the top two buttons open.

She checked herself out in the mirror over the sink. She was shooting for Lauren Bacall aplomb, but her critical eye told her she didn't quite make it. "You look like what you are—an embarrassed virgin. Why didn't I do it with Eliot Randall while I had the chance?"

"D'you say something?" called Travis.

"Uh, no."

She quickly opened the door. The lights were out in the room, but the fire he'd built gave off a warm orange glow. Travis was standing right there, one arm against the wall, leaning toward her in the sexiest manner imaginable. He, too, had shed his sweater and unbuttoned his shirt—all the way down his chest. She caught a glimpse of the golden fur on his body in the moment before he caught her around the waist and pulled her into his arms.

"You look great." He pressed his face into her hair. "I love this dark, sexy mane." He got his hands into it and tugged until her face came up. "Kissin' cousins," he whispered, then covered her mouth with his.

He kissed her gently at first, lips only, tender, teasing kisses. Then he tilted her head back a bit more and changed the angle. His mouth shaped hers, pressured it. Something hot and wet darted along the surface of her lips—his tongue. It advanced, courting, coaxing. Gingerly, she touched it with her own and felt the shivers run through her. His kiss turned rough. He pressed himself against her and slid his thumb slowly down the middle of her spine.

Delilah moaned and returned his caresses avidly. It was going to be all right, she told herself as he walked her slowly backward toward the four-poster. His kisses were deep now, fire kisses. Very exciting—lots of driving, demanding tongue. Yet smooth, real smooth. Experienced.

She felt the edge of the bed behind her knees. She sat down with a thump. Travis remained standing in front of her, his long legs on either side of her thighs. Dominant. She liked that. She was a strong and independent woman, yes, but for this she needed an even stronger man. He was undoing the rest of her buttons. Down, down, all the way to her waist. The bottom of the blouse was snagged within the waistline of her pants, so he jerked it out, then his hands were on her bare flesh. He covered her breasts with his palms, which felt very good to her. Her arousal mounted; she could feel the dampness between her legs.

Gently, he pinched her nipples between thumbs and forefingers. Her back arched and she made an involuntary sound. He bent his golden head and brushed his lips across one breast. She caught his head and held him to her while he laved the nipple with his tongue, then sucked it into his mouth.

"Oh God," she chanted. "Oh God, oh God."

He raised his head. "I've got some Trojans in my wallet. Do we need them?"

Had he brought the condoms knowing in advance they'd sleep together? Or did he routinely carry a few, just in case he got lucky? "I have a diaphragm, but I left it at home. If I'd known we were going to do this . . ."

"Okay, no problem. I'll take care of it." His hands were on her pants. "Let's get rid of these."

"I'll do it. You take your own things off and come to bed." Now, that sounded sophisticated, didn't it? "Hurry," she added.

"Impatient, huh?" His voice was a husky laugh, teasing, yet pleased. And he did hurry, coming under the covers with her, his strong naked body so hot and ready against hers. Delilah rolled to her back, expecting him to start immediately. She was anxious to get it over with. Now, quickly, before she got nervous again. Before he guessed.

But Travis had other ideas. He pressed up on one elbow beside her and pulled the sheet aside so he could look at her. "Your body is perfect. I always knew you'd be beautiful, Delilah. Your hair, your breasts, your long, long legs."

His blue eyes were full of compliments—that irresistible Travis Templeton charm. He touched her gently, whispering his praises over and over again. Her breasts, her belly, her thighs, and finally in between her legs. She was dazzled. He made her feel special, as if she were the only woman in the world he'd ever touched or looked at this way.

He kissed her passionately, then raised his head. He seemed stiff, and the muscles in his arms were trembling. "I'm trying to go slowly, but—"

"Travis"—once again she thought of telling him she was a virgin; once again she decided not to—"I don't want to disappoint you."

"Are you kidding? You could never disappoint me. I just hope I don't disappoint you. I'm the one with the overrated reputation."

They both began to giggle at this, which relaxed her briefly. But when Travis took her hand and guided it to his penis, which was warm and hard and, good heavens, terribly thick, she began to feel alarmed again. The description of Fanny Hill's first sexual intercourse came back to her with all its gory details. It had taken her first lover all afternoon to make any headway, and poor Fanny had suffered dreadfully.

He kissed her, rolled away for a few seconds, then came back. After that, everything happened very fast. He parted her legs with his knee, then brought the same knee up and rubbed it against her mound until she writhed in a most abandoned manner. His hand moved down to caress her. She was panting now, trying to pull him down atop her. He drove a finger inside her, then quickly covered her. His hard chest pressed against her aching nipples as he found the place and thrust.

Delilah tensed. His finger had penetrated easily, but . . .

"God, you're tight," he whispered, sounding amused and even a little pleased about it. Then she flinched and he held back for a moment. "Am I hurting you?"

"I'm okay."

He pressed deeper, and this time there was a brief, wrenching pain. She made an involuntary sound. Travis controlled himself enough to raise his head. "Delilah?" Blue eyes raked her, demanding honesty at last. "Is this your first time?"

"Yes. Don't stop. You're not going to stop, are you?"

"Does it feel like I'm stopping?" He thrust again, sliding completely inside her. She yelped. "Shit! I'm hurting you. I don't want to hurt you, love."

"It doesn't hurt; don't stop." She clasped her arms around him and moved her hips in what she hoped was the approved fashion. This felt good to her, so she did it again.

Travis groaned. "A virgin. My sexpot cousin's a virgin."

"Was a virgin." She was feeling better already. There was a stinging sensation, but nothing she would call excruciating pain. She stroked his naked back, sliding her hands to his buttocks. She closed her fingers on him, giving him a taste of her nails. "Do you like it? Tell me what to do."

"You're doing just fine." He covered her mouth with his and kissed her hard, then began to move with more authority. Delilah held him tight, feeling proud of herself, feeling as if she'd finally joined in the sisterhood of other women. Loving her man, feeling his weight upon her. She felt almost motherly toward him, especially when he stiffened and seemed to lose control for a few seconds. He moaned her name and shuddered in her arms.

"A virgin!" he crowed afterward, laughing at her. He laughed his blasted head off. Delilah joined in, although she didn't think it was all that funny. Now that it was over, she felt a trifle disappointed. She'd expected her initiation to be more remarkable somehow. When she surreptitiously looked for the traditional blood on the sheets that was supposed to mark her passage into womanhood, there wasn't any.

"How come I didn't bleed? Fanny Hill bled all over the place. I was a virgin. I was supposed to bleed."

Travis was still laughing. "You probably devirginated yourself years ago horseback riding or something."

"I never did much horseback riding—I'm afraid of horses. Maybe it was the Tampax. Grendam always said twelve was too young to be using Tampax. I didn't even have my period yet; I was just practicing."

He howled.

"Why didn't I feel as if our two bodies had suddenly become one? You know, like it says in romantic novels . . . 'She couldn't tell where her body ended and his began.' It wasn't like that. You were you and I was me and that was that. I mean, it was very nice, but the earth didn't move."

Her lover's hilarity waned. "You didn't come. I'm sorry; that was my fault."

"No, no, it wasn't. I was too tense."

"We'll work on that. It takes a while, sometimes, to get it right."

"You don't think I'm frigid, do you?"

He started laughing again.

"Travis, stop it! I'm serious."

He wrestled her down on the bed. "Nobody comes the first time. Stop being an idiot. If you're frigid, I'm an Eskimo."

Later they did it again, and Delilah concentrated so hard on trying to reach an orgasm that she didn't enjoy the sex at all, although he certainly seemed to. "I am frigid," she said mournfully. "That's what comes of waiting till the age of twenty-one. I must be all dried up."

"You've got performance anxiety; that's what's wrong with you. Relax. Nobody's keeping score."

It wasn't until a couple of weeks after the start of the affair, when she and Travis were both a little drunk, that Delilah lost her inhibitions enough to come to climax. When it finally happened, she laughed out loud. "I came, I came!" she crowed, as if she were the first woman in the world it had ever happened to. "Thank God!"

Travis nuzzled her throat and folded her, heart to heart, against him. "Silly girl. You're full of life and passion. I told you there was nothing wrong."

Her joy bubbled up. "I love you. I think I've always been in love with you."

His response came without hesitation: "I love you, too, Delilah. Forever and ever and ever."

17

"Have you seen Travis today, Delilah?" her father asked.

Delilah looked up from the letter she was drafting to the New England congressional delegation, imploring them to urge Congress to act on ending the war. She was in the dining room of her father's Walker Street house, which had become the command center of his protest activities. His student assistants were in and out all the time, sleeping there, eating there, typing position papers, using the half dozen phones. Someone was smoking marijuana upstairs in one of the bedrooms, and in the living room the Beatles were singing "Maxwell's Silver Hammer." The place was beginning to resemble a Haight-Ashbury commune.

"Not since this morning."

"Will you let me know if he comes in? I've got several important matters to discuss with him."

"Sure," she said, beating down the little voice inside her that said, "With him, Daddy? Why can't you discuss these important matters with me?"

This was unreasonable of her, she knew. She ought to be glad her father and Travis seemed to get along so well, particularly since David Scofield didn't like the Templetons. It was just that she hadn't expected them to get along quite as well as this.

"How's the letter coming?" asked her father.

"Fine. It'll be ready for you to sign in half an hour or so."

"As long as you're at the typewriter anyway, maybe you could answer some correspondence for me? When you're finished with that, come into my study and I'll dictate a couple of letters."

"I don't know how to take dictation."

"Oh yes, I keep forgetting. You really ought to take a night course and learn, Delilah. Useful skill, especially for a woman."

As he left the room a young woman she didn't know strolled over from the archway that led to the living room and offered Delilah a toke from the joint she was smoking. "Men," she said. "When the revolution comes, they'll run the world while we make the coffee."

"You're probably right."

"There wouldn't be any war if it weren't for testosterone," the girl went on. "Males are such aggressive shits. What we ought to do, of course, is get together with the women in North Vietnam and follow Lysistrata's example. We'd see the end of the war pretty damn quick then."

"No sex, no procreation. The cure could be worse than the disease."

"Sisterhood is our only power. These guys are no different from General Westmoreland when it comes to their attitudes about women."

"I'm sure you're right," Delilah said coldly, and went back to her letter. It was all very well for her to criticize her father. But her back went up when somebody else did it.

That night when she was alone with Travis, Delilah asked him if he thought her father knew about their love affair.

"No. I'm quite sure he doesn't. I certainly haven't told him."

"Neither have I. But people always think nobody knows, only to find out later that everybody does."

"Some of our friends know, undoubtedly. But your dad sees us as cousins, friends. I think he's totally out of touch with what goes on around him, particularly if it has to do with something as mundane as sex. The man lives his life on another plane of reality. He doesn't seem to require much in the way of ordinary human contact. Has he always been like that?"

"Yes." Her voice was sad. "Since my mother died, anyway."

Travis hugged her. They were in the living room of the small apartment he had rented near Radcliffe. "You said at the start you didn't want him to know. You wanted this to be our private business, our secret, our universe of two."

"Yes, yes, I know."

"Have you changed your mind about that?"

"No. I don't want anybody else involved. Not now, not yet." It seemed imperative to her that she and Travis keep their relationship private. She had told no one, not even her best friends at school. The world would crowd in soon enough; it always did. For now she wanted Travis all to herself.

Her lover was a woman's dream—handsome, good-natured, and romantic. He knew his way around the best night spots, restaurants, and private clubs. He had plenty of money and he loved to spend it on her—taking her to dinner at the Ritz, Joseph's, and the Cafe Budapest, lavishing her with roses and Dom Perignon, and teaching her all the different varieties of caviar. When she protested that his lifestyle was oppressing everybody from grape pickers to Russian sturgeon fishermen, he laughed and called her a Communist. It was one thing to work for peace, he insisted, another to martyr himself on the altar of social guilt just because he happened to have been born rich. "I've always liked the finer things in life," he said. "No doubt I always will."

When he took her out on the town, Delilah had to admit that she, too, felt the seductive pull and dazzle of great wealth. She wasn't used to it the way he was. Travis had grown up living a life of ease and privilege and taking these things for granted. In her case, although she would come into a considerable trust fund at age thirty, she was accustomed to David Scofield's Spartan ways, his dislike of ostentation of any kind, his seriousness. Travis wasn't serious at all.

"You don't seem to feel strongly about anything," she complained one day. "You just shrug your shoulders and smile."

"Come on. You know that's not true."

"And you're so even-tempered. Don't your emotions ever get out of control?"

"What emotions? Maybe I don't have any. Maybe I'm just a shallow son of a bitch."

"Don't joke about it."

"Nick said that about me once. I don't think he was joking."

"Well, he was wrong." Was he claiming to have no passion, no deep feelings? She remembered the rare temper tantrums he'd thrown as a boy—the times he'd beaten up his brother, the obscenity he'd carved in the apple tree. Both he and Nick had grown up trying to repress their emotions. Nick had been less successful at this than Travis; it had never been hard to tease Nick into a fury or dissolve him into tears. Travis had better control, but there was passion in him, nevertheless.

There was also a strong will, somewhat disguised by his charming, easygoing manner. This enabled him to be single-minded about the things he wanted, even his mental equanimity. "I wouldn't want to reel through life the way Nick does, that's for sure. He's always in the middle of one crisis or another, nervous and melancholy as Hamlet. It amazes me the shit some people put themselves through. I like my life just fine the way it is, thanks. I have emotions, but I'm certainly not going to wear them all on my sleeve."

Delilah thought about Nick, whom they saw now and then at peace demonstrations. He was a junior at Brown, and more than either she or Travis, he seemed to fit into the hippie category. He wrote bizarre poetry, refused to eat meat, and was—last she'd heard—a Zen devotee. Although Nick was extremely intelligent, he was a semester behind his classmates because he'd dropped out of school two years before, claiming to be depressed. "Life is absurd," he'd told Delilah at the time. "There's absolutely no point to it. I'm thinking of killing myself, as a matter of fact, so I won't have to face years upon years of wondering how I'm going to die and being terrified of death." He burst out in tears. "I can't face it, I really can't."

Alarmed, Delilah hugged him until he'd stopped crying, then called Grendam, who ordered Nick into therapy. It seemed to have helped. Nick went back to school, but he was still weird. The last she'd heard, he'd dropped some acid and seen God. He switched his major from history to far eastern religions and spoke longingly of making a mystical retreat to some mountain in Tibet.

Travis, in comparison, was the epitome of normal.

So far their love affair had been remarkably lighthearted and smooth. Although Travis had found himself an apartment, he kept putting off the starting date of his job at Templeton Tea. He had nothing to do but join in the war protests and amuse himself with his lover, and he made an art of the latter.

They didn't often argue—Travis didn't believe in wasting his energy arguing—and on the rare occasions when there was tension between them, he would disappear for a while. The first time this happened, Delilah went into a paroxysm of fear thinking maybe it was over, maybe he'd left her. She fended off her anxiety by telling herself that they were bound together forever. He could never walk out. Even as children they had sensed the power of their mutual love.

Her faith was rewarded: Travis returned later that night with chocolates in his hands and a silly grin on his face, and they fell into bed and made love for hours.

She loved him; she was content. Yet even so, she sometimes felt a shadow lurking, just out of sight.

For one of her senior seminars, Delilah was writing a paper on the history of the tea industry, and in the process she learned something that seemed to buttress her recently forged opinion about the imperialistic excesses of the family business.

"Listen to this," she said to Travis. She was sitting in his apartment with a fat history book propped up in her lap. "The tea business got nasty during the early nineteenth century, and the Templetons were right in the thick of things. Our sainted ancestors got rich trading in opium."

"Nice."

"Yeah. Grendam never told us any of this when she was extolling the family business. The East India Company started it, apparently, and soon everybody was following suit. China was the only place you could grow tea, and—"

"How about India?"

"Cultivation in India didn't start until the middle of the nineteenth century. The Chinese had a lock on tea production, and there were terrible penalties meted out to Chinese who revealed their secrets to the foreign devils. They were notoriously xenophobic and didn't care to be trading with Westerners at all, so they put all sorts of restrictions on the tea trade. The most important one was their absolute refusal to take goods of any kind in exchange for tea. They demanded payment in silver bullion."

Travis, who was reading a murder mystery, yawned. "So?"

"So tea had become such a necessary staple in the West by the beginning of the nineteenth century that the British began to suffer huge deficits in their balance of payments. Silver was pouring out of their coffers. They needed to find a commodity that would be even more in demand in China than tea was in England."

"Opium?"

"Right. It was illegal in China to grow or import opium, but British merchants found subtle ways to circumvent the Emperor's official policy. They grew poppies in India and auctioned the drug off to their Chinese agents, through middlemen. The setup was all very elaborate, but the bottom line is that more and more opium was funneled into China, resulting in huge problems with drug addiction, particularly in the port cities. But this is the best part—what do you suppose the East India Company demanded in payment for the opium?"

"Tea, I presume."

"Nope. Silver bullion. They got the silver, used it to purchase tea, produced more opium, demanded more silver, and so on, and gradually the balance of payments shifted back the other way. Soon China was facing financial disaster. The result was the Opium War, and the eventual breakup of the East India Company monopoly. Soon after that, tea was found growing wild in Assam, India, and Chinese domination of the market ended."

"So everybody lost?"

"The big guys lost, yeah, but in general it was good for the tea trade—more tea, lower prices. The smart importers, like our ancestors, made their money in the opium trade but got out of it in time to keep up with the changing picture. That's one thing they were always good at—adapting to the winds of change. But the great bulk of the Templeton fortune was made during the opium years."

She closed the book and thought for a minute. "I wonder what would have happened if I'd been alive then. Would I have been so intent on making a profit that I'd have traded in opium too?"

He shrugged. "Probably."

"I'd like to think not. What about you, Travis, would you have done it?"

"Yes," he said without hesitation. "From what you just told me, it sounds as if the opium connection was the only pragmatic course to take."

"What if that's how we had to do business now? What if we had to trade, say, heroin, to get tea?"

He shrugged. "It would be shitty, sure, but as they say in the Mafia, it's business." He grinned at her. "You're very idealistic, you know."

He was teasing her, surely. She stuck out her tongue at him. "And you have a criminal mind!"

"Uh-uh," he said, removing the book from her lap and tossing it on the floor. "I have a sex maniac's mind. C'mere."

When he kissed her, it was a simple matter to forget everything else.

Delilah sat in the office of her Beacon Street gynecologist and worried. Her period was three weeks overdue, and she felt tired and queasy all the time. Over and over she had told herself that she couldn't possibly be pregnant. She and Travis had been responsible about birth control. She inserted her diaphragm religiously, right before lovemaking, messy nuisance though it was. She probably had a virus. In a couple of days she'd be swallowing Midol for cramps.

"Your uterus is enlarged," Dr. Goldstein told her. He was middle-aged and comforting, one of the few physicians she knew who held an excellent reputation at the Boston hospitals yet still managed to come across as warm and human. "We'll run a test to be sure, but that's a technicality."

"I'm pregnant. In spite of the diaphragm, I'm pregnant."

"It's unusual, but it happens. These things have a failure rate of about fifteen percent."

Fifteen percent. She was caught because of a lousy fifteen percent.

"Do you intend to complete the pregnancy?"

"Do I have a choice?"

"Not in the state of Massachusetts. But there are other states where abortion is legal, if you can afford the travel expenses and the clinic fees."

Delilah thought of champagne breakfasts, nights at the opera, the thin gold chain ending in a diamond heart she was wearing underneath her blouse. "Money's not a problem. But abortion . . . I don't know." Automatically her palms drifted down to cover her belly. She felt strongly that the operation ought to be freely available to any woman who chose to terminate a pregnancy. She just wasn't certain that she, personally, could elect to have it done.

"It is a difficult decision," Goldstein agreed. "Go home and think it over. Discuss your options with the baby's father. If you decide to continue, that's fine; we'll make all the necessary arrangements. If you choose an abortion, I can refer you to several excellent colleagues in other states."

"Thanks."

Delilah walked out onto Beacon Street and caught the Green Line train for Park Street. As they jerked and squeaked their way into the center of Boston, she wondered what Travis would say. She hadn't told him her suspicions, but now, of course, he would have to know.

Why hadn't she told him? Because she already knew what he'd say? He wouldn't abandon her; she was sure of that. He'd probably insist they get married. She wasn't certain she was ready to take such a step.

"We have to talk," she said as they were getting into bed that evening.

"Later."

He leaned over to kiss her, and she realized that he did this all the time. Whenever she wanted to talk about something serious, he seduced her instead. By the time the sex was over, she was usually too cozy and contented to do anything but sleep.

"No. Now."

"Okay. What's the trouble?"

"I'm pregnant." She said it less diplomatically than she'd planned.

Travis laughed.

"I'm not kidding. I'm really pregnant, Travis. I went to the doctor today, and he confirmed it."

"Jesus." He sat up in bed and switched on the light. His handsome face was carved into a rare expression of dismay. "Are you sure? I mean, we've been careful."

"Birth control isn't infallible, it seems." She described her visit to the doctor. Travis questioned her as she spoke, and before she finished, she was on the verge of tears. "I feel so awful. I feel like such a jerk. I'm not some teenager who doesn't know any better.

We've been so damn responsible, Travis! Why the hell does this have to happen to me?"

"Hey, hey, Delilah, don't." He pulled her into his arms and held her while she struggled not to cry. He patted her shoulders awkwardly and said soothing things, but she knew he'd be much happier if he didn't have to deal with her emotions. He didn't like conflict. He wanted everything to be smooth and easy and trouble-free. "C'mon, it's not all that bad. As you say, we're not teenagers—we've got the money and the means to find a way out of this situation."

"Are you referring to an abortion?"

"Well, it's one answer, certainly."

"It's not an answer for me." She tore herself out of his arms, surprising herself with the intensity of her reaction. She knew she was being ridiculous, but her emotions were out of control. He didn't want the baby, obviously. He didn't want her. "I'm not having an abortion. I'm not going to kill our child, even if it would be the easy way out!"

"Hey. Calm down."

"Don't tell me to calm down. I'm sick of being afraid to raise my voice in front of you."

"As if that has ever stopped you."

"I'm pregnant, you son of a bitch! It's just as much your responsibility as it is mine."

"Jesus, Delilah, did I deny that? I've heard women get ornery when they're pregnant, but this is ridiculous." Travis rose from bed and pulled on his clothes. "I'm damned if I'll stay here and get screamed at."

"What's the matter—is a little screaming going to melt you, Travis? Why don't you scream back? Why are you so goddamn afraid of losing control?"

"I'm not afraid. I'm just—" He stopped, apparently unable to define what he was. "Shit. I'm going to find a bar and get drunk."

Delilah flung herself facedown on the bed. "Don't bother to come back."

He did come back, though, sometime in the middle of the night. He didn't seem drunk, but there was a faint smell of fine whiskey about him. No cheap beer or rotgut wine for him.

He came with a peace offering, a chilled magnum of champagne. Easing off the cork, he poured a glass of the golden liquid and put it to her lips as she lay propped up on her elbow in bed. With his other hand he gently patted her stomach. "You're pregnant, and there's a small miracle in that. One tiny, determined sperm fighting his way past spermicide gel and rubber and all the other natural obstacles in your womb to stick it to that microscopic egg and start a new life. I propose a toast to the little bugger."

It was moments like this that reminded her why she loved him. She opened her arms to him and they kissed.

They drank to his sperm and her egg and their baby, then he poured a rivulet of champagne over her belly and between her legs and knelt to lick it off. The familiar melting began in her belly and she drew him down on top of her. "Don't leave me," she heard herself say. "I get frightened when you leave me."

"I'm not going to leave. I promise. I love you. Forever and ever and ever."

In the morning he suggested they get married.

"Oh God, Trav, I don't know."

"What do you mean, you don't know? You're supposed to be thrilled at the idea. Half your friends are engaged to be married the Saturday after graduation. You see more diamonds in the hallways of a women's college dorm during spring of senior year than you see in Cartier's." He paused. "Don't you love me?"

"Of course I love you. You're my soulmate, my forever love. It's just that—I don't know—we're so young."

"Bullshit. People as young—or younger—get married all the time. Listen. I was thinking about it last night in the bar. We're going to have a child—a son or a daughter, the next generation of Templetons. Gran will be delighted."

It occurred to her that of all Minerva Templeton's grandchildren, Travis probably had the strongest sense of tradition. He was the crown prince, the heir. And unlike herself or Nick, he had embraced that role without rebellion.

"I've been screwing around with my life for months. Maybe this is a sign that I ought to settle down. Get my ass in gear and start learning about the tea business. Got to be a responsible husband and father, right?" He kissed her playfully. "You're not smiling. What's the matter?"

"We're cousins, Travis. I don't even know if it's legal for cousins to marry in this state."

"Sure it's legal; I checked. There's a whole list of people you can't marry—your mother, your sister, your grandmother, your mother's sister, and so on, but nowhere does it say you can't marry your father's sister's daughter."

Delilah frowned, leaning her chin on her palms.

"C'mon, cheer up. I know it's a big step, but I love you, babe. We'll be okay."

He was so sweet and affectionate that Delilah's heart opened. She reached for him and held his hands. Grinning, Travis went down on his knees beside the bed. "Got to be romantic about this." He kissed her fingers and looked deep into her eyes. "Will you marry me?"

"You ham," she said, beginning to laugh.

"Speak, I beg of you, fair lady. Make my dreams come true."

"Yes," she said, falling to the floor and knocking them both over with her momentum. "Yes, you idiot, yes!"

Later that morning, however, Delilah wasn't so sure she'd made the right decision. She fretted about it in class, hardly hearing anything her professors had to say. In the afternoon she rode the Red Line over to Boston and got off at Park Street. She came up from the subway station into the bright light of a spring day and began to stroll aimlessly through the Boston Common. She had to walk; she had to think.

She walked through the park, which had been the grazing place for the city's cows up until the middle of the nineteenth century. The trees were bursting forth their leaves, as fruitful, she thought with a smile, as her own body.

Without having any clear intention in the matter, Delilah found herself standing on Beacon Street just opposite the offices of Templeton Tea. She realized she wanted to talk to her grandmother. She needed her advice. It was odd how strong her need was to run to Minerva Templeton when she had a problem. She smiled as she imagined going into her grandmother's office, kneeling down and bowing her head, and saying, "Help me. I'm in trouble again."

"Shouldn't you be in class?" Grendam said when she entered her office.

"I've got one later this afternoon."

Her grandmother took a quick survey of Delilah's blue jeans and India peasant blouse. She was wearing an alpaca shawl from Peru and her generation's ubiquitous love beads looped around her neck. "I'm surprised you're not demonstrating somewhere about the evils of capitalist exploitation," Grendam said. There was more than a trace of bitterness in Minerva Templeton's voice. Along with her diatribes against the corporation and its policies, Delilah had scathingly renounced any ambition to run the company one day, and she suspected this was a disappointment to her grandmother. Of course, if she married her cousin, she'd be stuck with the tea company, like it or not.

On the wall behind the desk was a painting of a Yankee clipper with its sails full of the wind. Gazing at it, Delilah felt the barest ache to share some of that glorious past. Her hand settled for a moment over her flat belly, where past and future intersected. Imperialist whoremongers, her father called the Templetons. Minerva had retorted that that was rhetorical claptrap.

When the revolution comes, the men'll run the world while we make the coffee.

"I'm really quite busy, Delilah. Do you want something?"

Delilah imagined herself saying, "Remember that diaphragm you insisted I get four years ago? Well, it didn't work." Instead she said, "No, I guess not. I was nearby and I thought I'd come over and say hello."

"That seems a rather odd thing for you to do. Are you in some sort of trouble? Your ridiculous father hasn't gotten himself arrested again, I hope?"

"No, Grendam, it's nothing like that. Actually, I've been thinking of doing something rather conventional for a change. I'm sure you'll be delighted."

Minerva Templeton waited in skeptical silence.

"I'm thinking of getting married."

Her grandmother laid down the papers she had been perusing. "To whom? Some greasy-haired anarchist without a penny to his name?"

"No, Grandmother. To a well-educated, well-dressed, exquisitely mannered young man with an inheritance equal to my own.

He comes from a very nice family, he graduated from Yale, and you know him quite well."

Minerva Templeton blinked, obviously at a loss as to who might fit this description.

"Travis. I've fallen in love with Travis, and we're going to be married."

Grendam blinked again. Her face had gone rigid; she raised one hand to her throat in a quick, odd gesture as if she were suddenly unable to get her breath. "Your cousin Travis?"

"Well, of course. He's the only Travis I know. It's not exactly a common name, and . . . Gran, what's wrong?"

Minerva had risen from behind her desk. Her face was dead white. "You can't marry Travis. Absolutely not. I forbid it."

"Really, Gran, this is 1970. You can't forbid it." She was shaken by the intensity of her grandmother's reaction. There was an expression in her eyes that Delilah couldn't remember ever having seen before. It was as if Grendam was feeling deep, unrelenting anger as well as something stronger, an inchoate emotion that Delilah couldn't fathom.

"You and Travis are first cousins. It's out of the question that there should be a union between you. It's incest, Delilah. I can't believe you would even consider such a thing."

"It's not incest, nor is the marriage of cousins forbidden by law."

Minerva sat back down again, a little more color coming into her cheeks now. But she still didn't look very steady, and for the first time in her life Delilah thought, she's in her sixties. She's getting old.

"Does Travis know about this?"

"Of course he knows about it. What do you think—it's a fantasy I made up? We discussed it this morning." Delilah didn't even notice that her own doubts about the marriage had fled in the face of her grandmother's opposition. What right had she to dictate whom she should or shouldn't marry? Dryly, she added, "I wanted you to be the first to hear the good news."

Grendam's voice sounded breathless again as she asked, "Is he your lover?"

Delilah felt the heat come up into her face and neck. "I'm not going to answer that question. My sex life is none of your business."

"Keep your voice down!" Her grandmother was up again, going up and down in her chair like an elegant, Chanel-clad jack-in-the-box. "Do you want everybody in the building to hear you?"

"Why not? They'll hear soon enough that the two branches of the family are going to merge."

"They'll hear no such thing, by God! I don't know what could have possessed you, and I would have thought Travis, of all people, would have had more sense." She paused, her face whitening again. "Are you pregnant?"

Delilah realized she'd lost the initiative entirely. Grendam was the only person on earth who could do this to her. She might have been twelve or fifteen again, caught in some transgression and awaiting chastisement. And yet, this was worse somehow. It seemed as if, after years of getting into scrapes, she had finally done something that went completely beyond the pale.

"Are you? Dammit it, girl. Don't tell me you've been stupid enough to get yourself pregnant?"

"No, I haven't been stupid enough." Unlucky enough, yes. "And I'm not going to answer any more personal questions. I love Travis, and he loves me. That's all you're entitled to know."

"Love! I suppose you love him the way you loved that history teacher of yours, and God knows how many other males since. You're only twenty-one. You don't even know the meaning of the word."

"And you do, I suppose?"

Her grandmother's expression tightened. "What are you implying?"

"You've always claimed to love me, but I haven't seen much evidence of it lately. You hate my father, you denigrate my friends, you have no patience with anything I do—"

"You're right, I don't. You're a disgrace to the family, you and your father both. Getting arrested, dragging the Templeton name through the mud with your ridiculous left-wing activities. You're immature, disrespectful, and irresponsible, and quite frankly, Delilah, I'm tired of putting up with your outrageous behavior."

Delilah was reeling. Her eyes were burning and her heart had begun to beat very fast.

"I don't expect to hear another word on the matter, do you understand? If you are pregnant, which I sincerely hope you are not, you will have an abortion immediately. Do you understand me? There will be no marriage."

It was, suddenly, too much. Delilah did something she'd never done in the face of her grandmother's anger. She turned and fled.

Minerva Templeton slipped bonelessly to her knees beside her desk. She leaned her face against the cool metal of her typewriter table and saw a dusty plain outside Bombay. She and Edward had passed through the area on their way from Calcutta to Boston just after their marriage. There they had seen the Towers of Silence, where the Parsees offered up their dead to the sun, the wind, the elements. And the birds. When a Parsee died, his body was placed on a stone bench atop the tower. The vultures, waiting overhead, would descend and pick the bones clean of carrion, in a matter of minutes sometimes.

Why this image? She hadn't thought of it for years.

Her mind made the link at once: the stripping of the bones at a Parsee funeral and the melting away of the flesh on her daughter-in-law's body. Sarah Templeton had died of complications from an eating disorder. For dark, unconscious reasons that were beyond her control, poor Sarah had starved herself to death. Sweet-tempered, graceful Sarah, who had innocently contracted a marriage that Minerva had known in advance to be a travesty.

All actions have consequences. Before dying, Sarah had made a confession, entrusting to her mother-in-law a secret that Minerva had faithfully kept all these years. A secret that had frightened her, because of its uncanny resemblance to the long-concealed sins of her own life. As far as she knew, Minerva was the only person alive who understood the true circumstances of Travis's birth. According to Sarah, neither her husband nor David Scofield had ever faced up to what they must both have suspected to be the truth.

Travis and Delilah were innocent, but there was no excuse for her own blindness. What a fool she had been never to have foreseen the danger! It had never occurred to her that the two of them might fall in love.

They had to be stopped, of course. But how, how? For the first time in years Minerva heard the slow, anticipatory flapping of vultures' wings.

18

Two weeks later, armed with blood tests and a marriage license, Delilah waited for Travis on the steps outside Cambridge City Hall. He was supposed to meet her there at two P.M. At two-thirty he still hadn't shown up.

She was nervous. She had dressed for the occasion in a flowing white India muslin dress with silver embroidery on its fitted bodice. The dress was not expensive; she'd bought it in a Harvard Square boutique that featured various counterculture items like water pipes and Buddhist prayer wheels, but it was delicate and more feminine than her usual attire. She'd left her long hair loose, ornamented only with a silver ribbon, and instead of a pair of clunky stack heels, she wore silver ballet slippers with long ties that wrapped around her ankles.

Standing there on the concrete steps, Delilah fidgeted with the lacy sash around her waist and mused about the difference between her fantasies and real life. She supposed she'd always expected to have a traditional wedding ceremony—candlelit church, uplifting music, fresh flowers, a host of friends and relations, and herself emerging from a white limousine on her father's arm, gowned in a stunning silk organza original from Priscilla of Boston. As for the bridegroom in his dark morning suit—she couldn't quite picture him. She tried to superimpose an image of her tall, handsome cousin on the faceless man of her fantasy, but for some bizarre reason he didn't seem to fit, and this frightened her. Why couldn't she imagine her husband's face?

Despite the chill of a rainy spring day, Delilah felt a dampness beginning under the arms of her new dress. She scanned the sidewalks of Massachusetts Avenue and paced back and forth, impatient now. Where was he? Maybe he'd decided not to marry her. Maybe she was going to be left on the steps like the proverbial jilted bride. Maybe Grendam's disapproval had influenced him after all.

She couldn't account for the way her grandmother was treating her. Although it was true that she and Grendam had been increasingly at odds in recent months, this hadn't stopped Delilah from loving her grandmother and assuming that her love was reciprocated.

I don't understand it," she'd said to Travis. "I've always taken her love for granted; it was a given, I thought. She was there when I needed her, every time. But all of a sudden . . . it was just as if she despised me, Travis. I know I've been a trouble to her at times, I know I've caused her pain, but I never thought I could push her beyond the point of loving me."

"There must have been something else wrong. Some worry about the business, some difficulty occupying her mind."

"She acted as though I'd committed some criminal act." Delilah was profoundly upset, which, she could tell, made Travis uneasy. Once or twice he'd muttered that he wished she weren't so emotional.

"It's a shock to her, I guess," he said. "She was like a mother to us, so I suppose it never occurred to her that we could fall in love with each other. Maybe she hasn't faced the fact yet that we're grown-up. She'll think it over and change her mind; you wait and see."

He was wrong. Grendam had shown no signs of relenting. A day or two after that first confrontation she telephoned Delilah, saying that if she and Travis were still intent upon marriage, there were certain financial arrangements to be discussed. Delilah was amenable, until she realized where these discussions were leading.

As trustee of her dead husband's estate, Minerva Templeton had always determined the amount of the monthly allowance her grandchildren received from the Templeton Corporation. Now she made it clear that neither Delilah nor Travis would receive their quarterly allowance if they married. Since by the complex terms of the Templeton Trust they were not due to come into control of the capital until the age of thirty, this would mean that they would have no income from the family fortune for at least seven years.

"I don't care," Delilah said. "I don't need that money. In fact, I'd be perfectly content if I never saw a dime of the Templetons' filthy capitalist fortune."

"Wait a minute, Delilah," Travis protested. "Let's not be so hasty."

Frightened, Delilah lost her temper. She accused her lover of caring more for his inheritance than he cared for her. "You're used to being rich! You can't imagine not being rich. I can see it all now—she's going to *bribe* you to leave me!"

He did his best to reassure her, but Delilah worried herself into a frenzy anyway. Travis had admitted often enough that he enjoyed the pleasures that money provided. If he were forced to choose between his inheritance and his pregnant lover, would she really be his choice?

Travis continued to smile his golden-boy smile and tell her that everything would turn out all right. He loved her, he insisted, forever and ever and ever.

He went along with her hurried plans for the wedding, doing everything that was required in terms of blood tests, license, and plane reservations for a week's honeymoon in Bermuda to coincide with Delilah's spring break from classes. He was patient with her mood swings, which were more dramatic than usual, due to pregnancy hormones, she supposed. He was loving and affectionate when they slept together at night. He was going to be a sweet husband, a fine father. Despite the wicked old witch, they were going to live happily ever after.

Delilah was telling herself these things there on the steps of City Hall when the limousine pulled up a few yards away. As she watched, the chauffeur opened the back door for her grandmother. For an instant Delilah's spirits rose; perhaps Minerva had had the change of heart Travis had predicted so confidently. Perhaps she'd decided to give her blessing to their union after all.

But the hope faded when she caught a glimpse of Grendam's face. "Get into the car, Delilah. The wedding is off."

Travis Templeton was not introspective, but he knew himself well enough to realize that money was one of his weaknesses. In Europe he'd learned that not only did you have to have wealth to live the good life, you had to have great wealth. And Travis had every intention of living the good life.

Because of this slight flaw in his character, he lectured himself for several minutes before knocking on the door of the China Tea House Tavern, where his grandmother was waiting for him. It was the morning of his wedding, which Minerva Templeton had done everything to stop. It looked as though she was going to have one more try. In a way he admired her. The old campaigner never gave up.

Travis was proud of himself for resisting her arguments so far. Although it was true that he'd sat in a bar on the night Delilah told him she was pregnant and contemplated a quick retreat to Brazil or Morocco, he'd come to his senses, hadn't he? It was natural for a man to think about blowing town when a woman tried to reel him in. It didn't mean he didn't love her. It didn't mean he wouldn't accept his responsibility as her lover and the father of her child. All it meant was he wished the goddamn diaphragm had done its job.

Gran had been hounding him ever since she'd heard about their plans. She'd made threats. Tried to bribe him. "No," he'd said when she'd offered to triple his monthly allowance. "Forget it," he'd told her when she'd suggested a cash sum, payable immediately, of one hundred thousand dollars. (That had been tough, but he'd kept the image of Delilah strong in his mind.) "I love her. What kind of heel do you think I am?"

He hadn't broken down, and this seemed to him a milestone of sorts. He sensed that he was at a fork in the road, a point of moral decision which would determine the course of the rest of his life. He could choose the easy, carefree existence of a man who consistently slipped the knot of his responsibilities, or he could follow the path of commitment, the path of love.

He'd opted for love, and he felt good about that. He was getting married today, and nothing could stop him.

He knocked on the dragon lady's door. She received him in the parlor, in front of a mammoth fireplace that took up most of one wall. She said: "I understand the wedding is still on."

"Yes. Two o'clock this afternoon at Cambridge City Hall. Why don't you come? It would make Delilah happy. She's heartbroken over the way you've been treating her."

"Please sit down, Travis. I had hoped to avoid this. I had prayed there would be an easier way out. But you leave me no choice. I have something to tell you. It's going to come as a shock."

Now she's going to say I'm disinherited. She's going to threaten to cut me off. Let her—I'm not that stupid. I'll get the millions left to me in the Templeton Trust when I turn thirty whether she likes it or not. She loves to control everyone and everything around her, but she has no control over that.

"I'm telling you this in confidence," she went on. Her voice, he noticed, had begun to quaver. That was odd. She was so flinty, so tough. "You must promise not to reveal my words to anybody, not even Delilah. Especially not Delilah. Do you agree?"

Intrigued now, he promised.

"Delilah is your sister," she said.

Travis found it difficult to concentrate on the rest of their discussion. His grandmother, who was not really his grandmother, it seemed, gave him a faded letter. She explained that his mother had written it while in the hospital, dying. "It was a last confession. Sarah and I were close. She told me her secret. I didn't want to hear it, but she insisted she couldn't die with such a heavy burden on her conscience."

The letter was old; the stationery was dry and the ink faded. It was dated February 1952, shortly before Sarah Templeton's death.

The letter began with the words "To My Son." It went on to describe an affair Sarah had had with David Scofield, Delilah's father. The sentences rambled and failed to give specific dates, but his mother stated quite clearly that he was the product of this affair.

It was almost impossible to take in. Travis supposed that later he would feel both anger and grief. Now he was just trying to understand. "You're telling me that I've been sleeping with my own sister and that our child was conceived during an incestuous union?"

His grandmother's pale face grew paler still. "She's pregnant, then? I was afraid of that. Dear God." Minerva was pacing back and forth, her high heels clicking on the wide boards of the floor. "You're going to have to leave her, Travis. You see, don't you, why the marriage cannot go on?"

"Shit," he whispered, burying his face in his hands.

"Listen to me. She mustn't be told the truth." Minerva was no longer making any effort to appear calm. "She's so passionate, so dramatic. She might overreact. She might even . . ." Her voice trailed off, which was so unlike her that Travis looked up.

"She might even what?"

"After her mother died, she grew very despondent. Like Sarah, she stopped eating. I'm afraid for her. We Templetons don't respond very well to crises, do we? We have a long history of suicide."

"Yeah, the family curse." *We Templetons.* If what she had told him was true, he wasn't a Templeton. He no longer knew who or what he was.

"Delilah would never kill herself. She's too strong, too life-affirming." But even as he spoke he remembered how different she'd been lately, how short-tempered and nervous. Her emotional intensity frightened him sometimes. "She's not the type," he added a little uncertainly.

Minerva passed her hand over her brow. She was perspiring slightly, which was also unusual. Why is she so upset? he wondered. It's not as if *she's* the one who's committed incest.

"I wish I could be sure of that," she said. "To sleep with one's brother, to conceive his child . . . I'm afraid the guilt associated with that could be unbearable. It will be easier for you, Travis. You're not carrying within your body a constant reminder of your sin. You can't imagine what it's like to hold under your heart the issue of a forbidden union, to fear the consequences, to wonder if people will find out and how they will revile you . . ."

Again her voice trailed off. Travis stared at her, feeling the ghost of something move within his memory. She's not talking about Delilah now. She's lost in some grim accounting of her own sins. He didn't know exactly how he knew this. Something dark lunged up briefly from his unconscious. A man, drunk and violent. A woman, driven to the edge. And himself somewhere nearby, huddling, terrified. *I know her secret. It's not Delilah's guilt she's afraid of; it's her own.*

But he couldn't bear to examine it, this thing that was pushing at him. He forced it back down.

"Promise me you won't tell her the truth," his grandmother was saying. "You understand, don't you? We've got to protect her, Travis."

"I promise," he said slowly. "But she'll have to be told *something.* You've got to help me think of something to say."

"I don't want you to say anything. I don't think you should see her again. You can write her a short note. I'll give it to her. I'll take care of everything."

"But she'll think I've abandoned her. Jesus, Gran, it's our wedding day!"

"You're going to have to let her think that, Travis. You're going to have to make that sacrifice for her sake."

Something in him rebelled at this. Why should I, dammit? She'll hate me. Why do I have to be the one to play the part of her betrayer? *It's not my fault.*

But in the end, he agreed to it. He let Minerva Templeton manage this crisis just the way she'd always managed all the previous ones in the Templeton family. He didn't ask what she was going to say to Delilah. He didn't want to know.

In a way he knew he *was* betraying her, for he certainly didn't have the guts to face her. His grandmother gave him a plane ticket to London and a huge bank check. No longer a bribe, the money was the means of his escape. Incest, after all, was not your typical venial sin. He'd never been good at the ordinary confrontations of everyday life, and he certainly wasn't going to attempt to play out a scene that belonged in a goddamn Greek tragedy.

The fear of confrontation, anger, and the violence that could follow anger was so deeply rooted in Travis that he couldn't imagine doing anything else but running. He didn't want to face Jonathan Templeton, the sad-eyed wanderer who had joined the Peace Corps two years before and been sent to Africa, or his biological father, David Scofield, who was in Chicago at a peace rally. He didn't want to have to go to them and say, you fuckers, you ruined my life.

For his life *was* ruined. He had no doubt about that.

"I spoke with Travis this morning," Minerva said to Delilah from the velvety interior of the Mercedes.

"He asked me to change my mind and attend the wedding," the stiff little woman went on. She was dressed in a stark gray suit with a high white collar that made her look like a nun. "Travis has usually wheedled anything he wanted out of me. But some things cannot yield to Travis's charm. I was forced to draw the line this morning. I showed him the written order that would stop his allowance and yours. I also showed him the prospective changes in my will. And I made it clear to him that the job he thought was waiting for him at Templeton Tea would go to someone else if he dared to go ahead with this travesty of a marriage."

"I don't believe this. Why are you doing this to me?"

Minerva pretended not to have heard. She reached into her purse and withdrew a cigarette, which she lit with an enameled gold lighter. I've got to be strong, she told herself. If I am strong, she will continue to model herself upon me. She will come to understand that a woman can square her shoulders and survive even in the face of the most crushing disappointments.

"It wasn't difficult to convince him to break it off," she went on. "He knuckled under as soon as he understood that I was serious. Apparently he didn't believe that until this morning."

"Where is he?"

"On a plane. I have sent him away on an extended summer vacation—an all-expenses paid trip to Europe. You won't see him again for months. By the time he returns, you'll have gotten over this."

"You're lying." Delilah spoke confidently. "What is this, divide and conquer? He wouldn't leave me. He'd never just leave me without a word."

Minerva opened her alligator purse. She withdrew an envelope. Delilah's name was inscribed on the outside.

Delilah took it and ripped it open, trying, with the quick, careless action, to show her contempt. The note inside was short. She recognized her lover's handwriting.

For the first time she felt afraid. She felt her grandmother's power rising up between them, filling the car. When Minerva Templeton set her mind on something, she almost always accomplished it.

Delilah—

I love you, please don't ever doubt that.

I'm also ruining your life, and because of that, I'm going to have to leave.

She blinked. The letters had begun to dance unintelligibly before her eyes. She could make out only a few more phrases, something about not knowing exactly what he wanted, not being ready yet for such a serious commitment, not wanting to hurt her. They were both so young. They had so much ahead of them. All the usual excuses, in other words. He hadn't even come up with something original.

At the bottom of the paper he had written, "I'm sorry. Forgive me."

No, she thought. I'll *never* forgive you.

"We'll have to take immediate action on the matter of your pregnancy," her grandmother said. The smoke from her cigarette had filled the car. The smell was unfamiliar; Delilah had never known that Grendam smoked. "I've already begun making arrangements. The sooner the better. I presume you're no more than a few weeks along?"

"He told you?" Delilah was strangely calm. Now that she knew Travis had betrayed her, nothing further could surprise her.

"I asked him. I was afraid you might be pregnant. Having a baby at your age is out of the question, of course."

Delilah instinctively crossed her arms over her belly. "You're incredible. You actually think you have some say over what goes on in my body? You actually believe you have that right?"

"In this case, yes."

"Go to hell, Grendam." She spoke quietly; her voice was still very calm. "Maybe you have some power over Travis, but you're not taking my baby away from me."

"You don't want that child, and no doubt you'll come around to my way of thinking in a day or two. If not—" Grendam paused to stab out her cigarette, then resumed, "If you continue to be stubborn, I'll have to take stronger action. You're not having a baby, and that's final. But for now, I'm taking you home."

Her calm shattered. Delilah's entire body seemed to expand, stretching and stretching, faster and faster, victim of a madcap entropy that would scatter the particles of her being too widely ever to be regathered. Travis had betrayed her, and so had Grendam. Both of them, goddamn them. Both of them. What was wrong with her that the two people she loved most in the world could do this to her?

She pounded on the glass that separated them from the chauffeur. "Stop this car; I'm getting out."

The driver's shoulders hunched slightly, but he didn't respond. Delilah cursed him. When the car stopped at the next light, she ripped open the back door and jumped out into the chilly rain.

"Delilah!" Minerva sounded alarmed now. "Get back into the car. Where are you going?"

She didn't answer. She ran.

In the back seat of the limousine, Minerva burst into tears.

19

Delilah wandered for several hellish hours through the streets of Cambridge in the pouring rain. She felt impermeable; the water couldn't reach her through the glassy layers of pain that encased her. Her hair frizzed around her face, her dress stuck to her body. She didn't care. She was coming undone and it didn't matter at all, not to her, not to anybody.

I love you, please don't ever doubt that.

She hadn't doubted it. He'd been so convincing, after all.

Had he really left her? How could he have left her? Travis, her forever lover. Oh, foolish, foolish girl. So many women, so many short-lived, lighthearted experiences with the opposite sex—he'd left them, too. No doubt he'd been the perfect romantic hero to them as well.

She'd thought she was different. Special. They were playmates, soulmates. He would never leave *her.*

The rain still beat down, she still felt numb. In Harvard Square she stood on the island near Out of Town News and watched the students, hippies, and winos weave in and out of traffic. In front of the Coop, the Hare Krishnas danced, their tiny brass cymbals twinkling. Should she cut off all her hair and don a saffron robe? Dance and sing all day long like a child, face innocent, body pure?

She wandered into the old burial ground and walked among the gravestones. Many of the inscriptions had been smoothed away by the elements. Here lies Nobody. Dust thou art, to dust thou shalt return. As she stood there the world around her faded, buildings vanished, and nothing was left except a few small clearings carved from the great eastern forest. So had it been in the seventeenth century during Helen Templeton's time. Helen Templeton, who had loved a man and borne an illegitimate child. Betrayed and abandoned—it was woman's lot. You love a man and give him your body. He gives you a child and leaves you to bear the flesh of his flesh alone.

She passed the Episcopal church where she had been christened at the age of three months. Her mother, her father, her grandmother all must have held her in their arms. She hugged herself, thinking of the child in her womb, imagining how she—for surely it was a little girl—would look when she was born. *You're not having that baby.* The arrogance of Grendam! What had she meant by stronger action? Delilah envisioned herself being bundled off into a car and taken to some private clinic for a forced abortion. Was her grandmother that powerful? Did she hate her so much that she could kill her unborn child?

She crossed the street to the Cambridge Common. A black girl in a poncho and ripped blue jeans offered her a hit from a wetly smoldering joint, but she walked right past her. The rain had let up a little. She trudged up Mass Ave toward North Cambridge, past the law school, past Walker Street, where her father lived, past the College Grill, where she and Travis had gone for pizza that first day. On a plane. She was carrying his child and he was on a plane.

Houses, shops, apartment buildings, and restaurants passed in a dream. Parking lots, department stores, donut shops, gas stations, and junk shops. Churches, funeral homes, furniture showrooms, and used car dealers. How they amused her—all the myriad trappings of life. She crossed a highway and a river. She walked into Arlington. She walked until her feet felt thick and her back ached, low. She felt a little crampy, the way she felt when she was getting her period. But she wasn't getting her period. She was pregnant with an illegitimate child.

When she finally gave out, a couple of miles farther up Mass Ave, she simply sank down on the curb and rested her head on her knees. The afternoon had faded to dusk, and soon it would be night. She wondered, without caring very much, how long it would be before someone reported her and the cops came.

Her grandmother's Mercedes got to her first, its Nazi nose sniffing her where she sat as it pulled alongside. Delilah rose, shivering with cold and unable to believe that Grendam had come after her. As it turned out, she hadn't. A blue-jeaned, long-haired hippie got out of the car—her cousin Nick. While she sat there on the curb, blinking stupidly at him, he came around, took her arms, jerked her to her feet, and shoved her in a very un-Nick-like manner in the direction of the car.

"Get in. I've been cruising the streets looking for you for hours."

"Did she send you?"

"Yes. I was about to give up. How'd you get this far anyway? You're in fucking Lexington."

"I'm not going back with you. I never want to see her again as long as I live."

"I'm not taking you to her place. Come on, let's go."

"Do you know what happened?"

"I know a little," he said grimly. "I know enough."

"Where are you taking me?"

"Wherever you want to go. I'm trying to get you off the streets, Delilah. At this rate, God knows what's going to happen to you."

"I don't care what happens to me."

"Maybe not, but I do."

"Dear old faithful Nick. Always ready to do somebody a good deed."

He opened the door on the passenger's side and pushed her inside. When he joined her in the front and restarted the engine, she said, "I can't go back to the apartment. I don't think I can stand to be in that place."

"Your father's?"

"No." Her father had been no help at all during this mess. He, too, had insisted she couldn't marry Travis. In fact, he'd denounced the idea almost as passionately as he'd been denouncing the Vietnam War. Everyone had been against their wedding, and now they'd all won. Delilah hoped they choked on it.

"How about a motel?"

"You can take me to the river for all I care."

Nick made an exasperated sound and pulled out into traffic. Half an hour later they checked into a room at the Marriott in Newton. Delilah walked straight to the bed and collapsed upon it.

Her stomach was aching, a low, dull pain. She almost welcomed it —physical pain was preferable to the mental agony she'd been suffering all afternoon.

"I'm not just leaving you here," said Nick. "How will you get home?"

She didn't know.

"You're drenched from the rain. You should take off your clothes and get into a hot shower."

"Is Travis really on a plane?"

"Apparently. The chauffeur told me he'd driven him to Logan Airport." He spoke tersely, and she could see that his hands were clenched into fists. "Jesus, Delilah. How could you do it? Travis of all people? He's a shit!"

"He's your brother."

"He's a selfish shit and he always has been. You knew that; you must have. Do you have any idea how many girls he's sweet-talked into bed over the last several years?"

"I don't care. I love him."

"He uses people—charms the pants off them, then tosses them aside when he's through. You grew up with him, for God's sake. Couldn't you see what he was?"

"How can you say such things about your own brother?"

"Just because he's my brother doesn't mean I have to like him. Jesus. I feel like following him to Europe and throttling the son of a bitch."

"You're a pacifist."

"He's a shit."

"I can't believe he left me. I just can't believe it, Nick." All of a sudden her body began to vibrate with a new emotion—anger. "I'll never forgive him for this. I hate him, and I hate Grendam, too."

Nick pushed a hand through his stringy dark hair—he was wearing it down to his shoulders, tied back in a ponytail like so many of the war protesters she knew. He was skinny—all arms and legs—and his blue jeans were ragged. He said, "You shouldn't lie around in those wet things."

He's probably right, she thought vaguely. It's probably not good for the baby. She touched her belly. Hi, kid. I love you. Your father's a shit and it's just us now, you and me.

In response, her belly cramped. A current of fear ran through her. Why's it doing that? It's never done that before. There isn't anything wrong with the baby, is there?

"I hate to leave you," said Nick. "Are you sure you're going to be all right?"

She rolled to her side, pushing herself up to one elbow. Nick had retreated to the threshold. She saw him cast a surreptitious glance around, as if he had just realized they were alone together in a motel room, and that he had suggested she take off her clothes. "Why did you come after me? What do you care what happens to me? Nobody else does, so why do you?"

"Our grandmother cares."

"Don't lie to me!" She screamed the words at him. "Everybody else lies to me, goddamn it, but not you, Nick!"

He left the doorway and crossed the room to her side. "I don't lie."

"Then you're blind, because it's obvious she hates me. She's proven it. I've disappointed her once too often, and now she's lost patience with me. But I don't know why, I don't understand, and between them, she and Travis are killing me."

He sat down beside her and put his arms around her. "That's not the way it is. There's something funny going on. I don't understand it either. I don't know about Travis. He puts himself first and always has, but Gran loves you, Delilah; I'm sure of that."

But he was wrong; he had to be. It flashed upon her that the worst betrayal was Grendam's because maybe Travis *was* a little self-absorbed, and maybe she'd always known that. She'd trusted him, yes, and loved him, but there had been moments when she hadn't been sure, moments when she'd almost seemed to sense something like this was coming.

But there'd been no such moments with her grandmother. Grendam might not be effusive or outwardly affectionate, but Delilah had never doubted her love. Ever since that night so long ago in the China Tea House Tavern when Gran had come to her and calmed her fears and held her close until the dawn, Delilah had taken that love for granted. It was there for her, strong, steady, unconditional. She had not thought it possible to sever that bond.

"Oh God, oh God," she whispered as the room appeared to close in upon her. She felt as if her mother had died again and that strong, protective force she needed to sustain her had been withdrawn. She was frightened; she wanted to howl out her rage, her pain. She wanted to grieve as she had grieved that long-ago night. She was crying already, inside.

"It's okay, it's okay," said Nick. He turned her so her face was against his chest and rocked her while she cried. He held her as Grendam had held her; he filled that empty place. When her body went limp and her head drooped, he lay down beside her the way Grendam had done and she burrowed against him, trying to make herself smaller, trying to hide, to disappear. He was her cave, her rock. He was warm and kind and surprisingly strong. He wasn't sexy like his brother; he didn't know how to seduce, to charm. He was just Nick. Safe, shy, comfortable Nick.

As her tears slowly tapered off, her brain began making the inevitable comparisons between Nick and his brother. He wasn't handsome. His face was too thin and pale, and his eyes—if you could find them behind his Coke-bottle glasses—lacked Travis's vibrancy. His lips were thin, severe almost, and his front teeth slightly askew. He had a high-arching forehead, shoulders that slouched from bending over his books, and a body that was almost as uncoordinated at it had been when he was ten.

He was introspective, sometimes painfully so. He suffered greatly from periodic depression and nervous attacks that left him weak and shaking. She remembered these bad periods from their childhood; one night she had held his skinny body in her arms, trying to comfort him while he trembled ceaselessly over some nameless, faceless terror. "The stairs," he'd repeated over and over. "The stairs."

He'd confessed to her that during one of his meditations, he'd looked into the void at the center of all existence and reexperienced the primal moment of creation. "I saw this tree. It was ancient and beautiful, with strong yet delicate branches, and roots that probed deep into the earth. As soon as I saw it, I knew it was the symbol of all life. It sprang out of the void and filled my spirit with joy."

He was too imaginative, Grendam had often said. That imagination, she predicted, would either be the making or the ruin of him.

As they lay there, passionlessly embracing on a motel bed, it struck her that she knew more of Nick's inner life than she had ever known of Travis's.

"Are you okay?" he asked. "No more tears?"

"I guess so. Thank you. You're really nice, you know that?"

"No I'm not." He turned her face slightly with his palm and looked into her eyes. He smiled. He bent his head. Very naturally, it seemed, he kissed her. He stopped for a moment to take off his glasses, then started in again. She thought of nothing except that his kisses were unthreatening, sweet. But they were not shy kisses; neither were they awkward.

He's the first boy who ever kissed me, she thought, and the memory made her smile. She shifted to her back and he came with her, half covering her, his chest hard against hers. The kisses deepened; his tongue slipped between her lips and probed tentatively. Soon she felt the light touch of his hand on the side of her throat. It slid down to her collarbone, her breasts. His fingers were long and sensitive; they skimmed but did not press. He felt good to her, very good, but the feelings had nothing to do with passion. She just needed him. She needed somebody.

Nick lifted his head and took a deep breath. His eyes—it was strange to be able to see his eyes—were slightly dilated. Delilah shifted, and her thigh made contact with the bulge in the front of his jeans. Awareness shot through her. He was male and she was female. Call it comfort, but spell it S-E-X.

Her expression must have altered, for he sat up, shaking his head. "I'm sorry. God. I didn't mean that to happen, I swear." He pushed off the bed.

Delilah felt an elemental panic. He was leaving her.

"It's all right." Quickly she rolled onto her side and reached over her shoulders for the buttons of her delicate white dress. They eluded her. "Help me, Nick. Help me, please."

Nick backed away from her. "What are you doing? Don't, Delilah."

She was wrestling with the wet muslin and kicking away her sodden slippers. "I want you to make love to me. Lock the door. Then come here."

"No! We can't. Jesus. Stop acting crazy."

"I need you." She got the dress off and balled it up and threw it on the floor. She hated it—her wedding dress. "Come back here, Nick."

"Stop it. You're in love with my brother. You don't want me."

"Don't tell me what I want. And don't tell me you wouldn't enjoy doing it. You can't hide the fact that you're turned on."

She heard him blow out a shaky breath. There was a short silence, then he walked determinedly toward the door.

"No!" She could hear the desperation in her own voice. "Don't leave me. Please, Nick. Don't you leave me, too."

"Shit!" The door slammed with him still on the inside. He twisted the lock, seeming to fumble, then reluctantly turned to look at her again. "You don't even know what you're doing. It's as if you're drunk or something. If I stay, you'll be sorry afterward."

"I don't care." She wrenched off her bra, her slip. No stockings; that was easy. Her panties. She tossed them all haphazard on the floor and sat on the edge of the bed, shamelessly naked.

"Stop saying that." He was staring at her body. His eyes had darkened to black and his face was flushed with arousal. "You'll care when you come to your senses, believe me."

She ripped back the covers and crawled into the bed. It occurred to her that Nick wasn't like Travis—he'd never had an army of girls hanging about. In fact, she'd never really been able to imagine him with a girl—he was so awkward and clumsy and, for all she knew, too nervous ever to have tried his luck. He was still keeping his distance, still looking as if he might bolt at any second. "Can you fuck, Nick, or are you still afraid of girls?"

"Shut up. Just can it, Delilah."

"Remember—F-U-C-K? A vulgar way of referring to sexual intercourse. Ever tried it, Nick? Your brother's pretty good at it."

"You're pushing too hard. You always do that, don't you? You push until somebody feels inclined to push back."

"I can't wait to see how hard you push."

"You're fucking stupid, you know that?" He was beside her again, and he was furious. She lifted her chin, unafraid. Anger she could deal with; anger she could understand. "What the hell do you think I am, a goddamn Hindu ascetic? I'm a man. But you don't recognize that, do you? You don't even see me. You never have. It's always been Travis this, Travis that."

"You're jealous of him. You're jealous of your own brother."

"That's right, I am, because he's all flash and no substance, and nobody seems to realize it except me. He's a shallow, greedy, egocentric bastard, but you'll never see it that way, will you? Well, screw him! And screw you! You want it? Fine, you got it."

He ripped off his shirt. His shoes hit the wall with two loud thumps. "Maybe it'll change a few things around here. Maybe it'll make you realize that I love you, that I've always loved you, and that I'm probably a whole lot better for you than my brother could ever be."

And that ruined everything, for as soon as he said the words, she knew he meant them. And she saw—Oh God, she saw it so clearly now—how much she was torturing him. Until that moment she'd been too wrapped up in her own pain to recognize his.

"No," she whispered, covering her ears with the flat of her hands. He was bare-chested now, wearing only his jeans, and his fingers were fumbling with his leather belt.

"No," she said again as he sat down beside her and placed his hands on her shoulders. They weren't gentle now. His head swooped down and he kissed her, a bruising kiss, a kiss of domination. He might be shy, he might be younger, he might be no match for his brother, but nature had made him far stronger than she.

She flinched and tried to twist away, but he got his hands in her long hair and held her head still. He kissed her hard. Down deep she felt something stir, but she suppressed it. She was in love with Travis; it was unthinkable that she should feel anything physical for Nick.

She thrashed. "Stop it, Nick. Don't!" But inside her a voice hissed, if he forces you, it'll be your own fault.

"Shh." His eyes clouded and he bit his lip, no longer quite so angry, nor so confident. "Take it easy."

"You're hurting me."

The fingers against her scalp loosened. He sighed deeply. "Okay. Relax."

She let herself go limp. His arms went around her, gently now. "Forgive me," she said, low. "You're the only one who's helped me, the only one who really cares about me, and look how I've been treating you." She took a breath and blew it out. "I love you too, you know."

"Not the way you love Travis." His voice wasn't bitter anymore, just sad. "Not romantic love, not sexual love, not obsession."

Obsession? That's a bit extreme, she thought.

"I understand," he added. "I mean, I've always known how you feel. I've accepted it. It's just that kissing me, taking off your clothes, taunting me like that . . . it was too much. I'm sorry if I scared you. I'd never do anything to hurt you. I'd never force you, Delilah; you must know that."

She hugged him hard.

"I've had sexual feelings for you for as long as I can remember. The other kids were all in latency, but not me. When I was seven years old I used to dream about touching your hair and looking up your skirts."

The image was startling. Skinny little Nick with the huge glasses and the inevitable book under his arm. "But you were so shy. You used to run away from the neighborhood girls."

"Yeah, run to my refuge in the woods and huddle there dreaming about how I'd capture them, one by one, and make them play doctor with me."

"Oh, Nick." What fantasists we all are, she thought. What dreamers.

"You should have come to me if you wanted to sleep with one of your cousins. I'd have treated you a whole lot better. I'd have loved you, Delilah."

She reached up and stroked a lock of curly dark hair off his forehead. She felt compassion and a need to return his tenderness. She touched him again, caressingly. What is it to me? If it'll make him happy . . .

He understood at once. He shook his head. "Uh-uh. It wouldn't work. I want more than you're able to give."

"Oh, Nick, I'm so sorry."

"Just let me hold you. Wait." He rebuckled his jeans. "I'd better lock up my chastity belt."

Which made her smile.

"Come on, let's lie down together here and pretend we're kids again. I won't leave you, Delilah. For as long as you need me, I'll be around."

Delilah dreamed that night that she was with her lover, the

soulmate whom her spirit had known and cherished for a thousand years. But sometime in the middle of the night she woke and found it was only Nick sprawled beside her, barefoot and bare-chested, his lower body clad in ragged jeans to protect her from a complication that she didn't really want. He wasn't sleeping. His eyes were glittering behind his lashes, watchful as a predator of night.

"I love you, Delilah," he said, his voice so soft she wasn't sure she heard right. "I've always loved you; marry me instead."

Forgive me, forgive me, she was thinking as she said no, it was too soon, she didn't want to marry anybody now. I don't love you, Nick, my darling. I'm using you, that's all.

Delilah woke at dawn with a knife-sharp cramping in her belly. She stumbled to the bathroom to find that she was bleeding. Terrified, she stared at the blood and tissue that emptied from her womb into the toilet. "Oh no," she whispered. Then she screamed.

You're not having that baby. Dear God, was there no arena in which her grandmother could not win?

Nick came running. He knelt on the floor beside her and cradled her while she clapped her hands over her mouth and tried to hold in her sobs. Those she could contain . . . barely. But she couldn't hold in the fragile life that was dripping from between her thighs.

"I didn't know you were pregnant," Nick said, white-faced. "Jesus, Delilah. You were so upset, and I made it worse for you. You should have told me . . . I'd have never attacked you or frightened you or—"

"It's nothing to do with you," she told him quickly. "You didn't attack me. Please, please don't feel guilty."

Bending over, clutching her cramping belly, she thought, it's my own fault. She'd walked herself into exhaustion in a cold, driving rain. She'd had cramps. But she hadn't known, hadn't realized. She hadn't thought you could lose a baby so easily, getting upset, taking a walk.

Maybe it was a punishment. She loved the man who didn't love her, she didn't love the man who did. God was getting even by taking her child away.

God doesn't work like that, Nick insisted, but she didn't believe him. She didn't even believe in God. Certainly she'd never known the comfort of an all-powerful, all-compassionate transcendent presence.

"She's all I have left," she whispered, tears streaming down her cheeks. "I want my baby, Nick."

"We'll save your baby," he promised her. "Pregnant women bleed sometimes; it doesn't mean anything."

He telephoned her doctor, who asked a few pointed questions, then told them to come right in. Nick dressed her, wrapped her in a motel blanket, and carried her out to the car. He drove tensely, and too fast, reaching over periodically to squeeze her hand. "You'll be okay," he kept telling her. "The baby'll be fine."

He was lying, and they both knew it.

An hour later Delilah underwent a D and C in the Boston Lying-In Hospital. "We don't know why it happened, but we see this all the time," the doctor said briskly after it was over. Nick had hung around the hospital all morning, and the nursing staff obviously thought he was the father. "Many people don't realize that twenty percent of all pregnancies end in miscarriage. Don't worry about it. There's no reason why you two young people shouldn't be able to have another child."

Delilah heard his words, but they didn't console her. She knew she'd never have another child, for she was finished with sex, finished with men, finished with yearning for love that didn't exist from people incapable of giving it. Never again, she vowed. She was through with men forever and ever and ever.

20

On the third day of her hospital stay, Delilah thought she heard footsteps in the hallway outside her door, but when several seconds went by and no one entered, she decided she must have been mistaken. About a minute later there was another shuffle of sound. Delilah pushed herself up on one elbow. "Who's there?"

Her father pushed open the door. He stood there on the threshold, looking unusually weary and gaunt. Delilah let her body flop back down again. For the first time ever her thought was not, does he love me? but, who cares?

Her release from the hospital had been delayed because she'd developed a uterine infection. She wanted to go home but they wouldn't allow it. She'd hated hospitals ever since her mother's death; she hated them even more now.

Nick came faithfully every day, but the sight of him could not cheer her. She felt guilty about Nick. He loved her. She didn't love him back. She wanted Travis but he was gone.

Grendam had also come to see her, but Delilah had asked the nursing staff not to let her in. She tried phoning instead. Delilah wouldn't speak to her. She didn't want to speak to her father, either.

"What are you doing here?"

David Scofield pulled a chair up and sat down beside the bed. "How are you feeling, Delilah?"

She didn't answer.

"You were pregnant, weren't you?"

Delilah's throat ached, and there was a stabbing pain in her eyes. Thoughts of the baby oppressed her—she imagined a tiny creature crying out in pain and terror as its life was being washed away, and several times she had dreamed of a small white coffin. "It wasn't the right time, little one," she told her lost child in the quiet of the night. Oddly enough, the baby was more real to her now than it had been during the short period of her pregnancy. "I wouldn't have known how to be a good mother to you. I'd have screwed you up for sure. I wasn't ready, and obviously, your father wasn't either. I'm sorry, sweetheart. Forgive me; I'm so sorry."

She wondered if she was crazy to be talking to a dead child, a child who'd been so tiny and underdeveloped that she'd barely existed at all. Being crazy didn't scare her. Her body was empty and her soul felt stretched out, transparent. Frequently she drifted, not minding that her energy was scattered all over the universe.

Sometimes, lying there in her hospital bed, she remembered the Templeton curse. Under its influence, her forbears had been known to sink into depression, even commit suicide. Although she didn't actively fantasize about dying, the thought of being dead didn't frighten her the way it would have if she'd been in a normal state of mind. If death began to pull at her, she didn't think she'd bother to resist.

"You were carrying Travis Templeton's child," her father said. He had put his head in his steepled hands. The hands, she noted dispassionately, were manicured and elegant—a dandy's hands.

"Don't worry, you've been spared the shame of it, Daddy." She was surprised at the bitterness with which she spit out the word *Daddy.* "He's left me, but hallelujah, I won't be an unwed mother. I miscarried, or had a spontaneous abortion, as the doctors call it. The kind that isn't illegal because you don't have any intention of ending the pregnancy, because you mean to have your baby, and nobody, not even your powerful grandmother, is going to stop you."

"Delilah."

"I wanted that baby. Travis is gone, and she was all I had."

"Jesus." He sat there, looking stricken.

"You weren't around to help me. You've never been around to help me."

"I couldn't have helped you this time, Delilah. This child you lost, it was a mercy. You'll be grateful for this someday."

Grateful. Rage shivered through her. Listen to them—he and Grendam both. They thought they were God. "You have no right to say that. Only a real callous son of a bitch would even think it."

Her father's eyes met hers briefly, then drifted away. "I suppose I haven't been a very good father to you, have I?"

"You've been lousy, as a matter of fact."

"Some people don't make good parents. I never should have married. I certainly shouldn't have had children."

He spoke vehemently, yet there was no real apology in his tone. He was stating a fact. He seemed bemused by it, and sorry for her, yes. But she wanted more. She wanted him to say he would change. Become a different David Scofield from the one she'd known for twenty-two years.

But that was impossible.

Something had changed in *her.* It was as if her blinders had been removed and suddenly she could see. Travis, her father, her grandmother, Nick—none of them were exactly what she had always believed them to be. *When I was a child, I spake as a child, I understood as a child, I thought as a child; but when I became a man, I put away childish things. For now we see through a glass darkly, but then face-to-face.*

She saw them now for what they were.

She remembered a discussion she'd had with her father a few weeks ago: she'd asked him to tell her more about her mother. She'd felt she was losing her mother all over again because even her memories of that laughing, warm-hearted woman were beginning to fade. She'd been dead so long, she was so far away. Delilah didn't want to lose her completely. She'd hoped her father could tell her more about what Elizabeth Scofield had thought, felt, believed.

But David refused to talk about her. In all these years, he'd never wanted to talk about her. For a long time Delilah had respected this, fearing that questions on the subject would cause her father pain. But she'd been gone twelve years. Surely her father had exhausted his grief.

Instead, as always, he'd changed the subject to the Vietnam war, waxing passionate about the evils of the Nixon administration.

Delilah paid little attention. To the youthful Vietnam protesters he was a firebrand, a hero. But the truth was that David Scofield could love an idea, a principle, a noble cause, but not a real human being. Not his own daughter. And all her struggles to get his attention—for this was the light in which her childhood and adolescent pranks suddenly appeared—had been futile because he simply couldn't connect.

Her insights were confirmed by his behavior today. David Scofield had abandoned her at every turn. He was sufficient unto himself. He didn't need her companionship, and he could live without her love.

"It's over, Travis is gone, and I trust you'll be more careful in the future," he was saying. An unusual intensity came into his voice as he added, "We all make mistakes, especially when we're young. You've got to put them behind you. You've got to pick up the threads and get on with your life."

"Is that the best you can do? You the brilliant Harvard professor, you the articulate moralist whose speeches stir so many to outrage at what's going on in Southeast Asia? A bunch of hackneyed platitudes; is that really all you have for me?" Her fingers clenched into fists. "You're a shit, Daddy, a real shit."

He rose, pushing his chair back against the wall. "Obviously I can't communicate with you. Someday, when you're older, maybe things will improve."

"We can't communicate because you're a cold, unfeeling bastard who's never given me any love!"

"I see no point in continuing this discussion, Delilah."

His voice was implacable, his expression even more so. She recognized that look. It was as if a switch had been shut off.

So here they were, in the same place they'd been so many times before. Silence. Closed doors. A series of images from the past came back at her. Herself running through the rain, pigtails slapping against her shoulders, coming home from school to find her father out and the house locked. So many doors, always closed. Her father's study, her mother's hospital room. One day all the doors would open, she swore to herself. She'd force them open and walk through.

"Good-bye, Delilah."

He left the room, closing another door behind him.

Delilah jerked a Kleenex from the package beside her bed to blot her gush of tears. "I'm not going to cry over him," she said aloud. "I'm not, I'm not." The tears kept coming. "By God, this is the last time I'll ever cry over any man."

When David Scofield left his daughter's hospital room, he found a bathroom, went inside, and threw up into the toilet. A virus, he told himself, that's all it was. A virus, complicated by the fact that he always felt queasy in hospitals.

Afterward he washed his face carefully. Looking in the mirror over the sink, he combed his dark hair. There was a little silver around the edges, which added maturity and gave him a distinguished air.

He studied his face from one angle, then another. He had always been a little vain about his appearance, but surely vanity was not a grave character flaw. There were worse sins. *You're a shit, Daddy, a real shit.* He quickly blocked the memory. Where had she learned such coarse language? Certainly not from him.

None of this was his doing. How could he have known, all those years ago, that the actions he had taken to help a friend would have such disastrous consequences? He felt sorry for Delilah, of course, but she'd always been so reckless. Sleeping with Travis was a foolish thing to do, and there was no excuse for getting pregnant in this day and age.

He felt slightly queasy again at the thought of Delilah carrying Travis Templeton's child. If she hadn't miscarried, they would have had to tell her the truth, a course of action of which he highly disapproved. His daughter had no right to know something of so personal a nature. It was bad enough that Sarah had apparently told Minerva and that Minerva had now gone ahead and told Travis. He himself had never said a word to anyone. In fact, he'd never really been certain until last week, when Minerva had telephoned with the news of Delilah's plans, that Travis *was* his son.

David felt a twinge of guilt as he thought about Travis, whom he liked and was even proud of in a perverse sort of way. The boy's values were all wrong, of course, but David thought he recognized something of himself in him. He would have liked to have him continue working with Peace Now, but that was over.

No doubt Travis hated him now for something that wasn't even his doing.

Dimly, David envisioned himself back in college, listening to swing music, quoting poetry, getting drunk . . . he and Jonathan standing on the heights with the world spread out before them, both of them bursting with limitless potential and grandiose plans. Somehow, each year, the vista had grown increasingly narrow, the colors less vivid, the passions less intense. You chose a road and traveled it, then encountered a dead end. You took an action and lived with it, never dreaming that it could have such unexpected repercussions in your life. It didn't bear thinking about. If you allowed yourself to dwell on the myriad disappointments in life, you'd have little choice but to sink into despair.

Individuals were foolish, careless, and prone to making ridiculous mistakes; that was human nature. He'd decided years ago that the only way to hang on to that broad vista was to study movements, not individuals. The goals and feelings of a large group were far more important than those of any single person. By yourself you were nothing; life was absurd. Only in masses could you hope to accomplish anything at all.

David straightened the collar of his shirt and turned away from the mirror. He was giving a speech at Boston University in a couple of hours on the moral urgency of civil disobedience. He wondered if there was any chance of prevailing upon his daughter to resume her work at the peace campaign headquarters. His mail was piling up.

Delilah got out of the hospital in time to fumble through her final exams and graduate with her class, many of whom were wearing black arm bands mourning the deaths of four students shot by the National Guard at Kent State. Nixon had sent bombers into Cambodia, and on college campuses all over the United States students and faculty had gone on strike. The furor swept over Delilah, never quite touching her. The sixties had seen the murders of the Kennedys and Martin Luther King, and now it was unarmed students; who could be surprised?

Minerva Templeton came to Harvard commencement. At the end of the ceremony in the Yard between the Widener Library and Memorial Church, she marched up to her granddaughter and tried to embrace her. "Don't touch me," Delilah said, tearing herself away. "Don't you ever touch me again."

"Delilah, please, this has gone far enough. You can't ignore me for the rest of your life."

I'm sure going to try, Delilah promised herself.

"We're a family," Minerva said. "We stick together. Blood is thicker than—"

"I have no family," Delilah interrupted.

Her grandmother's stiff shoulders drooped. Delilah turned her back on the sight of those hard man's eyes filling up with tears.

To Nick, who was always around, like a guardian angel or a knight-errant, Delilah said, "Someday I'll get them. Grendam and Travis both. Someday I'll pay them back for what they've done to me."

"I wish you wouldn't say such things," said Nick. "I don't like to hear you talk that way."

But her fantasies of revenge were just about all that kept her going; that and the plans she was making to start a new life far away from the people who had hurt her so much.

A week after graduation, Delilah packed her belongings and left Boston.

PART FIVE

For her own breakfast she'll project a scheme,
Nor take her tea without a stratagem.

—Edward Young

Los Angeles, 1970

21

Delilah arrived in Los Angeles in the summer of 1970 with four suitcases that contained the only things she wanted from her former life as a member of the illustrious Templeton family in Boston. She knew no one in L.A., which was part of the reason she'd chosen the city as her new home. She intended to remake her entire life. She was going to become a new person in a city that was hot, brash, metallic, and hard—the qualities she intended to acquire for herself. Where old money didn't matter, and it was chic to be flashy and new. Where balls were more important than brains. Where nobody would care that her ancestors had come over on the *Mayflower,* although they might be intrigued with the one who'd been tried for witchcraft. She could become a witch herself in California and nobody would think it the least bit strange.

It was hot in L.A. The air smelled bad and looked worse, casting a brownish pall over the city. There were palm trees, big cars—lots of convertibles—and more limousines than she'd ever seen in one place. As she walked along Wiltshire Boulevard, people-gazing, she noted that both the men and the women were thinner, fitter, and less flabby than the average Bostonian. There were lots of good-looking men, many of whom had sun-bleached hair and weight lifter's muscles. Delilah amused herself with the thought that they probably spent their leisure time surfing.

She did have the address of one person in L.A. Dory Lester was a former girlfriend of Nick's who had dropped out of Pembroke to return to life in the sun. "She's okay, a nice girl," Nick had told her. Nick was the only one of the Templetons Delilah had informed about her plans. He had called her almost daily after graduation, not saying much, just letting her know he was there for her, should she need him. "She'll help you get settled in, I'm sure."

"Did you sleep with her?" Delilah asked.

"Yeah, for a while, but we parted friends. She still likes me, don't worry."

"Why d'you split?"

He shrugged. "Dory isn't the faithful type. I couldn't hack it. We were too different."

"Are you the faithful type?"

"Me? I guess so." He grinned. "One woman at a time's about all I can take."

He came to see her off at the airport. As they said good-bye Nick leaned over and hugged her, and they both shed a few tears. It was a special moment, fraught with affection, but on her side, at least, without passion. Despite those hours they'd spent together in the Marriott, she couldn't imagine ever feeling passion for Nick. The skeins of life were so tangled. How different it all would have been, she thought wistfully, if she could have met Nick's soul in Travis's body.

"I'll miss you, Nick. You're the only one of the Templetons I'll miss."

"I'll miss you, too. If you need anything—ever—let me know."

She had enough money to check into a cheap hotel in Hollywood, which was the only neighborhood in L.A. she'd ever heard of. She was amazed at the sleaziness of the place—it reminded her of Boston's Combat Zone. No glitz, no glamour, just run-down buildings, seedy-looking people, and porn. She went to bed early that first night, tired from traveling and from the excitement of starting her life over, but she was up at dawn to begin looking for a job.

A week later she was depressed, despite the beneficent effect of the constant sunshine. For some reason she'd thought her Harvard education would be the passport to a wonderful career, but such was not the case. She was forced to remember that she was part of the baby boom generation, and that there were thousands of other kids her age graduating from college and seeking jobs. Anyway, her education was impractical. Nobody wanted to hire an English major in 1970. Who cared about literature anyway? Did she know anything about computers? According to one personnel director, that was the field to be in. "Computers are about to boom. If I had some bread, I'd invest it in computers."

Delilah didn't know or care about computers. She wanted to work with people, preferably in social service of some kind. She was a good administrator; she knew that from her work on her father's peace campaign. She thought perhaps she could get a job with a nonprofit corporation, but they all seemed to require more experience than she'd had.

Unlike many of the other young women she met in personnel agencies, Delilah had no desire to be an actress, a rock singer, or a TV star. Nor was she interested in modeling. At one job mart where she'd gone to apply for a management training position—open only to men, it turned out—the counselor had examined her slim five-foot-nine frame, dramatic black hair, exotic bone structure, and sulky mouth and said, "You ever considered working as a photographer's model? How well do you shoot? Can you move in front of a camera? You got any objections to taking off your clothes? What about those legs; are they really as long as they look? And your tits—you wearing a push-up bra or do they really stick up nice and firm? Take off your jacket and let's see."

Delilah walked out. She'd heard of the casting couch, but she'd thought that custom only applied to the film industry. It had never occurred to her that a personnel manager might expect a payoff before sending her out on a job interview.

Later, when she'd considered the conversation dispassionately, she realized the guy might have been on the level. Out here women didn't seem to take offense at having their physical attributes assessed for potential commercial value. It was so hot and sunny in L.A. that bodies were pretty much on view year-round. You couldn't hide a less than perfect figure for six months under several layers of warm clothing the way you could in Boston or New York.

After two weeks of frustration, Delilah broke down and called Nick's friend Dory. She had been reduced to applying for clerical positions now, but even those were hard to come by since she couldn't type sixty words a minute or take shorthand. The hotel where she was staying no longer seemed so cheap. She hated to admit it, but she needed some help.

"Delilah? Of course Nick told me about you. Come right on over. Do you need a place to crash for a while? Maybe you can stay; my roommate just moved out and I was about to start looking for a new one. This must be destiny. What about a job? I think there's an opening at the place where I work."

Delilah liked her on the phone and liked her even more when they met outside the door of Dory's apartment on Sunset Boulevard in West Hollywood. Dory had bright red hair that frizzed around her face. She stood about five foot four and looked like a Barbie doll. Her waist was tiny, but her hips and breasts were voluptuous, and her legs were long in proportion to the rest of her. The freckles scattered across her nose made her look like a teenager, but the merry glint in her eyes was a long way from innocence. "My God! You look just like Nick."

"I do?" Delilah was taken aback. No one had ever told her she looked like Nick. She found the idea rather insulting.

"Not your face, your body," Dory insisted. "Slim-boned and skinny. You're a lot more graceful, though. How is Nick? I miss him. He was great in bed, one of the best fucks I've ever had."

Nick?

Delilah's surprise must have shown, for Dory laughed and added, "You wouldn't think it, would you? Good old Nick was full of surprises. He used to chant, though. In the middle of the goddamn night sometimes. Drove me crazy, all that meditating and chanting. I'm the one who's psychic, but he's the one fascinated with crystal balls and the I Ching and such."

"What do you mean, you're psychic?"

"Oh, I am. I have prophetic dreams, ESP, clairvoyance, that sort of thing. It's not always reliable, though. I mean, I should have known you were about to enter my life, but I didn't. It's a complete surprise. Come on in."

Dory's place was sunny and pleasant. The furniture was brightly colored, the air smelled fresh as flowers, and everything was spotlessly clean. There were paintings on the wall, portraits mostly, of indistinct faces done in bright, splashy colors. The execution was skillful and the emotion in the art extremely powerful. "Did you paint these?" Delilah asked.

"Yes. Awful, aren't they?"

"I think they're rather good."

Dory's smile radiated pleasure. "You do? Oh, well, thanks. I just fool around. I don't have any real talent, not for painting."

"What do you do for a living?"

"I'm an actress, of course, just like everyone else. Dreaming of the movies, going for auditions, never getting hired. To make ends meet, I work in a health foods store."

It was a story Delilah had already heard several times before while sitting in employment agencies and making conversation with the other clients. She couldn't believe how many people dreamed of making it in show business. They worked other jobs to put food on the table while they waited for their big break to come along. "What's it like working in a health foods store?"

"It's not bad at all. You meet lots of skinny vegetarian freaks." She winked at Delilah. "Some of those guys really show the benefits of consuming tons of vitamin E."

When Delilah looked blank, Dory laughed and added, "Vitamin E's supposed to increase sexual potency. I'm very into men, I'm afraid. Just can't resist them." She gave Delilah an anxious look. "You're not a lesbian, are you?"

"No."

"Oh, good. I had a lesbian flatmate once, and she had to leave because, as she put it, my heterosexuality was too rampantly disgusting. Another girl moved out because she said I make too much noise when I screw and she wasn't getting enough sleep." She looked concerned. "Will that bother you?"

Delilah began to laugh. "Don't worry. I'll stuff cotton in my ears."

Avatar One, the health foods store where Dory worked, was expanding and needed another clerk, so Delilah applied for and got the job. The pay was low and the work demanded that she be on her feet all day, but after she got used to it, Delilah liked the place. It appealed to her strong sense of the dramatic. The store was decorated in New Age chic: the walls were brightly painted with psychedelic, cabalistic, and astrological symbols and dotted with posters that offered information on macrobiotics, Transcendental Meditation, witchcraft, the Tarot, palmistry, natural childbirth, Zen, the I Ching, trance channeling, and sun worship. The shelves and refrigerator cases were loaded with such essential products as brown rice, wheat germ, bulgur, lentils, sesame seeds, whole wheat flour, unrefined sugar, brewer's yeast, tofu, alfalfa sprouts, organically grown vegetables, raw milk, lecithin, and every conceivable vitamin and mineral.

The customers were many and the prices were outrageous.

Chicken Rodriguez, the proprietor of the store, was a former Hollywood stuntman who had been seriously injured a few years before when the car he was jumping over a canyon didn't make it. He'd spent ten months in a rehabilitation hospital learning to walk again. What had got him through, he claimed, was the vitamin C he surreptitiously took when the nursing staff wasn't watching. He insisted it had accelerated the healing process.

"Why do they call him Chicken?" Delilah asked Dory during the first week of work.

"Apparently he was always terrified before every stunt, even though he pulled off some of the most reckless and dangerous ones in the business before cracking himself up."

"He's attractive, isn't he?" Indeed, Rodriguez was one of the most handsome men Delilah had ever seen: six one, curly dark hair, broad shoulders, and large brown eyes that radiated warmth and affability.

"Don't even think it," said Dory. "I can't tell you how much time I wasting drooling over him before I found out he was gay."

"What?"

"I know. Waste, isn't it?"

"Waste! It's a crime."

"Yeah. If only he were even a little bi . . . but no, I've tried, and so have lots of other women. Not even a flicker of interest. But some guy walks in barefoot and wearing a saffron robe, or better still, some biker in spurs and leather, and Chicken practically faints with ecstasy. Why d'you think business is so good? The gay community supports its own."

It was true that there were a lot of attractive young men coming in to buy dietary supplements. But there were also plenty of straights, some of them hippie types, but many others ordinary businessmen and housewives. The heterogeneous nature of the clientele convinced Delilah that unless it was a fad, the health foods industry could become big business. And business, for some reason, was something that she was increasingly fascinated with. It was in the genes, she supposed.

How do you know if something's a fad? She studied the customers. The barefoot young hippies who ate nothing but brown rice would grow older, get jobs, join the establishment, and go back to eating burgers. They didn't interest her much. But the housewives who were feeding wheat germ to their families did. Most people have kids sooner or later, and all parents want their children to eat the foods that will make them healthy and strong. "I grew up eating hot dogs, canned hash, and candy bars," one young mother told her. "My arteries are probably already clogged with crap. I want something better for my kids."

The other group who interested her were the aging beauties, both male and female. They were the ones who dropped the real bucks in the place, investing not only in organic meats and vegetables, but in vitamin E creme and PABA. They wanted to age gracefully, or better still, not at all. Everybody gets old, Delilah thought. There was always money to be made by seducing people with the fountain of youth.

One year at Radcliffe she had written a paper for an economics course relating consumer buying patterns to demographics. She knew that she and her fellow baby-boomers represented a huge bump on the population charts. As they grew up and got good jobs, they would have increased buying power. Aim a product at the baby-boomers and you had a chance of getting rich.

Her contemporaries were beginning to marry and have children. A few years down the road they were going to start aging. Taken together, these facts suggested to her that the health foods craze was destined to be something more than a fad.

There were possibilities in this; she was sure of it. She didn't know for what, exactly. Her plans and goals were still nebulous. The idea of going back to grad school for several years to learn a profession didn't appeal to her, and the other path that had always been available to her—following in Grendam's footsteps at Templeton Tea—was clearly out of the question now.

Somehow, someway, she was determined to make a success of her life, if only to show her father and the Templetons that she didn't need them; she didn't need anybody.

So she worked hard, learning the business, reading every book in the store from Adelle Davis to *The Whole Earth Catalogue.* She ate the stuff, too, everything from waxy lecithin to carrot juice and bone meal. She didn't go so far as to become a vegetarian, and she was damned if she was going to replace chocolate in her diet with carob, but she learned enough about the tastes and food value of the different products sold to recommend them with authority to the Avatar's customers.

Delilah wasn't sure exactly when she realized that her interest in the health foods business was turning into an obsession. It might have been the morning she discovered Chicken's sloppy accounting procedures. One of their wholesalers called to complain that his bill had gone unpaid for three months. Delilah relayed the message to Chicken. "Jeez, I'm sure I paid that guy," he said.

"Get me the canceled check and I'll send him a Xerox. That'll get him off our backs."

Chicken couldn't find his canceled check. Delilah asked to see his books. "What books?" he asked.

"The guy is great with customers but a complete idiot when it comes to managing money," she told Dory. "I told him I'd do his books."

"Do you know how to do books?"

"Nope," Delilah admitted. She nodded to the stack of accounting textbooks that she'd just checked out of the library. "But I'm sure as hell going to find out."

It turned out to be easy. Within a month she had a comprehensive accounting system plugged into the business, and she took charge of all Chicken's ordering and bill paying. In her spare time she boned up on other financial matters at the library so she could advise her boss on where he should invest the profits that were rolling in.

"Look at you, you're really into this stuff," Dory said one evening as she moved a stack of business books off the kitchen table to make room for the pizza she'd brought home. "My roommate, the capitalist."

Ruefully, Delilah remembered the various scathing remarks she'd made to her grandmother about the tea business during her protest years at college. The truth was, like Grendam, she had a flair for this kind of thing.

Chicken Rodriguez was impressed. About six months after she'd started, he bought another shop—on Delilah's advice—which he named Avatar Two. He made Delilah the manager of Avatar One and gave her a substantial raise.

In the meantime, Delilah was enjoying living with Dory, whose flamboyant character was perfectly suited to Delilah's own. They did crazy things together. On days off they went to the beach, where one of Dory's many boyfriends taught Delilah to surf. Or to the chic boutiques and art galleries on Rodeo Drive to browse among the rich. Nights they went dancing, never lacking for partners. Sometimes they just hung around the apartment, smoking grass while Dory painted or read the Tarot and Delilah boned up on corporate strategy.

Dory was into what she called her Black Period. At first Delilah thought she was referring to her painting, but it quickly became evident that Dory was talking about her sex life. "I've had six black lovers over the past year," she confided to Delilah one morning after ushering the most recent kinky-haired stud out the door of their apartment. "You know what they say—once you go black, you never go back. Want me to fix you up?"

Dory was always offering, but still smarting over Travis, Delilah kept saying no.

"You've got to unload your grief over that creep. I've asked the cards, you know, and the answer's always the same: he was wrong for you. A disaster. The relationship was doomed from the start."

"I don't need a psychic to tell me that."

"C'mon, let me turn you on to coffee-grounds thighs, rhythmic fingers, and palms so pale in comparison, they glow in the dark. And the moves, Delilah. You won't believe the moves."

"Dory, I think you're a nymphomaniac."

"I know. Isn't it wonderful?"

One evening after a hard day of auditioning for a TV part she didn't get, Dory came home with the latest stud of her Black Period, an unemployed actor named Sam. He was six-six, hefty like a football player, and his head was shaved completely bald. He wore leather trousers with a purple shirt that was open at the throat, revealing smooth, muscular chocolate flesh. When he smiled, his teeth could be seen all the way to New York.

Sam Harris had gone to UCLA on a basketball scholarship, then joined the Black Student Union and gotten himself into trouble with the college authorities by demonstrating on behalf of a variety of causes, including racism, Vietnam, gay rights, abortion, grape pickers, and freedom of religion for Black Muslims. He lost interest both in basketball and in his studies (for which, unlike some college athletes, he'd had unusual aptitude), decided school was irrelevant, and dropped out with only one semester left before graduation. He'd avoided the draft because he had a slight case of scoliosis of the spine that had unexpectedly been responsible for his 4-F classification.

Sam proved to be the seventh and last of Dory's experiments in improving racial relations. Within a week he'd moved in with them and was keeping Dory busier than she'd ever been in her life. He laid down the law—"You're seeing me, Mama, and you ain't seeing any other men, black, white, yellow, or chartreuse. You got that, Dory-babe?"

"I got it, Sam." To Delilah she'd grinned and whispered, "Boy, have I got it! I just hope it lasts."

It lasted a year. At the end of that time, Delilah woke up one morning to find Sam on his knees beside her bed, tears pouring down his cheeks. Dory had broken up with him and asked him to leave, explaining, in part, "I love you, Sam, but you're too damn possessive."

Delilah put her arms around him and hugged him hard. "I'm sorry, Sam." She remembered Nick's words on the subject. "Dory just isn't the faithful type."

Sam moved out, but his friendship with Delilah continued. When Dory quit working in the health foods store to take a job as a commercial artist, Delilah asked Chicken Rodriguez to hire Sam to take her place. He was a vegetarian, and he knew as much about health foods as Delilah did. He was also a good salesman—he could sweet-talk anybody into buying just about anything, and he was such a colorful character that Delilah promised Chicken that customers would come into the shop just to look at him.

When Chicken got a look at Sam, he was convinced. "I'm in love," he whispered to Delilah. "Please don't tell me he's straight."

"Sorry, Rodriguez. Anyway, it's bad business to ball the help."

Over the next several months, Sam made every effort to lure Delilah into bed with him, but this was one bill of goods he didn't succeed in selling. "It'll be cool, babe. Very cool, very smooth, nice and sweet and slow. And it'll be hot, babe. Fire-hot, so you can't breathe for the burnin'. You ain't never had it so good as you're gonna have it with me."

"Forget it, Sam."

"What's the matter, babe? You afraid I'm going to break your pretty little honky heart?"

"Business and pleasure don't mix. You want to work with me, fine—we work well together. You want to be my lover, that's something else. Get yourself another job, then seduce me."

"I like this job fine, babe. Can I help it if I've got the hots for the manager?"

"I don't sleep with my friends, Sam. Look what happened to you and Dory. You're only just getting to the point where you can talk to her without getting that hangdog expression plastered all over your face. You and I have a good relationship, and I'm not going to screw it up with sex."

"You don't know what you're missing, white lady."

He took rejection good-humoredly, though, and they went on as before. Delilah wondered at herself sometimes, for Sam was a sexy, attractive man. The fact that he was black didn't affect her feelings one way or the other. Despite the myths Dory was always expounding, Delilah figured it would all be the same with the lights turned out. Men were men, and she didn't feel any need to experiment.

Now and then during that first two years as she slaved for hours among the bean sprouts, Delilah asked herself if there was something wrong with her. Since losing Travis and the baby, she'd felt no desire for any intimate involvement with the opposite sex. "I think I'll buy myself a vibrator," she laughingly told Dory. "It doesn't lie, it doesn't cheat, it doesn't bring home VD, and it's always hard."

"It doesn't hug or kiss or keep you company at night, either."

"True. But I can survive without that."

"Keep telling yourself that, Delilah. Maybe someday you'll believe it."

So she lived in California, land of hot tubs and orgies, and the sexual revolution was passing her by. *It's not important* became her litany. She was too busy creating a future for herself.

Now and then it occurred to her that Grendam would be astonished and, probably, proud. But this was a thought she invariably squelched.

Within two years, Delilah was managing not only Avatar One, but Avatars Two, Three, and Four as well. She liked the work, but what she really wanted to do was branch out on her own. One day, purely by accident, she found the perfect way to do it: like a true Templeton, she was going to specialize in tea. Herbal tea.

22

Delilah was having supper one evening with Sam in a sidewalk cafe on Melrose early in 1972 when she got the idea that would change her life. It had been one of those excruciatingly hot days when the Santa Anas roar through the canyons, chasing up dust devils on the sidewalks. She felt lethargic, and even Sam, with all his energy, seemed to be drooping a bit. His silver shirt was open all the way down to his waist, and his glossy brown skin was flecked with sweat.

"This stuff is awful," Delilah said as she sipped the tea she'd ordered with her sesame-grilled chicken breasts. "It's bitter and too strong, not refreshing at all."

Sam toasted her with his beer mug. "Be like me. Forget the calories for once and order a nice cold beer."

"There should be something you can drink if you're on a diet and can't stand the saccharin taste of low-calorie soft drinks."

"How about water, babe?"

"Water's okay for lunch, I guess, but in the evening with my dinner I usually want something hot."

"They make good coffee here."

"Drinking coffee at night keeps me awake. Tea doesn't have as much caffeine, but this stuff is lousy. My ancestors would scream if they could see what the American tea bag industry has done to the taste of tea."

She rested her chin on her hand and thought. "What I want is something hot that won't make me jittery. Something that tastes delicious. Something that will calm my nerves and soothe my stomach and make me feel good."

Sam grinned. "Delilah, what you want is a man."

She laughed. "No, listen, Sam. I've been thinking. Over and over, you know what our customers are asking for? Recipes for making their own herbal tea. I can't tell you how popular that stuff is. I guess because of the mystique that herbs will cure all your ills. Wouldn't it be great if you could sit down in a restaurant like this on a hot L.A. night and top off your supper with a nice cup of peppermint tea?"

"Just give me a beer, thanks. I may be a vegetarian, but I'm not crazy."

Delilah didn't allow his skepticism to dampen her enthusiasm. The dried herbs stocked in the Avatar stores were selling very well, but customers complained that there wasn't enough choice, and that it was too much trouble to grow herbs themselves and brew their own decoctions. There was definitely a demand for herbal remedies, she insisted to Chicken, who had recently taken her on as a full partner.

"I don't know, Delilah. We don't need to specialize in any one product. We got it made already as it is."

Indeed, business was so good they now owned eight stores in various sections of Los Angeles. Chicken had visions of starting franchises and going nationwide, the McDonald's of health foods. But Delilah wasn't so sure. There was something inherently individualistic about the health foods movement. A golden arches of tofu burgers was something that simply wouldn't materialize in her mind.

But she didn't agree with Chicken. You were better off if you could concentrate on a single product. Everything was so much simpler that way.

She began reading up on the herbal tea markets, and the more she learned the more it seemed to her that all factors were working in her favor. There had been some bad press recently about the possible dangers of caffeine, which had stimulated many coffee drinkers to scour the shelves for something else to drink. At the same time, an expanded awareness of the stresses of modern life had promoted new interest in diet and health. In California especially, where people were always looking for new tricks to keep them youthful and fit, the appeal of herbal teas was strong. Herbs were an ancient remedy now coming back into vogue.

Delilah came home one Saturday with several pots from a garden shop and a bagful of seed packets. She laid them all out on the kitchen table, much to Dory's amusement. "What on earth are you up to?" her roommate demanded.

"Herbs. I'm going to grow my own herbs."

"Why?"

"I want to understand them, that's why."

She read every herbal she could find, ancient and modern. The more she read, the more intrigued she became. "Listen to this, Chicken," she said while munching a honey-bran bar at her desk one day at work. "Herbal medicine has been around for millennia. According to this plant historian, the Neanderthal race were well versed in the preparation and use of medicinal herbs, a fact proved by the various plants, seeds, and stems that've been found in their ancient burial grounds."

"Plant historian?" said Chicken, raising his eyebrows.

"Several authorities have even suggested that knowledge about herbal medicines is so ancient as to be almost instinctive. In other words, we humans once possessed a natural herb-dousing instinct which enabled us to isolate medicinal herbs from all the thousands of varieties of plants that grow, many of which are poisonous. How else did people know which plants were safe for human consumption? Or, more to the point, how to prepare said plants, and what particular ailments they were able to cure?"

"Trial and error?"

"Maybe so, if they were willing to poison their first few patients. I don't know. This is sophisticated stuff. Highly complex knowledge that's not easily induced from trial and error. It's a mystery, Chicken."

The question of how the medicinal lore was preserved in any individual culture was less mysterious. Shamans and their apprentices would memorize vast amounts of data about where and when to harvest and prepare herbs, and what ailments they could be expected to treat. The esoteric knowledge would be passed down from one generation to the next, preserved by a highly secretive oral tradition. This was still the case in many countries, Delilah learned. Indeed, right there in California she came in contact with several women who claimed to be descended from long lines of witches, who had been transmitting information about herbal brews to each other for centuries.

She learned that herbal remedies really work, and that some of the most efficacious drugs in modern pharmacies are derived from plants—digitalis from common foxglove, morphine from opium poppies, atropine from belladonna.

She experimented with valerian (natural Valium, she called it), which was good for insomnia and nervousness. From the flowers and leaves of mullein, she learned to make an infusion that relieved bronchial inflammations. Boneset reduced fever, coltsfoot was an excellent remedy for coughs, and mugwort had been famous for centuries as a diuretic that also brings on menstruation.

Interesting also was what she discovered about some of the ancient remedies that had *not* stood the test of time. In Helen Templeton's day, for example, an apothecary would carry not only a wide range of simples and infusions, but also the popular and prohibitively expensive compounds known as mithridatum. These mixtures often contained as many as fifty exotic ingredients, including precipitate of coral, oil of yellow amber, raw silk, lapis lazuli, ground pearls, musk, gold leaf, dried mummy, oil of swallows, antimony, and stag's heartbone. Dead man's skull, she learned to her horror, could be bought by the pound in seventeenth-century London, and unicorn's horns were widely advertised, even though no one had ever actually seen a unicorn.

"I suppose it was no more unusual to hope a little dried mummy would cure your asthma in the sixteenth century than it is to swallow laetrile nowadays for cancer," she said to Dory. "With a lot of hope and a positive attitude, some of these remedies probably worked."

Initially Delilah grew her herbs in planters on the sunny balcony of the apartment she shared with Dory, but she soon ran out of space. "We're going to have to move to a new place," she told Dory. "I need a garden."

"Are you serious? We can't afford a new place."

"Yes we can. Chicken's giving me a nice raise."

"Does he know about that yet?"

"No," Delilah said, laughing. "But I'll talk him into it, never fear."

They managed to find a small apartment on the first floor of an old Laurel Canyon home that had once belonged to Jean Harlow. Delilah loved the place. It had a view of the L.A. basin and a third of an acre of overgrown lawn in back that she was free to do whatever she wanted with. She cleared it and tilled it and planted her herb garden, carefully arranging the order of her plants so the ones that needed sun received it, and those that needed plenty of water were easily accessible to her hose.

She soon developed a routine. She planted and watered and pruned and staked, talking shamelessly to her herbs all the while. Following the advice of the friendly witch who lived up the road, she worked in the garden barefoot, and was careful not to let the iron of her knife touch the earth. When the herbs were ready to be plucked, she gathered them carefully and sorted them, separating them into roots, leaves, stems, and seeds. Some she dried, some she boiled, some she pounded, relying on her herbal books, her intuition, and Mara—the witch's—advice.

Careful though she was, she made an occasional mistake: once she broke out in a vicious rash from handling a potent distillate; another time she made herself violently ill from drinking too strong a mixture of one of her first herbal teas.

Chicken, Sam, Dory, and most of her other friends regarded her obsession as a harmless, if rather bizarre, hobby. Apart from Mara, very few of her acquaintances realized that Delilah was creating a potent, even dangerous, pharmacopoeia right in her own kitchen.

"You should study this stuff with me," she said to Dory. "I would think someone with your interest in psychic phenomena would want to learn the ancient methods by which witches and other practitioners of the paranormal operate. There are certain herbs you can take that will enhance your ESP, or even induce a trance. Witches used to 'fly' by making ointments of such narcotics as aconite, henbane, and deadly nightshade, which would be absorbed through the skin. The witch would then hallucinate her flight, or—if some of the legends are to be believed—actually free her spirit from her body and soar with the help of the drug."

"I don't do hallucinogens," Dory said. "I dropped some acid in college and bounced off walls for about a week. Saw visions and everything." She shivered. "Several of them came true. That was when I found out for sure I was psychic. I've always sensed things about people, even when I was a kid, but I didn't realize I was different. My great-aunt Agatha was a medium, you see. She was pretty famous back in the twenties and thirties."

"You mean she communicated with the dead?"

"Spiritualism, they call it. Yes."

"That's all been debunked, hasn't it? Weren't most of the mediums of that era frauds?"

"Some were frauds, yes. Other may have been genuine for at least some of the time. And some—Aunt Agatha among them—have never been adequately explained."

Delilah's dabbling in witchcraft had started her thinking a bit about metaphysics. She and Dory had rarely discussed such matters. "Do you believe we have souls that live on after death?" she asked.

"Yes. What's more, I think we're reincarnated. I'm sure of it, as a matter of fact."

"How can you be sure?"

"Ever since childhood I've had dreams of other places, other times."

"Everybody has dreams of other places, other times."

"This is different. I go somewhere—Rome, for example—and I know I've been there before. It's not just a vague sense of déjà vu. I can find my way around in the streets. Sometimes it's changed because of modernization, and I get so confused. Things aren't where they're supposed to be anymore. It's a weird feeling."

"Jesus, Dory, you've never told me this."

"I don't like to think about it. It makes me nervous. I saw my parents' death six months before it happened. They were killed in a private plane crash. I saw it all—even the serial number on the plane and the dress my mother was wearing that day. When I had the dream, she didn't even own such a dress. She bought it the week before her death."

"My God!"

"There have been other things like that, nothing quite so dramatic, thank goodness. I know I could see more if I pursued it, but the power frightens me. Who needs visions of tragedies, particularly if you can't do anything to avert them? Anyway, I'm not infallible—I've had visions that didn't come true, too. Predicting the future, it seems, is a very tricky business."

"I wish you could predict the future of my herbal tea business."

Dory grinned. "I don't need psychic powers for that. It's going to be an enormous success."

Although she was experimenting with herbal drugs, Delilah's real goal was to develop a cheap and appealing line of herbal teas. They had to be mild, without strong pharmacological properties, since anything billed as medicinal would have to pass muster with the Food and Drug Administration, a hassle she would just as soon avoid. She needed something innocuous enough to be considered a safe food at any dosage, yet potent enough to convince her customers that drinking the stuff would have some sort of beneficial effect upon their bodies.

There simply weren't all that many herbs that fit these requirements, but after endless experiments, she developed six blends of herbal tea using such ingredients as peppermint, chamomile, rose hips, lemongrass, coltsfoot, valerian, scullcap, fennel, cinnamon, hawthorn berries, and ginseng.

"Okay, Rodriguez," she said one day in the fall of 1972, "I'm ready to try and market this stuff."

"How?"

"I thought we'd start by slinging a couple of pounds of each of my six mixtures into a cannister and simply selling it over the counter. We'll have to come up with some promotional gimmick to call attention to the new product—a tea tasting, perhaps? Yes! Let's give our customers a party to inaugurate my new herbal teas."

"Okay, Delilah, sure. But if you poison anybody with that stuff, you're fired."

"Relax. I'm gonna make you rich."

The party was a big success. The herbal tea moved even faster than she'd expected. Her customers didn't hesitate to offer suggestions as to which blends they liked and which they didn't. Delilah altered the composition of three of the mixtures, eliminated one and replaced it with something new, and left the other two as they were. Then she offered the stuff again.

After a few weeks of this, she had her six blends down to a firm recipe. The next step, she decided, was marketing her teas on a wider basis, to other health foods stores. She paid an exorbitant amount to have her mixtures sealed into tea bags and packaged into boxes of twenty-four. What to put on the boxes presented the next big problem. Right from the beginning it seemed to her that the design on the cartons was very important. She'd learned from watching people shop that many items are bought on impulse, depending on their reaction to a container or a display. She tried a few designs herself, but quickly gave up . . . she might be gifted in other respects, but art was one area in which she simply had no talent.

She consulted Dory. "Okay, hotshot artist, how about doing something useful with that talent of yours? Design me a box for my herbal tea. Something colorful, something different, something that will make the packages so irresistible that they'll leap from the shelves into shoppers' market baskets."

"Tea packages are always pretty staid," Dory objected. "Look at Templeton Tea, for example. It's come in the same powder-blue boxes with Gothic lettering for as long as I can remember. I mean, who buys that stuff? It looks as if it would put you to sleep, not perk you up in the morning."

"Exactly. Templeton Tea is consumed by proper old matrons like my grandmother. We're not interested in that demographical group; we're going after the counterculture, which is why we're going to be so different."

"You need a name for this company, Delilah," Dory pointed out. "Something exotic, something magical, something that will look good on the package. You need a name and I need a theme."

At the time Delilah was reading Mary Stewart's *The Crystal Cave*. Her company's name came to her spontaneously: "Merlin's Magical Brews!"

"That's terrific!"

Within a week Dory had several provocative designs. Brightly colored like all her other work, they were offbeat enough to capture the eye. She drew Merlin as a stylized figure, much younger and sexier than he usually appeared, and had him directing a sorcerer's staff at a large pentangle on each box that described the properties of the herb. Each variety of tea was to come in a different-colored box, and around the edges Dory drew astrological symbols.

Delighted, Delilah signed a contract with a printer, then plunged into the hassle of figuring out how to move from mock-ups to actual packages. When she got depressed or intimidated, her habit was to sit herself down and say, "This wouldn't have stopped Helen Templeton, and she lived in an age when women were not even taken seriously. If she could do it, so can I."

Her next move was to try to get her product onto the health foods stores' shelves. This involved advertising in the trade papers and doing a mailing proclaiming a special introductory offer. Then she sat back, chewed her nails, and waited.

The response exceeded her wildest fantasies. Orders poured in until she couldn't keep up with the demand. She had to quit working for Avatar Enterprises, Inc., as Chicken's company was now called, in order to devote herself full-time to making herbal tea in her kitchen.

By the beginning of 1974 it was obvious that Delilah needed a physical plant and some employees. The trouble was, she'd run out of money. Her start-up costs had run higher than she'd estimated, and as with all new businesses, she was running in the red.

She went to her bank, prepared to give them the best spiel they'd ever heard on why they should loan her the money she needed. To her surprise, she had no trouble getting the loan, but it wasn't because the bank was impressed with her business forecasts. It was because she was borrowing it against the inheritance she was going to come into at the age of thirty. For the first time in her life Delilah learned that her inheritance from the Templeton Trust amounted to several million dollars.

"Can you believe it?" she said to Dory. "All these years I've been scrimping and saving, and I'm going to be a millionaire. Not just a millionaire, a multimillionaire. It's humiliating."

"Humiliating? Are you crazy?"

"I want to make my money on my own, dammit! I don't want to owe anything to them."

"To them? You mean to your grandmother back in Boston?"

"Yes. Listen, Dory. I have this fantasy, and it's growing stronger all the time. Tell me if you think it's perverted, okay?"

"My ears are burning. C'mon, 'fess up; I love perversions."

"Ever since I left Boston I've had an 'I'm gonna show them a thing or two' attitude toward my family. Or at least, toward my father and my grandmother and Travis." Delilah excluded Nick, whom she still kept in touch with by an occasional letter or phone call. Nick was studying for a Ph.D. in history and planned to teach college. "It's childish, I know, but someday I want to be in a position where I can get back at them somehow."

"I think that's perfectly natural. If I know you, you'll do it, too."

"I want to compete with them, Dory. I want to expand my herbal tea business so much that I begin to draw customers away from tea into herbal tea. I want to eat into Grendam's profits . . . and then, when I've expanded as much as I possibly can, I want to move into other products, maybe even *Camellia sinensis,* real tea. Compete directly, in other words. And break them. You want to hear the final act in this little scenario? I go back there, ten, twenty years down the line, head of a rival tea company so large and so successful, it's got them running scared. I go back, laugh in their faces, and take them over, Dory. Buy my grandmother out, fire her, and run Templeton Tea myself."

"I love it. It's the perfect revenge. What will you do to Travis?"

"Well, he'll be out of a job, for one thing. Now that I'm gone, he's the obvious choice for the next Director of Templeton Tea."

"Not good enough. He deserves a far more painful fate. You want perverse? We'll chain him in some damp Beacon Hill cellar and use him as a sex slave for all the women in the company. That's what he's good at, right?"

"That, and opening champagne."

"Ah, an extra refinement to our torture—luxury deprivation. If he does a good job and makes me come, I might be merciful and let him lick Chardonnay off my breasts, but no Dom Pérignon for him, and not a single dab of caviar!"

"That'll fix the SOB!"

By the spring of 1975, Delilah's company occupied a small factory building, complete with herb gardens in the rear, where her plants sucked up the warm California sun. Her herbal brews were being carried by health foods stores and food co-ops all over the Southwest, and she was expanding to meet the increasing demand from other regions as well. Merlin's was growing at the extraordinary rate of 40 percent annually.

Sam and Dory, who were friends again, worked with her full-time, and Chicken, who regarded Delilah as his protégée, was proud of Merlin's success. They all had a party for her to celebrate her twenty-seventh birthday, which was also the occasion for her to move, without Dory this time, into a modest home of her own in Bel Air. Sam proposed a toast to her, saying, "You've done it, babe. You're the fuckin' queen of herbal tea."

It's not enough, Delilah thought silently. She wanted more.

23

Delilah walked around the newly converted warehouse that was going to serve as the headquarters for Merlin's Magical Brews, feeling great pride in her accomplishment. Nine years ago she had arrived in L.A. with no job, no practical training for a career, no friends, no place to live, and very little money. Now here she was in the spring of 1979, the president of her own successful company and the boss of over a hundred people. Merlin's had shown very respectable profits in the last fiscal year, and projections for the future were even better.

"Hey, babe, lookin' tah-riffic," said a voice beside her as a dusky arm descended around her shoulders.

Delilah turned with a smile. "Thanks, Sam. Lookin' not bad yourself, considering you're such a mean, ugly brute."

"I meant the factory, white lady. You could look good, but only if you got yourself some flashier duds."

He fingered her lace top and silk shawl with some distaste. "Now that you're a big lady president and all, this junk shop chic style of yours has got to go."

"Ha. Just because you're suddenly Mr. Fashion Plate, don't expect me to start patronizing Dior and Yves Saint Laurent."

"Dior? Me? You got to be kidding." He looked down at his massive chest. The white silk shirt was open at the collar, revealing absolutely no chest hair, a fact of which he was inordinately vain. Delilah had no idea why, since she herself liked hairy men, but Sam had a thing against body hair. He was the only man she'd ever known who couldn't wait to get bald and resented the time he spent shaving his head.

"Well, whoever. Your recent sartorial splendor has not escaped my notice, Sam."

"I've always been interested in fashion, babe. Just never had the cash before to see to my equipage. But now, thanks to you, partner, I'm swimming in funds."

She grabbed his hand and squeezed it. "Isn't it great! Look at this place. Let's check it out from the inside, all right?"

"Sure, babe. You the boss."

"I wish you'd stop with that. You're my vice president, remember."

"Yeah, I know." Sam laughed his booming, hearty laugh. "The boy ain't done so bad after all. Bring on the dancing girls for the president of vice."

The new premises for Merlin's Magical Brews delighted her. As they walked through the renovated building watching the finishing touches being put on the walls and woodwork, Delilah felt terribly proud. They had more than three times the area of their former plant. She could have fit the entire Avatar One into one end of her new office.

In addition to its herb-processing, blending, packaging, and shipping departments, the new factory had ample office space for management, marketing, advertising, and all the necessary clerical functions. There was a solar-paneled greenhouse, where special herbs could be grown and tested for the development of new teas. Delilah was particularly pleased with the art department, where the distinctive package designs that Merlin's was known for were created. Dory Lester had stayed on as her art director, and a damn good job she had done.

Sam was right about her clothes, she reflected as they walked slowly around the plant, taking everything in. She was moving into a new role, and it was time she started spending some money on herself. The sixties were long over, and women were dressing for success. She was thirty-one years old and a businesswoman. She wouldn't have been able to maintain what Sam called her junk shop chic style in New York or Boston, but things were more casual in California. Besides, people in the health foods business were expected to look a little odd.

Last year on her thirtieth birthday, Delilah had finally come into the money from her grandfather's trust fund. She had plowed a good chunk of it into Merlin's; there would have been no new factory if she hadn't invested in the business. But now that this was done, she made up her mind to put some of what was left into a new wardrobe, new make-up, maybe even a spiffy new car.

"So," said Sam as they finished their tour and retired to Delilah's new office for a hot cup of Golden Ginseng, "What next, girl wonder? Here we are set up in a hot new place, but you're not satisfied, are you? I can almost see the wheels spinning in that creative little brain of yours."

"You know me very well, don't you?"

"Yup. No sooner do you get what you want than you're reaching for the next goal."

"The next goal's mainstreaming, Sam. Merlin's is on the shelves of health foods stores all over the country, which is great. But it's time to move out. Instead of continuing to sell our product only to the relatively small number of people who patronize health foods stores, I want to reach ordinary shoppers in supermarkets and grocery stores. I think we should change our specialty item image. I think we should go for the heart of the American beverage business."

"Okay. How?"

"PR. What we need now is some slick PR. I'm going to hire one of the top public relations firms to spruce up our image. The counterculture tea company idea is not going to get us onto the shelves of the big food chains. We need a new approach. Something less, uh, California."

Thinking about this later that day, Delilah concluded that she was basically happy in California. She discovered that she was one of many people who had ended up on the westernmost coast of the country for similar reasons—a desire to break with the traditions of the East and create a new, independent life. Some people, like herself, were relatively new transplants; others were descendants of adventurers who had made the decision years before. But in both cases, rebellion was an underlying theme.

Californians did not necessarily put work first the way New Englanders did, and in this respect Delilah did not fit in. It was, she believed, one of the reasons she'd been so successful so fast. One night at a party she spoke about the difference in lifestyles with a physician who had moved to California from the East Coast several years before. He was convinced that many Californians shared what he called the Make-Me-a-Star complex—they were sitting at the drugstore counter of life, hoping to be discovered. All they had to do to achieve success was be in the right place at the right time.

"Rot," Delilah argued. "Nobody's successful without long hours, hard work."

"That's the old Puritan ethic coming to the fore in you," the physician said. "You've brought your Boston mentality to L.A."

If so, it seemed to be working, in her professional life, at least. She wasn't so sanguine about her personal life. She'd been feeling stressed lately, plagued with various degrees of free-floating anxiety. She was itchy for a change of some kind, for a steady man, perhaps, as she moved into her thirties. She'd been so busy building up her business during her twenties that she'd had time only for a few short-term love affairs, none of which had tempted her to abandon her single state. But now, at this rate, she'd be old soon, too old to have children. She wanted children. Families were important—that idea had been bred into her at a young age. She wanted a family; she wanted a steady man.

That's the trouble with you, Delilah, she said to herself. You want it all.

Two weeks later Delilah was ushered into the office of Max Kaplan, founder and president of one of the top PR firms in Los Angeles. He had been recommended to her by a number of people. Max, they said, was the best.

Max was also one of the most obnoxious men in California—or at least, so she decided on the afternoon they met. From the moment she walked into his office on the twenty-ninth floor of a new building in Century City, something clicked between them, clicked in a way that Delilah didn't care for at all.

"Well, well, Ms. Scofield. You're not at all what I expected."

Delilah put a hand on her hip and stared back at the suave executive who was smoking a foul-smelling cigarette and evaluating her personal assets in a decidedly insulting manner. Delilah had taken Sam's advice and dressed conservatively in a navy wool suit and an ivory silk blouse. Her hair had been twisted into a no-nonsense chignon, and her make-up was light. Her mirror this morning had given back the image of a serious, even prim, businesswoman, so she couldn't imagine what Kaplan was leering at.

"No?" she said.

"You sure don't look as if you subsist on a diet of brown rice and herbal tea."

"You're not what I expected, either, Mr. Kaplan."

"No?"

"You're considerably ruder."

In his late forties, Max had that fit, California-trim body Delilah had come to expect in the men she met in L.A., although the lines on his face and the gray in his hair fully revealed his age. His features were distinctive rather than handsome. He had some Mexican blood which showed up in the dusky color of his skin and the faintly slanted black eyes, and his nose jutted aggressively. He bore a livid scar on his left cheek that was the only outward sign of a troubled Texas childhood and his mother's succession of violent live-in lovers. Delilah learned later that in a town where your face was your fortune, he was sensitive about his looks.

Delilah had heard on the grapevine that Max had started his professional career as a shipping clerk in a major Hollywood studio, and later worked his way into the promotion department. He'd risen quickly through the ranks, jumped to a promotional director's job at a rival studio, made hundreds of useful contacts, and finally set up on his own.

That had been fifteen years ago. Kaplan's clients now included some of the top entertainment corporations in L.A., as well as numerous high-tech and commercial businesses.

"So you think you can take the country by storm with herbal tea?" he said. His tone mocked her dreams, and made her doubt, for the first time ever, that she could realize them.

"How do you know what business I'm in? I made no mention of it when I called for this appointment."

"When people make appointments with me, I try to have them checked out in advance. It saves time. Before I meet the prospective client I already have some idea whether or not I can do anything for them. I'll tell you right now I haven't been holding out a helluva lot of hope for you."

He rose, cigarette in hand, came around his mammoth mahogany desk, and blew smoke a little too close to her face. Delilah retreated a step, annoyed because he made it necessary. He was playing the sort of power games that she didn't care for at all.

Max Kaplan was taller than he had appeared behind the desk. He seemed wound-up, full of a tension that was partly emotional, partly physical. He was dressed in a finely tailored dark gray herringbone suit. Although every detail from his Italian leather shoes to the tiny gold stickpin on his tie was impeccable, his rough edges still managed to show through.

His eyes, which were dark, lively, and constantly shifting their gaze, passed over her figure again. He seemed particularly interested in her legs. "There was some publicity on you recently as a result of the opening of your new factory. No picture, though. I confess to being pleasantly surprised."

"Because I'm not wearing love beads and an India print dress left over from 1968?"

"Because you've got a body we can do something with. That outfit's got to go, though. Too stark, too frumpy. You've got legs and breasts, honey; you ought to be exploiting them."

Delilah bit down on her rising temper. "I thought we might try exploiting the assets of my product. I'm not selling myself."

"You ought to be. All smart salespeople sell themselves before they sell anything else."

"I don't suppose it's occurred to you, Mr. Kaplan, that you, too, might be required to sell yourself? If I engage your services, you'll be working for me."

He sucked another drag from his cigarette and flicked ashes on the Karastan rug. "If my manner offends you, there's the door. It's no longer necessary for me to sell myself. I've got more clients than I can handle."

She wanted to leave, and she wasn't sure why she didn't. It might have had something to do with her dislike of being the reactive person, the one who was forced to respond in a certain manner to someone's else's manipulation. So instead of stalking out, Delilah eased herself gracefully into the nearest chair. She crossed one leg over the other, leaned back, and smiled. "Tell me about your services, Max."

She made deliberate use of his first name while giving his trim body the same thorough scrutiny to which he'd been subjecting her. As she did it came to her that she found him attractive, despite his manner and the rough-hewn features of his face. He exuded an aura of sophistication and power that might be quite exciting in bed. The idea boosted her confidence immensely. Let him see what it felt like to be regarded as a sexual object.

"Convince me that I need you more than you need me." Very gently she added, "Because I assure you, *honey,* you do have to sell yourself to me."

There was a lethal silence. Then, unexpectedly, he grinned. "Okay, Ms. Scofield. Let's talk."

Max Kaplan's fees were outrageous, but he was damn good. Within a couple of weeks he knew almost as much about herbal tea as she did. And he knew a great deal more about marketing and promotion.

One thing that he particularly liked about Merlin's tea was the art on the boxes—the bright colors and the exotic pictures. He suggested they emphasize it, still going with a counterculture approach, yet done in a slick, upbeat manner.

"There are three major stages of marketing here. You've done very well at the first, which is appealing to the aging hippies and health freaks who already enjoy herbal brews and would like to acquire them more easily. But you have to remember that's a small segment of the population, and the hippie element is getting smaller all the time. To really make this business grow, you've got to pull in other customers."

"The baby-boomers in general," Delilah said. "My own generation. We're the largest demographic group, and will be for our entire lives. Anyone who can exploit that market will always be able to make money."

"You're right. You're at one extreme end of the baby-boomers, though, remember. There's a large group of them, several years younger than you, who were children during the sixties and babies when Kennedy was shot. They didn't demonstrate against the war in Vietnam, and if they're into health foods, it's because they're the latest thing at some upscale gourmet shop. To reach them your packaging should be chic, not hip. It never hurts to pick up on the snob appeal."

"That's the second element, then. Baby-boomers who are just hitting the job market and suddenly having money to spend."

"Right—the young professionals. And the third element is the health-conscious of any age. The joggers, for example. All of a sudden everybody's out there jogging to improve their cardiovascular fitness. Taking care of the heart is the thing to do. Well, it's becoming more and more evident that caffeine needlessly excites the heart. Stress is bad for us, and coffee drinking's beginning to look almost as dangerous as smoking." He paused, taking a long puff from the cigarette in his hand. "Not that I personally have any intention of relinquishing either of those vices, but smarter people might."

"Just don't blow your smoke in my face, okay? I hate that."

"Sorry. So who's going to benefit from this raised health consciousness? The tea industry, to some extent, since there's only about half as much caffeine in a cup of tea as there is in a cup of coffee. But in most herbal teas there's no caffeine. And that's something we've got to emphasize. My advice would be to put 'No Caffeine' in prominent letters on the front of your boxes."

Delilah took his advice. Merlin's expanded its art and design department and instituted some major changes in the packaging. Max orchestrated the publicity for this and got some great coverage, not only in L.A., but in major cities all over the country. Sales went up immediately to wholesalers and health food stores.

"Not good enough," Delilah told him. "I want our product in supermarkets. The aim is to see our brightly colored boxes right there on the shelves beside Templeton Tea."

"Tell me about you and Templeton Tea, Delilah. I don't know as much as I need to know about your past."

Delilah felt she knew Max well enough now to tell him the same thing she had once told Dory. Her fantasy hadn't changed. The thought of cutting into her grandmother's business with Merlin's still made her blood rush.

"You won't be able to do it with herbal tea," Max said. "No matter how popular it becomes, it's still a very small percentage of the total market. If you want to compete with Templeton's, you'll have to deal in regular tea, Delilah. Are you prepared to do that?"

"I'm not sure. Not yet. First things first."

"Right. We'll file that problem away as something to consider in the future."

"Do you think I'm wrong to want to get them, Max?"

He considered. "Is it really revenge that you want? Or is it simply your heritage?"

"What do you mean?"

"You're a businesswoman, Delilah, and a damn fine one. You're a natural to take over Templeton Tea after Minerva Templeton retires. I'm sure even your grandmother recognizes that by now."

But Delilah had had no contact at all with her grandmother for nine years. Her father had remarried two years before, and Joyce, his wife, a graduate student two years younger than Delilah, seemed to want to be friends. Joyce had telephoned a few times and sent Christmas cards, but Delilah was cool to her. On the few occasions when she had spoken with her father on the phone, their conversations were restrained.

She still heard from Nick now and then, but nothing from Grendam, and nothing, of course, from Travis.

"There'll be time for all that later," said Max. "Let's not worry about it now."

It took several months to get Max's changes off the ground. While it was happening, Delilah saw him frequently, for they worked well together. More and more, she grew to like him. He was quick, smart, and macho, but there was an inner wisdom in him that she didn't notice at first because he didn't flaunt it the way he flaunted so much else. Max was more introspective than she would have expected a man like him to be. He seemed to understand and accept himself better than most people she knew. And he was perceptive about others.

"You know why you like me, duchess, don't you?" He started calling her duchess early on in their relationship. He preferred it to Delilah, he said, because to a man with thinning hair, the name Delilah had ominous overtones. "You like me because I'm twice your age and remind you of the father you never had."

"I've got a father, whom you don't resemble in the least. And you're only sixteen years older than I am, Max."

"At sixteen I was plenty old enough to father a child. And don't tell me you're not looking for Daddy, because from what you've told me, yours is a zero."

"I'm not looking for Daddy in you, that's for sure," she returned with a sexy come-on in her voice that Max, annoyingly, ignored.

The sexual chemistry she'd felt from the start continued to beat between them, but Max didn't pursue it. Delilah began to doubt that he wanted to. Maybe he felt threatened by her. He was nearly fifty and he'd been divorced for many years. He was not the world's most liberated male, and the women he dated were certainly nothing like her. As PR consultant to a number of film companies and celebrities, he often showed up in the gossip pages with some half-dressed starlet on his arm. "Airheads," Delilah would sniff, and toss the paper aside.

If the time had seemed right, she might have done the pursuing, but she figured her old rule about separating business from pleasure still applied as long as Max was putting in a lot of hours consulting for her. When the job was over she would give the matter more serious consideration.

In the meantime, because of Sam's scathing remarks about her clothes and her own images of Max escorting some actress dripping in designer clothes to the Academy Awards, Delilah secretly began investing in a new wardrobe. "I could get used to this," she laughed one Saturday morning as she and Sam sat on a velvet banquette sipping sherry from delicate crystal glasses in Saint Laurent's while she waited for a fitting. Sam continued to be her self-appointed fashion consultant.

"Don't even look at Ralph Lauren this season—he's even more boring than usual. Valentino's the dude for you, or Ungaro maybe. And don't buy the Hermès alligator belt, not this year, anyhow. Alligator won't do it, although snakeskin might, provided you get the right kind of snake. And don't make faces at me. You still ain't got no style, though you're learning, babe, you're learning."

Her transformation was subtle at first, then, as her confidence grew, more dramatic. Sam was right—she found she didn't really care for clothes with classic or conservative lines; she wanted more flare. Her personal style had always been dramatic; now she added a touch of elegance as well. She threw out the junk store chic but kept its theme of slightly defiant flamboyance by having her clothes cut along classic lines, then deliberately hemming her skirts to the wrong length for the season and mixing hot colors with eclectic designs. "I want to start trends, Sam, not merely follow them. I guess I'm a bit of an exhibitionist at heart."

"Tell me about it."

Six months after she and Max met, Delilah went to his office one morning with her latest financial reports. She took pride and pleasure in showing him the strong upward trends in all her business indicators, including the order that had just come in from Safeway to begin stocking Merlin's herbal teas in their supermarkets all over the country.

"We're doing it, duchess," he said with great satisfaction as he surveyed the reports. "It's finally happening."

"I have a lot to thank you for, Max. Are you busy tonight? I'd like to take you out to dinner to celebrate."

"No," he said so forcefully that she felt an instant of dismay. She had dressed with particular care for their meeting today, in a slinky raspberry silk confection from Giorgio's that emphasized her breasts and showed a long expanse of the legs that Max so admired. She'd had a facial at Elizabeth Arden, and her hair had been styled only an hour ago by Rudolph, the A list's current "in" coiffeur. Her make-up was perfect; she'd checked it out in the lady's room on her way to Max's office—three applications of the best sable mascara to separate and emphasize each eyelash, a touch of salmon blush under each cheekbone, darker salmon lip gloss, artfully applied with a delicate brush imported from Paris, and a touch of light, translucent powder to give her a subtle glow.

She knew she was looking unusually seductive. She was ready to put an end to the waiting between them.

"I'll take you to dinner, Delilah," said Max. There was a husky note in his voice that she'd never heard before. "Back where I come from, that's the way it's done."

He was smiling slightly and there was a new and special warmth in his dark eyes. "I've never asked about your men," he went on. "Since you're usually free when I suggest we work at night, I assume you're not terribly attached to anyone."

"Am I to draw the same conclusions about your women? I know there are a lot of those—I read the gossip columns. There's no one special?"

"There's someone special, but I've never touched her. When I finally do, she'd better be faithful to me or I'm likely to break a few heads."

His rough words excited her. She tossed her hair in what she knew was a provocative manner, thrilling to the darkening this produced in his eyes. "I'm not dating. It's been a long time for me."

He leaned forward. "Please don't tell me you don't need or desire lots and lots of sex, because for weeks I've been fantasizing about giving it to you."

"Weeks? Is that all?"

"Okay. Months."

"Six months. That's how long it's been since we met. Six interminable months, Max."

"Six months, a week, and three days."

He wants me, she thought, hugging that knowledge close to her heart. He's wanted me all along, the sneaky devil.

"I love sex. But the casual flings that everybody seems to be into nowadays don't do anything for me. I like monogamous relationships—that's all I'll sign up for, as a matter of fact. So if you want to start something with me, you'll have to be faithful in return. No more bubble-headed starlets with gowns slit to the navel."

"Fair enough." He came around his desk and sat down on the arm of her chair. He still didn't touch her, but he leaned close. "Let's start something. Come to my place this evening. We'll pretend it's for dinner—I'll even cook. I'll drug you with wine and seduce you with sophisticated sexual banter. Then I'll carry you to bed and make love to you until we die."

He touched her hair with the palm of his hand—his first caress. Delilah's eyes closed; she leaned into him. He smelled good, exotic and masculine. Beneath her cheek she felt his throat move as he swallowed convulsively. "What time?" she managed.

He cupped her cheeks and stared at her mouth for a second or two. Then he bent his head and kissed her. She saw his eyes close just before his lips touched hers, and there was something sweet and vulnerable about that, something that made her slide her arms around his neck and return his kiss with a fervor she had not felt in years. At last, she thought. *At last.*

When Delilah showed up at Max's that evening, she was so nervous she was sure the apricot silk top she was wearing with her Saint Laurent palazzo trousers was going to be ruined with perspiration. Max was nervous, too, she realized when he came to the door. He put one cigarette in an ashtray and lit up another without noticing that the first was still burning. And he apologized about the dinner: "Just steaks and baked potato and salad, I'm afraid. I'm not a gourmet cook. Jesus, you're not a vegetarian, are you?" He actually blushed at the thought. "I forgot about your health foods store, and—"

"I'm not a vegetarian, Max. I love steak."

"Good." He grinned sheepishly. "I thought I knew so much about you, but I don't have any idea what you like to eat. Or your other likes and dislikes, for that matter."

"You've never asked."

"Yeah, well, I knew if we ever got too deep into the personal side of things, I wouldn't be able to keep my hands off you."

"Why have you always played it so cool with me? I was beginning to think you just weren't interested."

His expression grew more serious. "The truth is, duchess, you frighten me. You're so young, so vital, so beautiful. What do you see in a used-up Lothario like me?"

"My dear man, you are very far from being a used-up Lothario. And besides, all the women you date are young and beautiful. Most of them, in fact, are younger and a lot more beautiful than I!"

"Yeah, but you're special. You, I could really fall for. You could spell the end of my serene, comfortable love-'em-and-leave-'em bachelor existence. That's what scares me, sweetheart."

She put her hands on either side of his face. "Don't be scared," she said, even as it crossed her mind that she was a little frightened, too. She could fall for him, yes. But the people she'd loved in the past had always let her down. Don't worry about that now, she told herself. Anyway, you've been cautious for too many years. You've got to take a risk sometime.

"I feel just the same about you. I've been waiting for you, Max. I've been waiting forever, it seems."

"Christ," he said, then backed her against a counter and put his hands on her waist. She could feel his heat through the silky fabric, and it made her tremble.

"You smell great. You look fantastic." He leaned into her and slid one hand up until it paused just beneath her breast.

Delilah put her lips to his and kissed him. She felt him harden against her. Her own hormones responded, flooding her with a desire so intense that her mouth went dry and her knees seemed about to buckle. She moved her hips invitingly. Max groaned and tore his mouth from hers. "The hell with dinner," he said.

Max proved to be one of those men who are altered by sexual arousal. She had observed that most men were pretty much like themselves in bed: selfish and superficial if that was their usual personality; gentle and thoughtful if that's how they behaved in other respects. Since Max was sophisticated and controlled when he wanted to be, Delilah had expected Beverly Hills-smooth. What she got was East L.A.-tough.

He all but dragged her into the bedroom, and if she hadn't protested, he would have ripped off her clothes. "Wait a minute, Max. Let's savor this."

"I can't." His own clothes went sailing into the air like great birds flapping and fell haphazard in all corners of the room. "I been dreaming about loving you for so long. We've got the rest of the night to savor it; right now I just want to possess you in the most primitive way."

There was something appealing about this, so she objected no more, but let him take the lead in everything . . . not that she could have stopped him. He was at a fever pitch. When they were naked he pressed her down across the bed and straddled her; the faintest trace of a Texas drawl colored his speech as he murmured dark suggestions about what he intended to do to give her pleasure. His language was earthy and explicit, his technique rough. He worked her nipples until they ached with arousal, then kissed them until she moaned. As her excitement built, he touched his teeth to her breasts—not painfully, but hard enough to make her feel as if they were doing something a little wicked, a little dangerous.

Holding her down, he explored her with his mouth, darting his tongue over every inch of her. When his fingers played between her thighs, brushing, teasing, piercing, she went wild and tried to caress him in return. But he wouldn't allow it. He manacled her wrists in his strong fingers, pinned them to the mattress on either side of her head, and let her writhe.

There was a hint of a threat about him, a potential violence that might have frightened her if she hadn't trusted him so much. He was a fantasy lover, arising from deep within her psyche. He was the personification of all her most fantastic sexual images.

"Are you ready for me?" he whispered after she had struggled for a bit. His voice was tender now.

"Yes, you kinky Neanderthal. I'm practically climbing the walls of your cave."

"You're beautiful. Look at you—all lush and zestful and aglow." He bent his head and licked a drop of perspiration from her breast. Then he parted her legs and fell upon her, sheathing himself inside her, deep.

When he thrust, her body yielded exquisitely. The sensation of his joining himself to her was mystical somehow, as if their union were taking place on several levels, of which the physical was the least significant. She wrapped her arms and legs around him and fell easily into the rhythm he established. In only a few seconds, it seemed, they were both over the edge into wave after wave of excruciating pleasure.

As she climaxed, she laughed, so great was her delight in him. "I think I'm in love," she whispered as they rolled to their sides and kissed.

"Me, too."

It was true. It was instant and all-encompassing, and very much a joy. "Oh, Max, I want to hug you and hug you. I want to talk all night. I want to know everything about you. I want to get inside your head."

He winked diabolically. "That's fair—you want to get inside my head and I want to get inside your body. A perfect male-female relationship."

"Sexist jerk."

He ran his hand over her flank, then back up to capture a breast again. His thumb on her nipple sent a renewed jolt of excitement through her. She made a faint sound in the back of her throat. Max grinned and pressed her down on her back once again, his intent obvious.

"I can't," she said. "I mean, all that stuff about multiple orgasms is a myth, isn't it?"

She felt him laugh, his firm stomach muscles dancing against her softer abdomen. "No myth, duchess; you'll see."

He slid down so his mouth could take her, and it felt so good, she knew she would come again if he kept it up. He did. And she did, making so much noise that she giggled afterward, wondering if his neighbors would call the cops.

"Who cares?" he said, and covered her, for her pleasure had made him hard again.

She playfully tried to push him off. "You animal. How old are you, nineteen?"

He rolled onto his back, keeping himself firmly planted inside her. "Middle-aged and tired. Do me, baby. I love you liberated lady types. You want to marry me, you'd better show me all your stuff."

"Marry you!"

"Yeah, you're auditioning for the role of my wife. Didn't I mention that?"

"No," she said, laughing. He was joking, of course.

He caught his fingers in her long hair and pulled her face down to his. "Of course, it all depends on whether or not you can make me come again." Delicately, he bit her lower lip, then soothed it with the tip of his tongue. "I haven't done it twice in a row since 1953 or so."

Delilah smiled. She never could resist a challenge.

24

Delilah was working in her office one morning in mid-1980 when her secretary put through a call from the East Coast. "Delilah?" said a voice she hadn't heard in ten years, "This is your grandmother."

How easily those simple words could cut right through everything else that was in her mind. Market research, sales figures, new varieties of herbal tea all went flying out of her head as she focused on the telephone. "Yes?"

"How are you, Delilah?" Was there a hint of wistfulness about the question? As if, perhaps, she cared? Had she called to try to find a way to put things right between them? The yearning that rose in her was almost overpowering. Oh Gran. I *miss* you.

"I'm fine. How are you?"

"I'm afraid I have some rather distressing news."

Delilah's heart began to slog. Who, she thought? Not Travis, surely? Funny how her mind leapt immediately to Travis.

Grendam cleared her throat, then said, "Your father had a massive heart attack late last night. His wife rushed him to the hospital, where he died at a little before nine this morning." When Delilah didn't respond, she added, "His wife is distraught, of course, and under sedation. She asked me to call you."

"Thank you," No, she thought. *Daddy, Daddy.* Knowing she must somehow keep this conversation normal, rational, *under control,* she said, "I don't know what to say. I'm shocked. I hadn't realized he was having trouble with his heart. He is—was—relatively young."

"He was fifty-six. The same age as Jonathan."

Delilah closed her eyes. She could see her father sitting at his desk in the house on Walker Street, his picture of her mother propped there in front of him. *He can't be dead.* "I'm very sorry to hear about it. When is the funeral, do you know?"

"There isn't going to be a funeral." Grendam sounded disapproving. "It seems he left instructions ordering his remains to be made available for medical research."

"I see." *Oh, Daddy, how could you leave me without saying good-bye?* "Yes, that sounds like something he'd do."

"He expressed some similar wishes when your mother died, but I nipped that idea in the bud. Joyce wishes it, however, and she is now, officially, the next of kin—"

"It doesn't matter to me what she does," Delilah interrupted. "My father and I have never been close."

Another silence, lengthier this time. Why don't I cry? Delilah asked herself. I'm not really so callous! Why don't I say something that makes it sounds as if I care?

Instead, she said, "If there's to be no funeral, I don't suppose there's any reason for me to come to Boston, is there?"

At her end of the wire, Minerva Templeton felt like screaming her frustration and disappointment; if David Scofield's death didn't bring Delilah home, what would? My death? Minerva wondered bitterly. That, no doubt, would affect the girl even less.

She wanted her back, she wanted her home, devoting her energy and talents not to some fly-by-night herbal tea operation, but to the family business. Minerva had been following her granddaughter's career, and everything she'd learned convinced her that she'd been right all those years ago in her assessment of Delilah's capabilities. How could she have been so right about that and so wrong in her estimation of the way Delilah would react to the forced separation from Travis?

Minerva had always regretted the way she had dealt with that calamity. She'd expected Delilah to be depressed—suicidal, perhaps—but for some reason she hadn't expected her to be angry. After all, she had acted in the girl's best interests, shielding her, protecting her.

But of course, Delilah had had no way of knowing that. I always tried to be so strong for her. Perhaps I should simply have tried to be kind.

She'll be back, Minerva continued to tell herself as the years slowly passed. Someday she'll forgive me; I must be patient, I mustn't give up hope.

Now her hope was rapidly waning.

"Delilah—" She stopped. She didn't know how to proceed. She wanted to tell Delilah she still loved her, but that was something she could only do face-to-face. She had to be able to see her eyes, to know the girl wasn't going to reject her outright. "If you don't wish to return at this time," Minerva went on, "that's entirely your own affair."

There was a pause, then Delilah said, "I'm afraid I'm rather busy here at present."

"No need to trouble yourself, in that case. You've cut yourself off from the lives of your family. There's no reason to alter that for their deaths. Good-bye."

Delilah was left holding a dead receiver. She dropped it onto the desk and let her face fall into her cupped fingers. Pain ripped through her, so intense it seemed physical. She wasn't sure if it was for her father, her grandmother, or herself.

"Hold me, Max," she said to her lover late that night.

"I'm holding you, baby. I'm never going to let you go."

"I miss him, you know. I never thought I would. I miss him."

"Of course you do."

All day since she'd heard the news, her images had all been of her father—graceful and distinguished, his dark hair always neatly groomed, his handsome face hidden behind a newspaper or a book. She remembered an isolated incident from her childhood, when he had tossed her up toward the ceiling, only to catch her safely when she tumbled back down. How she'd screamed in love and joy and terror. How she'd laughed when he'd capered around on the floor with her while she rode him like an elephant into a jungle of dining room table legs and chairs.

Her father had rarely indulged in such high-spiritedness, and after her mother's death, he had grown considerably more reserved. But even so, Delilah admitted to herself that deep inside she must have been harboring the dream that someday he would favor her with at least a glimmer of warmth and love and laughter. Now that dream was blasted.

"I could have done more to keep in touch these last few years." As she spoke she was thinking not only of her father, but of Grendam, too. "I could have made some attempt to heal the breach between us. But I didn't even try."

"You tried for years, Delilah. He was not a loving man. You are a loving woman. If you hadn't backed off from that one-sided relationship when you did, he would have gone right on making you miserable. You did the right thing."

Maybe so, but love does not dissipate, she realized, even if it is not returned. She had loved David Scofield, and now she wept for him. She mourned the intimacy they'd never been able to achieve.

"He was a lousy father. He was a real shit. Even so, there's a part of me that still believes the failing can't have been in him. That fathers are supposed to love their daughters, and if he didn't, it must have been my fault."

"There are few things more brutal to face up to than a parent's inability to love," said Max. "It's too bad you didn't have the opportunity to form an adult relationship with either of your parents. It's bound to make your own personal conflicts more difficult to resolve."

"What personal conflicts?"

"I was thinking of your unwillingness to commit yourself to me."

"Oh, Max. I can't think about that now. Anyway, it's only been a few weeks—"

"It's been five months since we started making love, and I asked you to marry me on our first night together."

"You were joking!"

"I was serious, and I think you knew it. You certainly know it now; I've asked you a dozen times and you keep putting me off. I understand—you've been abandoned and you're afraid of intimacy. But I'm not David Scofield or Travis Templeton or your grandmother. I'm not going to leave you; I promise you that." He kissed her roughly. "I know this isn't the time. But think about it, Delilah. I love you and I want you in my life on a permanent basis."

"I will think about it. I love you, too."

Max began to caress her in a manner that offered passion as well as comfort. "Let's get rid of this nightgown."

For the first time ever, she was tempted to refuse him. "I keep thinking of him dead. I keep wondering how he felt, if he knew."

He persisted, undressing her with hands that were both demanding and gentle. "Death is always there, always a possibility. You and I are going to celebrate life."

"All right," she whispered. "Make me forget."

"Dory, I'm unplugging my vibrator," Delilah said in the fall of 1980, a few weeks after her father's death.

Her arch statement was greeted with shrieks from her best friend. "You mean you're finally going to move in with Max?"

"We're getting married, Dory."

"Oh my God! When's the wedding?"

"Next weekend. Will you be my matron of honor?" Dory herself had married an aging rock star a few months before. Delilah was skeptical about the marriage, but so far it seemed to be working. "It'll be informal; Max doesn't like a lot of fuss."

"Do you love him, Delilah? Really love him?"

"Yes. It's taken a while for me to admit it, but I love him with all my heart and soul and mind."

"Well, it's about time! I'd just about given up on you with men! Every time I've read the cards for you, I haven't been able to catch any glimpse of a permanent relationship, at least not in the near future. I've seen you mated with a dark man, but I had the impression that he was taller and younger than Max." She chuckled. "I guess that just goes to show how wrong we psychics can be!"

It wasn't as if there were no problems—there were at least two that presented serious obstacles to the marriage. The first was her money. When Max found out how much she was worth, he was appalled. "I thought you'd been cast off without a dime by your family."

"Not exactly. I came into some money from the Templeton Trust on my thirtieth birthday. It was organized several generations ago by my ancestors, to be sure none of us could blow the entire family fortune. I've spent a lot of my inheritance, though, on Merlin's."

"But you've got a hefty chunk of it left."

"Well, yes. And I guess you could say I've been lucky with my investments."

"How lucky?"

"Four and a half million, give or take a few bucks."

He whistled. "Jesus Christ."

"Is it some kind of threat to you to find out I have money of my own?"

"Oh God, I don't know. Maybe."

"From the start you've been like a mentor to me, my advisor, my wiser friend. But we can't go on like that forever. We're getting married. To me that means an equal partnership."

"I know, baby, I know." But try as he might, this was difficult for Max to accept. If he hadn't been so much older, it would have been easier for him, but the dynamics of male-female relationships had changed a lot since he'd been her age. Max tried hard not to be a male chauvinist, but he held some old-fashioned values nonetheless.

Then there was the problem of children. Delilah was dismayed to learn that he didn't want any. "It was one of the reasons my wife divorced me," he explained. "I don't like kids."

He was surprised at the extent of her disappointment. He'd always thought she was one of those modern women who would be perfectly content to go through life without a family. "You're over thirty, Delilah. Most women have already had their children by your age."

"I probably wouldn't make the best mother in the world," she agreed, but there was a wistful look in her eyes, and when she left him late that night to return to her own apartment, Max was frightened for the first time in their relationship. He could lose her over this. Losing her was something he could not even contemplate.

Max knew there were things about her own family life that haunted her. Sometimes at night when she was asleep beside him, breathing softly and cuddling close as if unconsciously seeking security from him, he worried that he was too old for her, too jaded and too cynical. And no matter how much she denied it, he knew Delilah loved him because he was older. Max suspected that to some degree he was a substitute for all the people in her family who had betrayed and abandoned her. It bothered him that she might confront this in herself someday and outgrow her dependence on him.

Could he bind her with a child, or would a new family bring her unresolved emotions to a head all that much sooner? He remembered his own childhood as nothing more than year after year of pain and misery. His mother had been dreamy, half out of touch with reality, and her various lovers were always drunken, violent bastards. He'd never wanted children of his own; he wouldn't know how to treat them, he'd screw them up—they frightened him.

"I guess I don't need to have children right away," Delilah told him the next time they talked. "But I can't honestly say I'll never want them. Families are important to me; that sense of tradition, of the previous generations looking over my shoulder, is still a powerful force in my life."

"What good is your family to you now, duchess? All this wonderful sense of tradition doesn't make you any the less cast off."

She admitted this, but it didn't alter her feelings. "I'd like to know that having children is at least an option, Max. I don't think I can marry you without it."

Max gave in. They'd keep the possibility open, he assured her. Who knows, maybe he'd change his mind and ache to see his baby at her breast.

But he doubted it.

The early 1980s were wonderful years for Delilah, more stimulating and at the same time peaceful than any other period in her life. Everything seemed to go right for her: Merlin's continued to grow until her product was on the shelves of ninety percent of the supermarkets in America. And she, too, came to the attention of the public. With Max acting as her press agent, she soon found herself being courted by the media for feature pieces on herbal tea and women in business that boosted sales even more. Dramatic, witty, and stylish, Delilah was a PR man's dream. She did a good deal of public speaking, and her picture appeared on the pages of several national magazines, including *People* and *Business Week.*

She and Max lived in a whirlwind of social engagements; suddenly Delilah found herself on the A list for parties in Malibu and

Beverly Hills, hobnobbing with people she'd seen in films or on TV. Not that she was overly impressed with the glamour of these situations: "I finally know what the A list stands for," she said to her husband after the first couple of parties she attended with him.

"What?"

"Assholes."

He laughed. "Yeah, you're right."

"So why do we go?"

"For fun, babes, and to maintain our professional contacts. You never know when you might have need of an asshole."

Max liked to travel, but Delilah had always been too busy working to go anywhere. He changed all that. "Let Sam run the place for a few days," he'd say to her, and off they'd go for a long weekend of sun, wind, and gourmet dining in Aruba, or scuba diving on the black coral reefs of Cozumel. They spent their honeymoon in Paris—what could be more romantic than that? thought Delilah as they strolled the Left Bank by moonlight and dined in three-star restaurants. They rented a car and drove south to the vineyards near Beaune to wander in cool wine cellars and sip the full-bodied red wines. They spent a week in Erice, a mountaintop village in Sicily, gazing out past an old Crusaders' castle and squinting against the sun as they tried to catch a glimpse of Africa across the blue Mediterranean. In the winters they skied in Gstaad or Vail; in the summers they rented a boat and sailed the Aegean.

They rarely fought, which seemed remarkable to Delilah since she and Max both had very definite ideas, which didn't always agree. Sometimes she had the sneaking suspicion that this was because her husband was just a bit patronizing. "I'm too lazy to argue with you," he would say, grinning. "When you get to be as old as me, you'll see the error of your ways."

"And the wisdom of yours, I suppose? You're full of it, Max."

Yet there was a certain wisdom about him, and her admiration grew the longer they stayed together. Some people never learned or grew with their years, but Max had. She respected him, for more and more she understood that there were many things he could teach her about the never very simple business of living.

In 1983, when Delilah turned thirty-five, she went through a period of extreme depression over her childless state. For several nights in succession she dreamed of the baby she'd miscarried in 1970. She woke one night in a sweat, haunted by the uncanny feeling that the spirit of the child was near her, seeking another route to come into her life.

"Max, I want a baby," she whispered, clutching her empty belly. "I love you; why won't you have a baby with me?"

"Don't romanticize it, Delilah. Babies cry. They shit all over the place and wake up every two hours to be fed. You can't take them hiking in the Rockies or parachute-sailing in Acapulco. And they grow up—very slowly, I might add—to be teenage coke addicts and sex maniacs."

"I don't care. I want a kid and I'm going off the pill."

"Oh Christ. Let's wait a little longer. A few more months. I don't want to share you yet."

"That line's exhausted, Max. You've said a few more months for the past three years. What have you got against children, anyway? You'd make a wonderful father."

"I just don't like them. I never have. And I enjoy our life the way it is. I don't want to upset the equilibrium between us."

But the equilibrium was already upset, for Delilah's maternal desires increased as her biological clock continued to measure off the last few years of her childbearing abilities. As threatened, she did go off the pill. She was tempted to do it on the sly and trick Max into fathering a child, but she was too honest to pull something like that. When she told Max she'd flushed the pills, he responded by breaking open a box of condoms.

"You've got to give me a little more time to get used to the idea."

Very reluctantly, she agreed.

One day not long after this Max came home from his office with a stack of library books, which he dumped unceremoniously on the butcher block table of their Bel Air home. Delilah hefted a thick tome. "*All About Tea?*"

"Yes," said Max. "I think it's time we researched the subject. If you're still serious, that is, about your old fantasy of competing with the Templetons."

Was she? The truth was, her fantasy had dimmed considerably over the last couple of years. Now that she was married to Max, it didn't seem important anymore.

"You've done about as much as you can do with herbal tea. You need a fresh challenge. I can tell from watching you stalk around your office that you're itching to take on something new."

She wasn't so sure about that. In fact, Delilah suspected that Max had come up with this as a way of distracting her attention from the question of children. But she attacked the books, and before she knew it, she was hooked. The tea business was fascinating.

"Templeton Tea does most of their business in this country, Max, but companies like Twinings are worldwide operations. I wonder if it would be possible for Templeton's to get more of the world market. In specialty teas, for example, like Earl Grey and Irish Breakfast. Surely my grandmother's thought of that."

"Your grandmother's getting old. It's been years since she did anything new with the company. She's nearly eighty. She'll either die soon, or retire."

"She always said she would retire on her eightieth birthday. Nobody should have to go to work every day, she'd say, at the age of fourscore. Of course, when she retires, Travis will probably succeed her. He's been working for the company all these years."

"You're a better administrator than Travis."

"And you're biased! You know nothing about him."

"I know he's a shit."

"Lots of good businessmen are shits."

"You could go back, Delilah. I mean it. We could move to the East Coast. I've been thinking of opening an office in New York."

She embraced him, touched by his support. "Not yet. It's a big decision, and I don't know how much I really want it, to tell you the truth. I like California. It's become my home."

"I want you to be happy, sweetheart."

"I know. And I love you for it, Max. Just don't call the moving vans yet, okay?"

That summer they spent a week together in Istanbul, where Max was doing some PR for an opulant TV miniseries about the Ottoman Empire.

"They grow tea in eastern Turkey near the Russian border," Delilah told him one afternoon as they whipped along the winding road that ran along the Bosporus, past outdoor cafés where small glasses of tea were served, elegant wooden *yalis,* or villas, where the Ottoman viziers had spent their rich and lazy summers, young boys fishing and swimming in the none too clean waters where refuse and spent boat fuel was carelessly dumped. "Why don't we fly out there tomorrow and have a look at the tea gardens?"

Max agreed, and when his work was finished, they flew to the ancient port of Trabzon on the Black Sea. They hired a rattletrap taxi to take them up the coast road to the tea-producing city of Rize ninety kilometers away.

The countryside was lush. Delilah knew from her reading that tea required a great deal of rainfall. It also grew best at high altitudes, and the Black Sea region they were visiting was hilly, with towering peaks rising to the right of the highway, dotted with terraced gardens of the dark green herb.

In the company of a friendly and knowledgeable official from the Çay Kurumu, the Turkish Tea Council, they drove up into the hills surrounding Rize to see an actual tea garden. "You are lucky," Erdal bey said. "The women are gathering here today."

Dressed in bright smocks and trousers, often with broad straw hats on their heads to repel the hot sun, the women laughed and chatted as they bent over their task. Several of them worked the terraced gardens together, clipping the new flush from the tea bushes into small cloth bags, then emptying these at intervals into large wicker baskets.

"They have always done this work," the guide explained. "Their mothers did it, and their grandmothers before them. Their daughters will work in the tea gardens someday, too."

"What do the men do?" Delilah asked.

"Some work for the tea council, some in the processing factories." He shrugged. "Some go for their military service and never return to the village."

Their next stop on the tour was a visit to a processing factory, which was a long two-story stone building. At one end there was a receiving dock where trucks unloaded huge piles of fresh cuttings, which consisted of the top two leaves and a bud from the tea plant. These were spread out on the top level in shallow bins with fans underneath that blew warm air through the leaves.

This was called the withering process, their guide explained. It softened the tea leaves and removed excess moisture. After withering, the tea was dumped onto the none too clean floor of the factory and raked by laborers into a series of cylindrical holes that led to the lower level.

Delilah stared with a hygenic American's horror at the sight of the laborers, some barefoot, some wearing old rubber boots, wading through knee-high mounds of tea, which they raked into the holes. "Those leaves might end up in my cup someday," she said under her breath to Max. "After this I may never drink tea again!"

As they walked down a dark flight of stairs to observe the second of the four major steps in tea processing, rolling, the distinctive odor of tea began to permeate the air. "Smells delicious," Delilah said.

Their guide laughed. "That is the poorest-quality tea you are smelling. The finest leaves do not release their aromatics until they are brewed."

The tea that had been raked down the holes was now being crushed in huge, noisy presses that rolled the leaves, breaking up the skin and the stalks. When this process was completed, fermentation began. It was fermentation, the guide explained, that distinguished the black teas so popular in the West and the green teas consumed in China and Japan. Many Chinese restaurant teas, Delilah knew, were of the green variety—pale, subtle, and more astringent than black teas.

"We stop fermentation by removing the tea leaves to an oven and firing them," Erdal bey explained. "That is the fourth and final step."

He showed them through the firing area. Flat racks of tea leaves were conducted through the large ovens by a conveyer belt, which then moved the processed tea along to a machine that sieved and sorted it into seven different grades.

"This is tea," Erdal bey said, holding up a handful of dry, coppery brown leaves. "All that is left now is for it to be blended and packed and shipped to the grocery store shelves." He solemnly presented Delilah and Max with a plastic-bagged, newspaper-wrapped packet containing about a kilo of the best grade. "Take it, please, and enjoy."

Back in Istanbul that evening, Max commandeered a taxi and had the driver take them to a hill overlooking the darkling city—the sultan's palaces and the ornate mosques, the slender Bosporus bridge linking Europe and Asia, the winking lights of the night fishermen.

It was romantic, but Delilah couldn't stop thinking about everything they'd seen in Rize. When they returned to their hotel, she flopped down on the bed and said, "It's such an old-fashioned process in so many ways. So hard on the women who must bend over for so many hours each day, gathering the tea on those steep hillsides. There must be a better way to do it. There must be ways to improve the yield, and at the same time make life easier for the workers."

Max grinned. "You sound as if you're starting to think like a Templeton."

She rolled over and supported her chin on her hands. "Is that what you want for me?"

"You know what I want for you, duchess. I want you to be fulfilled and satisfied with your life, no matter what product you choose to sling."

"I am fulfilled and satisfied, Max. Merlin's keeps me busy, and I'm still not sure I want anything more from the professional side of my life. On the personal side, however—"

"Children," he finished. "You're not going to give up on that, are you?"

She smiled at the wry look on his face. "Don't worry, darling, we're on vacation, and I'm not going to bug you about children now. I love you, you know. You make me very happy."

He sat down beside her and took her into his arms. "C'mere, tea lady."

"Where do you get your energy?"

"Tea's an aphrodisiac; didn't you know?"

"Animal."

25

One Saturday morning a few weeks after their trip to Turkey, Max looked up from his morning coffee to find Delilah crying over something she'd received in the mail. It was a card from Julie Barnaby, her roommate from St. Crispin's, proclaiming the birth of her third child, an eight-pound, ten-ounce son. Max took the birth announcement from Delilah's limp fingers and read it in silence. She had not said a word, but tears were streaming down her cheeks.

Max crumpled the card. "Listen, love. Cheer up. We'll go out tonight, eat some fine food, drink some of the best champagne. We'll laugh and flirt and court each other all over again; we'll dance till dawn. Then when we're all primed and ready, we'll go to bed and try to make a baby."

Delilah flung her arms around him. "Oh, Max, you won't regret it, I swear."

He didn't believe her, but her pain over having no children was something he couldn't endure any longer.

The next couple of months were joyous—another honeymoon almost, with lots of lovemaking and laughter. Delilah filmed a couple of TV commercials for Merlin's Magical Brews that were so vivid and humorous and effective that Max advised an expensive national campaign on network TV. They went ahead with it, and Delilah's face was suddenly familiar to viewers all over the country. Sales of Merlin's herbal tea shot up once again.

But the longed-for pregnancy did not take hold, and at the end of five months Delilah was drooping again. "I don't understand it," she said one evening to Max. She had just started her period, which was still coming promptly every twenty-eight days. "It was so easy to get pregnant when I was twenty-one, even with a diaphragm firmly in place. Ever since that accident I've assumed myself remarkably fertile, and taken strict precautions never to be caught again. It's so ironic! Now there's not a single barrier to prevent the union of sperm and egg, yet the union doesn't occur."

"Well, it's certainly not for a lack of trying."

"I know, my darling. You've been performing your part with exceptional vigor and skill."

Delilah started charting her temperature every morning to make sure they would know when she was ovulating. "It's a good thing you're so damn sexy," Max growled early one morning when she insisted they make love before they both dressed for work because she had the slight pain in her lower abdomen that signals maximum fertility. "It's not easy for a fifty-one-year-old wreck like me to get his dick stiff on demand."

"I don't see you having any trouble."

"That because I'm basically a dirty old man who gets off on the idea of screwing a sweet young chick like you."

She laughed. "Shut up, Gramps, and come here."

Maybe this time, she thought afterward, examining her belly in the bathroom mirror and wondering if a child was growing inside. She had become very tuned in to her body. She knew that her breasts tended to become tender about a week before the start of her period, and that three days before the bleeding commenced she would experience some mild anticipatory cramping. The tender breasts were also a sign of pregnancy, she assured herself when she developed this symptom a week later. But when the cramping began promptly on day twenty-five, it brought with it a deepening depression. There was no child. They'd been trying for six months. Something was obviously wrong.

Delilah had read enough on the subject to know that fertility drops off sharply in women over thirty-five. And she was plagued by secret fears that the uterine infection she'd had after miscarrying Travis's child all those years ago might have resulted in some kind of tissue damage or scarring that could now be preventing a pregnancy.

She made an appointment with her gynecologist. The preliminary examination revealed no anomalies, but the doctor explained to her that a thorough infertility work-up involved a great many more tests, some of them exceedingly painful and unpleasant. "I don't care," she told him. "Let's go ahead with whatever you need to do."

The doctor explained that the first thing they'd better do was make certain Max was delivering potent and viable sperm.

"Terrific," said Max. "They think it's my fault?"

"It's not anybody's fault. They just want to rule some things out at the start, that's all."

"Well, what if it is my fault? Are you going to leave me for some stud with higher testosterone levels?"

Delilah heard something in his voice that convinced her he was only half joking. She went to him and put her arms around him. "Never. I wouldn't trade you for all the newborns in the maternity ward."

When he came home from his appointment with the urologist, Max slammed the front door much harder than usual, which frightened her a little. She wasn't able to tell from his expression what the verdict was. Please don't let it be Max, she was saying silently. For some reason it was easier to cope with the notion that she was the one with the problem.

"What happened?"

He lit up a cigarette—one of the particularly foul-smelling ones that she hated—and puffed away. "It was humiliating. 'We need a specimen,' the nurse tells me, waving me into the john. I had to jerk off into a cup, which wasn't easy since I sure as hell wasn't in the mood."

Delilah tried to joke about it. "Did you think about my sexy body?"

"As a matter of fact, I made up a little S and M fantasy involving your sexy body and a whip."

Which made her laugh. His face was more readable now. She started to relax. "So how about it, Mr. Macho? Are you man enough to give me a child?"

"You'll be delighted to hear I checked out. Apparently I don't have as many of the little buggers swimming around as some men do, but I've got enough, they assure me, to knock you up."

"I knew it. Look at all that hair on your chest."

He pulled her close and kissed her. "It seems there are a lot of things that could be wrong, including a possible immunological reaction of your body to my sperm. My age, not to mention yours, is against us, too. Your tubes could be blocked or your hormones askew or any number of other things. It could take several years to achieve a pregnancy, the guy told me. But there's been a lot of progress in infertility work over the last few years, he said."

"Test tube babies and all that. Want a drink? I could sure use one."

"Let's go out to dinner, love. Put on one of those gorgeous getups of yours and let's have ourselves some fun."

It was not until late that night, after they'd made love, that Max casually mentioned that he'd been referred to an internist for some other tests.

"What other tests?"

"The usual—chest X-ray, EKG, blood cholesterol, and so on. It seems I haven't been in for a physical in nearly ten years. Don't like doctors. Never have."

"Are you going to go?"

"I suppose. With any luck they'll tell me having a kid would be too strenuous for my heart."

Delilah felt a trill of anxiety. Max had lost weight recently, even though he had not been dieting. He had a smoker's cough that worried her sometimes. She thought of her father, felled by a heart attack at fifty-six. Max was fifty-one. "There isn't anything wrong with your heart, is there?"

"Not a thing, darlin'."

It was true, Max's heart was fine. It was his lungs that were full of cancer.

1984 was the worst year of Delilah's life. Max was dying. The love she had for him had grown into the single most powerful emotion she'd ever known, but despite his promise, he was leaving her. She couldn't deal with the fact that once again she was going to be left alone.

Because she couldn't deal with it, she denied it. She wouldn't even discuss it, not with him, not with anyone. She fiercely pretended there was nothing wrong.

She sat through the appointments with surgeons and oncologists without asking a single question. She refused to read any of the cancer literature or statistics that Max himself pored over. She drove him back and forth to the hospital for chemotherapy chatting about every other possible subject, constantly seeking his advice about matters at Merlin's that no longer needed his attention. And she didn't cry. Not once in the first few months after the diagnosis did she shed a single tear.

Max didn't press her; he himself denied the truth for the first couple of months. He didn't feel as if he was dying. He had a cough, yeah, but he'd had that for years. He could still climb a flight of stairs without getting winded, and he felt more inclined than ever to make a lot of love. He told his doctors they were on his A list.

"What does that mean?" one of them asked.

"Asshole," said Max. "You're one of the biggest ones I've ever met."

He even accused the hospital of mixing his X-rays up with somebody else's.

But after chest-crushing surgery on one lung and the horrors of several weeks of rigorous chemotherapy, Max's perceptions changed. He grew angry. At fate, for screwing him over. At his doctors, who were insensitive jerks. At himself for being stupid enough to smoke steadily for thirty-five years. And at Delilah, whose attitude wasn't helping him.

She was strong and brave in so many ways, but she wouldn't face up to this. He wanted to talk to her about what was happening to him, but Delilah wouldn't discuss it. He needed her, and she wasn't there for him.

He still desired her, even when the heaviness of his mortality began to weigh upon him. He had always been strongly sexed, and even now, when he was weak and nauseated from the drugs, there were good days when he was as obsessed with her physically as he'd ever been. Yet, for the first time in his life, lovemaking became a source of anxiety. He was afraid his increasingly gaunt body would disgust her, and he felt there was something obscene about a healthy and beautiful young woman opening her body to a cancer-ridden old man.

She never mentioned her longing for a baby—indeed, she seemed to have forgotten all about it—but Max fantasized all the time now about fatherhood. His erstwhile arrogance on the subject appalled him. It seemed horrible and unnatural that he had been so adamant about never having children. There would be no human legacy of his years on earth. He was going to dissolve into dust without leaving anything behind, and there was something intolerable about that. He began to pray to a God in whom he did not believe that Delilah would conceive and bring forth a son or a daughter whom he could hold in his arms for a little while, at least, before he surrendered to the night.

But Delilah didn't conceive. And Max went into a rage one night because he caught her in the bathroom inserting a diaphragm before she came to bed.

"You goddamned ball-breaking bitch!" he screamed at her. "I thought you'd do anything for a baby. What's the matter—are my genes too tainted for you now? Afraid the kid'll be born with cancer? Or maybe you think you'll catch it yourself and follow me gasping into the grave?"

"Stop it, Max! Don't talk about this thing as if it had already defeated you. You're not going to die. You're going to get better, you're going to be fine."

"Like hell. Stop being such a fucking coward, Delilah. If I can face the facts, so can you. Take that obscene object out of your body. Take it out right now, by God, or I'll rip it out of there myself."

"But you never wanted a baby; you only agreed to it to please me. And I thought you had enough to worry about now. I thought it would be best not to add any additional stress. Stop looking at me like that! You insisted you didn't want a child."

"I want one now, you selfish, stupid bitch. I want to leave something behind me besides a pile of dust. Get that thing out of there and lie down on the fucking bed. I'm not dead yet."

Delilah did as he asked. She lay shaking in their bed while Max stripped off his clothes. He'd dropped thirty pounds and was no longer well toned and muscular. He had an ugly surgical scar on his chest, and his skin was sallow from the drugs. He'd lost all his hair, even his eyebrows. Much as she loved him, she was afraid to look upon his body. If she did, she would cry, and if she started crying, she knew she'd never be able to stop.

"Open your eyes," he ordered as he lay down beside her. "No?

Open your legs, then; you'll do that, won't you?" He slid atop her and shoved his knee between her thighs. "If you don't have to see me, you can pretend I'm someone else. Someone healthy. Someone whole."

Delilah's eyes snapped open. "You son of a bitch."

"There's anger in you, is there? Well, that's something. I'm sick of looking at your blank, emotionless face."

Oh God, she thought. What's happening to us?

Max was usually the most considerate of lovers, but this time he took her without tenderness. When he finished he was panting for breath that wouldn't come. He reared up over her, his face grayish and soaked with sweat, his eyes full of bitter self-reproach. "I disgust you, don't I?"

"No," she whispered. She raised one hand to stroke his slack jaw, his hollow cheek. His bones felt fragile, his skin papery. "I love you so much."

"You haven't had an orgasm in weeks. You're dry as bone down there when I touch you. I don't blame you. Who in their right mind would be attracted to a corpse?"

"Shut up, Max! You didn't give me enough time, that's all."

"Don't lie to me. And stop lying to yourself."

"I love you," she repeated dully.

"You should go out and have an affair. Find yourself some healthy young stud who can screw the daylights out of you and make you come. I won't complain—how could I? I may feel like shooting the creep, but I won't."

"I don't want that, dammit. And even if I did, I wouldn't do it. I'm your wife, Max. I took a vow, remember? To love and to cherish from this day forward, for better for worse, for richer for poorer, in sickness and in health, forsaking all others . . ."

"Till death do us part," finished Max.

Silence hung between them. Then, to Delilah's horror, Max began to cry. Delilah had never seen him cry, and the sight unnerved her so much that she turned away, curling her body into a tight ball. I can't take this, she thought. I really can't. She felt herself stretching, floating, and vaguely remembered it as a feeling she'd experienced before. There was nothing to hold her together. Max was her center, her glue. Without him she had no more connection to the earth than a hot air balloon.

Her husband reached out for her. Each sob was a harsh, agonized sound. "Don't touch me." She clapped her hands over her ears. Her mind was about to shatter into tiny pieces and she was terrified.

"I need you, Delilah. Please, please, help me."

"Oh God!" She rolled back to his side, assailed by guilt and self-disgust. *You selfish, stupid bitch.* He'd never asked for help from her before, not directly. But all at once she understood he'd been asking for it nonverbally, and that she had let him down. "Oh, Max." She wrapped her arms around him, she cradled his head against her breasts as if he were the child she'd ached for. She had to be strong. For his sake, she had to reach deep inside herself and find the courage she'd been lacking.

"I'll help you; of course I'll help you. Forgive me, my darling. Forgive me for forcing you to ask."

When he was a little calmer he said, "You've got to face this thing. You've got to help me face it. D'you understand?"

"I couldn't believe it, that's all. I didn't want to believe it. There's nothing for me without you. And you promised me, Max. You promised you'd never leave."

"I know, baby. How do you think that makes me feel? I never should have married you. I can't give you your child, I won't be here to love you. It's killing me to know I'm abandoning you."

"Don't say that. Don't ever regret our marriage. I'd rather have a day with you, a week, a month than no Max Kaplan in my life. Do you understand? And you're not abandoning me. You're being snatched away."

"I need to be able to talk about it, Delilah. I need your courage. I haven't got enough of my own."

She stroked his poor bald head. He felt so fragile; not like the old Max at all. "Are you afraid?"

"Not of death, I don't think. Of suffering, of dying, yes. I know enough, have read enough, to understand what's going to happen to me. You're going to have to help me face it. Do you think you can do that?"

She hugged him so tight she could feel his bones. "Yes, dammit. But that doesn't mean I'm going to give you up without a fight."

"That's okay. I'm not going without a fight, I assure you. Fighting's fine. It's denial that isn't going to work anymore."

"You're right. I'm so sorry, Max. We'll fight it together, I swear."

Her words seemed to comfort him. She kissed his mouth, his throat, his chest. It was not the healthy body of the man she'd married, but it was still his body, still the only physical vehicle he had for expressing his love. "Max? Will you love me? You're right; I haven't had an orgasm for weeks, and it's driving me crazy."

He raised his head, the tiniest hint of a gleam coming into his eyes. "Jesus. The poor guy's dying and the lady wants to fuck again?"

"The lady would settle for a slow hand," she said coyly. "If you're not too exhausted, that is."

His kisses courted her, enflamed her, carried her up to the place where she hadn't been for far too long. "Laugh, sweetheart," he whispered. "Laugh in my arms again."

She couldn't laugh, but she did manage a smile.

Delilah couldn't sleep that night. She cradled Max close, imagining her body to be a shield that could protect him. She would not relax her vigilance. She alone could keep the chaos from him. She alone could hold back the night.

Sometime near dawn she lost her grip on consciousness and passed into the shadowed landscape of her dreams. She awoke sobbing, and this time Max held and comforted her. She cried for a long, long time.

When at last she rose, weary and weakened, to face the new day, Delilah had begun to accept in her heart what she had known in her mind for months. Max wouldn't be around much longer, but she was determined to seize every moment of every day that remained.

26

"I've decided to kill myself." Max's voice was calm, fully assured. It was early 1985 and he was a shadow, barely in this world at all. "Dying of cancer stinks. I've had enough, thank you very much. It's time to get a little more assertive here."

"You're too weak to kill yourself, Max," Delilah said lightly. Amazingly, his weakness had become something they could occasionally laugh about.

"I know. That's why you're going to have to help me."

"Don't be ridiculous." Delilah heard the nervousness in her own voice. Her brain told her he was serious, but her heart insisted he could not be. He'd talked this way a couple of times before, particularly after the agonizing sessions of chemotherapy.

"Can't you give me something to end this shit?" he'd said to his doctor during one of his excruciating stays in the hospital. "Take me off this wheel of torture with a nice, fast-acting lethal injection?"

Arthur Caffrey, his doctor, obviously embarrassed, had mumbled something about his Hippocratic oath.

"My life is over, duchess. I'm not being maudlin, just stating a fact. The doctors admit it, you know it, I know it. The cancer's spread all through me. I get weaker every day. The pain is unrelenting, and it's going to get worse. Death I've accepted. But torture? I'm no masochist—why put up with that?"

"Because your time hasn't come yet, Max."

"Bull. My time has come. I can't control the fact that I'm going to die sometime within the next few weeks. But I can control which day."

She hoped he would drop the subject; he always had in the past. But this time he didn't. This time he meant it.

"I don't know why more dying people don't kill themselves. Maybe they can't relax their hold on life. Maybe they don't have access to a reliable method of suicide, or maybe they're simply too weak and helpless to take the necessary action. I'm not going to wait until I reach that point, duchess. I'm going to do it while I still can."

"Max," Delilah said slowly, "I don't think I want to talk about this."

He looked up at her from the bed that had become his rack of torment. His dark eyes were huge in a face that had shrunk until it was no more than a pale covering for the bones of his skull. "You promised me your courage, duchess. It's not pleasant, but talk about it we must."

And so they did, even though talking was difficult for him. You need air to talk, and air was a luxury to Max. But he forced the air in and out of what was left of his lungs until the muscles in his chest screamed with the strain.

"I don't believe in suicide," Delilah said. "There's been too much of it in my family. It's a sort of family tradition . . . or curse. I thought about it myself after Travis left me. I had nothing to live for, I thought. If I'd acted upon those depressive wishes, look at everything I'd have missed. No one has the right to take their own life."

"The circumstances are totally different. You were a young woman with everything still ahead of you. I'm under sentence of death."

"But life is all we have, all we're sure of. That light goes out all too quickly for each of us anyway. Why deliberately surrender to darkness?"

"If it's coming anyway, why not?"

"Because you still have your brain, your wits, your unique personality. You're still Max, and your life is worth something to me, if not to you."

"Delilah, look at me: bedridden, skeletal, impotent. I've put up with most of this shit without complaining, but enough is enough.

I'm saying to God or fate or the powers that be, okay, boys, you've had your fun. I'm taking over now."

He was beginning to get through to her. She was no longer so certain she was right.

"I'm going to end it. So let's get practical and discuss how it should be done."

That same night he entered what she had come to call one of his bad spells. He was violently nauseated, unable to keep down even a few sips of water. And he was in terrible, unrelenting pain.

"Can't we do something about the pain?" she asked Arthur Caffrey. Max's doctor was formerly from Boston, a cancer specialist from Mass General who'd come out to L.A. and made a reputation for himself as being innovative, and compassionate. He had gone to college with Nick at Brown and was still a friend of his, one of those odd coincidences that had made Delilah feel, irrationally, that Arthur had come out to L.A. specifically to save Max. Certainly he'd done his best. But there was nothing, he'd told her sorrowfully a few weeks before, that could save her husband now.

"How much worse can it get? How much longer is it going to go on?"

Arthur shrugged and looked embarrassed. "We'll put him back in the hospital. Up the morphine—"

"He hates the hospital! And the morphine makes him sick. How much longer?" she demanded. "He wants to die."

"I'd want to die, too, if I were in his predicament," Arthur admitted.

When she again tried to pin him down on how much longer the torture would last, he couldn't give her a definite answer. "A month, maybe two. Or maybe not so long."

"You're damn right, not so long," said Max when he recovered enough for her to relate this conversation. "I've made a lot of efforts over the years to take responsibility for my life. Now I'm taking responsibility for my death."

Delilah was sitting at his bedside, her face in her hands. She had cried for him; all night she had cried. He was so thin, and he had suffered so.

"How would you do it?" It was the first time she'd been able to consider the possible methods, and when she saw the relief in his eyes, she knew she couldn't turn away from this any longer.

"I've considered several ways. A gun—that would be easiest. A good, quick bullet in the brain. I could do it, I'm sure. But what if it didn't work? Sometimes you miss a vital area, and instead of dead, you end up a vegetable. Besides, a gunshot wound would be unpleasant for you to deal with . . . afterwards."

Delilah shuddered, but Max remained calm. "I could open my veins, but that might be a little hard for me. I've never much cared for the sight of my own blood. That leaves drugs, I guess. I'm too weak to hang myself, and there are no convenient tall buildings around here to leap from."

"What drugs?" she whispered.

"That's where I'll need your help. Prescription drugs are tricky to obtain in the quantity I need. I wouldn't want to risk ending up in the hospital getting my stomach pumped. But you know everything there is to know about herbal remedies. You're familiar with drugs that heal and drugs that kill. I want you to get me one of the latter." He smiled faintly. "Preferably a fast-acting, painless one."

Oh God! She didn't know what she'd expected, but it wasn't this. "No, Max. I can't. You're asking me to poison you."

"I'm asking you to get me the stuff, that's all. I'll poison myself."

"I can't do that. Please, Max." Her control had shattered. "I love you, but don't ask me to do that."

"Delilah—"

"No!"

"Okay, duchess. Take it easy. Don't cry. Shit." Max felt a wave of self-disgust. How would *you* feel, asshole? Could you poison *her?* Even if she begged you to do it, could you be the instrument of your beloved wife's death?

"You're right; I shouldn't have asked it of you. I'm getting obsessive. Forget I said it, if you can."

Delilah had turned away from him, attempting without success to control herself. "I have to be alone for a little while. I have to think."

"I'm sorry, love. I'd rather go out screaming than inflict this on you."

Delilah fled.

That evening Dory came over to visit Max. Unlike some of their friends who had difficulty dealing with Max's illness, Dory was never uncomfortable with him. She was invariably cheerful even though she knew and accepted that he was going to die. Delilah always felt some slight relief in Dory's presence, and Max seemed to feel it, too.

After he fell asleep, Delilah and Dory sat in the living room and talked. "He wants to die," Delilah said. "He wants to kill himself, and he wants me to help him."

Her friend did not seem shocked. "Are you going to?"

"I guess I'd do almost anything. But I don't know what's right or wrong anymore. We're talking about *murdering* the man I love."

"Not exactly. His body's dying anyway. You're talking about easing the passage for his soul."

"I wish I could believe that."

Dory hugged her. "I haven't said much about this because I know you don't believe it, but there is no death, Delilah. Max has finished what he set out to do here and he's moving on. Listen. You've been so upset lately, I haven't told you what's happened to me in the past few months. I want to tell you now, okay?"

Delilah nodded.

"I've stopped damming up my psychic powers. I've stopped being afraid. I used to hear voices in my head, Delilah. I used to have dreams that would sometimes come true. I used to be terrified I might be going crazy, but every shrink I've seen has pronounced me sane. I understand what was going on now. It's been explained to me."

"By whom?"

"By Shastra. She's a disincarnate entity. I'm channeling her now. She's been a big help to me and to a number of other people, too."

The easiness Delilah always felt with Dory began to fade. "What the hell are you talking about? What do you mean, a disincarnate entity?"

"She no longer takes physical form, or at least, not in this plane of existence. She's a spirit guide. I go into a trance state and she speaks through me."

"You mean you're a medium? Like your great-aunt in the twenties?"

"Yes. It's called trance channeling now."

"Jesus, Dory!" Delilah passed the back of her hand over her forehead, thinking, I don't believe I'm hearing this. Dory had been increasingly interested in what Delilah called her metaphysical bullshit lately, but she'd had no idea it had gone that far.

"It was scary at first, but I'm getting used to it now. Shastra says she's no less real than you or me. We happen to have a bodily aspect at the moment and she doesn't, but essentially we're all eternal beings of spirit and light. Max isn't going to die, Delilah. Not in any real sense. You can't kill him; he can't kill himself." She closed her eyes. "He helped you die in a former life. You were warriors, primitive tribesmen from somewhere in South America, the Amazon jungles, perhaps. You had an arrow through your chest."

As she spoke, Delilah felt a sharp pain knife through her breasts. She gasped. Dory touched the spot and the pain subsided. "Max was your friend, your comrade in arms. He knew you were dying, but you wouldn't go. The wound was killing you, but not quickly enough. He cried and held you. You pleaded with him to end your torment. He took his knife and cut the artery in your throat, and you left your body easily, peacefully."

Delilah jerked away. For the first time ever, Dory had frightened her. Her throat felt odd for a moment, too; she was strongly aware of the blood pulsing there. A slight dizziness took her, leaving her lightheaded.

"It's okay," Dory said gently. "It was a long time ago."

Delilah stood up and retreated several steps. "I'm not into this stuff, Dory. I don't believe it. God and reincarnation and everlasting life and spirit guides are nothing but powerful myths we've invented to disguise the fact of our own mortality. The mind is very powerful. It can trick you. I don't think you're crazy, but I do think you're deceiving yourself."

Dory shrugged. Her red hair was long now, and her clothes were exotic. She looked like the witch Delilah had befriended years ago while developing her first herbal recipes. "The mind is even more powerful than you think."

"I appreciate your trying to help and comfort me. But I've got to find my comfort in the real world somehow. Not in the realm of entities and myth."

"I understand. I'm sorry. I won't do it again."

Delilah went back and put her arms around her friend. "If I'm being short with you, forgive me. I'm not my usual self these days at all."

Dory hugged back, saying, "Let me tell you one thing that has nothing to do with the psychic realm, okay? Max is strong-willed. If he's decided to do something, he'll do it. The action is his. You can help or not help; that's your choice. But if he's determined to go, don't hinder him. He knows what he's doing, and it's not wrong."

"Okay," Delilah whispered. "That's something I can cling to, when the time comes."

The time came soon. Max took another turn for the worse, and his pain became unbearable. She found him rocking on legs that would barely hold him, rifling the medicine cabinet one night, removing every prescription drug he could find and dumping them into a pile. "How many Valium do you have to swallow before you die?" he yelled at her when she ran into the bathroom. "How many aspirin, for chrissake, how many Dalmane? Will these do it?" He shook a half-empty pill bottle at her. "It might not work, dammit, but I'm ready to take that chance."

She got the pills away from him and forced him back into bed, where he cried in that terrifying manner she remembered from once before. She held him close. His body was wasted now, thinner than a child's. "Are you sure, Max? Are you sure that this is what you want?"

"Of course I'm sure." Barely able to lift his head, he cast a sardonic look down the length of his pain-wracked husk of a body. "This isn't me, duchess. What you see lying here in bed isn't the man you love, the man who loves you. I have to get out of here, baby. Help me find the way out."

Put that way, it reminded Delilah of the image she'd held so many years ago—the doors that were closed to her, the doors she was determined to open. And she had opened them, many of them—the door to independence, the door to success, and with Max, the door to love.

She would help him. Like her, Max was not the sort of person who could endure being shut out, or shut in. Like her, he had to open the door and walk through.

Deciding to walk through into death and actually going ahead with it proved to be two very different things. Delilah knew of plenty of plant poisons, but they were difficult to obtain. And even if she could get them, many herbal drugs would cause violent discomfort if ingested in a lethal dosage. Despite her background in the subject, she wasn't a professional herbalist, and even though Max trusted her, she wasn't sure she trusted herself.

She thought of calling Jonathan Templeton and asking him to write her a prescription for enough morphine or barbituates to do the trick. He would do it, she suspected; of all the physicians she knew, her uncle struck her as the most humane. Although it had been many years since she'd talked to Nick and Travis's father, she'd never really included him in her feud with the Templetons, perhaps because, like her, he'd always seemed a bit of an outcast—Jonathan the gay activist, Jonathan the wandering M.D., who'd spent most of his life working for various charitable organizations in poor countries around the globe. "My father's a saint," Nick had once told her, with pride. "He's a weirdo," had been Travis's opinion.

She tried to reach him one day, calling his last known address in San Francisco. The young man who answered told her that Dr. Templeton was ministering to the sick somewhere in Latin America and likely to be away for at least two years. There were no other doctors she dared to ask. She was on her own.

She dug out her herbals. She wanted something gentle, fast-acting, and sure. It didn't have to be untraceable, for Max was very sick and his death would probably be put down to natural causes. But they did need something that wouldn't leave a telltale signature on his body.

"We'll have to be careful," Max told her after she'd been researching the problem for several days. "We don't want an autopsy. The only thing that worries me about this is the possibility that you could be held responsible. No doubt there's a law against doing what I'm asking you to do."

"I don't care about that."

"Maybe not, duchess, but I do."

Trusting her to find the solution, Max turned his mind to other worries, the chief one being what was going to happen to Delilah after his death. He knew she wasn't thinking that far ahead. The ending of his life was all that concerned her, not the continuation of her own.

"I think you should give some serious consideration to going back to Boston," he told her one evening. "You know a lot about the tea business now. Don't forget your old dreams and fantasies about taking over Templeton Tea and running it yourself."

"That's just what they were, Max, fantasies. It's been so long. I can barely remember what Travis looked like. As for my grandmother, she's an old woman now. Even if I still wanted to get back at her for what she did to me, how could I go after an eighty-year-old woman?"

"Im not telling you to do it for revenge. It's your heritage I think you should seek. A number of strong women have run Templeton Tea, and you're the obvious successor to Minerva Templeton. Seeing her again will undoubtedly call up some of those old angry feelings, but you'll be able to deal with that."

"Oh God, Max, I don't know."

"You've got to deal with that bitter period of your past, then put it behind you. Test the waters for a while, and if it's right for you, stay. Merlin's has reached its pinnacle; you know that. But you're still young, and ripe for another challenge."

She shook her dark head. "The Templetons . . . the tea company . . . they just don't matter to me anymore."

"You think not, but they do matter. You love your grandmother, Delilah. Listen. Love counts. Don't let your grandmother pass from this world with your love for her—and hers for you—unspoken. Go back. It will take courage, but you've never lacked for that."

"I'll think about it," she promised.

"I want to know you're going to be all right. You've grown far too dependent on me."

"Stop taking the world on your shoulders, Max." She smiled as she spoke, trying to call up some of the insouciance of their early life together. "I'll be okay."

Neither one of them entirely believed it.

"I think I've found it," she told him a few days later.

Max didn't ask what. He was in one of his bad phases again. Pain had him on its wheel, and there was very little breath for him to speak.

"It will work," she assured him, answering the mute question in his eyes. "The taste will be bitter, but there won't be any pain. Your limbs will get heavy and you'll go to sleep. That'll be it. You won't"—she stumbled a little—"wake up."

"Will they know?"

"No. No one'll know." In fact, she wasn't positive about this. Arthur Caffrey was well trained, and he knew that Max had been thinking about suicide. But even if he suspected something, Delilah didn't think he'd do anything about it. Why should he? They all knew a natural death was only a few weeks away.

"I'll write a suicide note, just in case. If there's any question, just hand over the note. In it I'll insist that you had nothing to do with it."

"If you think it's necessary," she agreed, even though she suspected such a note wouldn't help her much if the truth came out. Everybody knew she was an expert on herbal brews—who else but she could obtain the stuff for him?

She wasn't going to worry about that, though. Even if the worst happened and she was brought up on charges, she figured she could make a pretty convincing case for the right of a terminal cancer patient to bring a merciful end to his own life.

"When will you have it?" Max asked her.

Her hands clenched into fists. "I have it now."

Max looked at her, his dark eyes huge in his pain-ridden, wasted face. "Then what the hell are we waiting for?"

It was a Saturday in March 1985, a warm, breezy morning with brilliant sunshine and the scent of flowers in the air. Delilah pulled wide the curtains in their bedroom so Max could look out from the heights of their canyon-top home and see the entire L.A. basin. It was clear—the wind had swept away the air pollution for once. The downtown skyscrapers shimmered in the sun.

"I want you to leave, Delilah. Go to the beach house in Malibu and stay for the weekend. Let the neighbors see you there. I'll wait until evening. That way, when the doctor estimates the time of death, there'll be no doubt in anybody's mind that you were far away."

"No."

"I don't have the energy to argue with you, dammit. Just do as I say."

Delilah stubbornly shook her head. "I'm not leaving you, so don't waste whatever energy you have fretting about it. This is one argument you've got no chance of winning."

Max subsided. Standing there at the border separating life from death, he seemed to see all things differently. The material objects around him had no more substance than the vanishing flesh of his own wasted body.

Where did that flesh go? he wondered. He had seen his own body waste away to almost nothing, yet he was still here; he hadn't changed a bit. Did that mean he would still be here, still be somewhere, when every particle of his body had passed into dust? He'd never believed this before. He couldn't quite believe it now. Yet there were times when he seemed to float above his body, look down upon it, and smile. He felt glad to be leaving it. He didn't need it anymore.

But his tired old body could cause trouble for Delilah, and that was the only thing that made him doubt the course he had decided upon. "Go," he said one more time. "You don't want to watch me die."

"I love you. I'm going to be right here beside you, holding your hand."

He didn't argue any further. The truth was, he wanted her beside him. He wanted the last thing he saw on earth to be her face.

Delilah had dreaded this day. She had imagined so many times the way it would happen, the way it would feel, what they would say to each other. Despite Dory's pronouncements, she didn't believe there was anything after death. This was it, this was the end. They wouldn't meet again in some fantasy afterlife, they wouldn't come back in new bodies and love again. Max was a light about to be extinguished. The place where he'd burned would be dark.

She wanted to cling, to stop him somehow, but he was more cheerful and relaxed than he'd been in weeks. He was finally back in control.

"You know where my will is? And the suicide note?"

"Yes. I know where everything is, Max; don't worry."

"About the funeral, I haven't planned anything for that because I don't want anything. Cremate what's left of me. And don't keep the ashes in an urn on the fireplace like some crazy mournful widow or I swear I'll come back and haunt you. Scatter them over the ocean. No ceremony about it, please. You can dump 'em off the end of the Santa Monica pier."

She couldn't speak. The tears she'd been trying to keep back were streaming down her cheeks.

"Cry a little; that's okay," he said gently. "I'd be sad if you didn't cry. But don't get carried away. Don't turn your face from living on my account. You haven't had any good loving for months. Find yourself somebody soon. Get married again, Delilah."

"No." She shook her head violently. "No."

"Yes. You're still young, and there will be a man. When he comes, I want you to love him. I want you to have your children before it's too late. You were right about that, you know. It's the one thing I'd do differently if I had the chance. Say yes to life, Delilah. It's the no's you regret when you're lying down dying. I think we're all meant to say yes a lot more often than we do."

She was sobbing now. Max reached up and touched her face lightly, stroking away her tears. "I love you, duchess." He took the glass she'd placed on the bedside table and raised it in salute. "To your courage, Delilah. To your wholehearted, unselfish love."

He put the glass to his lips and swallowed the bitter mixture down.

Delilah had expected grief, she'd expected loneliness. What she had not expected was the nether depths of depression into which she was plunged after Max's death. During the first couple of weeks she was numb, just as everyone said she would be, but the numbness turned to a slow, burning ache in the center of her body, which became her body, became her heart. She looked at her life and saw nothing but a hole in the fabric of creation. She had no connections to anything. She had no parents, no husband, no child. The love of her life was dead, and she knew she'd never feel so intensely about anyone again. Don't turn away from living, he'd told her. But life had nothing she wanted. What she wanted was to be where Max was. To go into that hole and never come out.

In the beginning she fought the depression because she felt obligated to do so. Max had been worried about her, and she'd assured him she'd be okay. So she went to work every day at Merlin's, mechanically doing her job. She even filmed a new TV commercial, smiling and clowning for the cameras with apparent success, since the producers were pleased with the results. Her body moved through space, through time, yet sometimes when she caught a glimpse of her reflection in a mirror or a window, she didn't recognize that body. She didn't feel as if that slim, long-legged, dark-haired woman had anything to do with her real, essential self, which was off somewhere, searching for Max.

Her friends—especially Sam and Dory—were wonderful to her, visiting, bringing food, taking her out to restaurants and clubs, hugging her and telling her she was loved. She appreciated it, but they couldn't pull her out of the abyss. She wouldn't even reach up for the hands they thrust at her; she just kept sinking, gradually sinking, going so deep she could no longer see the sun.

On one particularly dark night of the soul, Delilah rose from her lonely bed—the bed where her husband had died—and wandered out into the room she called her herbiary at the back of the house. Mechanically, she gathered together the ingredients of the potion she'd given Max. It had worked exactly the way they had hoped—sweeping and swift, like a powerful sleeping draft. Arthur Caffrey had seemed a bit suspicious when he came to the house to pronounce Max dead, but he'd signed the death certificate without asking too many questions. Delilah sensed he didn't really want to know.

"I thought it would drag out longer. But he'd lost the will to live, and once that happens, death can come at any time. There won't be a postmortem," he'd added, and she'd had that, at least, to be grateful for.

The potion had taken Max from his agony of breathlessness and pain. After he'd gone, his face had been transfigured, all the agony faded, leaving an expression of serenity. She had kissed him and closed his eyes. She had lain down beside him and held him one last time. He was cold, so cold. She had wept and kissed him again and told him good-bye.

She hadn't been afraid. She had freed him; now she was going to free herself.

Delilah blended the ingredients and poured the mixture into a fluted champagne glass. She dressed herself in a silk peignoir by Chanel, brushed her hair, and applied a light dusting of her finest imported make-up. Then she propped herself up with satin-covered pillows and sat in bed holding the glass. She thought about writing a note, but to whom? Dory and Sam would be devastated, of course, but they would understand. They knew how much she'd loved Max. As for the Templetons, she'd been estranged from them for so long. She'd pushed away Max's suggestion about going back and resolving her problems with Grendam. Her grandmother was a phantom from her past, as were Travis and Nick. They weren't real anymore; nothing was real except the Templeton curse.

The ethics of suicide. How passionately she'd argued that with Max. It seemed odd now; she couldn't remember her side of the debate. Of course he'd been right to end it. When life was unbearable, what other course was there to take?

She put the crystal glass to her lips. It had a sharp, pungent odor . . . It will be the last thing, she thought idly, I shall ever smell.

But for some reason it called up another smell—a woodsy scent she associated with Grendam. She flashed back to the night they'd held each other and comforted each other in the China Tea House Tavern. She'd seen her own death then. She'd seen herself dying alone in a bed, the ceiling pressing down. She'd seen her death, and been terrified because she was ten years old and wanted to live.

Now she wanted to die.

"Coward," said her grandmother so loudly that Delilah jumped and nearly spilled the drink. She looked around wildly. There was nobody in the room except herself. It was three in the morning and the city was asleep. Delilah put down her glass; her hand was trembling so hard she could no longer hold it. She'd heard a voice; she would swear to it. She was hallucinating. She was having a psychotic break.

She listened, but the voice did not come again. Instead her

grandmother's image rose up in her mind: petite and ramrod straight, those hard man's eyes, that slight sneer of her upper lip. She recalled how cold and controlled Grendam had been on that day in Cambridge when she informed Delilah that Travis had abandoned her.

Bitch. Perhaps the time for a reckoning had finally come. "Go back to Boston," Max had told her. "It will take courage, but you've never lacked for that."

Delilah closed her eyes. She fell asleep with Grendam's image imprinted on her brain, but during the night, when she dreamed, it was not Minerva Templeton but an auburn-haired woman she saw, clad in the garments of another age.

In the morning when she woke, the sun was bright and warm upon her body, and the ache inside her seemed a little less severe.

She got up and poured the potion down the sink.

27

"I need your help, Sam," Delilah said. "I want to know everything there is to know about Templeton Tea. Past, present, and projections for the future. How does the company stack up against its competitors, Lipton, Salada, Brooke Bonds, Twinings? What are its strengths, its vulnerabilities? I want numbers, hard data, facts. Can we find these things out?"

Sam patted his computer terminal. "This baby can find almost anything out."

"I'm going to start on the historical research. But I'd like you to grind some numbers for me, do some financial analyses of the tea business in general and Templeton's in particular."

"You got it." Sam was grinning. "Do I detect a note of the old crusader spirit in your voice? What are you planning?"

"I'm not exactly sure yet."

"It's good to see you taking an interest in something again. It's been a long time, babe."

"A long, dark time. But I think I'm finally coming out of the tunnel, Sam."

"I'm glad. Max would be, too."

Delilah nodded her head vigorously. "I know."

At the beginning, she reviewed the things she'd known for years about the origins and development of Templeton Tea. She spent more time than she'd ever spent before analyzing her ancestors' characters. She studied their weaknesses, because it was the weaknesses in Templeton Tea that she was striving to find.

She kept running up against references to the Templeton curse.

Every time something went wrong, every time someone died young, the curse was blamed for it. There had been at least one suicide in each generation. Her great-great-grandfather had hanged himself after a scandalous love affair around the turn of the century. Her grandfather's uncle Earnest had blown his brains out after the stock market crash in 1929. Her aunt Sarah, Nick and Travis's mother, had starved herself to death. Even her great-grandfather Harrison, while not strictly a suicide, had drunk himself into oblivion so often that he'd finally fallen down the stairs in the China Tea House Tavern and broken his neck.

As for her own generation, Nick suffered from depression and had talked about suicide on at least one occasion that she could recall. And she herself had nearly drunk Max's potion.

Was there really a curse on the family? Some inner destructiveness, passed down genetically, perhaps, that was activated in times of sorrow or despair? The idea chilled her. How did one fight something like that?

Aunt Sarah hadn't been a Templeton, she reminded herself, so maybe it wasn't genetic after all.

I'm not going to worry about it, she decided. Dory was always telling her she shouldn't allow herself to get caught up in negative thoughts.

She delved instead into the modern history of the tea company, beginning from 1929, when Grendam and her husband Edward had taken over. The company had been in serious straits at the time, she learned, but her grandparents had anticipated the growth in the tea bag market, which had started out slowly but boomed after World War II. Her figures for 1950 showed that the sales of loose tea in that year had been almost twice as high as the sales of tea bags, whereas in 1983 tea bags accounted for 60 percent of the total market, followed by instant tea and iced tea mixes with 37 percent, and loose tea with only 3 percent.

At the same time that she had kept up with these changes in the marketplace, Minerva had maintained Templeton's image as a producer of quality teas. In recent years she had cleverly combined the two functions, producing quality blends in tea bags for discerning customers. Most American tea companies offered customers their standard tea bag blend—bland—but Templeton's offered such varieties as Darjeeling, Ceylon, Earl Grey, and English Breakfast tea.

Even so, Grendam's track record was not as good in the last couple of years as it had been throughout the fifties, sixties, and seventies. The market for tea had expanded considerably in the late seventies, partly as the result of a series of natural calamities in coffee-producing countries in 1975 that had driven up the price of coffee to record levels. She learned that 1977 had been a banner year for U.S. tea imports and sales. Since then sales had leveled off, partly because of higher prices caused by the increased cost of transport resulting from the oil crisis, but all in all the demand for tea was much healthier than it had been twenty or thirty years before. To her surprise, Delilah could find no indications that the tea company had profited from this.

"I think I've discovered my grandmother's weakness, Sam. In spite of the romance and ruthlessness of my family's early tea barons, Templeton Tea has always maintained a staid, conservative image. Grendam's efforts have been aimed at keeping her longtime tea-drinking matrons happy, rather than going after the Yuppie crowd that we targeted here at Merlin's. She hasn't kept up with the times. She needs new advertising, a new marketing approach.

"Then of course there's the herbal tea market. Templeton's produces it—largely in response to the competition from Merlin's Magical Brews—but their product is inferior, it doesn't sell well, and their distribution is poor."

"In short, you can see several ways to improve the fortunes of Templeton Tea. You're thinking of leaving us, aren't you?"

"Oh God, Sam, I don't know."

"I always knew this would happen someday."

Delilah threw down her papers and held her hands out to him. "I've made no decision yet, but if I do go, you can buy me out, Sam. You'll be the man, with nobody to answer to, and I suspect part of you has always ached for that."

He shook his bald head, which he no longer had to shave. "That's what you ache for, babe. You won't rest till you've got it. Merlin's isn't a big enough arena for you anymore. The challenges are met, the thrill is gone. You're aiming to beat the shit out of the next windmill, scale the impossible peak."

She didn't say anything. She knew he was right.

"When you gonna quit, babe? When you gonna start appreciating what you have, instead of reaching out for the next goal? When you gonna live in the here and now, instead of the future or the past?"

"Maybe never. I'm a type A personality, I guess."

"Merlin's is your baby, Delilah. How can you even think of selling your half?"

"Merlin's may be my baby, but Templeton Tea is my heritage. And sometimes I think that everything I've done here has merely been preparation for going back. Max thought I should. He wanted me to take on this challenge."

"And you? Are you sure it's what *you* want?"

"I'm not at all sure it's what I *want.* But I'm beginning to think it's something I have to do."

On the evening before she left California for the East Coast, Delilah drove to the beach house at Malibu where she and Max had spent many a happy weekend together relaxing, swimming, sunbathing, and simply gazing out to sea. She made herself a light supper, listened to some music, and tried to let her mind rest from all the planning and fantasizing she'd been engaged upon for so many weeks. When night fell, she put on a jacket and went outside to walk along the beach.

The moon was bright that night, the air was clear. Overhead she could see a vast dusting of stars flung upon the velvet face of night. As the moon climbed higher into the heavens, it trailed a path of silver across the black ocean. Delilah sat down in the sand, not far from the water's edge, and watched the moonlight dance as the waves rolled in.

Max had loved the sea. She felt closer to him here than anywhere. Delilah rested her face on her chin and spoke to him:

"I'm doing it, my love. I'm taking your advice and going back to confront all my old ghosts. I feel compelled to do so—as if you're pushing me.

"Are you still there, still *somewhere,* looking out for me, making sure I do the right thing? Sometimes when I'm just falling asleep I hear your voice. I know you're speaking to me, although I can't remember afterwards what you've said. Is that possible, Max? I don't really believe it's possible, and yet when it happens, it feels so real.

"I wish I could buy all this psychic stuff that seems to be so popular out here. Remember how we used to laugh at Dory's absurd beliefs? She's becoming quite a celebrity; her marriage has gone to hell, but she and her disincarnate entity friends are packing them in in lecture halls all over the West Coast. She has a huge chunk of clear quartz crystal in her living room. She sits in front of it when she meditates. She claims it focuses her awareness and increases her vibrational frequency or some such nonsense.

"She wants to channel for me—to bring you through, no doubt. You're a disincarnate entity yourself now, Max; how do you like that? I can hear you hooting with laughter at the thought.

"Oh God, Max! I feel so alone."

Delilah wondered if she was crazy, sitting on a beach, talking to the wind. "I don't know what I want. I don't know why I'm going back. I'm afraid it's not from motives that are particularly noble; I tell myself that I'm too mature and compassionate to want revenge, but in my heart I think that's exactly what I want. On the other hand, I know I can run the tea company better than my cousin Travis. And I want *her* to know it. Grendam.

"As for Travis, it's odd, but I don't have many feelings for him at all. He was just a kid, too immature to know what he wanted from life. We had an unfortunate love affair—so what? If it hadn't been Travis, it would have been some other man. I was too frivolous for a serious affair. It wasn't until I met you that I learned what it really means to love.

"Perhaps when I see him, I'll feel differently. Perhaps I'll want to get him, too. But at present all I want from Travis is his job."

She fell silent. For several minutes there was no sound beyond the lapping of the waves and the slight rustle of the wind in the grasses behind the beach. Staring into the moondance on the waves, Delilah felt a change come over her. She sensed she was on the verge of a great insight, an epiphany that would alter her view of herself, the world, reality.

She couldn't take her eyes away from the moonlight. It seemed as if she could actually go *into* that silvery light, become part of it. Leap and play as the moonbeams did on the rippling surface of the sea. What freedom, she thought.

Jumping to her feet, she began to run along the beach. The wind whipped her hair back from her face and her feet kicked up a spray of sand as she flew along, heart pumping hard but evenly, her breathing easy. She was one with the wind, one with the sea. Delighted, exhilarated, she laughed again as she ran, imagining the echoes of her laughter radiating outward in all directions and girdling the world with her joy.

Her spirit expanded, rushing upward, bursting free. She shot up, rising above the beach, skimming over the dark waters, following that trail of moondance toward its source. Below she could see the darkened beach where it collided with the even blacker Pacific, then, rising higher, the curvature of the earth on the shadowed horizon. She laughed. My God, she thought, I'm flying! I'm flying as witches do.

Then, briefly, she caught a glimpse of something else. Far away, in the distance. A woman. Herself? Although she could not see the woman's face, Delilah knew her as well as she knew her own image in the mirror. She thought she heard the woman speak, but her words did not carry across the vast gulf that separated them. Delilah strained toward her, for she knew the apparition had something important to tell her.

My God, where am I? What's happening to me?

No sooner did fear enter her mind than she snapped back into her body again. No, she corrected herself impatiently. Back to a normal state of consciousness. She hadn't really been *out,* for God's sake. What an absurd idea.

She flung herself down in the sand, panting. My God, what was wrong with her? Here she was, all alone in the middle of the night, running wildly down a darkened beach and laughing, as if she were happy, as if she were in love.

"I hate you, Max," she whispered. The next thing she knew, she was shouting it. "I hate you for breaking your promise! I hate you for dying and leaving me alone!"

She listened. She tried to hear his voice. She looked again for that woman, the phantom she'd thought she'd seen, but there was nothing, nothing. All she could see was dark water, dark sky.

She rolled over, face down in the sand, and cried.

PART SIX

The intellect of man is forced to choose
Perfection of the life, or of the work,
And if it take the second must refuse
A heavenly mansion . . .

—William Butler Yeats

Boston, 1986

28

In the China Tea House Tavern, the witch's brew was doing its work. Helen Templeton could not measure how much time had passed since she'd quaffed the drug. It did not matter. Time was an illusion. The Wisdom taught that there are no lines, only circles. Circles within circles, the serpent with its tail in its mouth.

Even so, she felt elated to know that it was the future she was seeing, for few are blessed with such vision. She couldn't be sure, though, that what she saw would come to pass. The Sight is not perfect, alas, and all human events are a mass of probabilities, not certainties.

"Can the future be changed?" she had asked. "Is it not immutable, fixed?"

"Nothing is fixed," Rebecca, her mentor, had told her. "Even the past is mutable; indeed, we change it all the time."

This she had never entirely understood. If she could change the past, there were so many things she would do differently! She would be more careful not to alienate so many of the good people of Boston. She would try (she doubted she'd succeed) to resist the temptation of loving Matthew. And, most important of all, she would tell her son, Charles, the truth he needed to know to save him from the tragic set of circumstances that had made him a murderer. Indeed, if she could alter these things, there would be no need to concern herself with the future.

But although the notion of probable futures made some small degree of sense to her, the notion of probable pasts did not. What was done was done. It was not actions, but consequences she must alter. If she could spare her descendants some of the pain she had suffered, she would be satisfied.

There was one in particular. One whose life she had seen in snatches, one with whom she felt a special closeness. The witch-haired woman, who laughed and loved and did not recognize her danger.

"Is she one of my own future lives?" Helen asked her guides. "I see her so clearly—I feel her energy, her grief, her joy. She has my eyes. Is she my descendant, or is she another aspect of my soul, another life, another chance?"

There was never any answer. No matter how deep her meditative trance, to this question there was no reply.

Whoever she was, the black-haired woman was in need of her. And the other woman, the old one who would die soon, she needed her, too. Helen was determined to help them, if she could. But how to reach them? Was she capable of slipping the chains of earth, of time?

This was her challenge and her task.

Two nights after her eightieth birthday, Minerva dreamed she was back home in Darjeeling, under the purple mountains, climbing the terraced gardens of tea, higher, ever higher, into the sun. When she reached the top, the sky was so near, it pressed upon her. All around her, as far as she could see, were hazy steppes of deep green tea, dotted here and there by the brightly colored saris of the tea pickers as they stooped over the bushes, fingers flying, tossing their gleanings to the wicker baskets strapped to their backs. There on her mountaintop, Minerva drew a breath of the clear, thin air and reveled in the fact that she was mistress of all this.

She heard a scuffling sound as someone else climbed the rocky path behind her. Her dream turned fearsome; her heart accelerated, and perspiration burst out on her palms. Even before she could see him, she knew those heavy footfalls, knew the face that had appeared so often to darken her dreams. She backed to the edge of the precipice, trying to make her small body smaller still.

"Thought I was done for, didn't you? Thought you'd won."

The voice. Oh God, *his* voice. She edged farther away from

him, that hulking body, grown coarse and ugly with age. The air around her darkened, the mountains became walls. She could still smell the tea . . . she knew it was there . . . but she couldn't see Darjeeling anymore.

He came closer. His gait was heavy and uneven; he was leaning on a carved walking stick. From where she was cowering she could see that the cane had an ivory elephant head knob on top.

"No, no." He was close enough now for her to feel his breath against her skin. She tried to flee, but there was nowhere to go. At her back was emptiness. And he was lifting the cane, thick and cruel, the big bull elephant, malevolent, closer, closer, until it was on her, *in her,* and she screamed.

Then she was falling, tumbling backward into the tea gardens, nothing more than a leaf destined to be crushed and twisted and fired, and dissolved in liquid heat. "The stone," a voice hissed. "Remove the stone."

Minerva awoke in her bed in the China Tea House Tavern. Her heart was galloping and her damp nightgown was twisted around her hips. For a second or two she couldn't breathe, and she panicked, thinking, this must be the end.

Slowly the terror eased its grip. Harry Cox, physician son of her old and dear friend Augustus Cox, had said she had a tightly wired sympathetic nervous system that reacted physiologically to stress with an outpouring of adrenaline.

"I'm going to change your blood pressure medication," he'd told her recently. "The one we've been using isn't doing as good a job as it used to do."

"Please, Harry, don't fuss."

But now she remembered the anxious look in his eyes as he'd given her the new prescription. Dammit, she couldn't die yet. There were things she had to do first. Delilah was back. She would be starting work on Monday. Minerva had a whole world of things to settle concerning Delilah's future, the company's future. Work to do, decisions to make.

Minerva rose from bed, wrapped a thin silk robe around her, and went downstairs. Mary Mango was asleep, of course, and she didn't wish to wake her. She went into the kitchen and put the kettle on.

Tea. Universal panacea. She took her cup back upstairs to the large book-lined library that had been one of the additions to the house and got a thriller from the shelves—*The Sodom Conspiracy,* by Nicholas Templeton. She'd read it before, of course, but it was a goody. Taking the book back to her room, she sat in the rocker to read and sip her tea. But after about ten pages, her eyes started burning and she set Nick's novel aside. Instead she stared into the blackened fireplace that took up most of the wall on the north side of the bedroom. Huge, cavernous hole; it seemed to suck her in.

She must have dozed off, for the next time she tasted her tea, it was cold. She'd been dreaming again. "The stone, the stone, remove the stone," repeated the voice in her dream. She jerked awake to find her attention still fixed upon the hearth.

The fireplace, one of the originals, dated from the early eighteenth century. One of the stones in the masonry around the fireplace was loose, and she'd been intending to call someone in to fix it. She didn't think the hearth had ever been restored.

A dream, just a dream. Yet something compelled her to obey its dictates, just as she had obeyed on the night when she had moved her bed into the charmed circle. She knelt at the hearth and played her fingers over the stones until she found the loose one. *Remove the stone.*

It wouldn't come out. She broke a nail on her left hand, then a couple of seconds later, another on her right. What am I doing? she asked herself, even as she went downstairs to the kitchen to fetch a hammer and chisel from the tool box under the sink.

Even with the tools, her task was not easy. The stone was heavy. When at last she coaxed it forth and wrestled it to the floor, the cloud of dust that arose from the violated hearth made her choke. She stared into the small recess. She could see nothing but blackness.

She stuck in her hand. The hole was cold and grimy. She half expected to feel the strike of a serpent from deep inside, even though she knew this was impossible. In India, yes, but this was Boston.

She remembered the tale her father used to tell of a snake attack at a posh Calcutta hotel. A krait—a small, highly venomous snake whose bite could kill you in under a minute—was coiled on the edge of the shelf in the closet of his room. As he opened the door, it fell out and landed on the stiff bib of his dress shirt, striking madly, then bounced off and hit the floor, where her father was able to crush it with his boot. The heavily starched formal garb had saved his life.

I've kept my formal garb about me, too, she thought. For years I've armored myself. But I am old now, and the starch is faded, the armor rusted. There is nothing to shield me now.

The recess was empty. Of course it's empty; what did you expect? She probed deeper, just to be sure. Her fingers scraped on something sharp. She tapped. It was cold. Metallic. And immovable.

In the end she had to chisel out two other stones to enlarge the opening before she was able to draw her discovery out. It was a rectangular tin box, battered and old. The hasp was ornate—a sort of filigree material. The box was locked, so Minerva used the chisel once again to get it open.

Inside the box she found a thick oilskin pouch. She cut the leather ties that secured it and peeled back the fabric. She was holding a sheaf of papers, hand-bound between two faded cloth covers. The ink was surprisingly dark. The script was ornate, but written in a bold, firm hand.

But she could not read the pages, which were written in Latin. Pamela Grainger had taught her only a little Latin before they had mutually agreed to abandon their study of Roman literature.

One phrase was intelligible to her. On the last page of the volume were inscribed the words HELEN TEMPLETON. 30 APRIL 1730.

Nick and his daughter Kelsey, who was with him for the weekend, came to visit Minerva a few days later, bringing her a birthday pillow that Kelsey had sewn and embroidered herself. Minerva hugged her great-grandchild, and her grandson, both of whom she loved very much. They took over her kitchen, making a cheerful mess as they baked her a cake and frosted it. Minerva kept hearing shrieks of laughter from the kitchen, and the seven-year-old girl protesting frequently: "No, Daddy, not like *that!*"

Minerva was not allowed to help, although she insisted on brewing tea for them to drink with the cake. She demonstrated to Kelsey the proper way of making tea. "You must let the water come to the boil, my dear, then take it off the stove immediately so the water doesn't lose too much oxygen. The pot must be warmed first, of course, then you measure in one spoon of tea for each cup and one for the pot. Now we'll pour the boiling water over the tea and let it steep for five minutes. Have you got the tea strainer, Nick? The British pour the tea in over the milk—in India we drank it very white indeed—but in this country I've become accustomed to adding the milk after the tea. Milk precipitates the tannin; did you know that, Nick? It's because of tannin that the caffeine in tea is absorbed slowly by the body, which is why tea doesn't affect our hearts and nerves as much as coffee does."

"What's caffeine?" Kelsey asked, reaching a grubby hand into the cookie jar.

"It's a stimulant found in tea and coffee. Tea is made up of several components, including caffeine, tannin, and the aromatic oils which lend it its flavor and its scent . . ." Her voice trailed off as she looked into the girl's green eyes. Her hair was short and curly and dark like her father's. She looks like Delilah, Minerva thought. She had enacted this same ceremony with Delilah years ago: boil the water, warm the pot, spoon in the tea, let it steep.

She hugged Kelsey, hard. The little girl squirmed in her arms, saying, "May I have the pretty cup, Gran? The white one with all the gold leaves on it?"

"You'd better be careful with it," said Nick. "That cup's an antique that's probably worth a fortune."

"She'll be careful," Minerva said.

Later she showed Nick the papers she'd found hidden in the hearth. She knew she could trust him not to laugh at the circumstances. She told him about her dream and her compulsion to chisel out the stone. "There's something funny going on in this house, Nick. I'm a rational-minded woman, as you know very well. But this is the second time I've felt driven to do something odd."

Nick took it calmly. "Let me see what you found."

She handed over the tin box with its sheaf of papers. "Be careful. They're very old."

Gingerly, he turned the pages. "This is Latin. I used to be able to read it, years ago, but I'm pretty rusty."

When she showed him the signature on the last page, he said,

"It's a journal, I think. It seems to cover several years. My God, Gran. 30 April 1730—that's the day Helen Templeton died."

"The exact day she died?" Minerva had not known that.

"It's your birthday, too. And it's also the date of the ancient pagan festival of Beltane. Mayday Eve, the night the witches dance."

As he flipped carefully through the papers, he sounded increasingly excited. "Gran, this is an incredible find. A biographer's dream. May I take the papers home and translate them?"

"Do what you think best. There's only one thing I ask, and that's that you inform me of the contents of the journal before you use the material in your book. I have the distinct feeling that I was being shown this material for a reason." Even as she said this, she shook her head. Such thinking was nonsensical. Minerva had never shared Nick's interest in bizarre phenomena like ghosts, ESP, and UFOs.

"Maybe you were," he said. "Helen Templeton had a troubled life. It's possible, I suppose, that her spirit's not at rest, although I've never heard anything before this about the Tavern being haunted. Have there been rappings or footsteps or other odd noises at night? Have you seen anything unusual?"

"No. Nothing like that. It's probably no more than the imagination of an old woman."

"Well, there are ways to find out. The next time anything odd happens, call me . . . I don't care if it's the middle of the night. We'll get a psi-sensitive in to check the place out."

"Really, Nick. Let's not go to extremes."

Again that night Minerva had trouble sleeping. It was as if the weight of all her sins was pressing down upon her, taking its toll. Sin. God's retribution. Although she had joined a church some years ago and contributed faithfully to their annual pledge drive, she rarely attended services. But now the words of the Communion service came back to her: *We have erred, and strayed from thy ways like lost sheep. We have left undone those things which we ought to have done; And we have done those things which we ought not to have done.*

What if she were required to answer to God? Or worse, what if God—or the devil—simply punished her loved ones instead? Gentle Edward, tortured and killed in the war. Elizabeth, who had died so young. Jonathan, whom she never saw because he seemed driven to wander the earth like Orestes, pursued by his own personal furies of guilt. Delilah and Travis, innocently guilty of a crime that had always made mankind shudder. Justifiably or not, Minerva held herself responsible for the circumstances out of which each tragedy had arisen.

Someday soon, she knew, she would pay. She felt as if she were poised on the edge of an immense drop-off . . . not an abyss, exactly; her vision was more of a dark and arid landscape, strewn with rocks, devoid of vegetation, devoid of light.

Beyond this spiritual desert she sensed another realm, a place of colors and teeming life, a place where sunlight sparkled off the still water, and the grass was thick and cool. That place was far more distant from her than the other. It would require a desperate struggle to reach it. She wasn't sure she was up to the struggle; she wasn't even sure which of the two landscapes she preferred.

She could see both these places with more clarity than ever before. The darkness, the shimmer of light. Such fancies had never troubled her before. There was no doubt about it: she was getting old.

29

The Monday after her grandmother's birthday, Delilah reported to the Beacon Street offices of Templeton Tea for her first day on the job as the new Director of Marketing. Grendam greeted her in the foyer and showed her to her office on the third floor.

"Clarence Parker, your predecessor, had an office down the hall from mine, but since you requested to be near your staff, I've assigned you this one," Minerva said. "The art, advertising, and public relations departments are all within a few yards of this room."

The office was about one quarter the size of her office at Merlin's. The furnishings were old, although comfortable, and the one window looked down on the interior courtyard rather than out on the Common. "This is fine. Thank you."

Grendam led her through a side door in the office to another, even smaller room, where a young woman in a prim gray suit sat typing on an IBM PC. She looked up as they entered, but her fingers continued to flash over her computer keys.

"This is Jane O'Brien, your secretary. Jane, this is our new Marketing Director, Ms. Scofield."

"Delilah," Delilah corrected, smiling and holding out her hand to the woman, who was, she estimated, in her early twenties.

The secretary stopped typing and exchanged a cool handshake. "I'm very pleased to meet you, *Ms. Scofield.*"

"She resents me," Delilah said to her grandmother a few seconds later as they walked out into the corridor. "Why? Was she particularly loyal to Clarence Parker?"

"Yes, I suppose there's bound to be some resentment. Parker was a popular man here, and I fired him."

Delilah stopped. "I wasn't aware of that. You told me he was retiring."

"I made the decision after hearing what you had to say about our inept marketing plan. You were quite right, Delilah. Parker was incompetent."

Delilah heard this with mixed feelings. On the one hand, she was glad that her grandmother had been impressed enough with her remarks at the business meeting to have made some immediate adjustments. On the other, she found the quick decision ruthless, not to mention pitiless toward poor Mr. Parker. I would have done it differently, she thought.

"Clarence Parker was an excellent manager in his younger days, but he had become lazy and uncreative," her grandmother said. "Everybody who works for me knows that I do not tolerate their giving less than one hundred percent of their talent and energy to the company. Lest they've forgotten, let Parker's fate be a lesson to them."

Delilah said no more. But two things were evident as she was introduced to the personnel in art, advertising, and sales: her own management style differed strikingly from her grandmother's, and she was beginning her tenure at the company with the onus of being the unwelcome replacement for a popular boss.

It didn't help matters, she suspected, that she was the owner's granddaughter. They knew who she was, of course; most of them had seen her TV ads. But the Merlin's commercials had been scripted to present her in a far different role than the one she meant to assume at Templeton Tea. The commercials were funny, sexy, lighthearted. Delilah the entrepreneur was businesslike and serious, although not nearly as iron-handed as her grandmother.

She spent her first day trying to get the feel of the place. She visited each department and chatted with everyone in a pleasant and nonthreatening manner, doing her best to ignore the undercurrents. She made no attempt to assert herself, nor to establish any particular personal style. Let them wonder for a few days.

By the end of the first week, she sensed that the staff was relaxing. There was more noise in the corridor, and more ease during the coffee (or tea) breaks, and even a few welcoming smiles when she entered a room. On Thursday afternoon, Jane O'Brien, who had been sullen all week, broke down and called her Delilah.

Excellent. They were beginning to accept her presence, if not her authority. It was time to shake them up.

On Friday morning, she called a staff meeting for all three departments. Everybody was asked to attend, from managers down to stock clerks. Delilah dressed carefully that morning in a black and white Ungaro suit that was more conservative than some of her usual clothing. She swept her dark hair up into a sleek chignon and wore severe black onyx earrings with a bracelet to match. She knew she looked dramatic and feminine, yet at the same time as tough as any chairman of the board.

She addressed them in a calm, low-key manner: "We've had several days to begin to get to know each other, but there have been some deceptions. You've been trying not to show how you feel about my replacing Clarence Parker, and I've been trying to make you like me, or at least, to make you relax in my presence."

She noted their collective surprise. They had not expected her to speak so candidly. "Most of you, I imagine, know little about me beyond the facts that I'm Minerva Templeton's granddaughter and that I've done a series of popular ads on television for Merlin's Magical Brews. You may not be aware that Merlin's is a multimillion-dollar business started fourteen years ago in the kitchen of a small flat in one of the seedier sections of L.A. Without any help from my family, I built the business into the enormous success it is today. I learned a lot along the way, and I intend to bring my experience and expertise to my work here at Templeton Tea.

"Although I have personally managed every aspect of my business from the cultivation of herbs to the distribution of product in the marketplace, I have a particular flare for marketing and promotion. This happens to be an area where Templeton Tea has not lived up to expectations in recent years. I am being frank with you about this. We're not doing as well with respect to our competitors as we were several years ago. I intend to turn this trend around.

"When I started here on Monday, I had several ideas for new marketing strategies, although I haven't settled on anything yet. I'd like to get some input from you. I urge you to come to me with any brainstorms. I also urge you to bring me your problems or complaints. I'll do my best to be accessible. I don't know how your former boss ran things around here, but you'll find my management style to be creative and informal.

"I expect each of you to give me your very best job performance. I hope you'll stretch yourselves to the limit and, in doing so, make our success even greater. For I have no doubt about our eventual success. You're going to help me restore Templeton Tea to its former glory.

"By the way," she added, flashing her famous smile, "To all of you, no matter what your age or position, my name is Delilah."

There was a spontaneous burst of applause. Delilah's grin widened. She'd made a start.

"I hear you gave quite an oration today, Delilah," Travis said that evening from the doorway of her office. She was gathering her things together to go home. "The place is buzzing with the news. I've been waiting all week for you to do something spectacular."

"Spectacular is not my goal. I wanted to build confidence, that's all. There's always a lot of apprehension when a new manager comes on the scene."

"You did an excellent job of it, if my spies are worth listening to. Good for you."

"Thanks." Delilah looked away from the sight of him lounging in the doorway, one shoulder pressed against the jamb, his sleeves rolled up over his bare, tan arms, and his jacket dangling over his shoulder by the crook of one finger. He looked very suave and very rich. His accessories alone must be worth several thousand dollars.

"Are you quitting for the day?" he asked. "Care to walk down to the Bull and Finch for a drink? I'd like to talk to you."

"What about?"

"Not about old times, if that's what worries you."

"I'm not worried." She shoved a few things into her briefcase. "I guess I could use a drink."

Fifteen minutes later they were seated in the Boston bar that was reputedly the setting for the popular TV program "Cheers." Busy with the Friday evening after-work crowd, the place was hot and noisy. After one quick drink and a few frustrating attempts at conversation, they opted instead for a walk through the Public Garden across the street.

"This refreshing greenery in the heart of the city is wonderful. We don't have anything like this in L.A."

"Yeah, it's great," Travis said absently. He was carrying his jacket over one arm now, and his sleeves were still rolled up. He had a perfect tan, even though this was only May and he had not, to her knowledge, been away recently on vacation. He did travel extensively, though, buying tea in producing countries around the world. Templeton Tea had agents to do that, of course, but importing was one of Travis's primary responsibilities, and he apparently took it seriously.

They walked over the bridge that crossed the pond where the swanboats peddled. She and Travis had sat together in one of these years ago. She could almost see them there, laughing, their earnest young faces mirrored in the dark waters of the pond. They'd cuddled on one of the rear benches and kissed themselves into a frenzy.

"I wanted to talk to you about the company," he said. "And about this little power struggle that seems to be shaping up between us."

"Little? You're making it sound as if it's not important."

He lifted his shoulders, and the white cotton of his shirt pulled tight across the subtle muscles of his chest. "Epic power struggle?"

"That's more like it."

Travis stopped walking and turned to her. His tall form in her path forced her to stop, too. "I don't want to battle with you, Delilah. And I don't see the point of it. Templeton Tea is big enough and rich enough for both of us."

"I don't think so. Only one of us can end up in control after Grendam dies."

"Why? The stocks could be divided equally between us."

"You know as well as I do that's never been done."

"My attorneys tell me it's possible, nevertheless. There are no legal contraints to prevent it."

"Passing the stock on to the next generation in its entirety is a family tradition."

"If that's so important to you, why are you challenging me at all? You have no children, Delilah. To whom are you intending to pass along these fine traditions?"

For a moment all she could think of was the child they had conceived together. Was he flinging that in her face? "You son of a bitch," she said mildly.

The color came up in his neck. "I didn't mean to be insulting. It's the structure of the corporation I'm criticizing, not your own personal situation."

"I haven't reached menopause yet, thank you, so don't count on my remaining childless forever."

"Delilah, I'm sorry. I didn't mean that the way it sounded, honestly. I don't have kids either, as you know." He shot her a wry smile. "Neither of my wives wanted the bother of children."

She sent out a mental feeler, trying to get a sense of who he was, what he had become. What a stranger he was to her. Her own cousin, whom she'd known since childhood, with whom she'd shared a bed. Who'd taken her virginity. Who was the father of the only child she'd ever conceived. She didn't know this man.

She tried to fix on little things about him—the big, almost clumsy hands, the perfect teeth, the tiny dimple in his right cheek that you could see when he smiled a certain way. Would their child have had that dimple? Would their child have inherited that dazzling smile that charmed people beyond reason?

They walked on in silence, down the wide avenue that led to the boundaries of the Public Garden, across the hectic streams of traffic on Charles Street which had marked the shoreline of Boston before Back Bay had been filled in. They entered the Boston Common.

The trees on the Common were just coming into bud, their tiny leaves uncurling in a pale green that would later darken to emerald. Delilah touched one with her fingertip, inhaling its fresh scent. She was so accustomed to the eternal summer of southern California that she'd forgotten the fragile beauty of Boston in the spring.

For an instant she wondered what effect such things as the changing of the seasons might have on a person's character. In this city one could hardly be unaware of the ever-revolving cycle of nature. Things were born, they grew lush and ripe, then they faded and died, only to burst into new life again in the spring. You could see time passing in ever-repeating loops and reels. In stark L.A., where asphalt and steel reigned and no trees grew, the days, months, and years all slid unnoticed into one another. There was something unreal about time's passage. Things changed, but you never knew when, or how, or why.

Had Travis changed? Or had he always been so elusive?

"Hey," he said. He reached out and captured her hand. She saw his strong, tan fingers close around hers and felt a ghost of the old spark. Some things never change.

"Cheer up. It's a beautiful day, and even though we're bound to do battle with each other over the next few months, I'm glad to have you back."

She warmed toward him; she couldn't help it. Despite all their problems, she still felt a special kind of intimacy with him, something that defied analysis and remained beyond articulation. Dory would say, no doubt, that they were soulmates who had loved each other more happily—or perhaps more tragically—in another life. That their karma bound them together, and would continue to do so in life after life until they worked it through and discharged its negative energy. It had not been so with Max, whom she had come to know and to love more slowly. Close though they had been, Max had been a stranger whose soul she'd had to learn. Travis, on the other hand, was a wavery reflection of herself.

She supposed this was why she had fallen for him—typical adolescent narcissistic attachment. Love is the mirror wherein we look and see our own face. They had both been bright, reckless, and rich. No doubt he'd seen in her the same qualities she'd seen in him.

She'd learned during her marriage that real love was not so straightforward. Loving and accepting someone who was different, who didn't always understand you and who couldn't instinctively communicate with you—that was considerably more of a challenge. Her relationship with Max hadn't always been perfect, but the rewards in the end had been greater: the feeling of accomplishment, of pride in seeing the solid structure you had labored to build—that had been infinitely more fulfilling than anything she'd had with Travis.

First love. She could look back on it now and smile.

She gave his hand a companionable squeeze. "I hope we'll be

able to put the past behind us and get along with each other, Trav. You've never enjoyed conflict, and even I'm getting a little old for it, I think."

"Listen." His voice had gone low, intense. "I think you should know that I had a very good reason for leaving you."

She was amazed how easily the old hurt welled up. Suddenly he was too handsome, too smooth. Suddenly she didn't believe a word he said. "It's a bit late to make your excuses." She ripped her hand out of his and strode down the path. Travis followed her, touched her shoulder, blocked her way. She stopped, ordering herself to stand and face him.

"You haven't put the past behind you, Delilah, so don't lie about it. Let's lay it on the line, shall we? You want my balls."

"Let go of me."

"Not yet." The hand that was heavy on her shoulder moved down her arm in an unmistakable caress. Delilah shivered. His other hand slid up into her hair, holding her head still. "It's still there, isn't it? Why should I let you pretend it's not?"

God! Her old desire for him was like a snake uncoiling in her belly. Like her anger, it had not varied in sixteen years. The aggressive sweep-me-off-my-feet lover had always been an exciting fantasy for her, and Travis did it now, just as he had done it years ago, with an appealingly macho style. He even looked like the hero on the cover of a historical romance: a little rakish, a little dangerous, and what did they call it?—drop-dead handsome. An emblem, an archetype. The real man no real woman could resist.

She couldn't believe the strength of her urge to surrender to an adolescent fantasy. It was a mockery of her autonomy, her maturity, her independence. There under the budding trees of the Boston Common the validity of her years with Max was being called into question. Had her sexual response to her husband ever been as spontaneous, as violent, as mindless as this?

My God. I'm afraid of him. He drew her closer; he seemed about to kiss her. She jerked away, furious with herself. "Really, Travis." For the first time she noticed the crinkly lines around his eyes. The intense blue of those eyes had lured her once, but now it seemed to have an arctic quality. "Save your energy for Templeton Tea."

She turned and retraced their steps through the Common and the Public Garden toward the townhouse apartment she'd rented on Marlboro Street. When she was sure she was out of his sight, she increased her pace to a brisk walk that was almost a run.

30

At the end of Delilah's second week at Templeton Tea, the art director quit. His style and hers, he said, were different. This was certainly true. When Delilah had told him she wanted to see sketches for new designs on the tea cartons and packages, he'd blinked and said, "But the design on those boxes hasn't been changed for fifty years."

"That is precisely the point."

Delilah called another staff meeting. "I need some new ideas. I want you all to go home and turn on your televisions. Look at the way products are advertised and sold in this country. You'll see color, you'll see glamour, you'll see sex." She held up a package of English Breakfast Tea. The box was square and squat, the background color powder-blue, the lettering Gothic. "Now look at this. Tea is supposed to stimulate you, not put you to sleep. Can you imagine a woman stretched out half-naked in front of a romantic hearthfire luring her lover to join her with a cup of *this?*"

"You can't sell tea with sex," somebody objected.

"You can sell anything with sex. American advertisers do it all the time. But it's not necessarily sex I want to use. At Merlin's we made our pitch to health-conscious Americans, claiming that our herbal tea would be better for their bodies than other beverages. That was very effective. We need a marketing direction, in other words, a theme that will put across the idea that consumers should be buying and drinking Templeton Tea.

"That magical idea hasn't hit me yet. Maybe it will hit one of you first. That's why I want you to come to me with your thoughts on the matter—believe me, I'm open to suggestions. We need a new image, and a new theme."

Nobody spoke up. Delilah looked from one blank face to another. Her grandmother had not fostered group discussion of the company's policies; she'd made all the important decisions herself and expected her staff to carry them out. Delilah didn't want to work that way, but she could see that it was going to take a while to bring her employees around to her methods. She sighed. Things were not getting off to a very good start.

"May I speak to you a minute?"

Delilah looked up from her perusal of the latest statistics on world tea production. Jane O'Brien, her secretary, was hovering on the threshold between their offices. A week had gone by, and Delilah was still racking her brain for a comprehensive marketing strategy. Every idea she came up with was flawed.

"Of course. Come in and sit down." Delilah liked Jane. She worked hard, typed fast, and was obviously smart. She wasn't talkative, but Delilah's initial impression that Jane resented her had been replaced by the realization that she was shy. Never having been shy herself, she found that state of mind a little difficult to imagine, and she hoped, eventually, to see Jane loosen up. "Is something the matter?"

"Uh, no. It's just that, well, I'm sure you'll think it's stupid, but I had an idea about the new marketing strategy. You did say that if any of us had ideas, you'd like to hear them." She shot a look at Delilah's face, but did not hold eye contact. It occurred to Delilah that she didn't even know what color Jane's eyes were. Besides being hidden behind a pair of unattractive glasses, they were almost always directed toward the floor.

She was exactly the sort of girl who would benefit from one of those fashion magazine make-overs. Although she was nearly as tall as Delilah, her shoulders were always slouched. She had big, ringless hands with stubby nails that looked as if they'd never been touched with polish. Her nose was a trifle long, her mouth prim and narrow, but she had beautiful teeth and a graceful, swanlike neck. Her hair was a dun blond that cried out for a good highlighting job. Jane's clothes were neat and of good quality, but because she chose dark reds, blues, and browns instead of the pastel shades that would have been more flattering to her complexion, she invariably looked sallow and washed out.

Delilah indulged in a brief fantasy of taking the girl to a hairdresser, a manicurist, an ophthalmologist for contact lenses, and an exercise coach. The final step would be a shopping spree at the exclusive boutiques in Copley Place to update the girl's wardrobe.

Must be my maternal instincts coming out, she told herself wryly. Jane would be insulted if she suggested any such thing. "I'd be very interested in hearing your idea," she said.

"I'm sure you've heard better ones, or maybe you've already come up with something yourself, and—"

"Jane, don't be so hard on yourself. No one's come to me with anything so far, and I myself haven't had a good idea in weeks and may never have one again. Tell me."

"Okay, here goes. People drink tea all the time, right? But nobody really knows anything about it. Templeton Tea prides itself on its heritage, but I've been working here for a year and I still don't know very much about the company's history."

Jane's manner became more animated as she went on: "I've been watching TV the last couple of nights, and you're right—most of the ads use sex to sell their products. And you know what? I'm bored with that. I find those ads insulting. They assume such a low common denominator with regard to the public's intelligence. Why not conduct a campaign that flatters people, that assumes TV viewers possess at least a modicum of taste?" Jane's voice had grown passionate. "Our customers deserve our respect."

"You're right about that. It's always a mistake to condescend to the public."

"I think we should base our advertising campaign on the notion that people like to learn, to be informed, particularly if the subject is interesting. And tea *is* interesting." Jane pushed a lock of dirty blond hair off her face as she continued, "How many people know, for example, that it's the most popular drink in the world? That it's one of the cheapest? That there are all sorts of colorful legends about the origin of tea? The one about the holy man, for example, and his eyelids."

"You've been doing some research, haven't you?" Delilah said with a smile.

"I checked a stack of books out of the library."

"How would we inform people about the colorful history of tea?"

"Well, instead of a half-naked woman on a hearth rug, you could hire somebody to sip tea in a gracious drawing room while telling a humorous but informative anecdote."

"Okay. I like it so far. What else?"

"The most dramatic change would be in our packaging. I know you want to update it, but instead of creating a new look simply with color and design, perhaps you could come up with a variation on what you did with the Merlin's Magical Brews boxes. You know that little pentangle on the back where you describe the way some herb has been helping mankind for centuries? How about telling tea legends on our boxes? That way the consumers might feel they're getting more for their money."

Delilah picked up a pen from her desk and began tapping it along the tips of her crimson nails. The idea had possibilities. As with all good suggestions, now that Jane had formulated it, Delilah was amazed she hadn't thought of it herself.

"You're suggesting, in other words, that we create a mystique of tea. That we beguile the consumer into believing that in purchasing and drinking our product, they're joining a long tradition—a tradition we'll explain to them in some detail—and thereby becoming part of the great tea-drinking elite."

"Yes, exactly. It's become chic to drink tea, I understand. All the fine hotels are serving afternoon tea now, and instead of cocktail parties, some society hostesses are having people in for tea."

Delilah rose and began to pace back and forth in the brisk manner she employed when her brain was busy. Rapidly, she considered several angles . . . and liked the view from each.

"Maybe we could get some celebrities to do ads for us," Jane continued. "Not the usual movie star type. Someone with more class and high-style presence, like, uh—"

"Katharine Hepburn," Delilah put in.

"Or Alistair Cooke."

"Robert MacNeil."

"Princess Diana."

Delilah grinned at her. "How about the Queen of England herself?"

"No, no, Princess Diana would be much better. I mean, I'm not advocating *no* sex appeal for our tea . . . the Queen could have sold the current Templeton Tea, but not the new product."

"My dear Jane," Delilah said softly.

The girl met her gaze briefly, then seemed to falter. "I didn't mean to get so carried away."

Delilah returned to her desk and snatched up the telephone and dialed the extension for the advertising department. "Richard," she said to the young man who answered, "get in here with the rest of the ad staff right now." She hung up and pointed her pen at Jane. "Turn off your word processor. You're no longer my secretary."

The girl's face whitened. "What do you mean? You're not *firing* me?"

"Good God, Jane, of course I'm not firing you." She walked over and flung her arms around the girl. "Your idea is terrific. I should have thought of it myself, but I didn't, and you're going to get all the credit. I'm making you my new advertising director, starting immediately."

"But you can't! I have no experience. I don't know anything about advertising. No one'll listen to me."

"I just listened to you, didn't I?"

"But, Delilah, Ms. Scofield, the responsibility—"

"Shh. When I was your age I didn't know anything about the health foods business, but that didn't stop me from learning it. You're the person I want, Jane. You're smart, creative, hardworking, and you obviously have excellent instincts. I've given big responsibilities to inexperienced people before, and no one has ever failed me. You'll be fine in the job. No. You'll be great!"

She thought Jane was going to burst out in tears, but after what was clearly a struggle, the girl controlled herself. "Thank you. I'll try not to disappoint you." She managed a weak smile. "I'll try to live up to your reckless faith in me."

"Wrong adjective," Delilah said with a grin. "People who fail are termed reckless. People who succeed are regarded as innovative. I never fail, Jane."

"I sure hope this isn't going to be the first time!"

When Delilah got home that night she put a call through to Dory, who was freelancing as a commercial artist and doing her trance mediumship on the side. Delilah explained that she had just lost her art director, and asked if Dory wanted a steady job.

There were several seconds of silence, then Dory laughed and said, "Even for you, Delilah, I'm not sure that anything could induce me to give up California weather for the dubious pleasures of the East Coast."

"Not even on a temporary basis? I need some designs, Dory, and you're the person I want to do them."

"Well . . . Ra-ton did predict I'd be taking a trip east sometime soon."

"Who is Ra-ton, dare I ask?"

"He's one of the new entities I'm channeling. He only recently started coming through. He and I have had several lifetimes together—the last one was in Atlantis just before the cataclysm."

"I don't suppose you could leave the disincarnate entities in L.A.? This is Boston, for God's sake. We've got therapists here, yes, but they've got M.D.'s and Ph.D.'s and years of study at the Psychoanalytic Institute. They put a lot more stock in ancient Thebes than they do in Atlantis."

"I could raise a little consciousness out there," Dory said, unperturbed.

"So you'll come?"

"Well . . . yes, why not?"

Dory arrived within a week, breezing into town with trunks full of possessions, including astrology charts and books on psychic phenomena that she claimed she couldn't do without, and two huge hunks of rose quartz and amethyst crystal, which supposedly heightened her psychic powers.

"You're going to have to find yourself somewhere to live soon," Delilah teased her. "I don't have room in my place for all this junk."

"I don't imagine you'll let me do readings here anyway."

"Damn right. And if you ever so much as hint that Max is trying to contact me from the Other Side, I'll boot you into the Charles River."

"Delilah, my love, I wouldn't dream of it. But you would be much happier, you know, if you could accept that death is not the end."

Delilah quelled her with a look.

She was somewhat wary about introducing Dory to Grendam, but Dory charmed her. She didn't mention channeling or ESP; instead she chatted about the early days in L.A. when she and Delilah had shared a flat. It was the last thing Delilah would have expected her grandmother to show an interest in, but Dory's animation could render almost any subject fascinating.

Dory was a hit with the rest of the staff, too. Women began to confide in her almost at once, and the men appraised her hopefully. Dory was wearing her red hair long and natural these days—it fluffed out around her neck and shoulders like a mantle, a dramatic accent to her pale, heart-shaped face. She still favored low-cut necklines and short skirts. ("Are minis back in again at last? That's nice, but I've always worn them!") With her distinctive mixture of good-girl sweetness and bad-girl sensuality, she reminded Delilah of Dolly Parton.

About a week after Dory's arrival, Delilah called a meeting with Jane and the rest of the marketing staff in her office at Templeton House. She also invited Nick, whose research for his Helen Templeton biography had made him an expert on the history of the tea company. The purpose of the meeting was to work out the details of the new advertising campaign.

Nick had some interesting things to report, including the discovery—under unusual circumstances—of a number of papers written by Helen just before her death.

"Journals," he told them. "I've had them authenticated, and it looks as if they're going to add a great deal to my knowledge of her character. I'm in the process of translating them now. It's taking a while because her handwriting's hard to read and my Latin isn't as good as it used to be."

"And you say there was something paranormal about the discovery of the papers?" Dory asked.

"Seemingly. On the night she found them, Gran felt as if she were being guided. A voice came to her in a dream and told her where to look. She's wary of examining the phenomenon too closely. I've suggested we get a sensitive to check the place out, but that scares her, I guess."

"Dory could check it out," Delilah said, half-seriously. "She channels. Her great aunt was a well-known medium."

Nick regarded Dory with increased interest. Delilah had already noted his obvious appreciation for his former lover's tiny waist and long legs, and it occurred to her that Nick and Dory might do well to give each other another try. If anybody could put up with Dory's freaky lifestyle, it would probably be Nick.

"That's awesome, as my daughter would say," said Nick. "Do you hold regular sessions?"

"Not on any fixed schedule, but word gets around easily, so I usually end up channeling for clients a couple of times a week. I don't like to do it more than that. It's enervating."

"May I come to a session? I'm interested in that sort of thing."

"I remember," she said, laughing. "Sure. As long as you're not there to debunk me."

"I'm a little skeptical, I admit, but I have an open mind."

"That's something of an understatement," said Delilah. "The moment he hears about anything weird, Nick's there, taking notes."

"Hey, I'm a writer. I like to document all varieties of human experience, no matter how unusual."

Later that evening when Dory and Delilah were alone in Delilah's Back Bay apartment, Dory said, "Nick's improved over the years, hasn't he? He's turned into a real cutie. That trim, fit body, those soulful eyes, all that curly dark hair. And his manner—the success he's had as a writer must have given him confidence."

Ahha, Delilah thought. She pounced. "He's divorced, you know, and I'll bet he's lonely. But if you're thinking of adding him to your collection again, be gentle. Nick's the sensitive type."

Dory laughed and shook her head, sending long ribbons of red whirling. "I wasn't thinking of myself, Delilah."

Delilah was startled to realize she was thinking of *her.* She threw up her hands as if to ward off the suggestion. "Uh-uh. Get that gleam out of your eyes. He's Travis's brother."

"You mean there's something going on again between you and Travis?"

"No, of course not."

"Well, then. Why not? Nick's very good in bed."

"You've been telling me that for years. Has he got some special way of doing it? Upside down? Sideways?"

Dory giggled.

"Can he go all night? Did he find your G-spot? Is he kinky? What?"

"I'm not going to tell you. I don't want to spoil it for you. Just believe me, he's special."

"At one time he thought he was in love with me," Delilah admitted. "No doubt he realized the folly of that long ago."

"I'm not so sure. Haven't you noticed the way he looks at you? Give him a little encouragement and you can get firsthand experience of his erotic finesse."

"You're imagining things." The subject had ceased to amuse her. She still remembered how guilty she'd felt about hurting him in 1970, and the last thing she wanted was Nick in love with her again.

But once she got onto something, Dory was not easily shaken. "Delilah, when's the last time you had sex? When's the last time you took a man to yourself and loved him and moaned out loud while he did it to you?"

"Jesus, Dory!"

"Answer me."

Delilah thought—"1984."

"With Max, who's been dead for over a year."

Delilah said nothing.

"Look, grieving widowhood is very admirable and all that, but don't you think it's time you came out of seclusion? Max would have cheered you on."

"I'm not going to do it just for the sake of doing it. I've never enjoyed that. I have to know the man and care about him. You know that."

"I knew you were one of the world's great romantics back in the seventies, yes. But I figured that by now maybe you'd smartened up. Keep Nick in mind. He'd be good for you."

"Next you'll be telling me Shastra or Rin-tin-tin or whoever predicts that he and I'll get married and have a brood of baby Templetons."

Dory smiled in that infuriating oracular manner of hers and made no reply.

31

One night in mid-June, Travis was working late at the Templeton blending and packaging plant in East Boston. A new shipment of tea had just come in, ready to start the process of blending, tasting, and packing that would make it a marketable commodity.

Except for Mac Duggin, the night watchman, who was drunk, Travis was alone. He knew Mac was drunk because he'd personally provided the bottle. Mac wasn't unconscious-drunk, just feeling good-drunk. But it ought to be enough because the Red Sox were playing the Yankees on Duggin's TV, and the Sox were having a winning season this year.

Travis waited till the top of the seventh—the score was tied and the Sox were up—before leaving his air-conditioned office on the top floor and walking down a dimly lit corridor to the receiving area. The cavernous room was dark. There was a light switch on the wall, but Travis did not touch it. He pulled out a flashlight, keeping the beam directed at his feet.

The boards creaked violently as he walked. The building had been constructed in the thirties and, according to his grandmother, was quite innovative at the time because of its gravity system for moving tea from one level to the next. Most of the machinery had been replaced in recent years, but when Travis took over as Director, he intended to raze this place and rebuild.

He found the crates that had been delivered. There were two dozen of them, arriving in Boston via New York, the port of entry, where they'd spent some time in a bonded warehouse being tared and sampled to make sure they met all federal import standards. The lots were excellent—quality stuff like Darjeeling, Chinese Keemun, often referred to as the burgundy of teas, rich, tippy, high-grown tea from Kenya, and the tarry-flavored Lapsang souchong from Fujian Province in China.

There were also four crates from Brazil. Nothing special in terms of quality, this tea would be used in tea bags or reduced to powder for instant tea. Argentina and, to a lesser extent, Brazil had become major tea producers in recent years, and Travis enjoyed the trips he occasionally made to Latin America to buy the stuff.

The tea was ordinary, yes, but this was a special shipment. The crates had come safely through customs along with the rest of his consignment. They were officially tagged, labeled, stamped, and sealed. If some of these checks had not been as thorough as they should have been, this was due, no doubt, to the flawless record of trust that had been built up over the years—indeed, over the centuries—between Templeton Tea and the federal inspectors.

Checking once more to make sure there was no sign of Mac Duggin or anybody else, Travis severed the seals and pried open the first crate. This would cause no surprise to anyone—he inspected most of the tea personally when it came in. He'd been doing that for years.

The scent of tea rose up and engulfed him as he opened the inner seals, the inner protective linings. To him the smell was golden. Tea provided excellent cover because its aromatic oils gave off a scent that confused the dogs trained and employed by the U.S. Customs Department.

He rolled up his sleeve and plunged an arm into the coppery leaves. There were no false bottoms or false sides. "Customs can spot that a mile away," he'd been told by a man who'd been convicted of antiquities smuggling and had spent ten years in federal prison. "You want success? Keep it simple."

It took him ten minutes to find it. Carefully he drew out a long, slim packet, sealed in plastic. He unwrapped it and dipped the tip of one finger into the fine white powder. He touched a few grains to his lips. "Very fine," he said softly. No professional tea taster could have been more appreciative of his product. "Top quality."

There was a similar packet in each of the other three crates. Travis extracted them all and tucked the contraband into the briefcase he'd brought along for the purpose. He closed the tea chests and dusted off his hands.

Travis made it back to his office without incident. Gathering up his briefcase, he pasted on a smile and went to look in on Mac, who was still communing with his TV. "How's it going?"

"Ninth inning and the score's still tied. Yanks are threatening, though. They've got two men on. Hey, you jerk-off," Mac yelled at the Red Sox dugout. "Get that bum off the mound before he gives up another hit!"

Travis watched for a while, feigning interest, but when the bum got himself out of a tight spot and the game went into extra innings, he said to Mac, "I'd better get going. I've got a date tonight."

Mac wished him good luck with the lady.

Travis took the elevator down to the loading dock, where his car was parked. The elevator was one of those huge things with a wooden floor, a naked light bulb, and an accordion gate across the entryway. It creaked and shuddered as it moved downward, reminding Travis of that other elevator, the one that had almost killed him. An attempt at divine retribution? If so, God wasn't very efficient.

As he got into his car and transferred the cocaine to the hidden compartment he'd hollowed out under his seat, he felt exhilaration pour over him. He took a small shipment rarely, maybe three or four times a year. In the meantime he brought in a few other less risky items—gemstones, perfume, Russian caviar. Things that were easy to get rid of among the wealthy people who were his friends.

Perhaps he didn't need the extra money these transactions brought in; his income was large, yes, but his expenses were high. He had to maintain his three homes—an estate in Winchester, a summer "cottage" consisting of twelve rooms on Martha's Vineyard, and a ski chalet in Vail. He needed funds to invest in the downtown condos and the office buildings he owned in several major cities. The art he collected was a major expense, but he considered it a necessity to surround himself with objects of style and beauty. His clothes gobbled up quite a chunk, as did the private jet, the sailboat, and the cars. Not to mention the alimony he had to pay to both his former wives. What with women, jet-set vacations, the lavish entertaining he did so often to amuse his friends, it was amazing how creative his accountant had to be to keep him in the black every year.

Now that Delilah had returned and was threatening his future job security, Travis found it comforting to know that the proceeds from his "personal importing," as he thought of it, were slowly accumulating in a Swiss bank account.

As he let himself out the security gate at the plant and headed for the highway, Travis was thinking not of bank accounts, but diamonds. A few months ago he'd brought in six perfectly matched five-carat D-flawless stones that, if properly set, would make a lovely pendant. They would look stunning, he decided, around Delilah's slender throat.

Lily Stratham was waiting for Travis that evening in the bedroom of her Dover home. Beautiful, wealthy, and charmingly amoral, Lily had first invited Travis to share her bed about two years ago. Their relationship was casual, a convenience for them both. He knew she saw other men, and she had always declared herself to be fascinated with the details of his amours with other women.

She lived in an exotic Tudor-style mansion complete with a bell tower, a great hall, and a stable large enough to hold two dozen horses. The place had been designed and constructed by her late husband, industrialist Harold Stratham, whom she had married when he was sixty and she was eighteen. Hare-brained Harold, as she called him, had died a dozen years ago, leaving empty promises to his relatives and his entire fortune to Lily.

"You're late," she said when her lover entered her darkened bedroom. She was sitting at her dressing table, clad in a form-fitting ivory peignoir reminiscent of one of Jean Harlow's slinky gowns. Her head was tilted to one side as she languidly brushed her thick auburn hair.

"Sorry. Will this make up for it?" He produced a tiny pearl-inlay box containing a small portion of the cocaine he'd just harvested from the tea chests.

Lily lifted the cover of the box and smiled. "It might."

They each did a couple of lines of the stuff and got a nice buzz on. Lily had thoughtfully provided a bottle of chilled champagne.

"You look tired, Travis." Lily was regarding his reflection in the mirror. She leaned back on her stool so the back of her head brushed against his belly. "How's everything going at the office with your long-lost cousin?"

"Delilah is an excellent businesswoman. I'm sure her talents will prove a considerable asset to us."

Lily's laugh was indulgent. "Really, Travis. You're not talking to the press."

Travis stroked her hair, recalling the meeting he'd had yesterday with his primary East Coast distributors, a tough group whose approbation he'd spent years courting. They'd wanted to know how business was going to be affected by this new lady working for the company. "It's not going to be affected at all," he'd replied.

"We hear she's in there making a lot of changes. Real energetic, full of new ideas. Sounds like she's bucking for president."

"My cousin is very good at the public relations end of things," Travis had said. "We're using her to increase our name recognition, and thus, our revenues. Ultimately that will be good for all of us."

"Might not be so good for you, Templeton, if she snakes away your job."

"No chance of that, gentlemen." He took the leaders aside and addressed them with the charm that worked so well on both sexes. "Confidentially, Delilah and I are working things out together. She's a clever woman, dynamic and creative. But she's a woman, after all."

One of them chuckled. The other, the more cynical of the two, said, "Watch it, Samson. Be careful she doesn't chop off your hair. Or any of your other vital parts."

He'd laughed with them, of course, but he kept remembering his own words to her: *You want my balls.*

Lily was eying him in the mirror. "I haven't seen you as frequently as usual since she's been back," she said in a tone that was a combination of a scolding and a purr.

Travis's hands had moved from her hair to her breasts, and Lily arched her back to make the contact easier. She twisted around so she could reach up and loosen his tie. Pulling it free of his collar, she draped it around her own neck, then began on his buttons. As each released, she favored his throat, his chest, and finally his stomach with the pressure of her red sculptured nails.

Travis brushed aside one strap of her nightgown and bent to take her breast into his mouth. Lily arched and slid the palm of her hand up his thigh.

"You're wearing that floral perfume again. The one I don't like. You don't listen to me, Lily, do you? You don't do what I tell you to do."

"I'm sorry," she murmured. "Are you angry with me?"

"Yeah." He delivered a nip to the lobe of her ear. She was wearing a diamond stud earring the size of a cherry pit. He tugged at it with his teeth. "You'll have to be punished." Travis pushed her toward the bed. "Lie down."

Travis stripped off her gown, then tossed her unceremoniously onto the lavender satin sheets. He slid his tie from around her neck and used it to bind her hands. Then he raised them over her head and secured them to the cross bar of the mahogany headboard. Lily strained against her bonds, but her wrists were tightly constricted. She found this highly erotic. Between her legs the honey flowed.

Travis shed his own clothes and fell beside her. He caressed her body with a fervor she had not known from him in some time. Yes, she thought. *Yes.* She shivered as his teeth nipped her lower lip. Harder. When they'd first started sleeping together, he'd been too gentle. She was strongly sexed and desired more of a romp than he seemed inclined to provide. So she'd told him what she wanted, and he had proved willing—even eager—to comply.

"Spread your thighs," he ordered. "Wider. I want to see you, Lily. I want you to show me how obedient you are."

Shivering, Lily did as he required. Nothing gave her a more intense high than the feeling of utter submission and vulnerability during sex. It was not a fantasy she subscribed to at any other time of the day, but in the dark, with an inventive lover, she adored it.

He slid a hard pillow under her bottom to make her even more accessible to him. Then he knelt between her legs and ran his hands lightly over her, teasing, avoiding, making her wait. It went on and on. While his hands toyed with her breasts, his mouth made leisurely forays across her belly and down her thighs. He taunted her, refusing her the relief of a climax. Even when his mouth took her, he kept stopping the stimulation every time she approached the crest. Lily began to plead with him, which only made him smile. When he nipped her nether lips, she moaned. When his tongue plunged into her, she screamed.

Travis remained cool, very much in command of himself despite his obvious arousal. The tone of his voice never altered as he spoke to her, urging her to arch her hips, circle them. He released one of her wrists from its bondage and ordered her to caress herself. While she did so he pinched her nipples almost to the point of pain. After she had come violently, he made her kneel on the floor beside the bed and take him into her mouth.

Not until the end did he show her any tenderness. "I didn't hurt you, Lily, I hope?" he asked as she lay limp and peaceful in his arms. "Sometimes I worry about that."

"No, of course not." She stretched, catlike. She was well pleased. "I'm not fragile. You're a very exciting lover."

What you are is a shit, Travis was saying to himself. These games of Lily's excited him, but when it was over, he often felt a vague twinge of conscience. He could do anything to her, the kinkier the better, as far as she was concerned. And he enjoyed it. Maybe there was a part of him that had always enjoyed that sort of thing.

She brought out all his latent aggressions. She made him toy with notions he'd once thought were perverse. If anything was allowed, why not wallow in it? Why not rape? Why not incest?

After Lily fell asleep, Travis lay in the dark, thinking about Delilah. That day in the park. Wanting her. Touching her. What would it be like, he wondered, to press her close again, kiss her? Spread her legs and come inside her? The more he tried to suppress the fantasy, the more dominant it became. It was like this every night now, even after satisfactory lovemaking. He couldn't get her image out of his mind. He was becoming obsessed.

He envisioned her beside him, under him, laughing and moaning with uninhibited joy that was hers alone. He imagined her wet. He could almost feel her flesh gripping him snugly as he plunged into her hot, silky sheath and reveled in the pleasure of emptying himself inside her. Nothing, ever, had felt as good as that. She was his soulmate. The only woman he'd wanted to love forever and ever and ever. They were alike—attractive, aggressive, hedonistic. And they were bound, had been so since childhood.

They were bound, all right. And he was sick, sick, sick.

"Christ," he whispered in the darkness. From his office at the tea company, he often heard Delilah's husky, joyful laugh penetrating ceilings, carilloning off walls. He remembered himself as he had once been, pure and passionate, full of noble hopes and convictions. The man she had loved.

What had happened to that man? How was it possible for him to have vanished so completely?

On that long-ago night when she'd told him she was pregnant, he had chosen love and commitment over his more selfish impulse to desert her. How different everything would have been if he'd been allowed to go with that choice.

But he hadn't. Like Oedipus, he'd been cast out to wander in the dark.

Travis glanced over at Lily, at the tie he'd used to bind her wrists, at the remnants of the champagne and cocaine on the dressing table. He clenched his fingers into white-boned fists. "What a shit you've turned into, Templeton. What a greedy, calculating, amoral shit."

32

"Okay, Ms. Scofield, you're on next, as soon as they wrap up the news and weather segment. Watch the cables. No, don't worry about the mike; the technician will pin it on your chest."

"The technician can hardly wait, I see." Delilah grinned at the good-looking TV sound man whose fingers fumbled as he attached a tiny microphone to the collar of her blue silk blouse. Too bad he was so young. Everyone in the "Boston Alive" studio looked like college students, with the exception of one crusty cameraman and the producer, who was a professional woman of about Delilah's own age. Even the interviewer, Stephen Lord, who was Boston's latest celebrity hunk, couldn't have been more than twenty-eight or -nine.

She was there on the set of "Boston Alive" as a result of her efforts to get more media coverage for Templeton Tea. In the two months since she'd been working for the company, she'd given several interviews to Boston newspapers, but this was her first TV appearance.

Lord took the chair opposite Delilah. After glancing at the monitor, which showed Brad Preston, the weatherman, explaining the satellite pictures in another studio, Lord gave Delilah a shy smile. He held out his hand. "Nice to meet you, Ms. Scofield. I'm Stephen Lord."

Delilah took his hand and shook it firmly. "Hi."

"Do I call you Ms. Scofield or Delilah on the air?"

"Delilah's fine."

"Please call me Stephen, then." He took in her relaxed posture.

"You don't seem nervous. Most of my guests have to keep their hands clasped in their laps so no one will notice the sweat under their arms."

"I'm using astronaut-strength deodorant," she said with a laugh. "No, actually, I am a little nervous since this is live TV. But I've been in front of the cameras quite a few times before."

"I still get the jitters," he admitted. "Every day before I go on I feel as if I'm going to throw up. I can't help thinking what an eye-opener it would be for the good people of Boston to see me get up and rush headlong off the set."

Ahha, thought Delilah, Mr. Hunk's popularity had yet to go to his head. That was a refreshing change. Most of the TV personalities she'd run into over the past several years had been real full-of-themselves jerks.

"Sixty seconds," said someone on the floor.

"Damn," said Stephen, looking down at his notes. "I don't remember what I was going to ask you first." He looked up, his hazel eyes appealingly troubled. "What would you like me to ask you?"

"Ask her for a date," one of the camera operators yelled.

"Yeah, let's capture it for the viewers," said the assistant producer. "Mr. Sex Appeal begging for a date. Going down on his knees in front of tens of thousands of delighted Bostonians only to have the lady laugh in his pretty face."

"Go on, Steve, baby. I think she likes you. Maybe you'll have better luck this time."

"Shut up, you jerks." Stephen Lord was blushing. "They always do this to me. Every goddamn day it's something new."

"Thirty seconds."

"Steve here's too shy to ask for his own dates," the cameraman called to Delilah. "Can you believe it? The guy's single and rarin' to go, but he'd spend every night alone if we didn't help him out now and then."

"Go on, Steve. She thinks you're cute."

"He's real nice, Ms. Scofield," the young woman operating the second camera put in. "I'd go out with him myself if I weren't already married."

"Fifteen."

Delilah was laughing. For a moment she was tempted to take

them all up on it. Do the asking herself if Stephen Lord was really so reluctant. No, she decided, it would never work. He was too young.

"I'm sorry, Delilah; don't pay any attention to them. It's embarrassing. These monsters are insensitive as—" The sentence was cut off as the assistant producer jabbed a finger at him and the red light on camera one snapped on.

"Good morning, Boston," he said in a voice that was entirely free of anxiety. Delilah had one eye on the monitor and could see that what he projected was lots of sexy male charm. "I'm Stephen Lord, and this is 'Boston Alive.' We have a great show for you today, featuring Delilah Templeton Scofield, who is going to tell us all about the history of the tea trade and give us a professional tea-tasting demonstration. We also have with us Dr. William Stanton, an expert on a new method of treating people who've suffered one or more heart attacks, and Phyllis Manning, author. Now, Ms. Scofield, I understand you're a direct descendant of the woman who founded Templeton Tea nearly three hundred years ago. Will you tell us a little about her?"

Delilah looked into his eyes and began to talk.

In the conference room at Templeton House, Dory Lester was sitting in front of a portable TV watching "Boston Alive" with Mrs. Templeton, Travis, Jane, and most of the rest of the staff. On-screen Delilah smiled as the camera moved in for a close-up. Her royal blue blouse accentuated the color of her eyes. Her make-up was perfect. Had she done it herself, Dory wondered, or had the TV people helped her? TV aged most people, but Delilah looked no more than thirty-five, less perhaps. She looked good, dressed beautifully, and kept her figure with an infuriating ease. Dory saw what she usually ate for lunch: a peanut butter sandwich, if you please! If Dory so much as looked at peanut butter, she gained a pound.

Stephen asked Delilah about the origins of tea. Delilah leaned forward slightly, her face animated, and said, "There's a wonderful old legend about that. The Bodhidharma set himself the task of meditating for a lengthy period each day. One day when he was particularly weary, he lost his concentration and fell asleep. When he woke up, he was so disgusted with himself that he cut off his eyelids to make certain he wouldn't be able to fall asleep again."

"How ghastly," said Lord with a visible shudder.

"No, listen to what happened. He dropped his eyelids on the ground, and from them sprang a holy and wondrous tree, rich in dark green leaves. Soon everyone knew that these leaves, when dried and boiled with water, produce a liquor that possesses the property of retarding sleep."

"God, is that true?" Dory asked as the cameras cut to a commercial.

"It's one of the more famous legends about the origin of tea," said Minerva Templeton. "There's another one: back in the year 2750 B.C. the emperor Shen Nung, one of China's early scholar-emperors, heated a caldron of water to blend some herbs for a concoction of his. The leaves from an overhanging tree dropped serendipitously into the boiling water, creating a delicious smell. The intrepid emperor decided to taste the brew and declared it excellent. It soon became his favorite herbal drink."

"If that's the way it happened, I'm amazed Delilah didn't discover tea on her own," said Dory. "That's exactly the sort of thing she used to do with her herbs when she was first starting out. Our kitchen always smelled like one of the Medici's secret laboratories. It's a wonder she didn't poison anybody."

As she lightheartedly spoke these words, Dory felt her skin tingle. She turned inward, and in one of the flashes of vision that she was still not entirely accustomed to, Dory saw Delilah mixing a potion with a slow, heavy arm as tears ran silently down her cheeks. She poured the dark and evil-smelling brew into a fluted glass and gave it to—to whom? Dory could not see. She wasn't certain whether her friend was offering the potion to another person or quaffing it herself.

The vision changed. Now it was another woman who was lifting the glass. An old woman, dressed in—what? Ceremonial dress? Witch's garb? Or was it naught but a nightgown, and a modern one at that? The images faltered, seeming to flash back and forth between the present (or the future?) and the past. Dory's stomach churned. Something dark descended upon her, and she called silently for her guides. She saw blood, she saw fire. She saw someone stretched upon a ladder, and someone else loading bullets into a gun. My God, she thought, beginning to swim up out of it. There is danger here.

On the television screen Delilah had begun a tea-tasting demonstration for the "Boston Alive" viewers. She was standing in front of a table that was laid out with seven white porcelain tea-tasting pots. She bantered with her host while timing the infusions and pouring off the liquor, then she emptied the leaves from the first pot onto a saucer and tipped it toward the camera.

"You see how small these leaves are? This is Darjeeling tea, grown high on the slopes of the Himalayas. It's believed by many people to be the finest in the world. Note the light, clear liquor it produces." She reversed another cup and tipped the saucer toward the camera. "Now contrast it with this large-leaf tea, Lapsang souchoug, from the east coast of China. See the difference in leaf size, in leaf color? Lapsang souchong leaves are smoked with burnt oak, which gives it a unique tarry flavor. Here, Steve, have a taste. Hold it in your mouth for a few seconds and try to evaluate it."

Delilah put the china cup to Stephen Lord's lips, grinning sidelong at the studio audience, who were laughing and cheering them on. Watching, Dory folded her arms around her chest and shivered. The air around her was chill.

Travis, who was seated beside her, touched her shoulder. She jumped. "Is something wrong?" he asked in a low voice.

"No, no, I'm all right."

But she couldn't relax, and it didn't help to have Travis staring at her with no small degree of interest.

On the TV Delilah was explaining that fine teas have their own character and flavor, just like fine wines. But Dory couldn't concentrate. She had begun to wonder if there might not be a more important reason for her visit to Boston than the new design for the Templeton Tea boxes. Delilah needed her artistic talents, yes, but perhaps she needed her psychic abilities as well.

Delilah spent that evening with her friend in the apartment Dory had rented for the summer in Cambridge. It was a large, sunny one-bedroom in an old but well-maintained building near Harvard Square. Dory had looked at several flats and declared that in this one the vibrations were right.

They gorged on a large mushroom and onion pizza, a bag of

taco chips, a six-pack of beer, and a carton of Ben and Jerry's ice cream. Replete and a little drunk, Delilah lolled on the living room floor, pulled her T-shirt up to her breasts, and stared at her bare stomach. When Dory asked what she was doing, she said she was trying to reach nirvana by contemplating the pleasures of a full belly.

"I'd like to read the cards for you," Dory said.

"Only if you can discover a tall, handsome stud in my future. At this rate I'm going to have to begin an intimate relationship with my vibrator again."

Dory unwrapped her tarot deck from the silk cloth that bound it and gave the cards to Delilah to shuffle. When Delilah returned the deck for her to lay out, Dory could feel the energy charge upon them. Power, great power. Apprehensively, she spread the cards.

She had found a path, an opening. Her image was of threads crossing and mingling briefly, long enough to form a small corner of fabric substantial enough to support her weight and carry her message. In practical terms she did not know of what this fabric was made, but she had been taught to trust her images, as long as they were not generated through her own anger or fear. Sometimes it was difficult to sever vision from emotion, but this felt pure.

Her heart was thundering, and there was pain. She was too old. Finding the channel would not be sufficient if she lacked the strength to pour herself through the fabric on the loom. "You must devote your entire life to your gift," Rebecca had told her. Rebecca, whose beliefs had proved that despite the guilty denial suffered by the colonists after the ravages of Salem, witches had existed in New England after all. We were not devil worshippers, though. Oh no. We worshipped the Great Mother.

"You must learn to control it," Rebecca had said, "lest it destroy you."

She had paid no heed. She had poured herself instead into worldly pursuits, never learning to harness the beast that was now riding upon her back. It would very likely ride her to her death.

So be it. Her death was nothing. Despite her successful quest to make the people of Boston eat their words, despite the respect that she the adulteress, the witch, the pariah had eventually earned, life had been bitter to her ever since Matthew had died. "My love, my love," she whispered. "It's been so long, and I miss you so much." Was he waiting for her there across the borders of the night? Had he forgiven her for the curse she had inadvertently laid upon his children?

Those children needed her. Helen drifted near the opening that would take her spirit to their sides. Archetypal images began to appear to her—the Wheel of Fortune. The High Priestess. The Hanged Man. The Lightning-Struck Tower. Faster and faster the figures spun.

"Well?" said Delilah. "Why the downcast expression? No paragon of masculine virtue is headed my way?"

"You can have lovers if you want them," Dory said. "I see at least two. And I see danger associated with them. Are you sure you want to stay in Boston? Maybe it would be better for you to return with me to California."

"No, thanks. I don't need psychic abilities to know that I must make my future here."

Dory tried not to frighten her clients if the images she received for them were negative. Fear itself could tip the scales enough to bring about the very events that someone was trying to avoid. So all she added was, "I see an intensification of the conflicts around you in the coming weeks. You're going to have to keep your wits about you, Delilah. It's going to be a rather difficult time."

Delilah groaned. "That's all I need. Haven't I had more than my share of difficult times?"

Dory leaned forward and grabbed her friend's hands. "Let's go back to the West Coast. There's a lot of powerful energy hooked up with your family in some way, and I can't quite get a handle on it. Maybe it's because you're such a good friend, but I can't see clearly, and that disturbs me. I don't like it. You're a catalyst, I think. Things are going to happen because you've returned, and some of these things have the potential to harm you."

Delilah eased her hands away. "It's a good thing I don't believe in this stuff or I might be worried."

"Delilah, I—"

"I'm staying, Dory. I love working for the tea company. It's what I was always meant to do." She got up from the floor and gave Dory a hug. "You're my best friend and I love you, but as I've told you before, when it comes to fortune-telling and channeling, I'm a confirmed skeptic. Even if I believed it, I don't believe in hiding from shadows. Whatever happens, I'll deal with it. I'll bet even your own spirit guides would say we all ought to make the most of the present and leave the future to take care of itself."

"That's true, but—"

"But nothing. Night, Dory." She tossed her dark hair over her shoulders and looked back from the doorway. "Sit down with your crystal and meditate," she advised impishly. "You'll feel a lot better."

Dory could hear her laughing as she ran down the stairs to her car.

33

"You all know what our old packages look like," Delilah said, nodding to a powder-blue box of Templeton's Earl Grey Tea. "Now we'd like to show you the sketches for the new boxes." She held up a large cardboard display board painted with the design Dory had recently completed. Dory had traded the blue for a vibrant maroon. A modernistic block-style print had replaced the Gothic lettering, and the traditional Templeton logo—a clipper ship cruising full sheet to the wind—had vanished altogether. The new logo was a stylized drawing of the two leaves and a bud that symbolized the tea plant.

Delilah and Jane were making their presentation of the new marketing initiatives they'd spent half the summer developing. They had invited everyone from her grandmother on down to listen, and the room was full. Nick had taken the day off from his writing to verify the historical details. Travis, away at the London auction, was the only executive not present for the demonstration.

After Delilah finished showing off the proposed new boxes, Jane rose to explain everything that had been planned to update the image of Templeton Tea, including TV appearances, newspaper interviews, commercials, and print ads. Delilah knew Jane was nervous about her presentation, and was pleased to see the younger woman speak with relative ease and confidence. Jane had bloomed in her new position. After Delilah had made several artless remarks about how long it had taken her to discover which colors looked good with her black hair, Jane had begun showing up at work wearing new, more flattering shades. "You're paying me so much more money now," she'd said lightly one day, "I can afford to buy clothes."

When Jane finished speaking, Delilah took the floor again. In answer to a bland query from Grendam about how much all this was going to cost, she said: "Admittedly, it will be expensive. But it's not unusual in the beverage business for a company to budget a good deal more money for advertising than I'm proposing. Our competitors are doing it, and if we want to stay in the running, we must follow suit."

She cut the lights and showed a videotape of the new commercial that was being produced. It was rough at this point—just actors reading a script, without graphics or special effects. But the actors did an excellent job of relating a brief history of the glamorous tea clippers, and although the approach was soft sell, the script managed to include the Templeton name often enough to make an indelible impression on every viewer's mind.

When the tape ended, the staff gave a cheer. "I'd run right out and buy Templeton Tea after that," somebody in the back of the room shouted. Delilah and Jane looked at each other and grinned.

When the meeting ended, Minerva asked her granddaughter to come into her office. Delilah would have brought Jane, but Grendam shook her head. "I'd like to speak to you alone."

There was something in her tone of voice . . . something that called up memories of reproofs from long ago. Delilah sensed there was a problem, and grew tense. She wasn't accustomed to the necessity of having her decisions rubber-stamped. Oh, for the good old days of being the undisputed boss.

"I know I've presented you with a lot of dramatic changes," she said as the door closed behind them. "I'm hoping you'll trust me when I tell you they're necessary."

Grendam walked straight to the window. She looked frail standing there, her profile to Delilah, her petite figure almost washed out by the summer glare from the floor-to-ceiling window. Despite the heat, she was wearing a mauve knit dress with a high collar, and stockings. (Delilah's legs, as always in the summertime, were bare.) She looked smart and sophisticated, but there was iron running up her spine.

"Changes? You've been fomenting a revolution. You're not running this company yet, Delilah. Perhaps you never will be."

Delilah stiffened. "I'm well aware of that."

"We can't afford to spend so much on advertising. You'll have to trim your budget by at least fifty percent."

"I've already trimmed it. I'm no spendthrift, I assure you. This is as low as we can go."

"It's too high. I won't approve the expenditure. At this rate you'll put us out of business before the end of the year. For all I know, that's precisely what you have planned. A fine revenge that would be, wouldn't it?"

Delilah felt herself flush. "Don't be absurd."

"And as far as these go, I don't like them." She was holding the drawings of the new package designs. "The change is too radical. You've done away with all the traditional elements that one associates with the long history of Templeton Tea. No one will even recognize these packages as ours, and that, my dear marketing expert, would be a colossal mistake." She turned away from the window, walked across to her desk, and tossed the sketches into the wastebasket. "Get me something else."

Delilah rocked back on her heels as a wave of anger whipped through her. She stalked over to the wastebasket and retrieved the sketches. "Do you have any idea how hard Dory has worked to get the right images, the right print style? My God, Grendam! How dare you toss aside our suggestions as if they were nothing!"

"They're all wrong. You and Dory are going to have to come up with something a little more in the tradition of Templeton Tea."

"Traditions are all very well, but they don't necessarily sell product. What I'm trying to do is bring this creaking old company into the twentieth century."

Her grandmother advanced upon her until she was standing less than three feet away. Delilah towered over her, but she didn't feel it, at that moment. Instead she was a teenager again, being reprimanded for her latest escapade at school. "You're fifty years too late," Grendam said. "I did that, Delilah. I did it, nobody else. You wouldn't be standing here, talking back to me, if I hadn't taken a failing business and beaten it up off its knees. So don't try to tell me you're doing something that's never been done before."

Minerva was shaking. "You know nothing of my struggles, my failures, my victories. What this company was, and what I made of it in a time when, unlike now, women were not expected to do such things. How dare you belittle my life's work!"

Delilah was struck silent. She'd been so busy seeking out recent mistakes that she'd forgotten the way her grandmother had come into a faltering company and restored it to greatness. "I'm sorry. I certainly don't mean to belittle you. You did a wonderful job. But if I don't know as much about those years as I should, it's because you never talk about it." It was true, she realized; ever since she'd returned from California, she and Grendam had both striven to keep their relationship businesslike and impersonal. Neither of them had confronted the emotional rift between them, which was by no means healed. "We're not close enough anymore for you to talk to me."

"We're not close because you are stubborn. You don't listen. You insist upon having your own way."

"You make me sound like a spoiled child. But I'm no more a child than you're an all-wise, all-knowing adult. I'm your equal and I expect to be treated as such."

"You're an arrogant upstart, that's what you are!"

Delilah felt a crown of pain around her head. She was afraid she'd blow up, totally lose control. "I see no point in continuing this conversation." She moved toward the door. "Obviously, we can't work together. Our egos are too strong, and we don't seem to be able to compromise."

"So what are you doing, quitting?" Grendam said scathingly. "That would be like you, wouldn't it? What will you do, run back to California again?"

Delilah whirled back to face her. "I'm not a quitter. I'm going ahead with my plans. If you don't like it, fire me."

"Don't tempt me!"

"Hey," said Nick from the hallway. He came in, shamelessly, giving them both a crooked grin. "Let's not do anything rash, okay?"

"Listening at the keyhole, Nick?" Delilah snapped. "Playing knight in shining armor again? My God!" Clutching Dory's drawings to her chest, she stalked out, slamming the door behind her.

Minerva looked helplessly at her grandson, who was no longer smiling. "Damn her," she said.

"All I heard was the tail end of that, but it sounds to me as if you're both at fault, Gran. Why do you go after each other so harshly? If there was no love, no admiration between you, it might make sense, but . . ." He allowed his voice to trail off.

Minerva sat down behind her desk. Stubborn, stubborn girl. This was the latest in a series of flamboyant moves Delilah had made. She'd come into the marketing division with whirlwind force, initiating change after change without so much as a by-your-leave. "But you put me in charge, Grendam. You gave me a free hand," the baggage taunted her every time she protested. "I really think you ought to stand back and give me a chance before you criticize."

I should have known, Minerva said to herself. Her stomach was aching and her arthritis was acting up. No doubt her blood pressure was soaring, too. She was a mass of aches and pains, due to this exasperating girl. To think she had wanted her to come back and work for the tea company. To think she'd actually been relieved when the prodigal had returned.

The ironic thing about it was that most of her employees responded very well to Delilah's new approach. They love her, Minerva thought bitterly, in a way they've never loved me.

"I'm too old for this," she said to Nick. "I'm sick of the fights, the arguments, the constant battle of wits. Travis never argues. Of course, he always does what he damn well pleases, but at least he smiles and pretends to follow my wishes. Delilah makes no bones about the fact that she intends to do everything her own way."

"At least she's honest. God knows what Travis has been up to behind your back."

"You always criticize him."

"I don't trust him. I never have."

"I wish it could be you, Nick. I wish I could leave the company to you."

"Well, you can't. And the fact is, you don't want to leave it to anyone. You've been running it for fifty years, and you can't bear to relinquish control."

"I know," she said slowly. Silently she acknowledged that even in the days when she and Edward had managed the company together, she had needed to be in control. It went back to her youth —her need to hold her destiny in the palms of her hands. It was her strength . . . and her greatest weakness as well.

"I have my own methods, my own style. Delilah is untraditional . . . I don't know how to deal with her." She rested her head on the heels of her hands. "I thought that if she came home, we'd be able to be friends again. I thought things could go back to the way we were when she was a little girl. I miss that so much, Nick! But she's here, she's back, and we're still estranged."

"Have you talked with her about what caused her to leave? Have you ever tried to resolve it?"

"I can't talk about it," she said in a low voice. "Not now, not ever."

"That's too bad, Gran. Because it doesn't look as if anything's going to come right unless you do. I'd rethink the matter if I were you."

Nick left her then, trying not to feel guilty about badgering her. If somebody didn't push them, nothing was ever going to change.

Delilah took shelter in her own office, where she dry-swallowed two aspirin for her headache. This kind of thing never used to happen at Merlin's. The working atmosphere there was pleasant, genial. Nobody fought, nobody yelled, everyone got along just fine. Of course, at Merlin's, there was nobody around to tell her what she could and could not do.

She threw open the windows to get some fresh air. The small inner courtyard couldn't be seen, or reached, from the street. There were many such interior courtyards on Beacon Hill. She loved this one, for it was filled with hollyhocks and roses bathed in the summer sun. She leaned over the sill, breathing deeply. The flowers were in full bloom, and the leaves were now a mature dark green.

"Don't jump," said Nick's voice behind her. "We're a depressive bunch, we Templetons, but things are not that bad."

She whirled to face him. "Fat chance I'll jump. Don't you dare patronize me."

He crossed to her desk and sat down on the edge of it, picking up the tea growers' journal lying there and glancing through it briefly before tossing it down. Delilah leaned against the window sill and surveyed him. He made a few concessions to office routine during his frequent visits to the tea company by dressing more formally than usual, but he clearly didn't intend to sacrifice comfort. Today he was wearing jeans with a shirt, a tie, and a rumpled corduroy jacket. He must have been tugging at the tie, though; its knot was unraveling.

"I talked to her doctor the other day. Her heart's not strong. She can't take this sort of excitement."

"You never let up, do you? If she can't take it, let her go home to the China Tea House Tavern and live a quiet life like any other eighty-year-old woman in the city. Let her retire, as she promised to do."

"You've got to be patient. The tea company is her child. She's not ready to let it go."

"The tea company is the only child to whom she's ever given any love." The words burst out of her before they were fully formed as a thought, and Delilah wished she could snatch them back. Damn Grendam. Damn him.

"You're wrong. She loves you very much."

Delilah made a deprecatory sound.

Nick noted her stiff posture, the elevation of her chin. Her voice was tired, bitter, hurt in the way that she was usually so careful to disguise. He was catapulted back through the years to a night when Delilah had stood at the window of the Concord farmhouse, her face scrunched up against the glass, watching for headlights in the driveway. It was the day before school was due to begin, and her father was supposed to come and take her home. She hadn't seen him all summer. Her suitcase was packed, her eyes were excited, all day she'd been jumpy and falsely bright.

David Scofield had never come. Their grandmother had had to drive her home the next morning.

"It's easy for you to speak on the subject," she went on. "You've never given her any trouble, have you? Nick the sweetheart, Nick the angel. What have you ever done to cause her anger or distress?"

"You'd be surprised. She wasn't too pleased with me when I got divorced from my 'lovely wife,' as Gran called her. Nor did she care much for the way I 'let my feelings get the better of me' and had to start seeing a shrink three times a week and go on massive doses of tranquilizers to calm me down."

Delilah was ashamed. She'd been wrapped up in her own concerns; it was easy to forget that other people had problems, too. "When was that?"

"After I lost custody of Kelsey. I'd had anxiety attacks since I was a kid, but this was different. This was your proverbial dark night of the soul. Gran was worried about me, yes. But she doesn't have a whole lot of patience with people who can't keep a stiff upper lip. She's a smart, strong-willed woman, but she lacks imagination."

"That's for sure." She pushed a hand through her thick hair. "Did you ever figure out what was causing your attacks?"

"No. I've done lots of traditional talk therapy without uncovering the root cause. I feel as if something happened to me, something terrible, at an age when I was too young to understand it. All I've been able to come up with is my mother's death, but that doesn't seem to be it somehow. That was grim, but this is something even darker."

"Are you all right now?"

"I'm fine. A better person, as they say, for having gone through the valley and emerged safely on the other side. I don't regret it. I learned a lot, both about myself and about other people."

Her mouth thinned again. "Which gives you the right, I suppose, to give advice?"

"It's a rare bird who listens to advice. I'm giving you a warning, Delilah. The same one I gave you the day I picked you up at the airport. Stop hounding her. She's eighty. She's got high blood pressure, high cholesterol, and heart rhythm irregularities. She doesn't always take her medication. Her physician has warned that too much stress could cut short her life."

Delilah recognized a guilt trip when it was being laid on her. Look at him: those green eyes, how implacable they could be. There was an unsuspected strength in Nick, a kind of iron-willed determination that amazed her sometimes. "If she has a heart attack from overwork, I suppose you're going to blame it on me?"

He moved closer, cornering her there against the window. "I might. And by God, you'll wish yourself back in California if I do."

Delilah stood still, as angry at his use of physical intimidation as she was disconcerted by his intensity. Dear old unpredictable Nick. For a brief, wild moment she recalled Dory's remarks about his sexual expertise. For the first time in her life, she believed it. He was emitting the sort of energy that could be dynamite in bed.

"You're going to have to learn to compromise," he went on. "Unlike Merlin's, this isn't your show. It never will be, even if our grandmother chooses you to succeed her. You're going to have to work with Travis, even with me. I'm on the board of directors. I might decide to take a more active role."

"Who the *hell* do you think you are?"

"I'm a Templeton. Your family, Delilah. Like it or not, you're stuck with us." Nick picked up the drawings from her desk and leafed through them. "She's right, you know. These'll never work. You'd know it yourself if you could stop emotionalizing and see straight."

"Go fuck yourself, Nick!"

"I would, baby," he said, grinning. "But frankly, since my divorce I've been doing entirely too much of that."

He walked out of the office, leaving her trembling and closer to tears than she'd been since leaving California. The trembling she understood; she had a temper, by God. But the tears disconcerted her. As did the slight hint of warmth in the pit of her belly. It wasn't attraction, was it? Surely not.

I hate this conflict, she muttered to herself. ("I see an intensification of the conflicts around you," Dory had warned.) Is this what it was going to be like between herself and the other Templetons for the rest of her life?

Damn him, damn them all! She threw her things into her briefcase. She was taking the rest of the day off.

34

Delilah left the office, got into the Nissan Maxima she'd bought shortly after her arrival in Boston, tuned the radio to one of the local rock stations, and drove. She sped up I-95 to Route 128, the old highway that girdled Boston, until she came to the end of the road in Gloucester, the famous old fishing town. Remembering shortcuts she hadn't taken for twenty years, she found her way to Good Harbor Beach, where her parents used to bring her on summer weekends when she was small. Delilah parked the car, slipped off her snakeskin pumps, and tossed the jacket of her strawberry-beige linen suit into the back seat. Loosening the collar of her blouse, she set out along the boardwalk for the sea.

The afternoon was hot and the beach crowded. When her office attire raised a few eyebrows, Delilah grinned and loosened another button.

She had learned to swim along this stretch of sand. Her mother had bought her a pair of red rubber water wings, which she'd inflated and put on Delilah's arms. They buoyed her up enough to give her the confidence to go in over her head. Not that she'd ever been particularly reluctant. On one occasion she'd plunged right in, following her father as he swam out beyond the breakers. Yelling, her mother had jumped in after her while her father swam on, oblivious to the drama. The lifeguard had gone after her, too. "I wanted to see how far I could swim," Delilah had said when they hauled her back in. "If I got tired, I was going to tread water and let the waves carry me back to shore."

"That was brave of you, Delilah," her mother said, "but it's not a good idea to get in over your head."

"If you only knew, Mummy," she said now. "Getting in over my head is one of the things I do best."

She walked along the shoreline, enjoying the feel of her bare toes sinking into the sand. This was the first time she'd been to the seaside since that night at Malibu when she'd wept for Max. The coastline was harsher here. Missing were the greens and blues of California. Black rocks and wintery seas abounded, even in the summer. When the waves reached her, the chilly water turned her ankles numb.

You've got to go back and deal with them, Max had told her. Well, she was trying. But she wasn't doing such a hot job.

Her game plan so far had been to impress her grandmother with her innovative business skills, and at that, she believed, she was succeeding. Marketing was one area in which she felt she could make a significant contribution in a short period of time. With only one year to convince Grendam she was the right person to take over, it had seemed sensible to go all out.

But . . . *let's face it, duchess, you've screwed up.* Had she been too aggressive? Had her easy rapport with her coworkers alienated her grandmother? Had Merlin's been a special case, and its founder a fish out of water anywhere else?

There was no Merlin's anymore, at least, not for her. She'd sold her interest to Sam. Templeton Tea was all she had now. If she blew it, there was nothing else.

Nick was right. If she seriously wanted to run the tea company, she was going to have to find a way to get along with the Templetons—all of them, her grandmother included. Cooperation. Compromise. She was good at a lot of things, but maybe she wasn't so good at that. Maybe she'd better start learning. Maybe she'd better stop being so goddamn selfish and try to see the situation from her grandmother's point of view. Or from Nick's. Or even from Travis's.

She got back in the car again and drove. Back down 128 to 2. Out 2 west to Concord. Through Concord Center, past Sleep Hollow Cemetery, where Hawthorne and Thoreau and Louisa May Alcott were buried, along Monument Street past the "bridge that arched the flood." Off on a side road through rolling hills and forests that were dewy with the fresh scent of summer. It had been so many years since she'd been here, yet nothing had changed.

It was late afternoon when Delilah pulled into the private driveway that led to the farmhouse she'd loved to visit as a child. She parked the Maxima in front of the barn. She leaned against the warm hood for several minutes, just looking around. The house was buttercup-yellow with white trim. There was a trellis of tiny red roses to the right of the entryway, and an orange trumpet vine growing on the pillars of the front porch. Around the left corner, where the bay window was, she could see the old apple tree brooding in the distance, looking smaller than she remembered.

Nick didn't answer her knocking, but his car was in the barn. She let herself in through the unlocked front door. The inside of the house had been beautifully kept up; the floors and woodwork were waxed and shining, the wallpaper fresh. The kitchen had been modernized; the bathrooms, too. She wondered if he'd kept that wonderful old claw-footed bathtub in the master bath upstairs.

"Nick?" No answer. After exploring a bit, she found him down in the basement gym that had once been their playroom, working out with weights.

"Hi there, champ. Those biceps are looking good."

Nick stopped flexing for a second, then resumed, a little more slowly than before. "You startled me."

"Sorry. The front door was open. I had to talk to someone. D'you mind?" She kicked off her shoes and flopped down on an exercise mat. "I'm sorry about this morning. Are you still mad at me?"

Her cousin was doing bench presses on a formidable-looking metal torture machine. "I'm not still mad. But you can be a real bitch sometimes."

"Not usually. Only when I'm on the defensive, Nick. And she can put me there so fast, so easily. It's scary, the way she can still do that to me."

"Makes you feel like a kid again."

"That's right. A forty-year-old kid."

"Thirty-eight," he said with a smile.

Delilah ringed her knees with her arms, unmindful of the consequences to her skirt. "Dammit, Nick, I know I behaved badly, I know I've got to learn to work with her, to cooperate, as you put it, but how can I go against my best instincts and perhaps scuttle the very thing I'm trying to accomplish, just to get along with my grandmother? Can't she give a little, too? Can't she acknowledge me for what I am?"

Nick's green eyes locked with hers. "What are you?"

"I'm exactly what she always wanted me to be. A damn good businesswoman. A worthy successor to her. Why can't she take pride and satisfaction in that and let me fulfill my destiny?"

Nick freed himself from the machine and came to sit beside her. Clad only in a pair of shorts and running shoes, his angular body was slick with sweat. His muscles were surprisingly well defined for such a lean, spare man. She could see faint ripples in his arms, his belly, his legs. He had a strong, still-young body. Although she knew he ran, did karate, and worked out with weights, his physical competence had never made an impression on her before. He'd had so little of it when he was a child.

We remember the child. We see the adult, but the child is always there, penetrating our awareness, forming our impressions. The child never goes away.

"Maybe what she thought she wanted is not what she really needs," he said. "Maybe it's not your talents as a businesswoman she's craved all these years. Maybe all she really wants is your love."

She could almost hear Max saying, "Love counts. It's the only thing that does."

"Maybe," she admitted. "But what if I'm not a very loving person? I mean, it's *hard* to love sometimes."

He smiled. "You look as if you could use a good workout, Delilah. Blow off some of that negative energy. What do you do to keep in shape?"

"Not much these days. We had a pool in L.A., of course; everybody did. I used to swim every morning, but after Max got sick, I stopped. What's the point of it when being in perfect physical condition doesn't prevent you from dying of cancer? Nobody knows why some people live forever and others die relatively young."

"You don't get any exercise?"

"I run a little now and then. Don't start in on me about that. One guilt trip per day is all you're allowed."

He laughed. "No more guilt trips, I promise." He stood and walked over to a closet. "I've got an idea. Come here."

"Why?" she asked even as she followed him.

"I don't know if working out is going to extend my life span—that's not why I do it. For me it's a way of insuring I don't reach a critical mass and explode." From a shelf in the closet he withdrew several fat plastic objects that looked like boxing gloves. "Here. Put these on. You stick your fist in here and snap the Velcro around your wrists."

"What are they for?" Delilah did as he said and ended up with a soft appendage on the end of her arm. Beyond the small recess that enclosed her hand, the glove was filled, balloonlike, with air. It reminded her of the water wings at Good Harbor Beach.

"I'll help you with the other one. Hold still a minute." He equipped her other hand in the same manner. "Okay. You ready?"

"I'm not sure for what."

"A great form of therapy, and believe me, I've tried all of them. Close your eyes, Delilah."

"Nick—"

"Shut up and trust me."

"Okay, okay, they're closed."

"Now you know I'm here, right? Less than two feet away. I want you to focus on all your angers and frustrations. Just let them rise up. Don't try to control them. Let them control you."

"Are you crazy? I can't do that! I'll kill someone."

"You can't kill anyone. You can't even hurt anyone, thanks to these clown gloves. No, keep your eyes closed and focus on your emotions. Don't be afraid of them. They're just feelings, Delilah. Powerful, yes, but mental activity, nothing more."

His low, confident voice was like a drug. Images began to come into her head—unintelligible scraps that gradually grew more concrete. The supercilious sneer of her grandmother's upper lip as she'd tossed Dory's sketches into the trash. The cigarette lighter she'd held in her hand that long-ago day when she'd told Delilah her lover had abandoned her. Travis's naked body, his shocking blue eyes. Max lying motionless in their bed, not breathing because she'd poisoned him.

"Let the anger come," Nick said. "Let it rip."

She began to breathe faster; she could feel her muscles hardening as the channels opened up. Her heart raced. Her tension soared. With a sharp movement of her head, she tossed her hair off her neck. Damn hot hair. I'm going to chop it off.

"Hit me," said Nick.

"What!"

"That's what the gloves are for. You won't hurt me. Do it, Delilah."

"No. I don't want to. I can't."

"I really got to you this morning, didn't I? What right did I have to say those things? Am I more mature than you are, more emotionally stable? Me, the Anxiety King? Who the hell do I think I am?"

"Cut it out or I will hit you!"

"Pretend I'm Gran." His voice altered slightly as he added, "Pretend I'm Travis."

She shook her head, breathing hard. Don't push me, she was thinking. Don't push me any further or things are going to start flying all over this room.

She heard a rustling sound. "I'm putting on the gloves myself," he said. "I'm not afraid to hit you. You make me pretty mad sometimes. You've never taken me seriously. You come cry on my shoulder, relying on me to comfort you, but you don't really see me, do you? Not the way you see my brother."

"Stop it, Nick."

"Pretend I'm Max," he said in such a mocking voice that all at once she wanted to kill him. "Or better yet, pretend I'm your father."

She lost it then. A jagged series of images flooded her—closed doors, corridors lined with closed and bolted doors . . . *You're a shit, Daddy, a real shit!* She leapt forward and began to pummel him with all her strength.

Nick had put on one of the gloves, but he didn't hit her back or even try to defend himself; he just stood there and let her expend months, even years, of pent-up aggression on him. He was her target, rocklike, immovable. She battered against him like a bird against glass, not really trying to hurt him, just trying to . . . to *get free.*

When it was over, she was hysterical. Crying, laughing, hyperventilating so much he had to pull her face against his chest and hold her there for several seconds, forcing her to rebreathe her own exhalations until the giddiness faded and she went limp.

"My God," she whispered when she could control her voice. "Did I hurt you? Are you all right?"

"No damage, thanks to the gloves. Over here." He helped her over to the couch on the far side of the room.

"I'm shaking, Nick. I can't stop shaking."

"Don't worry; that's normal. Something to do with your body rebalancing itself after spending so much adrenaline. It'll stop in a little while. Are you cold?" He grabbed his sweatshirt from the arm of the sofa and pulled it on over her head. She could smell the faint but pleasant male odor she'd always associated with Nick. "Your pretty blouse is all wrinkled and sweaty, I'm afraid. I should have made you strip down first."

Delilah couldn't speak for a long time. Nick held her, petted her, spoke soothingly to her, and as he did so another image of the past came back to her—herself providing a similar kind of comfort to him one summer night in this same room after Travis had had one of his rare temper tantrums and beaten up his younger brother.

At last she said, "There's not another person on this earth who could have done that for me. Thank you, Nick. I love you."

He didn't answer. His arms were around her; his chin was resting on the top of her head. She felt him nod.

At Nick's invitation, Delilah stayed for supper. He broiled bluefish in white wine and shallots, which inspired her to inquire archly whether Drake had been taking cooking lessons from Spenser. After dinner he took her for a tour around the house, showing off the study where he wrote the series. He also showed her his gun collection, which Delilah taunted him about. "Hey, I acquired this stuff for research purposes," he protested when she accused him of being a closet Rambo. "This is a Colt .44 dating from the middle of the last century. And this is the sort of automatic pistol the feds used in the 1920s wars against organized crime."

"My God. Is it loaded?"

"Of course not."

She browsed among the rifles, pistols, and shotguns. "Do you know how to fire these things?"

"I belong to a shooting club, as a matter of fact."

She hooted. "My cousin, the former hippie radical peacenik, now a member of the NRA!"

"I'll have you know I'm still a good Democrat. But Drake's an expert with weapons, so naturally I have to know everything he knows."

"Yeah? And what are these for?" She was dangling a pair of police handcuffs.

Nick took them away from her. "I use 'em to restrain obnoxious guests," he drawled, making a playful grab for one of her wrists.

Delilah laughed and promised to stop teasing him.

They adjourned to the living room for coffee. Nick talked a lot about his daughter, proudly shepherding Delilah through seven or eight thick photo albums of Kelsey from birth (he'd been in the delivery room and had been the first to hold the newborn) to age seven. "I want you to meet her. She's heard all about you, of course. She'll be here again in a couple of weeks; maybe we can get together, the three of us."

"I'd like that."

He asked her about her marriage, so she told him all about Max. At one point she compared what she'd felt for Max with what she'd felt for Travis. "I didn't know who I was or what I wanted in 1970. In retrospect I guess it was mostly a physical thing with your brother. I thought it was true love, but love wasn't a very coherent concept to me then."

"It's been over a year since Max died, and you're not dating, are you? Aren't you lonely?"

She shrugged. "I suppose so. But there have been other periods in my life when I've done without men."

It was dark in the room, and although he was sitting close to her on the sofa, his legs stretched out and resting on the coffee table, his voice seemed to come from far away: "What do you do about sex?"

"I fantasize about all the wonderful affairs I could be having, and go to bed alone." Delilah turned her head to look into those green eyes that were so like her own and asked, "What do you do about it?"

"I'm seeing someone, actually. But it's not the most secure thing I've ever had going."

She was surprised. She had not realized he was involved with anyone. "Why not?"

"It's not serious. Her name's Karin and she's a corporate attorney. She's too busy to spend much time with me."

"Are you in love with her?"

He shook his head. "It's not love, just convenience. Which is part of the problem. I don't like sleeping once a week with someone I don't love. In the first place, I'm a sex fiend, and once a week isn't enough to satisfy me."

"Ha!"

Grinning now, he added, "And in the second, why spend even that much time with a woman who doesn't intend to make a commitment to me?"

"My God, you sound like most of the single women I know. Commitment? It's the men who won't make a commitment. They're too busy running around chasing all the sex they can get."

"Not me."

"What about that desire for sexual variety that's so common among males?"

"Among us hypochondriacs of the world, darling, variety is out. I'm not going to die for it, thank you very much." There was a short silence, then Nick shifted on the sofa and added, "One can have sexual variety without a lot of partners. I'd be content sleeping with the same woman year after year as long as she was willing to vary the roles we play together in bed."

"Her on top once in a while, you mean?"

He wriggled his eyebrows at her. "I had something a little more sophisticated in mind."

Delilah giggled. "Tell me, tell me. What are you into? Kinky stuff? Do those handcuffs you showed me play a part in your bedroom activities?"

"I'd be glad to give you a peek into my bedroom activities, but there's a catch. You can't just watch. You have to participate."

Delilah felt the heat come up in her face and neck. For the first time since she'd entered his house, she looked at him, really looked. His features had matured and softened over the years, taking away the sharpness of his youth. There was an air of confidence about him, the self-assurance that comes with successfully negotiating the twists and turns of life. As for sensuality, it was condensed in his strong, lithe body, his long-fingered, sensitive hands. His mouth, which was erotic. His eyes, which radiated an allure that was as old as time.

All this talk about sex . . . he had initiated it. She swallowed some coffee. It was lukewarm. "Watch it," she said lightly. "I'm liable to take you up on that."

He didn't speak. Delilah felt a curl of nervousness in the pit of her stomach. "You're not kidding, are you?"

His eyelids came down, curtaining off those too honest green eyes. "You're my cousin. Of course I'm kidding."

His voice was low, but the emotion broke through anyway, and Delilah caught a glimpse of something vivid and real. Something that had been in existence for far longer than she'd ever wanted to admit. Something that had lasted and renewed itself several times over the long passage of years that marked the boundaries of their lives together. *N. loves D.*

It only took her a few seconds to decide. *Say yes to life, Delilah. I think we're meant to say yes a lot more often than we do.*

She stood up before him. The room was dark; the fire he'd lit so many hours ago was the only flickering light. "If there's one thing I regret, it's what didn't happen between us in a motel room in 1970." She tugged her blouse out of her waistband and began unbuttoning it.

She'd only managed one button before Nick shook his head and said, "No."

"What do you mean, no? You can't reject me twice. Not allowed, Nicholas. No way." She rapidly slipped buttons out of buttonholes and parted the front of her blouse. Her bra had a front clasp, which she opened with a flick of one finger. Nick's eyes followed the gesture, but they didn't linger long on her breasts before coming back to her face.

"What was true then is still true now," he said. "What you're offering isn't enough."

"Bullshit."

"There's more between us than the possibility of some pleasant sex, Delilah. But you won't acknowledge it."

She shook her head. "I've had my grand passion, if that's what you mean. But there are many kinds of love."

He smiled thinly. "I'm not so sure I buy that old cliché."

She tossed back her hair. "Look at you. Lounging there so calmly, pretending you're not aching to grab me." Still holding eye contact, she knelt between his legs and stroked her palms up the inseam of his jeans. His thighs were lean and hard, as hard from tension, perhaps, as they were from exercise. She smiled as she felt the muscles flinch beneath her touch.

"I want you to stop." Each word he spoke was clearly and separately enunciated.

"Uh-uh." Her hands reached his crotch, finding, as she'd expected, that beneath the thick denim he was fully erect. Delicately, her fingers traced the shape of him. *Nice,* she thought. She sneaked a look at his face and saw the muscles in his throat convulse as he swallowed.

She was tugging at his zipper when his hands covered hers. "I said no, you stubborn woman. Do I have to fight you off? Are you planning to rape me in my own house?"

"If that's your favorite fantasy, sure. I'd like it, too, I think, a little gentle S and M with someone I trust . . ." As she spoke she dropped her head into his lap and nuzzled him. Let him try and stop me. Show me the man who can resist a woman kneeling before him, her mouth against his—

"Cut it out, Delilah!" He slid down to the floor and straddled her body with his knees. When she arched up against him, he shoved one hand under her skirt. The hand was warm and firm; it felt very good against her bare flesh, but before she could enjoy its caress, it moved under the silky fabric of her underpants. His index finger touched her, probing quickly, expertly. One second only, then it was gone. "You're faking."

"Jesus, Nick!"

He jumped up, leaving her sprawled on the carpet. "Try me again someday when you're wet."

"You son of a bitch! Hasn't anybody ever instructed you in the sexual response of women? It takes us longer. And it helps to have a man who does more than sit there like a stone idol!"

"I know as much as any man about the sexual response of women." There was no braggadocio in his voice, just a simple statement of fact. "I know I can make you want me, I know I can give you pleasure. But you don't yearn to make love to me the way I yearn to make love to you, and that kills me, Delilah. I don't need your touch to arouse me. I just look at you, hear your voice, think about you, and I ache as much as any fifteen-year-old kid."

Delilah winced. The guilt she'd felt years ago in a motel room rose up to assault her once again.

He made it worse: "I love you. But you don't feel that for me, and I've still got some shreds of pride, of self-respect. I'm damned if I'll accept a charity fuck."

"Nick, I love you, too. I just can't give you what you want. It's not in me anymore. When Max died he took everything that was hopeful and tender in me."

"That's crap and I don't believe it for a second. You're afraid, that's all. You've lost too often. I know about fear; I understand it. It's stifling, debilitating, and it makes you cold and self-absorbed. That's okay, that's human. But at some point you've got to fight it, to start saying no, this isn't the way I'm going to live the rest of my life. Whether with me or with Gran, you've got to open yourself to love."

Delilah rose from the floor to face him. "You'd better give me back those gloves of yours. I think I'm about to hit you again."

Nick surprised her by pulling her close and kissing her mouth, the slow, fierce kiss of a frustrated lover. She liked it; she felt the beginnings of a genuine arousal this time. But instead of continuing, he pushed her back from him. "One of these days I'll have you the way I want you," he told her. "I'm an optimist."

The night after Delilah came to his house, Nick kept a date with Karin Harvey, the corporate attorney he'd been seeing for several months. He liked Karin; she was easygoing and fun to be with. They went to the Red Sox game and screamed themselves hoarse when Jim Rice hit a two-run homer in the ninth to win the game. The Sox were on a winning spree, and pennant hopes were high.

Afterward they had a late dinner at Michaela's Italian restaurant in Kendall Square, then went back to Karin's place for what was usually some pleasant, mutually fulfilling sex.

It wasn't until they were in bed with the lights out that Nick realized he wasn't going to be able to do it. Karin's caresses left him cold. So. Life would not go on as usual after all.

"Is something wrong?" she asked.

"Yeah." He was comfortable with Karin, so he wasn't particularly embarrassed, but he was concerned about hurting her feelings. He enjoyed her, they were good at pleasing each other in bed, and until now his feelings for Delilah hadn't interfered with his ability to make love to Karin. But tonight he couldn't get aroused, not even when she stroked him.

"Maybe you drank too much at dinner."

"One glass of wine? No, I don't think so." He flopped back on the bed beside her, unwilling to tell her the truth. "Maybe it's the first sign of some deadly disease."

Karin knew about his half-serious, half-playful hypochondria. "Cock cancer," she said solemnly.

He laughed and held her while she snuggled to him, yawning. "Never mind," she said. "I had a rough day and I'm exhausted anyway."

"Let me caress you for a while. There's no need for you to miss out on this just because I'm incapacitated. My fingers, at least, are hard."

She declined the offer, explaining that she couldn't really enjoy it if he wasn't along for the ride.

Later, after Karin had fallen to sleep beside him, Nick began thinking about Delilah's long limbs and dark mane of wild hair. Her hands on his thighs, his cock. Her mouth . . .

There was an immediate rush of blood to his groin. Dammit, he breathed in the darkness. Something had changed.

He wasn't sure exactly what had released his feelings, but perhaps that pummeling had been as cathartic for him as it had been for her. Or perhaps the change had arisen from listening to her talk about the difference between her feelings for Travis and her feelings for Max. She'd seemed to put Travis out of the running forever.

For some reason, he'd never expected to have a chance against his brother. Wrong though Travis might be for her, there had always been a chemistry between them you couldn't deny. But now, for the first time in his life, Nick saw a path to Delilah that was not blocked by the genial presence of his brother. With that, Karin Harvey simply couldn't compete.

In the morning, he told her. She didn't believe him at first. "Don't be silly, Nick. It happens to everyone sooner or later. I'm not always in the mood either, for goodness' sake; it just doesn't show on me."

"That's not why." He hated this kind of thing. Some men would just walk out and never call again. Why couldn't he be like them? "I'm in love with another woman. I'm sorry, Karin. It wasn't exactly something I planned."

For a moment, but only a moment, her face revealed her hurt. Then she concealed it. "You're sleeping with her, of course. You probably slept with her yesterday, which was why you couldn't—"

"Actually, I've never slept with her. And I don't know if I ever will. She's not in love with me."

Karin said nothing. Nick put his arms around her, afraid she was going to cry. She jerked away.

"You're a lovely, sensual woman," he said gently. "You deserve something better than I have to offer."

"I haven't asked for all of you, Nick. I'm content with our friendship and I enjoy you as a lover. Why should we throw that away?"

"Because it's not fair to you for me to be thinking about someone else while you and I are in bed together."

"Christ, you're such a romantic! I think of other men all the time. Harrison Ford, for example. Don Johnson. Bill Kurtz."

"Who the hell is Bill Kurtz?"

"The computer analyst I see when I'm not seeing you. He's not as good a lover as you are," she added with a slightly acid intonation, "but at least he's living in the twentieth century."

"In other words, you've been unfaithful to me."

"We're not married, Nick."

"I've been faithful to you."

"Wonderful. You deserve a gold star."

She was hurt and angry, he knew; she was striking back. But he didn't feel too guilty after that.

Nick's problem with women, he'd decided long ago, was that he was too damn nice. He loved sex and thought about it a lot, but he'd never felt the need to rack up conquest after conquest. As he had indicated to Delilah, good, inventive, imaginative sex required trust and caring, and both these qualities required commitment. Commitment didn't scare him, but it certainly seemed to scare a lot of women nowadays.

Janet, his wife of ten years, had left him to "find herself," taking Kelsey with her. Nick was devastated when it happened; it had taken him months to come to grips with what had gone wrong. They'd loved each other. They'd had good sex. Their little girl was a darling. But Jan had given up grad school to have their baby. She'd wanted to do so; she'd insisted that a child needed her mother full-time during those important developmental stages of life. She'd devoted herself to Kelsey, who had thrived. Nick was proud of his wife, proud of their daughter. He and Jan laughed with their friends about their traditional roles—his going off to work at the university, her taking care of the kid and the house—because they'd always seemed such a nontraditional couple, such a throwback to the sixties.

Then Kelsey started going to day care for half a day. The following year she was gone from eight-thirty to three-thirty, and Janet had a lot of time on her hands. Such a common story. She talked about going back to school, but couldn't decide what career to pursue. She lost interest in sex. (She was sleeping with Kelsey's pediatrician, he found out later.) She began spouting opinions on the need for all human beings to be independent and free.

Beginning to be alarmed, Nick suggested couple's therapy. "Forget it," she said. "You're the one with the problem. You get therapy."

"What's my problem? If I've got a problem, I'll do something about it. Come on, name it. What?"

"You're too goddamn perfect!" she shrieked at him. "You're too understanding, too willing to put up with the foibles of everybody else! You're too polite, too gentle, too perceptive, too forgiving. You're the understanding husband, the skilled and inventive lover, the loving, supportive father. You're so goddamn wonderful, it makes me want to throw up."

"You're thinking of leaving me because I'm perfect?" He couldn't believe she was serious.

"I can't live with a man who makes me feel so guilty and inadequate. I'm sorry, Nick. I have to grow up, I have to come into my own. I can't do it the way things are."

"I'm not fucking perfect. If you leave me for such a stupid reason, if you insist on putting Kelsey through the pain of a separation and a divorce, you'll see very quickly the limits of my so-called perfection. I'll sue for custody, I'll nail you to the fucking wall."

He meant it. Good-natured though he was, when aroused to anger, he could be implacable. Within a few days, he and Jan were at each other's throats. Six months later they were divorced. She ended up with custody of Kelsey, whom he still missed so much, it was pitiful. Now that Jan had moved to the Midwest, he only saw his daughter one weekend a month, which wasn't enough.

Nick knew he wasn't perfect; he figured that whatever had gone wrong in his marriage had been as much his fault as Janet's. Jan was a strong woman, as was Karin Harvey. Nick had always been attracted to strong women, and they in turn were attracted to him. But for some reason, when he got involved with them, these strong women turned belly-up dependent on him. They liked the smooth sailing, they liked the good sex. But they didn't like being obligated to him for these things, and when they realized it, they got mad.

Delilah, he figured, would be no different. She was one of the strongest women he knew. And yet, in other respects, she was one of the most vulnerable. He knew her secret, and that gave him power over her. He knew how much she needed to be loved.

35

The day after her evening at Nick's, Delilah went into her grandmother's office just after nine A.M. and said, "I'm sorry about what happened yesterday morning. I'm not very good at taking orders, I'm afraid."

Minerva rose and came around the desk. Delilah could tell Grendam was surprised at her gesture, and thought, how arrogant must I seem to her that she's so astonished to hear me apologize.

"I'm sorry, too, Delilah. We must work harder to minimize our differences. It's bad for the company's morale for us to be in conflict with each other all the time."

"It wasn't the company's morale I was thinking of. It was my own." She paused. "And yours."

Her grandmother nodded. She looked weary; there were dark circles under her eyes. Delilah thought of what Nick had said about her general ill health, and she felt a shaft of fear. *Don't let your grandmother pass from this world with your love for her unspoken.*

"Gran—" she began, but Minerva interrupted her with a remark about the necessity to be conservative as they initiated changes in their marketing strategy. She wasn't going to risk herself in a more personal discussion, it seemed.

Go to her, Delilah said to herself. Put your arms around her. Say, please, Gran. Enough. Say, I love you and this nonsense has got to end.

She didn't know why she couldn't do it. She was afraid, perhaps, that her grandmother would turn away. So instead she said, "You may be right about the tea boxes. I was so anxious to get a bright new design that I encouraged Dory to give us something entirely different. But of course we don't want to lose our regular customers, who might be confused if those familiar boxes disappeared from their supermarket shelves. That was stupid of me. I'm meeting with the art department later this morning; we'll rethink the problem."

"I'd appreciate that," Grendam said.

Delilah left her office feeling frustrated. She wanted more than peaceful coexistence with Minerva Templeton. She wanted to feel secure about her place in her grandmother's heart.

Minerva was dreaming again of Darjeeling—the mountains, the tea bushes, the processing factories that belched smoke, the evil man who took her into the tea gardens and threw her down upon her back. "I'll kill you, I'll kill you," she screamed, and woke trembling.

Minerva couldn't shake the feeling that someone—or something—was trying to contact her. There had been several incidents in recent weeks. Once she'd woken suddenly from a deep sleep sure that a hand had touched her face. On another occasion she'd had the eerie sensation that the bedstead where she slept was glowing red, as if aflame.

Tonight she woke to the sound of a loud report that seemed to be coming from just beside her head. She sat up and switched on the light. The room was empty. But lingering in the air was the distinctive odor of gunpowder.

She was frightened. They had been coming more and more frequently lately—the nightmares, the panic, and the resultant insomnia. She'd spent so many nights wandering around the China Tea House Tavern in the predawn hours that she'd asked her doctor to prescribe sleeping pills. But she rarely took them; she'd never liked the idea of having to rely on medication of any kind.

At night her thoughts dwelt almost exclusively upon the earlier events of her life. It was odd how clearly she recalled those years. More recent things—her time with Edward, with her children—seemed much farther away. Her father, Pamela, and Harrison Templeton, how vivid they were, especially in her dreams.

Once again the nightmare images arose. Forcibly, she turned off the flow of memories. She would not think about it. Harrison

Templeton had deserved the death he had died on the narrow staircase of the China Tea House Tavern. If hell existed, he was surely afire there.

If hell exists, you'll join him.

Her heart was pounding arrhythmically. This time I'm really going to die, she thought. Trapped in the web of her panic, she did something she'd never done: she reached for the phone and called Nick.

After apologizing for the hour (it was two-thirty in the morning), Minerva tried to explain what she'd heard and how it had made her feel. "It sounded like a gunshot. I'm frightened. I think I'm going crazy. At this rate I'll end my days looking out a barred window at the finely kept lawns of McLean Hospital."

"You're not crazy," said her loyal Nick. "I'm going to talk to your doctor, though. There are medications that can help you if you're having panic attacks. I'm also going to call Dory Lester and ask her to do a psychic reading on that weird bedroom of yours."

"No, Nick, really—"

"I insist. This has gone on long enough."

She was so tired that she agreed, even though the idea of holding a séance in the China Tea House Tavern seemed to her to be an adventure in futility. Whatever was happening, it wasn't due to ghosts, she was certain. It was more likely to be a manifestation of the pent-up power of her own guilty conscience.

"I'm going to try to go into the trance state," said Dory. "Don't speak to me until it's obvious that the entity has taken control."

"How am I supposed to know that?" Minerva asked.

"Don't worry, you'll know," she replied with a grin.

"I certainly hope so," Minerva said dryly. She leaned back in her chair across from the medium and folded her hands in her lap. She, Dory, and Nick were up in her bedroom in the Tavern. Dory and Minerva were seated inside the faerie circle, and Nick, who had promised not to interfere, was stretched out on the bed.

Minerva leaned back in her chair to watch as Dory prepared. First she did several shoulder circles and stretches, then she placed the palms of her hands flat on the table, bowed her head, and expelled a forceful breath. Thereafter she was still, sinking into a state of relaxation.

"I'm going to disengage so the spirit energy of my guides can enter," Dory explained. "There are several entities who might appear. The most likely one is Ra-ton, who's lived many times on this earth and is particularly fond of assuming the persona of a priest from the lost continent of Atlantis. He's a highly evolved soul, a teacher, and he knows a lot about the great changes that are taking place in the world today."

Goodness, Minerva thought, this was even more outlandish than she'd expected. How had she ever let Nick talk her into it?

"The energy within this circle is very powerful," said Dory. "There is ancient magic at work here."

Then she was silent. When several minutes passed without anything extraordinary happening, Minerva began to wonder cynically if the spirits were busy elsewhere. Dory appeared to be asleep. She considered reaching out and giving her a little nudge.

The younger woman groaned. A spasm whipped through her body. Her hands lifted from the table and began to shake as if she were afflicted with some sort of palsy. A freezing blast of air penetrated the room. Tricks, Minerva told herself. Don't get all silly and scared over some parlor game.

Dory groaned again and lifted her head. Her features were contorted. Both eyebrows seemed to have raised up and tilted slightly, making her look like a female Mr. Spock. Her lips pulled away from her teeth.

Dory's throat moved as if she were trying to speak, but no words emerged. Minerva stared into her eyes and felt a prickle. She sensed strongly that the personality staring at her through Dory's eyes was not Dory. Minerva glanced over at Nick, who had sat up on the bed and was staring at his onetime lover with undisguised astonishment. Don't be a fool, she wanted to shout at him. Don't you remember Delilah's telling us that Dory had once intended to be an actress?

"Greetings," said a deep male voice. "I am Ra-ton. Please state your name and the nature of your business with me."

Feeling ridiculous, Minerva replied, "I am Minerva Templeton, and I'm here today because of some odd events that have been occurring in my home. I feel as if somebody is watching me, trying to reach me."

Ra-ton smiled. If this was really an entity possessing Dory's body, Minerva wondered, where was Dory?

"She is nearby; have no concern about her," Ra-ton stated. "I only borrow her physical form briefly, as part of a compact to which she agreed before entering her current incarnation. She suffers no harm, and together we are sometimes able to do great good."

Minerva felt a little less arrogant about the whole thing. Ra-ton (or Dory) was telepathic. "Are you able to monitor all my thoughts?"

"No, indeed." He had a slight accent, but she was unable to identify it. "Only if you consent to it on the subconscious level. You consented a moment ago because you wished for some proof of my independent existence. It will not satisfy you, though, for you are highly rational and skeptical, Minerva Templeton. And you are also, I think, afraid."

"I do not make a practice of participating in paranormal events. I confess I find this experiment startling."

"I do not refer to your current unease, but the fear that comes upon you in the dark of night."

She didn't think Dory could know about that. Nick might have told her something, but not even Nick knew the extent of her insomnia.

"You are afraid, Minerva Templeton, because you sense the presence of something unknown, something you do not understand. This would create fear in anybody, but the effect may be greater in your case because you have a guilty conscience."

Minerva's fingers clenched into fists. No one knew about that. *No one.* She cast a quick glance at Nick and wished she'd asked him to wait downstairs.

"Fear not; I will be discreet," the entity continued. "I will not interfere in the melodrama you have chosen to make of your life."

Ra-ton's voice was husky with wry humor, something that surprised Minerva, who had expected a disincarnate entity to take himself more seriously. She was getting strong vibrations from him now. She sensed warmth, compassion, and great humanity.

"Why do you call it a melodrama?"

"I do not mean to insult you." He sounded apologetic now. "It's just that from my current perspective, all existence in the physical plane seems melodramatic. I have lived many lives in the physical coordinates you know as Earth. I learned many lessons, the same lessons you are engaged upon learning now. The chief of them, perhaps, is that all passionate human suffering is illusory. Very real, of course, when one is actually enduring it, but illusory nevertheless."

Minerva wasn't particularly interested in being lectured to about the follies of physical existence. She wanted to know what was going on in the China Tea House Tavern.

"Indeed, and I shall endeavor to assist you," Ra-ton said, reading her mind again. "But you must be patient while I drop a few pearls of wisdom along the way," he added with a smile. "It is my current vocation to be something of a cosmic psychiatrist."

Minerva chuckled. He was charming. "I would like very much to believe you. Could you perhaps tell me something more about myself? Something that Dory Lester does not know?"

"Perform tricks, you mean, to improve my credibility? I am no stage magician. You must judge me by your intuition, for your reason will find a logical explanation for any trick I might choose to demonstrate. It is almost impossible to prove that entities such as myself exist and speak through channels such as the young woman whose vocal chords I am currently animating. Your twentieth-century science is still sharply limited in that respect. There is no instrument which can measure me.

"If I delve into the secrets of your heart, you will explain it later by concluding that Dory Lester is highly telepathic. It has been my experience that modern, sophisticated people like yourself find it easier to believe in ESP than in the eternal survival of the soul. Such nihilistic skepticism is a recent development on your planet, and fortunately, a temporary one. How dismaying you must find it to believe that you will die, and that oblivion will be your end."

"I find it quite a restful idea, to tell the truth. I begin to grow weary of this life."

"Now, that is a sorrowful state of affairs, although I remember lifetimes during which I would heartily have sympathized. If you will take a small bit of advice, however? Do not indulge excessively in such thoughts. Your civilization in its current stage of evolution has not entirely understood the power of mental activity. You understood it once, and many of you acknowledge it still instinctively, but in general, you have forgotten.

"Your thoughts have activating power. They are the means by which the physical universe comes into being. Consciousness always precedes matter. Think a thing too intensely and too often, and it will become manifest in the physical world. This is a danger, for you in particular. You must not continue to dwell upon your sins."

Minerva shivered. It was true she had been engaging in a great deal of negative thinking lately. "Are you suggesting that my thoughts are somehow responsible for the odd events in the China Tea House Tavern?"

"No. What is happening in your home is coming from something outside yourself, although you are intimately connected with it."

"What do you mean?"

"This is not easy to explain. Give me a minute." There was a pause of several seconds, then the voice continued, "The place where you live is located at physical coordinates which are highly charged with certain energies. I do not know precisely how to put this into words, for the physical world is not constructed at all the way you currently believe it to be. Linear time, for example, does not exist. It is an illusion necessary to the reincarnational dramas that are played out in the physical universe. Without linear time, you could not be born, grow old, die, and come back in your next life. In truth you do not do these things, you only seem to do them.

"The events you are perceiving in the China Tea House Tavern are not really happening now, in your present. They are happening in the past. But since the past and present are simultaneous, it is possible that something from another era can bleed through, as it were, and become perceptible to sensitive receptors in another era. Do you understand?"

"I think so. But I've never been very good at metaphysics."

Ra-ton chuckled. For the first time his glance was directed toward Nick. "You will discuss it with your grandson. He understands."

"I'm not sure that I do," said Nick.

The entity turned back to Minerva and continued, "You feel a special closeness with this man because you have known him in many other lives. The same is true of the woman Delilah. You three have played out many roles with one another, changing sexes, ages, relationships. This is true with some of the others in your current life, also. You have even reincarnated several times within the same family. The one you call Travis in this life has appeared with you, too, although not as frequently. You must watch him, Minerva Templeton. He is moving into a state of crisis, and it remains to be seen how he will choose to respond to his challenges."

"I am worried about Travis," Minerva confessed.

"The karma between you is heavy in this life." He paused a minute to clear his throat. "We must stop soon. The young woman who so graciously shares her body with me is growing tired. The contact is excellent today, but she cannot sustain so deep a trance for long."

"Please, explain to me about this house. What is it that's bleeding through?"

"This is not very clear, but I sense an entity who is obsessed by one of her incarnations, a life in which she explored certain tragic themes. She bears some relationship—I am not entirely sure what this is—to the young woman she is attempting to reach. Does this make any sense?"

"No," said Minerva.

"There is a good deal of interference. I'm not getting . . . wait a moment." The voice issuing from Dory's lips faded, then spoke again at greater volume. "There is danger. Physical and psychological danger to you and to others. The curse of repetition, or near repetition, of a family tragedy. This has happened before in your family. Repetition. Karmic forces are at work. Reincarnational dramas. The young woman is advised to understand the past if she is to secure her future."

"I don't quite follow—"

"Wait. The channel is clearer now. Ah." There was a short pause. "Of course. I see a very determined woman who was trained in the ancient mysteries and knows a great deal about the true nature of the universe. She was good and brave, but also proud and defiant, forever getting herself in trouble." He spoke with wry affection. "Her soul is weighted down with karma, yet at the same time, radiantly bright.

"This woman feels responsible for the string of bad fortune that has infected your family. She is adept enough to see into future probabilities. She is not responsible, of course, except for her own sins. But she is a bit of an arrogant soul, I'm afraid, who hasn't learned that lesson yet." He sounded more amused than disapproving. "You share her fault, Minerva Templeton, which may account for the sympathy between you. The phenomena that you have experienced are the direct result of this woman's attempt to break through and warn you about the thoughts and actions in your life that may call down the so-called curse. The repetition." Toward the end of this statement, Ra-ton's voice grew increasingly distant. Dory shifted easily; her eyelids fluttered.

"I don't know what you're talking about," Minerva said.

The expression on Dory's face grew stern and authoritarian, not like the lighthearted, flamboyant Dory at all. "Understanding is not beyond you, but you resist it. You have heard her voice, but you will not open yourself to her. You would do well to pay attention. This communication is sincere, and directed toward you with love."

A longer pause. Then: "I regret to say that we must stop for today."

"Wait!" she cried, but it was over. A shudder passed through the medium. Dory's features went slack and her face fell forward onto her hands.

"I think he's gone," Minerva whispered.

"Jesus Christ," said Nick. "He *is* a cosmic shrink, even to the last remark: your fifty minutes are up." He shook his head as if to clear it. "That was one of the most amazing things I've ever witnessed." He jumped up and crossed to Dory's side. Her head was still buried in her arms. "Dory?" He touched her shoulders. Minerva noticed that he seemed a little hesitant, as if Dory had been transformed into somebody who awed him.

Slowly, groggily, Dory lifted her head. She blinked a few times. Her face was pretty, a little impish, perhaps, but lacking in that special intelligence and wisdom that Ra-ton had radiated. She yawned hugely. "Well? What happened? Did anyone come through?"

"Ra-ton."

"Did he have anything interesting to say?"

Nick was massaging her temples with his thumbs. "You mean you don't remember?"

"I have some hazy pictures in my mind, that's all. Like dreams. It's a little like being asleep, although not exactly." She yawned again and stretched. Nick dropped his hands and stepped away from her. "Was it helpful? Did you get the answers you were looking for?"

Minerva rose, her arms folded tight around her petite body. She was thoroughly shaken by what she had heard. "I suggest we go downstairs and make ourselves a strong cup of tea."

"It was Helen Templeton," said Nick. Dory had had her tea and left; she had a date, she explained. "I never let metaphysics interfere with sex," she'd said, laughing.

"What do you mean? It was Ra-ton, supposedly—"

"Not him. The woman who is trying to contact us. Trained in the ancient mysteries, an arrogant soul, able to see into future probabilities, feeling responsible for our problems. It's Helen. I'm sure of it."

"I'm not sure of anything. It's all a lot of claptrap, in my opinion."

"I don't blame you for thinking that. This is getting scary. All that business about sin and repetition and the family curse. The whole thing makes me apprehensive, particularly in light of what I've been learning lately about our esteemed ancestor."

"Tell me."

"Well, those papers have turned out to be even more of a gold mine than I originally thought. In the first place, she really was a kind of witch, it seems. Among those papers are herbal recipes for various potions and drugs, along with pagan incantations and spells. And on the more mundane side of things, I think I may have discovered the identity of her lover."

"The man who was the father of her illegitimate son?"

"Yes. If I'm right, it explains several things, including why Helen could never reveal his name or marry him. The journals refer frequently to Matthew Broadhurst, and to the delicacy of his position. I've checked the name against the town records for the period and found that Matthew Broadhurst was Helen's brother-in-law. That is, his brother James was married to Helen's sister, Anne."

"The name means nothing to me."

"Broadhurst was a minister of the Lord, a protégé of Cotton Mather. A married man, during the period of which we are speaking. His wife was an invalid. It fits, you see. Helen would have known Broadhurst well because of her sister's connection with him. They must have fallen in love. Perhaps they resisted their passion for a time, but in the end were consumed by it. She conceived his child. Marriage was impossible. Once her condition became known, they were both in grave danger. Adultery was not tolerated in colonial Boston. The punishment was very severe."

"As in *The Scarlet Letter.*"

"Worse than that. Adultery was a capital crime. If convicted, you could be hanged."

"My God."

"If you examine the court records of the period, you'll find that juries usually refused to convict. Perhaps they felt guilty; perhaps extramarital affairs were no less frequent then than they are today. Most offenders were convicted of lesser charges, such as public lewdness, the corruption of innocence, and so on, but in at least one case, an adulterous couple was hanged from the great hanging tree on the Boston Common. The good people of Boston would have been particularly enraged to discover one of their ministers involved in such sinful behavior. Matthew Broadhurst was supposed to set an example of righteousness, not cavort in the ways of the devil.

"Also, you'll remember, our ancestor had already endured one trial. She was acquitted of the capital crime of witchcraft, for which quite a few Bostonians actually were 'turned off,' as Samuel Sewall terms public execution in his famous diary. If she'd been brought up on charges of adultery, no doubt she'd have been convicted and sentenced to hang along with her lover."

"So she refused to name him. Of course; anybody would."

"She herself was not married. If her lover was also unmarried, their sin could not be deemed adultery. Fornication was also a crime, but it wasn't a capital offense. Now, listen carefully. This is where my theory gets tricky. If I'm right, Helen's silence, necessary though it was, had tragic results."

"What do you mean?"

"It activated the curse."

"Suicide?"

"No. Not suicide, Gran. Incest."

"Incest is the Templeton curse?"

"The curse is early death, I guess, but it's the crime of incest that brought the curse upon us. It's an old tradition—the sins of the fathers are visited on the children, and so on. Of course, it's not really supposed to extend for hundreds of years.

"But to return to the point: Helen Templeton never told anybody who the father of her child was. Not even the boy himself. Matthew Broadhurst, who was the father of three other children, died a relatively young man. When Helen's son, Charles, grew up, he fell in love with and married Lucy Broadhurst, daughter of Broadhurst and his ailing wife. His own half sister, in other words. It all transpired when Helen was away in England attending to her business interests there. She returned to find her son wed to his sister, who was already pregnant with their first child."

Nick was so wrapped up in his story, he didn't notice the look on his grandmother's face. "Even then she kept her secret, fearing the consequences if she did not. Matthew was dead, and she was the only person who knew the truth. She wanted to keep it that way. Incest is an even graver sin than adultery.

"But somehow Charles found out. He had several children by this time, and the success of Templeton Tea had made him a wealthy man. He confronted his mother with his suspicions, and she confirmed them. Poor Charles couldn't cope with it. He shot his wife to death, then put the pistol to his own head. It's apparent from reading her journals that Helen blamed herself for their deaths. If she'd revealed her secret years before, she might have died for it, yes, but her son would have grown up knowing his parentage. The incest would not have occurred. No curse would have been laid upon his descendants. It was Helen's silence that sealed their doom."

"Oh God, oh God."

"Gran? Are you all right? What's the matter?"

Close now, very close, Minerva could hear the heavy beating of vultures' wings. Darkness cloaked her eyes, and she fainted.

36

In August Minerva received a report on a number of business indicators that described the recent status of Templeton Tea. She studied the computer printout, which confirmed that profits were up significantly since Delilah had come to work for the company. Market share was up, too.

Never had the tea company enjoyed so much publicity. Delilah had been interviewed in the lifestyle or business pages of every major newspaper in the region, and she'd appeared on several radio and TV talk shows. Every time she was interviewed, she managed to find something new to say about the endless fascinations of tea.

In the hallway outside her office Minerva heard Travis's charming voice saying, "Hey, lady. Nice legs."

To which Delilah's voice returned, "Nice ass. Bet you ride a horse or a bike."

"Well, I sure do spend a lot of time in the saddle."

Delilah laughed. Whatever comeback she had was muffled by the slam of a door.

Minerva dropped the computer sheets on her desk. Her fingers ached. Arthritis? Or just nerves?

She and Delilah were coexisting reasonably well these days. It was as if Delilah had made a conscious decision to try to get along with her. She had backed off on several of her demands for the marketing campaign. She'd cut the budget sharply and had Dory redo her designs for the new tea packages to something upbeat and slick, but less radically different from the original.

Minerva was pleased. She had begun to feel that there was hope for a reconciliation after all. If it weren't for her uneasy feelings about what was going on between Delilah and Travis, she might have begun to relax at last.

It had been happening more and more lately—Travis was flirting with Delilah, and Delilah was flirting right back. Once or twice Minerva had seen him looking at his former lover with an intensity that was only thinly disguised. It frightened her. She tried to tell herself that she was still jumpy from her encounter last month with the mysterious Ra-ton, but she couldn't convince herself that this was all it was.

Ever since Dory's visit to the China Tea House Tavern, Minerva had been in an agony of doubt and confusion. All this nonsense about reincarnation and repetition and incest curses; by the light of day it seemed laughable. But Nick had given her a copy of Shirley MacLaine's *Out on a Limb,* which suggested that there were all kinds of people, some of them very rational and intelligent, who actually believed in these things.

"Do you believe it?" she'd demanded of Nick.

"Let me put it this way: my rational mind rejects this sort of thing as wish fulfillment. We can't accept the fact of our own deaths, so we construct a sophisticated metaphysical system to provide us with gods and souls and eternal life. The human brain, which is powerful and mysterious, creates the sometimes very bizarre phenomena that inspire faith in metaphysics."

"So you don't believe it."

"The logical, reasoning part of me doesn't believe it. But when I meditate I enter a state of mind where such things as ESP, channeling, and spirit guides are not only possible, but absolutely real. *Of course* we reincarnate, I think at such times. I see and experience my former lives. I understand that we are all beings of light. I know the playful, creative, spontaneous joy of wrapping myself in a body and participating in this great festival known as life on earth." He paused, smiling at Minerva's astonishment. "The trouble is, such moments of clarity are fleeting. When I'm not in that meditative state, it's easy to dismiss my insights as preposterous."

He does believe it, Minerva thought. He believes with his heart, with his intuition, with his imagination.

"I know one thing," he said. "Since I began at least entertaining the possibility that reality doesn't end with what we can see, hear, and touch, my life has been easier. I have more self-confidence, more control over my own destiny. Less of the terror that comes in the night. Less anger. And more love."

"I think you're a more evolved soul than I am," Minerva said dryly.

He laughed and hugged her. "You're fine, Gran. You're strong and good and brave, and I love you very much."

No, she thought. *We acknowledge and bewail our manifold sins and wickedness, which we, from time to time, most grievously have committed, by thought, word, and deed, against thy divine majesty, provoking most justly thy wrath and indignation against us.*

I am a wicked, selfish woman, and if I don't believe in God, it's because I'm afraid He's going to punish me.

Travis sat in his office staring out the window. His mouth was dry, his stomach clenched. Delilah had just left his office. "Looks like we'll be working more closely together from now on," she'd said.

Their grandmother had told her this morning that she was so pleased with the work Delilah had been doing in marketing (profits were up, which she seemed to think was Delilah's doing) that she had decided to give her more responsibility. "Grendam wants me to learn tea buying next—the whole importing procedure from tea auctions abroad to what goes on in the plant. Distribution, too. You've been trained in every aspect of this business, Trav, but I haven't yet. I'm hoping you'll help me."

Travis couldn't help but notice that Delilah had been going out of her way to get along with him these days. She'd been courteous, friendly, affectionate, and the spell she'd been casting over everybody at Templeton Tea extended even to him.

To make it worse, he couldn't look at her without desiring her. Things had gotten so bad in this respect that he'd begun to tell himself lately that his mother must have lied. How could David Scofield have been his father? He didn't look anything like him. His mother had been neurotic, confused. Maybe she'd had the hots for Scofield and fantasized the entire thing. Or maybe it was really the dark-haired, green-eyed Nick who was Delilah's half brother. They even looked a little alike.

"I'll be glad to help you in whatever way I can," he told her, even while he was thinking, there's no way you're going to mess with importing. All I need is you poking around in the plant, seeing something you're not meant to see. Can't allow that, Delilah. No way.

But Christ, he wanted her. Lily no longer satisfied him; in fact, he'd been avoiding her. He didn't think it bothered her, for Lily, too, had someone new. "It is obvious that you're pining for your cousin," she'd told him the last time he was with her. "Why not just take her if you want her so much?"

Travis had told her to mind her own business and enforced it with a rough passion that had driven the subject from her mind.

It was not so easily driven from his. He'd never been good at resisting temptation. He was going to make love to Delilah if he could. It was wrong; of course it was wrong. But it was inevitable nonetheless.

"I want to talk to you."

Minerva looked up from her work. Travis was standing on the threshold of her office. It was late afternoon; many of their employees were beginning to leave. "Come in."

He settled into the chair opposite her with every indication of attentiveness and ease. "I have a complaint," he said with an apologetic smile. "I don't think you're being fair to me."

"In what way?"

"I've been working for you for nearly twenty years. I've worked hard, been loyal, and done a good job. But increasingly I get the feeling that you have already decided to give Delilah everything that I expected for years would come to me."

"I have decided nothing," she said, although inside a voice was crying, *That is a lie.* "I am trying to be fair to you. And to Templeton Tea. I want the best person at the helm."

"She and I are good at different things. I don't deny her skill at marketing and public relations—she's extremely talented. I'm similarly talented in the operations end of things. If you expect me to teach her about tea purchasing and distribution so she can deprive me of my heritage, you're overestimating my complacency. I don't want her interfering with my responsibilities. I don't want her going to auctions, and I don't want her in the plant."

"That's ridiculous, Travis. Of course she has to learn the various aspects of the business—"

"It wasn't part of the original agreement, which was to give us both a year to prove our skills with the things we do best. Keep her in marketing. Keep her away from me."

Minerva had tried to read him a number of times during the past few weeks, but that had never been easy with Travis. He covered his emotions well, but even so, she sensed passion in him . . . and anger. More of both than he usually betrayed.

She thought of the *kus-kus tattis* on the windows of the houses in Delhi. The woven reed mats were used as a primitive form of air conditioning. You would soak the mat in icy water and hang it over a window that was open to the sun and hot air. As the dry wind blew through the window, the kus-kus tatti would cool the air, lending it a steady if almost imperceptible chill.

Travis was like that. Strong emotions were filtered through him, coming out controlled and restrained on the other side. Yet the hot, dry wind was always there, on the other side of the mat. Strip away the kus-kus tatti and it would roar through your home.

He's moving into a state of crisis.

"Why are you so unwilling to work in proximity to Delilah?" she asked. "Are you still in love with her?"

Something leapt, then subsided in those blue-blue eyes. Travis shook his head, frowning. "How can you even ask that?"

"I've been considering telling her the truth. It's been long enough now that I think she can deal with it, don't you?"

"No." He came and leaned over her desk, his nose only a few inches from her own. "We agreed back in 1970 that she would never know the truth. I didn't want her told then, even though it meant I'd end up playing the role of the bastard who walked out on his pregnant lover on the day he was scheduled to marry her. I suffered for that deception; she's never forgiven me. But it's behind us now. I don't want a scandal, and neither do you. Leave it, Gran." He paused a moment, then added, "Leave it in the dark with all the other secrets you'd prefer nobody knew."

There was something about the way he said the last sentence that frightened her. When Travis and Nick were children, Travis would rarely tattle on his brother in the usual way kids did, but when he did come forward, it was always something big, something Nick was sure to be punished for, even though it might have happened months before.

He could keep a secret, in other words, until it suited him to reveal it. What secrets did Travis know, she wondered, about her? *We have done those things which we ought not to have done; we have left undone those things which we ought to have done . . .* "Are you threatening me?"

He straightened. "I'm asking you to respect my privacy, that's all."

Minerva thought about what Nick had told her about Helen Templeton's silence and its tragic outcome. She, however, had not remained silent. Fearing the Templeton curse of suicide, she had done her utmost to protect Delilah. Travis knew the truth. Surely his knowing was enough to insure that there would be no further "repetition" of the crime of incest, in this generation at least.

They flirted with each other, yes. But people flirted with each other all the time without letting it go any further than that.

She could trust Travis, surely. Even if he still loved Delilah, it wouldn't be the first time a man had loved and desired a woman he could never have.

"I won't say anything to her," she agreed. "And I will certainly try even harder to be fair to both of you. But in return, please set my mind at rest. Promise me you won't keep flirting with her the way you do. You're an attractive man, Travis, and I sense that she's still vulnerable to you."

His expression cleared of tension. He smiled, and when Travis smiled, the world was struck with sunshine. "No more flirting," he promised. But there was something about the way he said it that left her even more worried than before.

"Damn," said Delilah. The overhead light in her office blew, and the ceilings were too high for her to be able to reach the fixture without a ladder. The custodial staff had already left for the day; it was a hot evening in late August, and she'd just arrived at her office after spending the entire day riding a food distributor's truck, trying to ensure that the jobber gave Templeton Tea a prominent place on the shelves.

It had worked, too, although she had to admit to feeling mixed emotions in one shop when the jobber made more space for Templeton Tea by taking several perfectly good packages of Merlin's Magical Brews and stuffing them below eye level at the bottom of the rack.

"Ruthless," she told herself. "You've got to be ruthless if you want Grendam's job." But she made an excuse to run back into the store as they were leaving and sneak the Merlin's tea back into its original spot.

Delilah tossed her briefcase down on her desk and tried the desk lamp. It came on, but it didn't provide much light. "I don't feel much like working anyway," she said out loud.

"Good, neither do I," said a voice behind her.

"Travis?" Her tall cousin looked even taller standing there in the shadows of her doorway. "You startled me. I thought everybody had gone home."

"I think everybody else has."

"Working late, huh?"

"With you around, I gotta stay on my toes."

"Will you help with that?" She pointed to the dead light overhead. "If you can do it without making any cracks about how many tea company executives it takes to change a light bulb."

He laughed. "Sure. We keep the bulbs in the utility closet down the hall."

"I was concerned about you, out on those trucks today," he said a few minutes later from the stepstool he had mounted to dismantle the light fixture. "Some of those distributor types can be pretty rough. I decided to stick around and make sure you got back okay."

"Thanks. They treated me like a princess. I had fun."

"Do you think it'll do any good in the end, hobnobbing with truckers?"

"Sure, why not? Distribution's the bottom line, isn't it? We can't sell product if it's not on the shelves, and we'll sell more product if it's prominently displayed. Templeton's has never done a damn thing for its distributors as far as I can tell, but we depend on them, Trav."

She paused a minute, watching the long reach of his arm as he screwed in the light bulb. He was wearing a fine white summer shirt with the sleeves rolled up and a pair of exquisitely tailored gray trousers. He'd had his jacket over his arm when he'd come into her office; it was thrown casually over her desk chair now. His arms were tan, strong-looking. His hands were big and had always been a little clumsy in appearance until you saw—or felt—them in action. Face it, she told herself—there are moments when you're still drawn to him. When you still find him exciting. Those old memories die hard.

He gave the bulb a final twist and replaced the light fixture. "If I were you," she said, "I'd give a party, a big bash to which we could invite all the food brokers we deal with. Not just the big guys, but the men and women who drive the trucks, too. Show them we care about them and are grateful for the hours they put in getting us into supermarkets all over the country. I'd also send them Christmas cards, the company newsletter, all that personal stuff. Make them feel as if they're part of the Templeton family. A little old-fashioned courtesy, in other words. People respond to that sort of thing."

"You're something, you know that?" He climbed down from the stepstool and dusted off his hands. "Maybe I'd better start looking for another job."

"Maybe we'd better give some serious consideration to how we're going to learn to work together."

"What's this? Not a change of heart, surely? Last time I suggested we work together, you nixed the idea at once."

"I know. But I had just come back and I was nervous. Overly defensive, perhaps."

"I guess we were both pretty defensive. I'm sorry about that, Delilah." He paused, then added, "I'd like to have an easier, friendlier relationship with you."

Impulsively she laid her hand on his arm. Things were better, so much better these days with Grendam. Now, if she could only find a way to resolve her problems with Travis, maybe she would begin to feel comfortable with all the Templetons at last. "Would you like to go somewhere and talk about it? We've spent so little time together since I've been back."

"Why not? Are you hungry? I'll take you to dinner."

"I'm starving. But it's Friday evening, Trav. You don't have a date?"

He smiled and took her hand. "I do now."

They were not alone in the building after all. Minerva watched them leave together from her unlit office window. She had been waiting for Delilah to return from her jaunt; there were several things she'd wanted to discuss with her. But she'd sat down in the recliner that Nick had insisted on furnishing her office with a few months ago, and her old carcass had taken advantage. She'd fallen asleep, wakened too late, disoriented, and nearly walked in on Travis and Delilah, alone, talking in the dark.

Panic had flooded her. It was happening again. Incest. Repetition. The family curse. This, surely, must be what Helen Templeton had meant.

She'd slunk away, afraid to let them see her. Afraid to confront them. What would they do together? Nothing? Everything? She'd been a fool to trust Travis. She should have told Delilah the truth years ago. Secrets, so many secrets. Generation upon generation of secrets. *For they shall have prosperity, but neither joy nor peace.*

Now she'd left it too late. She had heard them on the stairs, conversing animatedly, Travis's smooth-tongued voice, Delilah's husky laugh. From the window of her darkened office she could see them now, leaving the building, walking out onto the sidewalk, Delilah's midnight-dark hair tossing in the wind, and Travis's hand hovering—but not quite touching—the small of her back. The closeness they'd known since childhood. The chemistry that anyone who came within ten feet of them could feel.

As they'd walked down the hallway Travis had said something about a restaurant called the Club Cafe. Minerva had heard of it. It was located in the South End, not an area Minerva herself frequented. But if someone, accidentally, were to meet them there . . .

She picked up the phone and dialed Nick's number in Concord.

"I've always regretted it."

Travis's voice was low and deeply sincere. All sounds seemed muted to Delilah—the many conversations flowing around them, the ripple of the piano keys, the quiet steps of the waiters passing by with their decorative platters of food. "It was one of those fateful decisions that somehow changes the entire course of one's life."

"I loved you so much." Her own voice seemed muted. Had she

drunk too much? A gimlet before dinner and a few sips of the excellent California cabernet sauvignon with her rack of lamb. Not too much, surely. What was she drunk on, then, if not wine? "I was wildly, madly in love with you, my beautiful cousin with the movie star smile."

"I felt the same."

"It was first love, maybe, but it was powerful all the same. It took me a long time, getting over you."

"It wasn't easy for me either, Delilah."

"What did you mean a few weeks ago when you said you had a reason? I've wondered about that several times."

One of his fingers traced a pattern on the linen tablecloth. "I don't know what I meant. We were too young. I didn't know what I wanted out of life. Marriage, a baby—those things frightened me. And I couldn't imagine living without money. Gran knew that and played on it masterfully. But maybe she was right. We'd probably have made each other miserable. We weren't mature enough to handle our feelings."

"No." She looked around at the dimly lit room with high ceilings and the art deco furnishings. The restaurant was sophisticated and romantic in an old-fashioned way, and the food was superb, although it was definitely not old Boston like the wood-paneled Locke-Ober's or the elegant royal blue dining room at the Ritz. The Club Café was contemporary, the current trendy place to dine, particularly if you happened to be gay.

The place seemed more crowded all of a sudden as a bluesy singer began to croon torch songs and the people at the bar end of the restaurant gathered around with their drinks. A young man wearing a black silk cape came in through the wide glass doors at the entrance and greeted his friends in a high-pitched, excited voice. His hair was brown and frizzy, but the ends had been dipped in gold.

Delilah glanced at table after table of well-dressed, handsome males. "Do you realize we're the only heterosexual couple in here?"

"We can leave if it bothers you."

"It doesn't." She looked into those blue eyes that had so mesmerized the young woman she had been. "I'd like us to be able to forgive each other, Travis, and coexist. Be friends again. Do you think that's possible?"

"No," he said.

Delilah felt the blood begin to beat at her temples. "Why not?"

He leaned forward slightly. She was intensely aware that the table was small and his face was only inches away. He could reach out and touch her if he wanted to, touch her arm as it lay across the table. Reach beneath the linen tablecloth and touch her leg.

"Listen," he said. "That day in the park, the day we walked by the pond where the swanboats cruise, I felt as though a door had opened, and I was young again. With feelings and desires that were also young. I acted badly then, and for that I'm sorry. It was because I couldn't control the emotions I felt. That's rare for me, Delilah. I never go out of control."

"Maybe you ought to sometime." She was thinking of Nick and his special boxing gloves. "I've always wondered what you do with the thoughts and emotions you dam up inside."

"I think the dam is breaking." He shook his head slightly. "It's scary."

"I know." She reached out and patted his hand. You shouldn't do that, Delilah. You know what happens the instant you do that.

His palm covered the back of her hand, sandwiching her between the two big, warm hands that had once caressed her body all over. Anticipation tightened the muscles in her stomach. What he said next made it worse:

"Do you think about it? Do you remember how it felt? Lately it seems I'm obsessed with those memories twenty-four hours a day."

She shook her head, but he swept on, "Sometimes when I remember how sexy you were, how warm and open and frank, how your skin flushed and your limbs danced and your soul came into your eyes when I loved you, it just about kills me. In sixteen years, I've never met your match."

"Still the charmer, Trav. Still the flatterer." She spoke lightly so he wouldn't see how disturbed she was.

"Give me a chance, Delilah. I'm still in love with you."

"Travis . . . I don't know. It was so long ago."

He sighed and lifted her fingers to his lips in one of those graceful old-world gestures she remembered so well. Then he released her hand. "It's crazy, isn't it, for me to be so obsessed by you."

"Very crazy." She was thinking, I ought to feel triumphant. If I wanted revenge, this is it. But he was too near, his eyes were too blue. She thought, he and I are special to each other. There's unfinished business between us, and one of the things I came home to do was resolve my feelings about the past.

To which another side of her, the more rational, monitoring side, retorted, resolve them, yes, not stir them up again.

She seemed to see a pit opening up in front of her, and she was uncharacteristically afraid to move a step in any direction. She had a strong mental image of Nick. Two brothers, both laying claim to her. The apple tree. A kiss, a fight, a flashing knife.

But things were rushing forward; she was already headlong upon a course that had been decided long ago. No matter what she did now, it wouldn't make any difference. Some chain of past action and intents stretching far away behind her, farther than she could see or even imagine, was already working out its effects.

The room was closing in on her. "Let's get out of here," she said.

Those blue eyes flickered, then smiled. He kissed her hand again, this time in the center of her palm.

The next few minutes never registered anywhere. He must have summoned the waiter, paid the check. Then his hand was there between her shoulder blades as he guided her out, had his Porsche brought round.

He took her dancing. She didn't remember, afterward, the names of the clubs they visited; they weren't important, her surroundings meant nothing to her. What mattered was being in his arms.

Don't think about Nick, she ordered herself. This is between Travis and me. A universe of two. Our private world.

Anyway, we're only dancing. And he's special to me. We were children together; we had our special place in the apple tree. Another image sprang to mind, a skinny boy, hurt eyes. *Cut it out!* she screamed at Nick, who wouldn't stop invading her brain. *Leave us alone. Why are you always following us around?* Just the two of them. Delilah and Travis. His swaying body, the imprint of muscle against muscle, blood against blood.

They danced and danced, then he drove her home. Incredibly, he found a place to park half a block from her apartment. As he slipped the car into it and cut the engine, he turned to her and smiled. It was a sweet smile; it made him look twenty again. His hand cupped her throat, his thumb stroked her chin. He murmured something; she wasn't sure what. He laced his fingers in hers. They were thicker than Nick's fingers. His brother had long artist's hands, very sensitive, very beautiful. *Go away, Nick!*

Travis leaned over and brushed her lips with his.

Delilah had gone very still. This is wrong, she thought, and gently freed her lips.

"I love you," he said. "And I need you. I'm in trouble. I really need you, Delilah. Please."

"Trouble?"

"I'm falling. There are stairs, plunging into darkness, and I'm falling down them. Just like—" He stopped, coughing a little. "Just like a tragic hero or something. Macbeth. The witches who tempted him. The agony of the first crime. The way it got easier and easier to do evil until he was nothing but a walking shadow. Do you understand? When I lost you, that was the beginning of it. The falling. The going down."

She had no idea what he was talking about, but he sounded desperate, and desperation was something she'd never associated with Travis. Oh God, she didn't know what to do. She was thirty-eight years old and a man wanted her and she didn't know what to do.

He seemed to hesitate a moment, then he tried the kiss again. More insistently this time. His tongue slipped into her mouth, and explored delicately. She didn't respond, but she didn't stop him either. The center of her body had gone soft and yielding.

It's been so long. I need it. Nick shouldn't have refused me. Why can't I stop thinking of Nick?

"Come on." He reached over and unfastened her seat belt, his fingers lingering briefly on her midriff. He reached farther and jerked on the handle of her door, opening it outward. Then his hand came back to sweetly caress her thigh.

Shakily, she got out her side while Travis got out his. She came around the front of the car, where he met her. He took her into his arms, pressed her back against the Porsche's low, curving hood, and kissed her hard.

"Great," someone said. "Terrific. Make my day."

The kiss broke off, and they turned.

He was standing there in the shadows, just beside them. He was tall and lean and not so vulnerable anymore. I'm a magician, Delilah thought. She could objectify her thoughts, conjure spirits from nothingness.

She'd conjured Nick.

37

"I feel like a spy," said Nick. He was standing with his hands thrust in his pockets in the doorway of the China Tea House Tavern, listening to his grandmother's instructions and thinking, I'm not going to go through with this, am I?

"It's very important," said his grandmother. "I didn't know what else to do, whom else to call."

"I'm not Drake, Gran. He'd do this kind of thing, sure. But not me."

She ignored that. "The Club Café. Do you know it?"

"It's a gay hangout, I believe. Is my brother a closet homosexual?"

"If he were, I wouldn't have had to call you."

"Look, Gran, you're not asking me to chaperone a couple of teenagers. Travis and Delilah are two mature, independent adults." *What the hell is she doing, going off alone with him?* "If they want to have dinner together, what business is it of yours? If they intend to resume their old love affair, my interference certainly isn't going to stop them." *I'll kill him if he touches her.* "Suppose you tell me exactly what this is all about."

"I don't want them together. You know that. It was wrong sixteen years ago, and it's still wrong now."

"Why? None of us ever understood why you thought it was wrong."

He saw his grandmother bite down on her bottom lip. "She thought it was because I felt she wasn't good enough for him. But it's the other way around. Travis has no heart; he'll hurt her all over again, and I think Delilah's been hurt enough, don't you?"

You're lying, Gran, Nick thought. The enormity of the lie rose up and shook its head at him so clearly that he was stunned he'd never seen it before. There was something more here. There had always been something more.

Nick felt his heart rate increase in that ominous fashion that heralds an anxiety attack. She was hiding something. Something dark. He was suddenly sure he'd be a lot happier if he never learned what it was.

"Let's try the truth, Gran, okay? Let's just try it on and see how well it fits. What's really at stake here? What was at stake sixteen years ago?"

Nothing. She said nothing. Her lips were trembling now, and she looked as if she might black out the way she had after the channeling when he'd told her about Charles Templeton's incestuous marriage.

If anyone knows a reason why this man and this woman should not be joined in holy matrimony, let him speak now or forever hereafter hold his peace.

His heart was really slamming now. Great, he thought. I'm going to go into cardiac arrest right here in front of her. "I think you'd better tell me. There are a limited number of possibilities, none of which I particularly care for."

His grandmother's hands remained clenched in her lap. "Can't you just stop them, Nick?"

"Without a reason, the way you did sixteen years ago? No, Grandmother, I can't. I'm the one who held Delilah in my arms after you did that to her. I'm the one who heard her cries, who watched her struggle to understand what she'd done to lose your love, the love she'd been so certain of since childhood. I'm the one who took her to the hospital when she began to bleed away the baby you didn't want her to have, the baby you probably killed because of the emotional wringer you put her through.

"You know how far she walked that day? Alone, in the pouring rain, half out of her head? She walked all the way from Cambridge to Lexington. And then she lost her baby and has never been able to have another. Did you know *that?* Did you know she and Max tried to have a kid and couldn't? That they went for medical help and were trying to solve the problem when he got sick and died of cancer? That she lost both her parents and her husband and the only child she ever conceived and that now she has *nothing?* And that you, whom she loved so much, rejected her and broke her heart?"

Minerva shattered. Sobs began to jerk from her, racking her delicate frame. "Oh shit," Nick said. He crossed the space that divided them and took her into his arms. She was almost insubstantial. He could have lifted her as easily as he lifted Kelsey.

Her sobs were ripping, tearing things. Nick couldn't remember ever having seen her lose control like this. He tried to soothe her, stroking her shoulders, patting her hair. "I'm sorry, Gran, I'm sorry. I shouldn't have said that. I got carried away."

"You're right." She had a hard time getting the words out, but he understood what she was saying. "God forgive me. What you're saying is true. I've done so much wrong to so many people, but to Delilah in particular. I have so much to answer for."

"We all do, Gran. We all do."

He took her to the sofa and laid her down. He kissed her hands, so frail and bony. She suffered from painful arthritis, but she never complained, nor did she ever miss a day of work. "I'm sorry, Gran," he said again. "It's just that I hate to see you and Delilah at odds when I know you love each other."

"We haven't been at odds lately, Nick. Not so much."

"She's been trying."

"I've been trying, too."

"But you haven't hugged each other, have you? You haven't held each other the way I'm holding you and said, I love you, it's okay, what happened in the past is forgiven and nothing can ever separate us again. When are you going to do that, Gran? I think you ought to do it soon."

Minerva withdrew enough to see his face. "You're in love with her, aren't you?"

"Bingo," said Nick.

"Can you take her from Travis?"

"I was beginning to hope so. Now I'm not so sure."

"You must. You've got to stop him. Now, tonight."

"Believe me, if I thought my interference wouldn't blow things with her forever—"

"You've got to," she interrupted. "Listen. I have something to tell you, Nick." She was still weeping a little, but her voice was firm. "I'm going to tell you, no matter what the consequences to me."

"Tell me, then."

She sat up first, trying to compose herself. He sat beside her. She took his hands and held them tight, and said, as she'd said sixteen years ago to Travis, "They are brother and sister, Nick."

He had gone first to the Club Café, but it was too late. They'd finished dinner and left. But the maître d' remembered them—a handsome couple, especially the man. Oh yes, he remembered them. They'd stood out; they were obviously so much in love.

Agony. Where were they? At Travis's place, or Delilah's? Delilah's was closer. And a gentleman's rules dictated that the choice was ultimately hers; she could invite him in, or send him home.

So he went to her apartment building on Marlboro Street, parked his car nearby, and waited. For hours, he'd waited. He'd been about to give up in despair when his brother's Porsche finally materialized in the street.

When they didn't immediately exit the car, Nick was relieved. She was saying thank you very much and goodnight. No problem. She was too smart to fall for whatever line Travis was dishing out this time.

But then they both got out of the car, and Travis kissed her. Nick felt dirty, filthy, like a Peeping Tom. It was Travis, always Travis. She loved his brother, wanted him.

"Great," he said. "Terrific. Make my day."

Dead silence for a moment. Even the wind seemed to have stopped hissing through the trees.

Then Travis said, "What the fuck are you doing here?"

Nick didn't look at Delilah, whom he couldn't face. He stood up to his brother instead . . . something he'd always meant to do. "Preventing you from doing something you're going to regret."

"Get out of our way."

Nick shook his head. "Can't do that. Sorry."

"Please, Nick," Delilah was saying, and he wanted to pummel her because she was touching his arm, and her touch was so *careful,* as if she was terrified of hurting his feelings. She'd told him on several occasions that she loved him, but pity was all it really was. Poor Nick. So nice, so gentle and understanding, but never able to compete with his brother's pirate charm. Why did women always fall for the shits?

He could have had her. Twice he could have had her. Charity fuck or not, it would have been good. And once he'd got her naked under him, who knows what might have come of it?

You're a real jerk, Templeton. Any other man would have seized his chance and made it pay. Certainly his brother—*her* brother—wouldn't have hesitated.

Travis pulled her away from him, actually jerked her back so she was no longer touching his arm at all. She took it from him, which made Nick feel even sicker. Strong, tough, independent Delilah just let him jerk her about, as if she were hypnotized.

"He wants you himself," Travis said. "He always has. As long as you've had feelings for me, Nick has been jealous of them."

"That's very true," said Nick. "You're more perceptive than I thought."

"Go fuck yourself."

Nick advanced a step. "Get out of the way, Delilah. I have a few things to say to my dear brother."

"No," she said, predictably. "This is none of your business, Nick."

"Let's just ignore him, Delilah, and go inside."

What do I do now, Gran? Hit him? "You're not listening, man," said Nick. "Get back in the fancy car of yours and get the fuck out of this neighborhood. If Delilah goes inside with anyone, it'll be with me."

Now red began to sweep into Travis's face—warning flags of the anger that was rare, but explosive. Delilah saw it and touched his arm. "Stop it, both of you. I'm not going to stand here and be fought over like some thirty-dollar whore."

Travis shook her off and advanced toward Nick, whose body tensed into readiness, adrenaline roaring along his nerves. He could take him, he thought, if he was quick and stayed calm. Travis was about an inch taller and thirty pounds heavier, but although he appeared fit, Nick knew he didn't work out on a regular basis.

Golf, yeah, and tennis—enough to keep the body trim, but not enough to give him an edge in a fight.

"I don't believe this," said Delilah. She stepped between them. "Stop it! Civilized people don't brawl in the streets."

Travis was shaking now. He pushed Delilah out of the way; she stumbled and nearly fell. Nick reached out an arm to steady her, and for a moment he felt the pressure of her hand. It was sweating. She was scared.

"Take it easy, Travis," he said. "She's right—we ought to be able to solve this problem with words."

"Too late, runt. I'm going to put you in the hospital."

Nick laughed softly. All at once he knew how much he'd been looking forward to this. How many times had his brother beaten him up when they were kids? A dozen? Twenty? It was time the balance of power shifted.

He backed strategically, taking a quick survey of the terrain. They were on the sidewalk. Delilah's brownstone apartment building was about twenty feet behind them. It was fronted by a low stone wall and, behind that, a patch of grass. On the other side of Travis, about six feet back, was the street, blocked off by closely parked cars.

"Retreating already?" Travis taunted. "You're a loser, Nick. You always were."

He threw the first punch a little sooner than Nick expected, getting him on the left shoulder as Nick pivoted away. Travis grabbed his arm and spun him around. Nick let the momentum take him, but ducked the punch when it came. He jerked free as Delilah let out a furious yell. "Stop it! Stop it, both of you, or I'll call the police."

"Just stay out of the way," Nick told her as Travis advanced again.

Well, of course she wouldn't, and Nick thought, I'd better finish this fast or she's going to get hurt. The possibility that he might get hurt himself was no small incentive, too. Travis threw a right that caught him smack on the side of his lip. He tasted the coppery flavor of blood. Dammit. And again. Nick ducked, but felt the impact in his left shoulder, which began to tingle ominously.

"Travis!" Delilah screamed.

Nick danced away, then feinted twice to the right and caught his opponent off guard. Time to get tough. He cut inside and slammed his fist into his brother's chin. Travis's head snapped back, but he shook it and came on again, too stubbornly mad to stop and consider what he was up against. He was breathing hard, tired already.

Travis threw two punches that Nick deflected by holding his lower arms up in front of his face. This made it look as if he was in trouble, but only an inexperienced fighter would miss the trick. Travis went slightly off balance as he struck again, and Nick hit a tight combination, right, right, and a pounding left on the jaw that he could feel reverberating throughout his own body. Travis swayed. Nick moved back and let him regain his balance. He was pumped up, exultant, and he could afford to be generous.

Travis threw a kick that got him in the kneecap, and Nick nearly went down. Jesus! He ought to have expected something dirty . . . Travis's gentlemanly veneer certainly didn't penetrate to his bones. He was rabbit-punching now, and Nick caught another blow on the side of his neck that might have put him away if his brother's aim had been better. Gasping, he feinted, twisted out of reach, then came back with another combination, two lefts and a right this time, all of which connected and sent Travis into a spin.

Travis came back one more time, much more awkwardly, but Nick was ready. He hit him high on the chest and once more on the jaw. Travis reeled backward and half fell against his car.

It was over. Travis was groaning, his breath tearing out of him and blood pouring from his nose. Nick knew if he hit him once more, he'd go down and stay there for a while.

"Don't you dare," Delilah said.

Nick looked at her, panting. He couldn't see her very well. His vision was blurred. Great, he thought. Don't tell me he hit me hard enough to do some damage? He hadn't felt it, but in a fight you often don't. But then he decided the only thing wrong with him was that he'd lost a contact lens. "I wasn't going to," he said. "He's finished."

Delilah did not go running to Travis the way some women might have done. She just stood there, looking back and forth between the two of them. Nick didn't think he'd ever seen quite so scathing an expression on her face.

Nick opened the front door of the Porsche, collared Travis, and shoved him into the car. Leaning his head in, he said in a low voice, "I want you to understand why this happened. It wasn't only because you've had it coming for years. It was because I know, Travis. *I know.*"

His brother shuddered under his hands. Slowly he managed to pull himself upright in the driver's seat.

"When were you going to tell her?" Nick asked in that same quiet voice. "In the morning? Next week? Next month? After you had a few kids, perhaps?"

Travis groaned.

Glancing around quickly to make sure Delilah hadn't heard, Nick added, "The game's over. I'm going to tell her everything. The next time she sees you, she'll know."

Before he could say anything else, Delilah dragged him out of the doorway. Jesus, thought Nick, she's strong. "I want to see for myself," she was saying. "Travis? Do you need a doctor?"

"No." Travis said. With more dignity than Nick would have thought possible, he added, "Listen. No matter what Nick tells you, nothing I said to you tonight was a lie."

"Travis . . ." Her voice broke in a manner that was unusual for her. "I'm sorry you're hurt, but what we were doing was wrong."

Travis wiped his sleeve across his nose and blood came away, staining what had probably been a two-hundred-dollar shirt. "Oh yes, it was wrong. But it was my last chance, even so."

"What do you mean?"

Travis did not reply. With one last lethal look at Nick, he started the car, pulled the door shut, and drove off into the night.

Nick felt like crowing. Don't, he warned himself. He turned to Delilah, who backed up a step. Someone had opened a window in the building behind them and was looking suspiciously into the street.

Delilah said: "Don't touch me."

"What makes you think I was going to?"

"Seems to me I've read this scene before. Drake beats the shit out of the bad guy, saves the woman, throws her over his shoulder, and carries her to bed. It's a lousy macho resolution, and it's not the way this scene is going to end."

"Everybody's an editor," Nick said mildly. "We've got an audience. Let's talk about it inside."

"I'm going inside. You're staying out in the street, where you're obviously very much at home."

Nick considered her. She meant it. He was still breathing hard, still pumped up. He needed a glass of water and an ice pack, and he wouldn't have turned down a little tender loving care.

"I have something to discuss with you, Delilah. I'm not leaving until we talk." He caught her wrist to prove he wasn't kidding and urged her toward the front door of the brownstone.

"Let go of me."

He shook his head. "This is important." He gave her arm the slightest hint of a twist. "I'm sorry, but I'm going to insist."

She wouldn't budge. She looked up at him, those deep green eyes alight with some intention he couldn't quite define. "Nick, darling, I'm impressed. After all these years, you finally beat up your brother. He underestimated you—always a bad mistake. And you know what?" She glanced down at the hand manacling her wrist. At the same moment, she half turned as if to embrace him. "You just underestimated me."

"Delilah, I would never—" The words were choked off as a sheet of pain engulfed him. He gasped and stumbled and thought, terrific, I'm going to throw up.

She had kneed him in the crotch.

"Go home, Nick. Call me in the morning if it's so damn important."

A moment later he heard the slam of her apartment building door.

Nick collapsed on the stone steps in front of her building, fighting the nausea. He could have cried; for a moment he thought he would cry. Then, despite the pain radiating through his vitals, despite the frustration, he thought about how strong she was and how tough, how he *had* underestimated her for a moment there, and how much he loved her. And instead of raging, instead of crying, he put his head down on his folded arms and began to laugh.

38

Nick got into his car, drove out onto Storrow Drive, and headed in the direction of his home. He was down in front of the Harvard Business School when he changed his mind. "Screw this," he said out loud.

In college he'd written a paper entitled "Hamlet: The Anxiety of Action." It wasn't that Hamlet was passive or afraid to act, he'd argued. It was simply that as a thinking man, a moral philosopher, he knew all too well that all actions have consequences and that some of them can never be anticipated.

But *Hamlet* was a young man's play. I am nearly forty years old. Am I afraid to act? *No.*

He exited Storrow, crossed the Charles at the Anderson Bridge, and backtracked toward Boston on Memorial Drive. He crossed the Massachusetts Avenue Bridge—a mess of reconstruction so the long span wouldn't collapse into the river—and turned left on Commonwealth Avenue to return to Back Bay.

This time there was no place to park near Delilah's building. He had to circle three times, then walk six blocks, which did nothing to improve his mood.

The door to the street was unlocked. He went into the building and walked down the short hallway to her apartment—1A. He put his finger to the buzzer, but stopped short of pressing it.

Instead he reached into his shirt pocket and took out his pen. He removed a business card from his wallet. He wrote something on it, then bent down and slid it under her door.

Travis also doubled back into the city after his initial flight away from the scene of his humiliation. His head was aching and he felt sick to his stomach, but the worst feeling was the pressure inside. There was a silo in the center of his body, loaded with something that felt ready to explode.

He thought briefly of the cottage on the Vineyard he'd bought as a refuge from the city three years ago. It was peaceful there. The house was built on a sandy bluff on a private stretch of beach; you could walk quite a distance without any company but the gulls. He could drive down to Cape right now and catch the first ferry across in the morning. He could lick his wounds in private and plan his next move.

But instead of heading for the Cape, he drove in the direction of the China Tea House Tavern. It was late, yeah, but he doubted his grandmother—who was not his grandmother—would be asleep.

Funny how hers was the only image he could see. He wasn't thinking of Nick or Delilah or what they might be doing together; it was Minerva Templeton whose small, neat, exquisitely dressed figure rose up before him like a beckoning ghost. They had an appointment with each other. They'd had it ever since his wedding day in 1970 when she'd stripped him of his bride, his child, his name, his heritage and set him on the road to who-the-hell-cares amorality. What he had become was partly her fault.

She'd spilled his secret. But she had a secret, too, and he was the only person alive who knew it.

It was time she understood that he could destroy her.

Delilah was lying on the couch in her living room, staring at a tea industry periodical. She hadn't read a word of it. In the back of her mind was the image of the tea bushes she'd seen in Rize, dark green and shiny, two leaves and a bud ready to be plucked, but the image kept slipping away from her to be superseded by the memory of Nick and Travis, brawling in the street.

Seeing them fight had been like going back through time. To Concord, to the apple tree where Travis had described what sex was while Nick had shown her what love was. And to a motel room in 1970 where, essentially, the same thing had happened. Travis was always there with his ready body and his charming smile, but if things didn't go the way he wanted, he raged or carved obscenities, or hopped on a plane. Nick, on the other hand . . . *You don't even see me. You never have.*

"I'm such an idiot," she said aloud, dropping the tea journal onto the floor. She saw him now.

There it was, the truth at last: she was in love with Nick. She'd realized it outside, but she hadn't been quite ready to accept it. The fight had been the catalyst. She'd expected Travis to win. Even though she'd seen Nick working out in his basement, she'd still expected his big brother to crush him, and that had scared her. Don't hurt him, she'd wanted to beg Travis. Please, please don't hurt Nick.

But Nick had emerged victorious, and that had scared her even more. It changed everything. Actually, everything had changed a long time ago, but the implications hadn't struck her until she saw Travis drive away. Something primitive had happened, something the twentieth century woman who'd witnessed it had trouble processing. Two men had fought over her, and the winner had turned to claim her. Nick had won; she belonged to him now.

Well, of course she couldn't accept that, so when he'd touched her in something other than his usual gentlemanly manner, she'd rebelled. She'd said, in effect, "Equal partners, Nicholas. You're the man, and yes, you're physically stronger, but don't you ever think that gives you authority over me."

On the other hand, maybe she shouldn't have declared her independence quite so forcefully. Poor Nick. Repentant, she'd gone back outside to find him, but he wasn't around. She told herself it was for the best that they have some time alone to think things over, but the truth was, her disappointment had been severe.

She picked up the tea journal again and tried to get back to the article. She had forced herself to read about three paragraphs when her buzzer rang.

Delilah jumped. She half ran to the door, which was locked and chained. *Closed doors.* If she opened it, everything would be different, and for all her courage, all her enthusiasm for life fully lived, there was something intimidating about that.

He knocked, a gentle knock, polite, deferential. For a moment it occurred to her that it might not be Nick at all, but Travis. Then she thought, no. She'd seen the look Travis had given her as he'd prepared to drive away. It was finally over with him, forever and ever and ever.

Another knock, a little more impatient this time. Standing there, hesitating, Delilah noticed the small white rectangle on the floor just inside the door. She stooped and picked it up. It was a business card, engraved with Nick's name and address. She flipped it over to find a lopsided drawing of a heart. In dark, neat letters at the center of the heart was the inscription N. LOVES D.

Her eyes closed for an instant. "I love you, too," she whispered, and opened the door.

He was standing there, leaning one shoulder against the doorjamb, grinning at her, wearing those scholarly glasses of his (had he lost his contacts in the fight?), one side of his lip swollen, one cheek already looking bruised, those disreputable jeans of his scruffier than ever.

"I thought you'd gone. Your car—"

"I did go. I drove for a couple of miles, then came back."

The jeans were tight, emphasizing his long legs and well-muscled thighs. (This had made it easy for her to know exactly where to knee him.) She could see the muscles in his bare arms, too; not brawn, but the supple sinews of a man who worked out with weights to keep himself in shape. Who was quick, and agile, and able to defend himself and her. Who was tall, and slender, whose hair was dark and curly and whose eyes were huge, thick-lashed, and honest.

And suddenly she understood that although she'd been impressed by his physical skill and competence, it wasn't Nick the brawler she loved. What she loved was the way he'd held back until the last possible second. The way he'd kept his head while she was screaming and Travis was going berserk. The way he'd refrained from landing the punch that would have put his brother on the ground.

"May I come in?"

"Yes." She stood aside as he entered, then she carefully closed and locked the door behind him. She was still holding his business card in her right hand. He nodded to it. "Did you read that?"

She lolled back against the door, smiling. "Um-humm."

"It's true."

"I know, Nick."

"You know something else? I've never loved you more than I did a little while ago when you nearly unmanned me."

She laughed, beginning to relax. "A streak of masochism, huh?"

"I've never cared much for women I could dominate." He braced one strong arm against the door and leaned toward her. "I'm sorry I came on to you like that."

She cast an arch glance to the south of his belt buckle. "There isn't any, uh, permanent damage?"

His other arm fixed upon the door, caging her there. "I don't think so." He touched his lips to the line where her dark hair sprang away from her forehead. "Shall we check it out?"

Delilah remembered her teacher, Eliot Randall, and how she thought she'd die the first time he touched her. It was like that now with Nick. She was a teenager again and her blood was hot, urgent. He caressed her jaw, then brushed his thumb across the surface of her lips. Her body flashed to full arousal, and she was feeling everything he'd wanted her to feel, everything she'd thought herself incapable of feeling for him. She took a step closer and shivered as his arm locked around her waist.

"Nick—"

"Don't talk. We're through talking."

When he lowered his lips to hers, Delilah's knees buckled. It wasn't at all the way she'd imagined Nick's lovemaking would be. Instead of being sweet, careful, and considerate, he was fierce, demanding, erotic. He kissed her as if drinking her, breathing her, as if he would die without her. He made everything she'd felt for his brother shrivel and fade away.

Nick's mouth was all over her face, her neck. His hands, fevered, were taking possession of the various curves and angles of her body. Her breasts swelled for him, the peaks pebbling as he brushed them. Pressing her back against the door, he leaned into her with his hips and circled them. She gasped. In the pit of her stomach the muscles clenched and loosened and clenched again as long-frustrated desire gathered and pooled.

He lifted and carried her into the living room. To the sofa, where he laid her down. He took off his glasses, which struck the top of the glass coffee table with a definitive crack. Such a little thing, yet it excited her. *He's taking off his glasses because he really means it this time.*

He fell upon her, settling well in between her thighs. Delilah writhed under his weight, trying to get their bellies and hips into the most pleasurable conjunction. He was iron-hard against her; she was loose and soft and damp.

Slowly, he lowered his head. She could see his eyes, smiling. His tongue slid into her mouth, touching and engaging her own. She caressed him, moving her hands everywhere she could reach. She loved it—those crisp tendrils of too long hair. The delicious weight of him crushing her into the sofa cushions. His slow, rhythmic movements against her belly. She rotated her hips, delighting in the size of his erection, loving the way he groaned against her lips.

Panting, she freed her mouth. "Nick. Listen. All evening, talking to Travis, dancing with him, I kept getting flashes of you. When I saw you, standing there on the sidewalk, I thought I'd conjured you up." Her voice was fierce. "When I understood you were really there, I was glad, Nick, so damn glad."

He cupped her face between his beautiful long-fingered hands, holding her motionless. "Then why were you with him in the first place?"

"I don't know. It was like being in a time warp. As if the real Delilah, the Delilah of today, of 1986, had checked out for a little while. Maybe it was an exorcism. I'm not sure. All I know is, you came, you were there, and that was a reprieve."

"Prove it, Delilah. Show me."

She kissed him, pouring her entire soul into the kiss. And as she focused her awareness so intensely upon him, something strange happened. She heard a buzzing sound and felt, for a moment, disoriented. The room darkened around them and Nick's body changed subtly—he seemed taller, broader, while she herself was much more petite. And he was aggressive, wildly so. But he wasn't hurting her . . . it was passion, and they both felt it. Strong, heady, send-the-world-to-the-devil passion, much more powerful than anything she'd ever felt in this life.

In which life? All at once there were two. And then another shift, and there was a whole corridor of lives stretching endlessly in both directions. He was there beside her, sometimes laughing, sometimes cruel, loving her, teaching her, kissing her, killing her, always, always around. Max was there sometimes, too, but not as often. And Travis, less often still. But Nick, Nick was her love. It had been Nick all along.

He raised his head. "Do you understand what I've been waiting for all these years?"

Was it possible he had seen the same thing? Surely not. Surely it was nothing more than an illusion that was already breaking up and fading. Or maybe it was telepathy, and he had sent the images to her. "I don't believe in that junk."

He smiled, those green eyes terribly tender. "How about this junk?" As he spoke he gave another quick grind of his hips, which she acknowledged with an answering jerk of her pelvis.

"That I believe in."

"Can we go into the bedroom? This sofa's too damn short for me."

He walked her down the hall to her bedroom, one strong hand riding the small of her back. Delilah was trembling. He closed the door behind them and began stripping off his clothes. "You, too. Hurry up, woman, get naked."

She was too slow, so he came to her and helped her. His hands were gentle—the gentleness she had always associated with the shy, sensitive Nick of her childhood—it was still there, after all. Somewhere along the way he had lost his clumsiness. Somewhere he had found grace.

As he smoothly followed her down upon the mattress, his powerful body surging between her thighs, she felt an absurd urge to laugh. Who would have thought the smaller, younger boy she'd teased so mercilessly would mature into a man of so much sexual energy and endowment!

He kissed her thoroughly, then pushed up on his elbows. "Jesus, I almost forgot. What about contraception?"

"I have a diaphragm, but I don't think we need it. My period's due in a couple of days." She smiled as she ran her hands over his shoulders and chest, then down to stroke his belly and below. He turned on his side to give her greater access. After a minute she took his hand and brought it between her legs where she was so moist, so hot. She wanted him to know she wasn't faking this time . . . not that there could be much doubt.

He caressed her deeply, murmuring his approval. But he took his hands away too soon and straddled her and kissed her breasts instead, his tongue a delicious instrument of torture. He was teasing her now. Devil.

She shifted fretfully as those magic fingers drifted over her stomach, her legs. When at last they returned to the delta of her thighs she arched her hips to encourage him, but he shook his head, taking his time. His mouth captured a breast again and suckled hard while his fingers more urgently explored her. When she began to moan, he slid slowly down her body, letting her feel his hard muscles and crinkly hair against her much more tender skin. She cried out as his mouth brushed her belly. She pushed her hands into his hair and held his head as he lapped at her mound, her inner thighs, and then, delicately, the engorged flesh between her legs.

"Look at you," he whispered. His fingers teased the petals, the cavern, the bud, then held her open to him while his tongue snaked into her. Her hips came off the mattress. My God, it's so good, she thought. It's never been so good for me before.

When he reared up over her, his skin was flushed and damp with arousal, and his arms were trembling. Delilah ran a finger down his chest, tangling it in the glossy hair growing there. "I love you, Nick."

The elation that came into his eyes made her love him even more. "I love you, too, Delilah."

The first thrust was tight, despite her intense arousal. "Relax," he whispered. He bowed his hips and drove harder. This time she gasped as her body stretched to accommodate him. "You okay?" he asked.

"Yes, yes." Wrapping her legs around him, she began to meet him thrust for thrust.

Nick's mouth covered hers and he kissed her passionately. Delilah whimpered with pleasure as his flesh knifed into hers. He quickened the pace. No sophisticated game of advance and retreat, tease and extend, this was a ferocious mating, violent in its pace and its energy. He was driving into her as if he wanted to melt her flesh and crush her bones.

She sensed he was ahead of her, and was straining to catch up, when she felt the goose flesh rise on his back. "Delilah," he breathed. He went in deep, then stiffened against her, bursting. Between her legs she felt the mighty pulsing of his orgasm. His arms collapsed and his face disappeared into the soft curtain of her hair. "Shit," he said.

"It's okay, I don't mind." She hugged him; her palms were bathed in his sweat. "I love you, I love you, it's okay."

He withdrew, keeping her pressed to him. She expected him to be embarrassed, but instead he was grinning. "Guess I'll roll over now and go to sleep."

She got her fingers into his hair and pulled. "Not unless you want to be the victim of a justifiable homicide."

He laughed. "Give me a few minutes and I'll be back in action, I promise."

"Well, I hope so! Dory's been giving me propaganda for years about what a great lover you are."

The expression on his face was so comical, she began to laugh.

"Dory Lester said that?"

"Uh-huh. And she's had lots of experience, believe me. You're right up there with the best of 'em, she assured me." She nipped the end of his nose. "Certainly the hors d'oeuvres were delicious, but I'm going to have to reserve judgment about the main course."

"My dear girl, I was a virgin when I slept with Dory. What just happened here was a masterful performance compared to that debacle. Of course"—he paused, giving her a leer—"she was a good teacher, and I improved a lot with practice."

"Yeah?"

He began nuzzling her throat. "Uh-huh. I love sex," he added seriously. "I think it's a great gift, a great joy. A way for grown-ups to play, to dramatize, to work off tensions. And the best way, of course, to love." He kissed her tenderly. "I love you so much. I've loved you for such a long time."

"A few centuries or so?"

"Don't mock it. We're reincarnational partners, you and I. Every time I've done a past-life regression, you've been there."

"Is that possible? Do people really reincarnate together?"

"Sure. A lot of the people who are in this life with us have been with us before, acting out different roles, varying the steps of the dance. But you and I are very old, very special friends."

Delilah laughed; she couldn't help it. "You really believe that stuff?"

His hand moved up her flanks and caressed her stomach. "Once we were homosexual lovers—males. Another time I was the chieftain of some violent nomadic tribe, and you, the young and lovely daughter of my enemy. I carried you off, raped you a few times, and when you continued to obsess me, took you as my wife. You were afraid of me, but deliciously responsive."

"Sure, Nick. Sounds more like sexual fantasy than past-life regression."

"Another time," he said, grinning, "you and this bare-breasted army of Amazons captured me and staked me out in the center of the village, forcing me to be the unflagging sex slave of a couple of dozen insatiable women . . . I was a celibate priest in my next life, so I'd have a chance to rest."

"And what was I, a nun?"

"You don't buy it, do you?"

"For a moment, when you kissed me in the living room, I believed it, yes. But now—"

He sighed. "I know. It's like that with me, too. Brief visitations, nothing concrete. And when you're a fiction writer, equipped with a vivid imagination, it's hard to believe in the objective reality of your dreams. But never mind that now. Why are we chitchatting when we could be making love?"

"I thought we were waiting for you to recuperate."

He whispered something in her ear and she giggled. "Okay, I can do that. Anything else you want, you depraved pervert?"

"I'm gonna make you dizzy the next few weeks, getting used to all the kinky things I want."

She hugged him convulsively. "How did I miss out on you for so many years?"

"Seems as if I've been dreaming about this forever." He moved against her again, reviving. He smiled as her eyes widened. "You can minister to me next time. I don't need it now."

"Big man!"

"Divine justice. I couldn't get you in 1970, so it's only fair that I should have a college kid's recuperative powers all these years later when you're finally mine."

"What d'you mean, I'm finally yours?"

"Barefoot and pregnant, that's how it's gonna be. Stay home and darn my socks. Maybe *I'll* take over Templeton Tea."

"Drake. You've turned into Drake. Is there a full moon tonight?"

He lowered his mouth to hers. "Shut up and kiss me," he said.

39

Nick raised himself up on one elbow and looked at Delilah beside him, her dark hair fanned out on the pillow, her lashes sooty against her cheek. "I have something to tell you," he said.

It was sometime in the middle of the night. He hadn't wanted to cast a pall over their lovemaking, but he couldn't put it off any longer. He had been tempted—as Gran had been—never to tell her at all, but he knew instinctively that this would be wrong. He would give her his support when she needed it, yes. But he would not overwhelm her with his solicitude, nor would he make her dependent upon him the way so many other women had been. He would respect her strength, her courage, her ability to deal with her problems her own way. He would not allow his love to become a suffocating, cloying thing.

Delilah reached out a hand and stroked his hair back from his forehead. "Did you know that when you're anxious, you get a tiny line right here in the middle of your forehead?" She touched it with her fingertip. "What's the matter?"

He remembered the way she'd screamed that night so many years ago when she'd miscarried Travis's baby. She was strong; she had endured a lot in her life, but who could predict how she would react?

"Delilah, I know what happened sixteen years ago. Why Gran treated you the way she did. Why Travis left. The truth is painful, but it's something you have a right to know. If you want me to tell you, I will."

Delilah considered the trepidation in his eyes, the serious, almost grim, slant of his mouth. Did she want to know? It was less important now than it had ever been. "Make love to me first."

He held her afterward for a long time while their bodies cooled and settled. Their fingers were laced together and her hair ran riot across his throat.

Delilah tipped her head up on one hand so she could see his eyes. "Now. Explain."

He held her a little closer as he began to speak.

"You told them, didn't you?" Travis said. He was there on the threshold of the China Tea House Tavern, demanding admission. Minerva was alone. Mary Mango had gone to Dallas for a few days to visit her daughter.

Travis was bruised and haggard; he had been beaten. By Nick? His eyes had never looked so wild.

She didn't want to let him in. *Don't be ridiculous.* She threw wide the door and led him into the parlor, then she turned on the light in the corner and sat down on a sturdy wingback chair. A quick glance at the grandfather clock in the corner told her it was late, after midnight.

"I told your brother, yes. I saw you and Delilah leave the office together, and I was afraid."

"She's with Nick. *Nick,* for God's sake."

Oh, Nick, you darling. All evening I've been fretting here, hoping you would find them, stop them, be in time.

"What you wanted was impossible. You knew that. As for Delilah, we should have told her years ago."

"You're right. Sooner or later all secrets come to light." He paced the room and stopped just in front of her, his big body blocking the dim light from the lamp. Quite suddenly she was afraid. Travis's voice was harsh and his golden hair looked brassy and unkempt. There was something in his eyes that reminded her of Harrison Templeton on the day he'd come back from India. *Repetition.* Travis isn't that type, she told herself. He's not evil. He's just entering a period of crisis. That was it, that was all.

"I want to talk about a secret of yours, Gran. I think it's time to air out all the closets . . . shine some light into all the dark corners, uncover the rot that's at the heart of the Templeton family tree."

Shivering, she said, "What are you talking about?"

"You know damn well what I'm talking about."

Her heart was beating much too fast. Too much adrenaline. Fight or flight, except she couldn't do either, of course. Damn being old! Damn being unable to defend herself against a man half her age who was suddenly more threatening than he'd ever been in his life.

He leaned over her chair, supporting himself on the arms. His knuckles were white. His eyes were winter-blue, and there was something so cold about him that she felt as if he'd exposed the snake within the skin. She began to believe in her dreams, her nightmares. Something unspeakable was going to happen.

The vultures were spiraling down from the heavens, seeking retribution at last.

Delilah took the news that Travis was her half brother more calmly than Nick had dared expect. The facts were startling, but she accepted them. What she couldn't accept was the way she had been left so long in the dark. "Why didn't they *tell* me, Nick?"

"I don't know. Gran had promised my mother, so that was one reason. The other was her anxiety about what she considered to be your fragile emotional state. She thought it was better to let you think your lover had abandoned you than to reveal that you'd slept with your own brother."

She was silent. After several moments there was a little catch in her throat. He cuddled her closer. "You were bitterly depressed after your mother's death. Gran was afraid, given the circumstances, and the family curse . . ." He let his voice trail off.

"That I'd kill myself?"

He nodded. "I told her I didn't believe you'd ever have gone so far. She insisted that incest is a heavy sin and that you wouldn't have been able to cope with such a burden of guilt. It's odd how passionate she was about it. It's almost as if she was talking about herself."

Delilah remembered that desperate night in L.A., the deadly potion, the voice calling her a coward. If that could happen to her at the mature age of thirty-seven, maybe Grendam had been right to worry about what she might have done when she'd felt betrayed and abandoned at twenty-two.

A new suspicion raced through her. "What about *you,* Nick? Whose son are you?"

"Gran assures me I'm Jonathan's son. I guess my father is capable of making love to a woman, he just doesn't enjoy it much. As for your father, by the time I was born, he was happily married to your mother. His thing with my mother had been over for four years."

"Good old Daddy," Delilah said with a touch of bitterness. "I can't imagine that he could have made Aunt Sarah happy."

"Nothing could have made her happy, I'm afraid."

"And now, except for your father, they're all dead. They must have loved, yearned, felt passion, guilt—and it's come to nothing now, Nick. It's all just—gone."

He couldn't think of anything to say to that.

"So Travis knew. When I first returned to Boston, he said he'd had a good reason for leaving me. I didn't believe him. I got mad. Maybe if I hadn't lost my temper that day, he would have told me. Instead, he—"

"Instead he ended up trying what he did tonight."

"He was going to make love to me, knowing we were sister and brother." Delilah moved fretfully. "We were guiltless before; we didn't know. But now—" She freed her hands from Nick's and pressed her fingers to her temples. "God! This hasn't penetrated yet. I've committed incest. It sounds so heavy, so portentous. But it doesn't *feel* like such a big deal. Not worth killing myself over or putting out my eyes. If I hadn't had the miscarriage, I suppose I might view it differently. I'd have feared the consequences for my child. That's probably why Charles Templeton did what he did, don't you think? He and his wife had children."

"And we're descended from them. It's the repetition Ra-ton spoke of. We're doomed to repeat the sins of our ancestors until we break the curse."

"So how do we do that?"

"No one knows."

"Do you really *believe* there's a curse?"

Nick sighed. "I don't know what to believe anymore. I wish I could convince myself there is no curse, particularly now that you and I are together. Our union isn't incestuous, technically, but we are first cousins, and I'd hate to think that our troubles might be magnified by our falling in love with each other."

She slid her arms around his neck and pulled him down on her. "We've suffered plenty of troubles alone, Nick. We've both survived. I think together we can handle anything the fates decide to fling at us, don't you?"

"You lying there so silky and receptive beneath me boosts my confidence, yeah." He moved his hips rhythmically against hers. "Forget the family curse."

In the China Tea House Tavern the chill of the night had settled into the corners. Minerva sat huddled in her chair staring at the handsome golden-haired man who was addressing her so intensely, and thinking, he looks like my childhood image of a god. Krishna, maybe. A god from the mountains. A god who had come down finally to say, you thought you could get away with it, didn't you? But we've been watching you.

"I used to have a recurring dream," said Travis. "One of those falling dreams that are so common. For a long time I thought the dream was symbolic, but there were certain elements that puzzled me. Elements that seemed very real.

"I'm not an introspective person, so I let it alone. I figured that if my conscious mind was going to so much trouble to repress something, it was probably better left repressed. But the dreams didn't stop. Indeed, they got worse, becoming more frightening and more specific all the time. So I went to a therapist, who offered to use hypnosis to regress me to my childhood and unlock the mystery of my dream."

He stopped for a moment. Minerva didn't speak. How does he know? she asked herself. He was only a boy. What must it have done to him all these years, knowing?

"When I went under, I became a child again, six or seven years old. Everything I saw was from the perspective of a child. Furniture looked bigger, doors and windows taller. I was wandering in a giant's house. It was an old house, dark. The floorboards creaked, and I knew there were monsters. There were monsters, it turned out, but not the variety I feared.

"One night I ran through a long, narrow corridor searching for my mother, but she was dead. I remembered visiting the hospital with my father, who was a doctor. I remembered the way he used to hang over her bedside, pleading with her to eat, to live. My grandmother took care of me during those years; Nick and I used to visit her often in the China Tea House Tavern. We both loved her. She smelled nice and she told good stories.

"I hated my great-grandfather, though. He was fat and cruel. He used to grab me by the ears and shake me, like a cat or a puppy. My grandmother didn't like him either. She never admitted this, but I knew it. Sometimes I would lie in bed in the China Tea House Tavern and listen to them argue. My little brother Nick would wake up and cry, and the nanny would comfort him. I'd lie in bed, silent, never letting anybody know I was awake. I'd listen to them fight, and plan the way I was going to kill him, that mean, ugly monster who made my grandmother cry."

"Travis, don't. Stop. I can't bear this."

She might have been speaking to the wind.

"One night I got out of bed and opened the nursery door. Nick was awake, too, whimpering a little, as usual. I told him to shut up and go back to sleep. Our nursemaid wasn't home that evening; it must have been her night off.

"The battle was raging more fiercely than ever. I crept slowly down the stairs from the third-floor nursery. I heard odd sounds coming from the bedroom where my grandmother slept. Slaps, followed by cries. I was scared, but angry, too. He was hurting my grandmother, but maybe I could save her. Didn't she always call me her little hero, her lovely little golden horseman?"

Minerva couldn't control herself. Her eyes had been burning; now they overflowed.

"But she didn't need my help. As I reached the bottom of the stairs at the dark end of the hallway, she burst through the bedroom door. Her nightgown was torn, her hair, all blond and wavy, was hanging down her back. I stared at her hair, more surprised by that than by anything else. It was long. She always wore it piled atop her head, and I'd had no idea it was so beautiful. I remember thinking it looked like Rapunzel's hair.

"He came bellowing after her. He had a whiskey bottle in one hand and something that I thought at first was a sword in the other. It wasn't a sword, of course. It was his walking stick, the one with the ivory elephant on top."

Minerva covered her face with her hands.

"He chased her to the spare bedroom at the far end of the hall. For some reason she couldn't open the door; perhaps it was locked. He laughed and took a swig from the bottle. 'Where are you going to run to, my love?' he said.

"She scuttled away from him, dashing back along the hallway in my direction. Just at the head of the steep staircase that led to the first floor, he caught her. He held her by that beautiful long hair. There was a crash as she lashed out at him and knocked the whiskey bottle out of his hand. He yelped—it must have struck his foot before it shattered. She whipped away from him, crouched down, and seized the broken neck of the bottle. I could hear her panting as she waved the broken bottle at him like a lance. 'I'll kill you, you filthy bastard,' she said. 'I've dreamed of killing you for years.'

"He laughed at her, not quite as confidently as before. 'Drop it, Min. Be a good girl now and put that thing down.'

"Instead she lunged at him, slashing the jagged glass at his throat. He backed away from her. He tried to hit her with the walking stick, but he was afraid of the bottle. He backed again, never seeing the dark stairwell yawning there behind him. She saw it, though."

"Travis, please. Travis—"

"She lunged once more, and he tottered on the edge of the top step, realizing, suddenly, his danger. He grabbed for the newel post, but before he could reach it, my grandmother threw down the bottleneck and gave him a powerful shove. He fell backwards into empty air.

"He didn't cry out as he fell. As for me, I was too terrified to utter a sound. It was dark, so I couldn't see him falling, but I could hear his heavy body careening down the steep stairs. He landed at the bottom with a thump and a kind of crack, then all was silent again. I crept backward the way I had come. I hid behind the door to the upper stairway, clutching my belly and feeling sick. My grandmother stood poised at the top of the stairs, then she sort of crumpled. Folded up and sank to her knees amidst the spilled whiskey and the jagged shards. 'God forgive me, but I hope he's dead,' I heard her say.

"And he was dead. An accidental death, according to the coroner's report. He got drunk, it seems, and stumbled in the dark at the top of the stairs."

Minerva raised her ravaged face. "I never knew. I had no idea you were there."

"I was there, all right. Christ, even Nick was there, although I'm not sure how much he saw."

"Oh God, oh God," she whispered. It had happened exactly as he'd described it, and when she knew her adversary was dead, she had exulted. For six hellish years she had given him shelter in her home and been his sometime mistress, always under coercion. She did it for Jonathan, to protect him from the secret of his birth. Knowing how much she loved him, Templeton took great satisfaction in tormenting her with threats about her son.

But he had never actually told Jonathan the truth. No doubt he'd known that if he did so, his hold over her would be lost forever.

As he aged, Templeton's drinking got worse and worse. In the final months before his death he became impotent, which was, to Minerva, a mercy. But violence could still arouse him, as had been all too obvious on that final night when he'd come after her with his cane.

Until the last terrible moment when she'd seen her chance and seized it, she had been his victim. But in the end, she'd pushed him. In the end she'd killed him. She had taken a human life, and she had borne the guilt of it for thirty-three years.

And now . . . all actions have consequences. That was one moral law in which she absolutely believed. She did not think she could be charged with murder. It had happened too long ago, and events recalled under hypnosis are not admissible as evidence in court. Even if the case had gone to trial thirty years ago, she could have made an excellent argument for self-defense. No. Travis had no legal recourse.

She said as much.

"I'm not threatening you with the law. You're right—they won't be interested in you now. The newspapers will, though. The good people of Boston will be fascinated to learn that a respected Beacon Hill matriarch was capable of killing an old man, her lover, who also happened to be her dead husband's father. That should be good for a few headlines."

Scandal, she thought. Reputation.

"I'm guilty of incest," he went on, "but so are you. How many months did you sleep with him before you killed him? How many *years?* Were you attracted to the drunken, violent type, or did he have some sort of hold over you? If so, what was it? People are going to ask themselves those questions. They're going to lust over the answers. Remember Jean Harris? You'll have the *National Enquirer* after you, *People,* Barbara Walters—"

Minerva's voice cut through his tirade. "What do you want?"

Travis smiled his genial smile. What was that line she remembered from her father's beloved Shakespeare? That one may smile, and smile, and be a villain. "I want the tea company. That's all that's left; there's nothing else for me now."

Minerva thought, I will not be blackmailed again.

"As for Delilah, I want her fired, I want her gone. I expect to see a copy of your will leaving everything to me by five P.M. tomorrow. Your competition to establish which of us will be better for the company has just come to an end."

"You're worse than your great-grandfather."

"He wasn't my great-grandfather, remember? To hell with the Templetons. I'm not descended from them; they're not my family, and they're no longer my concern. Fuck the Templetons."

The room was silent except for the ticking of the clock. Somewhere outside, a fire engine whined.

"Very well," Minerva said. "I'll do what you want."

But Travis didn't like her enigmatic smile.

Nick had an anxiety attack that night. He woke suddenly from a nightmare in which his grandmother was fleeing from a monster who forced her to swallow a cup of poisoned tea. Then the monster came after him. No, he screamed as someone put a pistol to his head. "Abomination," a voice said, and a finger moved on the trigger.

He woke beside Delilah, hot and sweaty from too many covers and the warmth of her body curled around his. She was deeply asleep. Nick managed to unclasp her arms and slide away from her to lie on his back, listening to his heart beat. The familiar sick tingling gripped his belly and he felt the run of sweat along his spine, under his arms, in his crotch.

He rolled over onto his left side and tried to calm down, but that was the trouble with the attacks that crept up on you at night—you were most vulnerable then. There was no warning, no time to bring the meditative techniques into action. Before you could even begin to organize your resistance, the thing escalated into a full-fledged adrenaline bath.

He sat up. Bad choice—he felt dizzy. Your blood pressure rises when you sit up, he remembered. Maybe he was better off flat. He flopped back down.

Coward! Hypochondriac jerk! Snap out of it, Templeton!

Delilah made a sound and turned over, her hand feeling for him in her sleep. He slid farther away from her. Stay asleep, babe. He didn't want her to see him like this.

Scraps of dream images were still flitting through his mind. He saw the stocks where the Puritans chained convicted criminals. And the China Tea House Tavern as it had looked in the early eighteenth century; he saw it as if he'd been there. Too much research. Too much imagination.

He closed his eyes and tried again to meditate.

Several interminable minutes passed before his heart stopped racing and the perspiration dried. He lay quietly, drawing white light into himself, spinning a globe of shielding love around this bed where he and Delilah were finally together. They were safe, safe. Thank God Gran had warned him in time.

He sat up. Gran. The dream images came back more clearly now. He and Delilah were okay, but what about Gran?

He should at least have called her to tell her he'd found Travis, intervened, stopped them in time. He remembered something she'd said about telling him the truth about Travis and Delilah, no matter what the consequences to herself. What had she meant by that?

He squinted, trying to see Delilah's alarm clock. Three-fifteen. He couldn't call her now—it would frighten her if he woke her from her sleep. He settled back down, still feeling queasy. It's just my blasted nerves acting up as they've done a hundred times before.

He'd call her in the morning, first thing.

40

In the China Tea House Tavern Minerva was not asleep. She was looking out her window and thinking many things, one of which was, hurry. You don't have much time.

In the morning they would come looking for her. Nick and Delilah would both come, if Travis was right about their being together now. She hoped it was true. Nick's wise and loving spirit would provide Delilah with the security she needed. Her lively, zestful manner would buoy him up when he was depressed. They would take care of each other, and perhaps, God willing, Delilah would have her children at last.

There was no sound but the rhythmic ticking of the grandfather clock that had belonged to Harrison Templeton's father. Minerva Templeton sat in the front parlor, enshrouded in darkness. Outside the moon was full, and there was something vaguely familiar about that.

She went to her desk and carefully examined her papers. There was a copy of her will; her attorney had the original. She glanced through it one more time and nodded. Everything was in order.

Minerva put out the light in the parlor and walked slowly up the stairs to her bedroom. Dory had telephoned earlier in the evening from California. Was she all right? Ra-ton, her friend from the great beyond, had delivered an ominous warning concerning the China Tea House Tavern, and Dory was worried. Minerva assured her she was fine, and asked her to tell Ra-ton to mind his own business.

But she was not fine. She was an old woman with a weak heart and more guilt on her shoulders than she could possibly bear.

All her life she had needed to be in control, both of people and of situations. From this had come her wickedness. At the age of seventeen she had sworn revenge on the man who had raped her and stolen her land; she would not be his victim; she would seize life in her hands. Somewhere along the way, control had become her obsession. She would run the tea company, no matter what the consequences to her husband's ego. She would restrict her son's sexual expression, no matter what travesty of a marriage resulted. She would keep Jonathan's paternity a secret, even if she had to submit to blackmail and stoop to murder.

The list of her sins went on and on. She had betrayed Delilah, whom she loved, and possibly caused her to miscarry her baby. She had failed to shield Travis from Harrison Templeton's death, and God only knew what witnessing a violent death at the age of seven had done to his psyche. She could scarcely blame him for the way he was dealing with her now. She had brought this tragedy upon them both.

Even now she was adding to her sins: instead of facing the consequences of her actions, she was running away. All her life she'd wanted respectability and approbation; she couldn't endure the thought that the scandalous details of her life would come out and she would have to face Nick and Delilah . . . not to mention everybody else . . . and acknowledge the true state of her soul.

Even at the end, she needed to be in control.

She and Travis were partners, in a way. There must have been some point in his life, as in hers, where he had taken the wrong turn, gone down the wrong road. At some further point perhaps they both could have turned around and retraced their steps, but it was too late for that now. She could see her destination, and the only thing she still wanted was the oblivion it promised.

It was over. She didn't regret what she intended to do. The Templeton curse was upon her.

She'd had the pills for a long time. She'd been squirreling them for several months—forty Nembutal, the barbiturate that her physician had prescribed to help with her insomnia. Forty ought to be enough.

They were small and looked innocuous, her bright yellow pills.

As she swallowed them, one by one, with water, she felt an odd sense of communion with Helen Templeton, who had died more than two hundred and fifty years ago, here, in the same place.

The drug worked fast. Before she had swallowed half of the pills, she began to feel drowsy and heavy-headed. She continued doggedly until they were gone, then lay down on her bed within the magic circle and closed her eyes. She thought of nothing . . . nothing but the home she had left so many years ago—the rolling hills of tea, the purple mountains where the gods reside.

High overhead, the predator birds circled. So. You have won. You have beaten me after all. Minerva smiled and made no resistance as the wings of darkness enfolded her.

Nick woke again at dawn. Delilah was deeply asleep, one arm flung out to the side. She was beautiful and he loved her, but the sick feeling he'd had in his stomach during his anxiety attack still lingered. Something was wrong; he knew it. Something was terribly wrong.

He pulled on his jeans and went down the hall to the kitchen, where there was a phone on the wall. He dialed his grandmother's number. She was usually up early. She must be worried, wondering what had happened last night.

The phone rang over and over. She was a light sleeper. The ringing certainly ought to have wakened her.

Nick hung up. His palms were wet. He went back into the bedroom, put on his shirt and his shoes, and bent over Delilah. "I'm going out for a while."

"Hmm?" she half woke, blinked at him through sleep-heavy eyes.

"Stay in bed, sweetheart. I'll be back soon."

"Mmm-kay. Don't be long."

He kissed her neck. "I love you."

"Loveyoutoo."

Nick ran the six blocks to the place where he'd parked his car.

Delilah was awakened around seven-thirty by the sound of the telephone. She groped for the extension beside the bed and put it to her ear.

"Delilah?"

"Nick?" Still half-asleep, she looked over at his side of the bed. He'd been here; now he was gone, but he'd said he was coming right back . . . "Where are you?"

"Delilah," he said again, and she shot to full consciousness. There was something wrong with his voice.

"What's the matter? What is it? Nick?"

"Oh, babe. You'd better get over here right now. I'm at the hospital, Mass General. Delilah, it's Gran." His voice broke and she knew he was crying. "They brought her in, they've been working on her, but I'm afraid she's going."

"Going? What do you mean, going? She's *dying,* is that what you mean?" Her voice rose frantically. "She can't be dying; I don't believe it, Nick!"

"You'd better come if you want to see her. Come right now."

"Oh my God," she whispered. When she'd fallen asleep, only a couple of hours ago, everything had been so good. She and Nick, loving each other. Confident, hopeful, ready to remake the world. And now . . .

"Just hurry, okay?"

She could hear her own hysteria as she assured him she'd be right there.

She remembered nothing of her drive to the hospital. She supposed she must have out-Bostoned the other Boston drivers, for she vaguely heard horns honking at her, but this was the last of her concerns. How could Grendam be dying? How dared she die before they'd had the chance to talk about the past and forgive each other?

You've had plenty of chances. But you let every one go by.

She was directed by the girl at the emergency room desk to Intensive Care. She rushed past orderlies and nurses, hardly seeing them. Don't let her door be shut. Don't let her body be covered with a sheet.

Nick met her by the nurses' station in the intensive care wing. He grabbed her and held her hard. For as instant as his body made contact with hers, she felt a flash of that physical obsession that a new love brings. "Nick?"

"They worked on her for ages. They've just moved her to a private room."

"You mean she's still alive?"

"Barely. She's in a coma. I don't think—" His voice broke and he tried to steady it. "They told me there's very little hope."

"Oh God, Nick, what happened? Was it her heart?"

Something came into his face then, something closed and hard and cold. "No."

"What d'you mean, no? A stroke? Did she fall? What?"

"She swallowed a whole bottle of barbiturates. It was a suicide attempt. She wanted to die."

Delilah felt the darkness coalesce around her. No, no, the voices began screaming in her head. Not again.

"She must have taken it during the night," he went on. "By the time they pumped her stomach, the drug had already been in her bloodstream for hours. And I knew, I knew. I woke up knowing I ought to have phoned her, but I thought, it's all right, it can wait till morning, it's silly to call in the middle of the night." Tears were streaming down his face. "Now she's not going to make it, all because I didn't trust the dream, my instincts, the warning I got."

She clutched his arms and shook him. "You can't have known. Don't be so foolish as to blame yourself."

"She depended on me so much. I can't believe I wasn't there to help her this time."

"But you were there. This morning—you got up and went to her house, didn't you? You found her and called the ambulance? If she pulls through, it will be due to you."

"She's not going to pull through. Somehow I know that, too. This is what she wants; she's chosen it. She's ready to go."

"Into her next life, I suppose?" Delilah couldn't take any of Nick's metaphysical crap right now. She pushed past him and accosted the nearest nurse. "I want to see my grandmother."

They were allowed in for a few minutes. Minerva Templeton was lying small and still on the hospital bed, covered with a sheet and a light blanket; her head was propped up on two thick pillows to help her breathe. She was hooked up to half a dozen monitors. Delilah could hear her breath, harsh and slow, being pushed in and out of her lungs by the force of the electronic respirator.

Oh God, she thought. Grendam wouldn't like this. She wouldn't like being kept alive by artificial means. It had been one of the things Max had most dreaded—to be trapped in a body that was no longer really alive.

She pulled up a chair beside her grandmother's bed and reached though the various tubes and wires to stroke her brow. She was cool to the touch—almost cold. Delilah remembered this, too, from Max. Her throat tightened and the tears began. "Why have you done this, Grendam?" she whispered. "I don't understand."

Nick sat down on the other side of the bed. He swept his unruly hair back from his forehead with a hand that shook. "I feel like tearing these tubes from her nose and mouth and breathing my own life back into her. I never thought you'd be so stupid, Gran! Or such a coward, either, damn you!"

But Delilah was thinking, no, no. Grendam wasn't stupid or a coward. And suicide was often much more carefully reasoned than the survivors thought.

"It's the fucking family curse," Nick said. "We're as guilt-stricken a bunch of sinners as have ever walked the face of the earth. And I knew it, dammit! I sensed she was projecting her own feelings about suicide onto you. You're a fool, Minerva Templeton," he said to the motionless figure on the bed. "Whatever you had to feel guilty about, it sure as shit didn't merit this!"

The ache in Delilah's throat had grown unbearable. "I wanted to talk to her," she said to Nick. "I imagined going to her today and telling her it was all right, that the past is behind us now, that I loved her. I haven't told her I loved her, Nick." Her tears were running freely. "She doesn't know. How can she die not knowing? My God, what a fuck-up I am! I never told my mother, I never told my father . . . but I always meant to tell Grendam. I always thought there would be enough time."

"Tell her now."

"She can't hear."

"Nobody knows much about coma states, but they say the hearing is the last thing to go. Tell her. I have a feeling she'll hear you."

Delilah took her grandmother's limp hands in hers and held them tight. They were so gnarled, so old. Eighty. She was already half that age herself. So many people I've loved have come to this. So much warmth dissipated, so many lights turned off.

How do you express the love you've felt for years but so often denied? What do you say? She leaned over and kissed Minerva Templeton's cheek. "I love you, Gran. Please hear me. Please don't go until you've heard me. I love you."

Minerva could see her body lying on the hospital bed, very straight and prim, very neat. She thought: I must be dreaming. In spite of all Nick's nonsense and Dory's, she hadn't really believed that consciousness was independent from the physical body; she wasn't sure she believed it now. She was still alive, that was all, and when the pills finally finished their work, this, too, would be obliterated. There would be peace at last.

Or so she hoped. Why was she still conscious? And why was she looking down on her own body in this peculiar manner as if she were out of it? She could see the machinery they had her hooked up to; she could see Delilah and Nick. She could hear them, too, and even catch echoes of their thoughts.

Nick was desperately telling himself that death isn't the end and that when the time came for him to cross over, his beloved grandmother would be there waiting for him, just like it says in all the books. But he didn't really believe it, and he was angry because his New Age philosophy didn't seem to be sustaining him at the time when he needed it most.

Minerva turned to see if anyone was waiting for her. Her gentle Edward. Her laughing Elizabeth. It would be wonderful if she could be with them again.

There was no one, and she quickly ordered herself not to wish for it. If she did, they would probably send Harrison Templeton to usher her into his eternal revenge.

If there's really an afterlife, what can I expect from it but punishment? *Forgive me, Father, for I have sinned.* My life has been one travesty after another. I've lost the love of everyone close to me, except Nick, but Nick is a blessed soul. I won't be there to meet him when he dies, because he'll be going to heaven while I'm burning endlessly in hell. Of course there's no one here to meet me. They never want to see my face again.

She did notice a light in one corner, though, an unearthly radiance that seemed to draw her. It was a peaceful vision, even a joyful one. It didn't bear any resemblance to what she imagined as hellfire, so perhaps things weren't as grim as she thought. She had sinned, yes, but there were worse sinners. Perhaps there was mercy, after all.

The wages of sin is death; but the gift of God is eternal life.

She turned her back on the light. Not yet. Eternity would have to wait. She hadn't said good-bye to Delilah.

She discovered that she could move. She wasn't exactly sure how, but she thought herself closer to Delilah, and in the next instant she was there, beside her, almost touching her.

Delilah was holding her hands (her body's hands, that is) and weeping. Delilah was saying, I love you, I love you, over and over again.

Concentrating, Minerva went inside her granddaughter's memories. She saw a little girl, ten years old, lying alone in a massive bed. She felt the child's terror, her loneliness. Then she saw herself of nearly thirty years ago, rushing to this child by night, summoned by her screams. She held Delilah, pressed her to her chest, felt how thin and fragile she was. Delilah was physically healthy, but her soul did no more than flicker inside that wan body. She wanted to go to her mother. She was close to going to her mother; Minerva had never before realized how close.

She—that earlier self—gathered the little girl close. She got into bed beside her—she who hated to share her bed with anyone, least of all a restless child.

I gave my love to her then, Minerva thought, even if I failed her so many times afterward. At least there was one moment when she knew and felt my love. One night in a long life of selfishness when I thought first of somebody else.

Is one moment all you need for redemption?

Minerva moved closer and touched Delilah, the adult Delilah, who, like her grandmother, was lost in a merciless litany of her own sins. Can she feel me touching her? Apparently not. Minerva tightened her arms around the girl's stiff shoulders, but it was like trying to embrace the air. Delilah's thoughts did not alter. She was castigating herself for every argument they'd ever had, and for the wholehearted reconciliation they had never achieved.

Perhaps I can touch her with love? I gave it to her once. There must have been other times also when I gave it to her, or she would not be so sad.

Minerva closed her eyes and searched deep within herself for a spark of that redeeming light. *Lighten our darkness, we beseech thee, O Lord.* How strange it was that the majestic language of those long-forgotten Sundays in the Anglican church in Darjeeling should come back to her at this time.

She found it, coaxed it, blew upon it until the spark became a flame. Then she drew it up out of her belly through her shoulders and down her arms to the tips of her fingers, which began to glow rosy-gold. She touched Delilah again, willing that light to radiate into her, willing her to feel and accept her love. *That true Light, which lighteth every man that cometh into the world.* It's all right, was all she could think of to tell her. All is well.

Delilah lifted her head. She said to Nick, "Did you feel that?"

"What?"

"I felt for a second as if someone touched me."

For an instant Minerva was back in her body and could feel the imprint of Delilah's lips against her cheek. There was a buzzing sound . . . or was it the rattle of her own breath? "Oh God, I think she's going," Minerva heard her granddaughter say.

And she saw Delilah as a newborn baby again, to whom she said, "You are very special, and you shall do so many marvelous things!" My love, my love. There's been no man for me since Edward died, but there was you, sweetheart, there was you.

It would be all right. Nick was there, and Delilah, the two people she loved. They were there, they were together. They would save each other, somehow.

I will not leave you comfortless.

Then she was going, as the girl had said. Going confidently, into the light.

41

I am the resurrection and the life: he that believeth in me, though he were dead, yet shall he live: And whosoever liveth and believeth in me shall never die.

Minerva Templeton was buried on a late summer day in the family plot where the Templetons had been laid to rest for decades. The sloping grassy knoll shaded by a sturdy oak was the same one Minerva herself had chosen as the final resting place of her laughing daughter, Elizabeth. Minerva lay beside her now, near the memorial stone she had erected in 1943 for Edward, whose body lay in an unmarked grave somewhere in France.

Delilah handled most of the funeral arrangements herself with the help of the instructions her grandmother had left with her attorney. Her grandmother had requested a short service at the Church of the Advent, the Episcopal congregation of which she had been a perfunctory member for many years. The service was crowded, and more elaborate than perhaps Minerva would have wished. Her gleaming mahogany coffin was carried by six pallbearers, including Nick and Travis; the minister preached a moving eulogy, and a full choir sang her favorite hymns.

Many of the same people who had been guests at Minerva's eightieth birthday party were also present at her funeral—friends, employees, business associates, tea industry workers. Nick's daughter Kelsey was there with her mother, looking solemn and a little scared. Harry Cox, Minerva's physician, wept openly, and Mary Mango, her housekeeper, wailed. The only immediate family member who was not present was Jonathan. He was somewhere in India, and so far they had been unable to reach him to inform him of his mother's death. Nick, in particular, was distressed about this. "Even though he's been gone so much in recent years, my father loved her very much. I know he'd have wanted to be here to lay her to rest."

"You must play his part," Delilah told him gently, "as well as your own."

Listening to the majestic language of the old Book of Common Prayer, Delilah was transported back through time to the family funerals she had attended in her childhood—her mother's, Sarah Templeton's, her great-grandfather Harrison Templeton's. So many deaths for a little girl to cope with. As with a wedding, a funeral inspires you to relive all other burials; as you weep for your present loss, your old ones are once again unlocked from your heart. Delilah's tears were given not only to her grandmother, but to her mother, her father, and Max as well.

When the mournful procession reached the gravesite and the final prayers had been said, Nick read a poem to close the ceremony. It was one, he said, that their grandmother had particularly admired. Delilah expected something from Shakespeare, but Nick read—or rather, declaimed, since he had it by heart—Gerard Manley Hopkins's "Spring and Fall, to a Young Child." And Delilah wept again, for she remembered standing here in the cemetery with her parents and Uncle Jonathan when they buried Nick and Travis's mother on a dark autumn morning as the leaves from the old oak had eddied in the wind and drifted into the open grave. Grendam had recited the poem then, and Delilah, not entirely understanding, had divined its essential message.

> Margaret, are you grieving
> Over Goldengrove unleaving?
> Leaves, like the things of man, you
> With your fresh thoughts care for, can you?
> Ah! as the heart grows older
> It will come to such sights colder
> By and by, nor spare a sigh
> Though worlds of wanwood leafmeal lie;
> And yet you will weep and know why.
> Now no matter, child, the name:
> Sorrows springs are the same.

Nor mouth had, no nor mind, expressed
What heart heard of, ghost guessed:
It is the blight man was born for,
It is Margaret you mourn for.

As she left the cemetery, Nick's arm clasped tight around her shoulders, Delilah thought of the Templeton curse and wondered which of them would be the next to be buried there.

The will was read two days later. Delilah assembled with the rest of the family in the State Street office of Cade Brenner, who for many years had been her grandmother's attorney. She was dressed smartly in black, and a look in the ladies' room mirror told her she appeared pale but composed. Travis and Nick were present, of course, the former looking frayed around the edges but still suave, the latter wearing his thickest glasses to hide his red eyes. Kelsey and her mother were not present. Neither was Jonathan, whom they still hadn't reached. It occurred to Delilah as they sat in the plush office and waited that the great Templeton family had been reduced dramatically in the twentieth century. You'd have thought there would have been more grandchildren and some other great-grandchildren by now.

The other people present in the room were old friends and retainers who had been summoned to appear because of the various bequests of the complicated will. Many of them, Delilah noted, had dried the eyes that had wept throughout the funeral and were now avidly anticipating the spoils.

Delilah felt strangely indifferent to the proceedings. Even though she knew her future—not to mention vast amounts of money and property—was at stake, she felt nothing more than a vague curiosity about the outcome. Perhaps this was because she'd prepared herself for the worst. Her grandmother had told them in April that her will left the tea company to Travis. She would change it—if indeed she decided to do so—at the end of one year. Only four months had elapsed since then.

Four months. If I'd known I would only have four months with her, how differently I would have behaved!

Brenner dealt quickly with the routine bequests to servants and family friends. No surprises there. Delilah tried to pay attention to the long-winded disposition of Grendam's personal collections of art, jewelry, crystal, and such. Travis got most of the art, Nick most of the books, Delilah herself most of the furniture and china, particularly the tea paraphernalia. Grendam had also remembered to leave her a number of small items she'd always liked as a child—an ivory elephant from India, a blown-glass vase of exceptional beauty that she had nearly broken as a child, a set of silver teaspoons dating from colonial times.

Brenner's voice droned on and on. Each of Grendam's descendants—Jonathan, Nick, Travis, Kelsey, and herself—were left two million dollars in addition to what they had already received from the Templeton Trust. My God, she must have been very rich, Delilah thought when she heard this. But she didn't really come to attention until Brenner began to read the final section of the document:

"As is customary and traditional in the Templeton family, one hundred percent of the voting shares in the Templeton Tea corporation are to pass to my successor, who will assume my duties and responsibilities as the Director of the corporation and Chairman of the Board of Templeton Tea." The attorney paused momentarily for a glance around the room. What wonderful WASP control, Delilah thought. He must know what was in the will, but he didn't reveal even a hint of that knowledge.

"I hereby appoint to this role my granddaughter Delilah Templeton Scofield, to whom I leave my entire holding of common stock in Templeton Tea and all its subsidiaries. Because I wish my granddaughter to have every advantage in her new position, I leave her an additional legacy of five million dollars for her to invest as she sees fit for the good of the company. To Delilah Templeton Scofield I also leave my residence known as the China Tea House Tavern and all the furnishings therein for her to hold during her lifetime under the terms of the Templeton Trust."

Delilah felt dizzy; for the first time in her life she thought she might faint. Nick said something under his breath, and Travis leapt to his feet. It was plain from the look of distaste on Brenner's face that he expected that most dramatic of confrontations—the angry relative's disbelieving challenge to the will. But Travis made a visible effort to control himself. He folded his arms across his chest and said, calmly enough:

"What is the date of this will?"

"It was revised in July of this year," Brenner replied.

"That was only a few weeks after Delilah returned from California," Travis said tightly. "Which can only mean that our grandmother's proposition about a one-year trial period had no substance to it at all. She had already made up her mind to bequeath the stock to Delilah."

"I'm not sure to what you are referring," Brenner said. "I know of no one-year trial period. If you will kindly resume your seat, Mr. Templeton, I have not completed my reading of Mrs. Templeton's instructions."

"I've heard enough." Travis shot a blistering look at Delilah as he strode out of the room.

Delilah's only reaction was to reach out and take Nick's hand.

She cried that night, in the privacy of her bedroom, in the shelter of her lover's arms. She was as astonished by the will as she was by the fact that Grendam had made these changes so soon after her return, before she'd seen comprehensive results of her granddaughter's efforts on behalf of the company. Grendam had obviously had more faith in her than she had ever let on.

She and Nick had talked about it all afternoon. Nick was not as surprised as Delilah. "I kept telling you how much she loved you, how much she respected your talents and abilities. Frankly, I think she's known for a long time that Travis couldn't cut it."

"Travis looked at me as if he'd like to strangle me."

"Travis has plenty of reason to be upset. Two million dollars won't go far with him."

"I'm worried, Nick. What's going to happen? Will Travis quit his job? Can I fire him? If we cast him out, what's he going to do with the rest of his life?"

"Screw him," Nick said, less sympathetically than usual. "I don't know and I don't care."

Delilah rolled over in bed, feeling hollow and numb. The full impact of this hasn't hit me yet. She touched Nick's back, felt the tension that was still twisting him in knots. Nick had taken Grendam's death very hard. Trying to be strong for Kelsey had exacted a toll on him, too. The little girl had never encountered death before, and despite the reassurance she'd received from

Nick and Jan, her mother, Kelsey had been distraught. Jan had taken her back to Chicago right after the funeral, and Nick had already called them several times, to make sure she was okay.

We're the adults now, she said to herself. Except for Jonathan, all our parents, all our grandparents, are gone. We're the front line now, the ones who stand between the younger generation and death.

In her case, though, there was no younger generation. Pressed to Nick's body, Delilah felt that familiar flash of heat. Not even grief kills the sex drive, she thought. Perhaps in some cases it makes it stronger, more fervent, more desperate. Replace me, whispered her body. Your task is to leave something of yourself behind.

"Do you want to make love?" Without contraception, she was thinking. I'll be thirty-nine on my next birthday. I have no child.

"I'm afraid I'll hurt you," said Nick.

"Hurt me?" she repeated, incredulous.

"I'm kind of pent up. If I let go, things'll explode."

She leaned up so her hair brushed his shoulders. "We could put on your special boxing gloves." She trailed her hand from his throat to his pelvis. "Or we could try this and see if it works just as well."

In less than a second he was on her. Not a word was spoken as his mouth began to assault hers.

Sex between them could be violent, she learned that night. But it was a healing violence, and under its passionate façade love was there like a guardian, keeping them both safe. They battled for dominance, and Nick, being stronger, got her down on her back beneath him, her body writhing between his thighs. "We're going to make it last," he told her after brushing her bare skin with hands that teased rather than gentled, aroused rather than satisfied. "We're going to see how many times we can go to the edge without falling over. You'll need me inside you more than you need your next breath."

"No way," she whispered, but she found his threat exciting. He had pinned her arms to the pillows on either side of her head. His long fingers were clamped around her wrists. She'd read somewhere that the wrists and ankles are highly erogenous, which is why so many people find it sexy to be tied up by a trustworthy lover. No one's ever done that to me. I never thought I'd want anyone to do that to me. But with Nick, I want everything, everything.

When he kissed and caressed her and loved her with his mouth, she closed her eyes, clawing the sheets, trying not to reveal how close to the edge she was. She was there, almost there. A little more, just a little . . .

He raised his head. She kicked at him, furious. He fell on her and she fought him like a wildcat, so crazy with lust she didn't care if she hurt him, nor would she feel it if he hurt her. They rolled over and over. He got her down on her belly and slapped her bottom several times with the flat of his hand. She felt nothing but pleasure . . . strong muscular ripples that were too erratic to be orgasms but felt almost as good.

He turned her over and blew on her breasts, nipped them. In return she flexed her long fingernails against his shoulders, delighting in the gasps she wrung from him.

Pushing up on his forearms, he poised himself over her, his green eyes glittering, his mouth snarling as if in agony. She spread her legs wide. "Do it, Nick. Do it now."

He bowed his hips and thrust. She cried out and wrapped her arms around his waist. His expression suddenly gentled. "God, I love you, Delilah."

She couldn't answer. She was coming already, and it was like nothing she had ever known before. Her soul seemed to shoot up out of her body and merge with something bright and luminous that she recognized as the essence of Nick. She knew from the tensing of his body that he was climaxing too. They were together in another place, another realm of existence. She laughed with the wild joy of it and cried at its beauty.

Later she told him something she'd never trusted anybody else with: the true story of how Max had died. She explained his determination, her reluctance, his desperation, her agonizing doubts. "I argued for as long as I could, but slowly I came to believe he was right. It was my final gift to him. But some people might regard me as a murderer, Nick."

"Well, I'm not one of them," he assured her.

"I've never regretted doing it. I thought I might be haunted afterward, stricken with guilt for breaking one of God's laws. But that hasn't happened. When I saw his face—afterward—when I saw how serene he looked, all that pain and torment gone, I knew I hadn't been wrong. I loved him so much." Her voice broke. "Why do I keep losing the people I love?"

Nick didn't trust himself to speak. His eyes were wet.

"I'm sorry if I'm hurting you," she said. "Are you jealous? I loved Max, but I love you, too."

He shook his head. "I'm not jealous. There's never any limit to love. You've got plenty for both of us." He wrapped a long lock of her hair around his wrists. "I share your pain. And I have a fierce determination to protect you, to make sure you never go through anything like that again."

She leaned up over him. "No one can guarantee that. When Max and I got married, he promised he'd never leave me. When we found out he was dying, I felt so betrayed. You'd think I'd be unwilling to risk everything again after that, wouldn't you? In fact, you accused me of that very thing once, remember? The night I tried to seduce you on your living room rug."

He nodded. "Maybe I was wrong."

"It's odd, but I'm *not* afraid to risk myself again. Just the opposite, in fact. Once, before he got sick, Max said something like this: death's always there, always a possibility. The only way to cope with that is to celebrate life." She put her lips to his and kissed him. "Will you celebrate with me?"

"Yes," he whispered. "Oh yes."

As she was relaxing for sleep, the reality of what had happened that day finally penetrated. She sat up in bed and said, "My God, Nick. I'm the Director of Templeton Tea."

PART SEVEN

There's a divinity that shapes our ends,
Rough-hew them how we will.

—*William Shakespeare*

Boston, 1986

42

"The building is old, but when it was built in the early thirties, it was considered to be the latest thing in terms of ease and convenience," Delilah said on camera as she led Stephen Lord and his TV crew through the corridors of the blending and packaging plant in East Boston. She explained the gravity system that deposited tea crates at the top-floor entrance that crested the hill into which the plant was built. From there the processed tea gradually moved down, floor by floor, until, packaged and ready for sale, it reached the trucking dock at the ground-floor entrance. "It's all quite ingenious, you see."

"Whose idea was this?" asked Stephen.

"I'm not certain, but it was my grandmother who supervised the construction of this plant."

Two months had passed since Minerva Templeton's death. As part of her effort to increase publicity, Delilah had agreed to do an hour program for "Boston Alive" on the intricacies of the tea business. Her appearance in July had prompted a lot of mail, so the producer of "Boston Alive" had settled upon an on-the-scene documentary about tea importing. Although it was local TV, Delilah knew that if the program was interesting, one of the networks might be in touch for something similar.

Delilah led the crew into the cavernous receiving room, where row upon row of tea crates were stacked to the ceiling. "There are several occasions during the whole process of buying and importing tea when professional examiners—sometimes buying agents, sometimes federal inspectors—must draw samples and test the tea. I'm going to show you how they do it."

She took a drill from a case and attached a special two-pronged bit to the end. Her task was to bore a small, round hole through which she could extract some of the tea with a small wire rake, being careful not to break any of the delicate leaves in the process. Delilah had only practiced this once before, but she'd had no problem. Now, however, perhaps because her hands were a bit sweaty from the hot TV lights, the drill slipped just as it completed boring the hole. It jarred forward into the crate, and a cloud of tea leaves and dust was thrown back into her face.

The cameras captured it all—the slip of the drill, the rain of brown upon her face, neck, and ivory silk blouse. For an instant Delilah was mortified, then, catching the expression of pained hilarity on Stephen Lord's face, she broke up.

"Stop the tape!" the producer shouted as the entire crew began to howl.

"Thank God that wasn't live," she said as the crew was finishing up for the day. They would be back tomorrow to try the shot again. "I'll practice until I get it right. I'll bore holes in a couple of dozen crates if necessary."

"I kind of like the version we have," said Stephen.

"My dear Steve, this is a serious program, not a farce! Still," she added wryly, "I guess I'd better wear a copper-colored blouse tomorrow, just in case."

As soon as the TV people had packed up and gone, Delilah went into her office—Travis's old office. There in relative privacy she attacked with her drill the half dozen crates that were stacked there. The crates had just come in yesterday, and Delilah wasn't quite sure what they were doing in her office. Travis was the consignee, but he hadn't been in to work since the reading of the will.

It was all a question of controlling the drill, she decided as she practiced. You had to press hard to get through the thick wood on the sides of the crates, but as soon as you felt the bit give, you had to let up.

She bored into four crates with increasing finesse, stoppering the resulting holes with bungs specially designed for the purpose. Sure she'd mastered the art of crate boring, she got a little cocky, and on the fifth crate the drill slipped again. This time it was not tea that came flying back into her face, but a fine white powder.

"It's Mr. Templeton," the night watchman on the ground floor told Delilah on the plant intercom. "You asked me to let you know when he arrived. He's on his way up."

"Thank you, Mac."

Delilah's hands were shaking and her clothes were none too clean. It was eight o'clock at night, and she'd been going through crate after crate of tea in the receiving room trying to see how many of them contained illegal drugs.

So far she'd found it in all six crates that had been stacked in Travis's old office, but in none of the others. She'd only searched a small percentage of the crates—there must be hundreds of them in here.

She was furious. Things had been difficult enough at the company since her grandmother had died. Having concentrated on marketing, Delilah had known very little about the rest of Templeton Tea's operations, and Travis's leaving her in the lurch had meant she'd been thrown unprepared into the myriad problems of distribution, blending, and importing. Were it not for her experience at Merlin's, she might have been in serious trouble; as it was, she'd been working eighteen-hour days and going home every night with knots in her stomach. After two months of intense stress, she was just beginning to see some daylight. Now this had happened.

Drugs. Travis was responsible; she was sure of it. He, personally, had purchased this tea in Rio de Janeiro and shipped it to himself.

Ever since Grendam had died, Delilah had been feeling guilty about Travis. She'd told Nick several times that Grendam's will hadn't been fair to Travis. That he deserved something for having worked so many years for Templeton Tea. That maybe they ought to rethink the policy of keeping the stock together in one chunk. Why not put their heads together and carve out a way for them to run the company together?

Nick told her she was crazy. It was good riddance to Travis as far as he was concerned.

"You're so tolerant of everybody else, but so unforgiving of your brother," Delilah protested.

"I think he's dangerous."

"Oh come on, Nick—"

"I'm not kidding. He's lost everything, Delilah. And he's capable of rare, but vicious, attacks of rage. If you want to do something for him, fine. But let's wait a few months until some of this blows over."

She agreed. This matter, however, wouldn't wait.

She heard the grinding of the elevator, followed by the familiar sound of his footsteps in the hall. She sat very still behind the desk, her hands clenched in her lap as he opened the office door and entered.

"Here I am, responsive to your urgent request. What do you want, Delilah?"

She was accustomed to seeing him in a chalk-striped suit and a silk tie, his face tan and handsome, his gold hair fashionably trimmed; so it was a shock to see how disheveled he was. He hadn't shaved today and his cheeks were rough with gold stubble —the "in" look among certain tough-guy television personalities, but not at all what one expected with Travis. His hair had gone weeks without a cut. He was wearing jeans and a turtleneck jersey that emphasized the width of his shoulders. And instead of his usual smile, his expression was grim.

Delilah didn't speak. She opened her drawer, removed the plastic package, and tossed it down on the desk between them. A small cloud of white dust escaped from the hole she had inadvertently bored.

Travis looked from her face to the package and back. *Now* he smiled, and in a manner that chilled her. "You've been busy, I see."

Delilah pulled the other five packages out and piled them on top of the first. "I'd like to know how much more of this stuff there is. If I searched every crate, I'd be here all week."

"That's it," he said calmly. "You found the entire stash. May I ask how? A psychic hunch from your friend Dory, perhaps?"

Dory had returned to L.A. at the end of the summer. Nick had attended several channeling sessions with Ra-ton, who had become legendary at the tea company by the time Dory had finished up her work and left Boston. The entity—if such he was—had passed on no specific warning about cocaine smuggling, but he had advised Delilah to watch out for Travis.

"I had a TV crew over here this morning," Delilah said. "Fortunately it wasn't until after they'd gone that I bored into the cocaine."

Travis said nothing. She almost wished he would. She wished he would come up with a smooth statement of some sort that would explain away this whole thing.

"I've checked the purchasing records. You bought this tea in Brazil and must have arranged somehow for the drug to be packed inside the crates. Now I understand one of your reasons for wanting to keep control of the company. You've been using your position to cover drug smuggling."

"Have you notified the police?" he asked, not sounding as if he particularly cared.

"I thought I'd give you a chance to explain yourself first. I had hoped there would be *some* sort of explanation."

He laughed harshly. "Like what? That I knew nothing about it? That someone else must be responsible? That the stuff in those packets is actually something innocuous, like sugar or powdered milk?"

"This stuff kills people, Travis! My God, it reminds me of the way the Templetons got rich on the Chinese opium trade. We thought it was reprehensible; we condemned our ancestors for that!"

His smile twisted. "You condemned them. I seem to remember thinking the opium trade had certain practical applications."

I never knew him, Delilah thought. I never knew him, even then.

"However, before you explode in moral indignation," he went on, "let me make it clear that this stuff doesn't end up on the streets. It's strictly a private supply for myself and my friends."

"And if Customs discovered it? Or the Department of Agriculture inspectors? Don't you care about what that would do to Templeton Tea? Or to you personally, for that matter? I can't believe you took such a risk."

Travis took a short walk across the office and back. He stopped in front of the desk and leaned over it. "Are you going to turn me in?"

"Believe me, the idea has crossed my mind." She rose, feeling more confident on her feet. "If I call in the feds, there'll be an investigation, alarms set up with Customs, bad press—the whole mess. I don't want that, but I'm willing to risk it, Travis. There will be a scandal, yes, but it won't last forever. When it blows over I'll get my PR people working on another advertising campaign that will erase the damage. Who knows, the publicity might even boost sales. As they say, there's no such thing as bad PR. Of course, none of this will matter to you. You'll be in prison."

A muscle spasmed in his jaw. "And the alternative?"

"You resign immediately from your job and from your position on the board of directors. You renounce all further claim to the company. I don't trust you, Travis, and I realize now that Grendam didn't either. You've got twenty-four hours to think it over. If you don't comply, I'll turn you over to the authorities. It's as simple as that."

"Is it?" He rounded her desk now, grabbed her upper arms, and pulled her to her feet. For an instant Travis saw a flash of fear in her eyes, which inspired in him a brief, guilty pleasure.

He'd known there was a possibility of discovery. The crates here in her office had contained the last of the stuff he'd picked up in Rio. It should have arrived weeks ago, but there had been a screw-up in the shipping arrangements.

Bad luck. He'd had a lot of that lately. No longer could he afford to rely on luck.

"Let go of me."

"There's something I want you to understand." He loosened his grip but didn't release her. "For the sake of what was once between us, I want you to listen to me."

Her hard expression—it was so like Gran's, he noticed for the first time—loosened just a little. "Okay. Talk."

"I know I'm not the man I could have been. I know that, Delilah. Something was destroyed in me that day our grandmother told me we were brother and sister. It was our wedding day; do you remember?" He shook her slightly. "Do you remember, damn you?"

"Of course I remember."

"When you told me you were pregnant I thought about ditching you. Leaving and never looking back. The thought of all that responsibility scared me. I loved you but I wanted to run."

"We were young, Travis; I'm not blaming you anymore for—"

"The idea was tempting, but I resisted it. I decided to draw the line. To make a stand. I decided to give myself over to love." Travis hadn't intended to go into this, but it was bursting out of him. Being alone with her, touching her, inhaling her heady scent was doing weird things to his body, his brain.

"And look what happened," he continued. "That decision was taken away from me. I couldn't give myself over to love, because suddenly love was wrong, a sin, a biological crime. Everything was going to be so fine between us, so perfect. We cared about each other; we had goals, dreams, ideals. We had everything we would ever need, until Minerva Templeton destroyed it all."

Delilah was shaking her head, and the sight of her thick black hair brushing her shoulders made his stomach clench. "It was destroyed before it was ever born," she said. "Your parents, my father, they destroyed it. We never had a chance."

"They're dead. Everyone we know thinks we're cousins. There's no legal reason why we shouldn't marry. Delilah, I still love you." He slid his hands up her arms and under that thick fall of her hair. It felt silky, luxurious. He wanted to press his face in it. He wanted to strip away her clothing and make love to her again.

She tried to squirm away, but he held her fast. "I still want you, and I know you feel the same." He dropped kisses along her jawline, the line of her hair. All the time she fought him, but he was stronger. He didn't even notice that his fingers were leaving marks. "It's you and me, Delilah. Forever and ever and ever. Remember the apple tree? Our secret place? I love you. Doesn't that count for anything anymore?"

"Travis, you're my *brother.* And besides, I'm in love with Nick." She said it gently . . . so gently he wanted to scream. "What I felt for you was the love of a girl, a girl dazzled by a romantic ideal that has no reality in fact. It's over, Travis. It's been over for years."

"No."

"Yes," she insisted. "You've got to give up this obsession. I love Nick and I'm going to marry him."

Travis put her back from him. His desire was twisting inside him like a snake. Coiling and changing, shedding a skin of need and replacing it with a patina of fury.

"We want children," she went on. "I've always longed to have a baby. Nick and I are going to be married in a few weeks. Travis, I'm sorry."

I'm sorry too, he thought. Because I can't let you marry him. I can't let you produce an heir who will supersede me. I can't let you take my job away, or turn me in to the feds. *I'm* sorry, Delilah. You just crossed the line.

He gave her one more chance. He kissed her, putting everything he had into it. And she shoved him away, the distaste plain on her face.

The wheel of fortune he'd been riding for years took one last agonizing twist, and falling away beneath him, he could see the ground.

Ten-thirty P.M, Halloween night. Nick was hard at work in the second-floor library of the China Tea House Tavern, where he and Delilah had been living since shortly after their grandmother's death. He was writing the latest Drake novel, which he'd neglected while working on the Helen Templeton biography. The Drake book was due at his publisher's in less than a month. It was going okay now . . . he would probably make his deadline, but only with a lot of hard work.

Delilah poked her head in the doorway. She smiled at the huge jack-o'-lantern burning in the window that overlooked the street; they'd had lots of messy fun earlier in the evening carving it. Not many kids had come to the door tonight, though, and those who had had been carefully supervised by their parents. The days of carefree trick-or-treating in the city were over.

"Still at it, huh? D'you mind if I go to bed?"

"Sure, love; I know you've had a rough day."

Delilah came over to the desk and kissed the top of his head. "Any chance of wrapping it up soon for the night?"

And coming to bed to love me? was the unspoken part of her question. Christ, he wanted to. But the story was really moving tonight, and he hated to interrupt the flow, even for the sake of life's greatest pleasure. "I'd better keep at it until I get to the end of this chapter."

"Okay." She put her mouth to his and kissed him. "Night." She felt so good his groin pulsed, and Drake's problems began to fade.

"The creative process is *so* easily disrupted," she said, clucking softly. "How are you ever going to write books if you're so horny all the time?"

"If you really wanted to help the creative process, you'd crawl under the desk, unzip my jeans, and do delicious things to me while I kept right on working."

Her eyebrows rose extravagantly. "Listen to you. Getting spoiled, huh?"

He sighed. "Why can't I be more like my hero? When Drake says, 'On your knees, woman,' the lady scrambles to obey."

Delilah gave him a slow smile. "Maybe I'll try to stay awake until your chapter's done." With that she blew him a kiss and sailed out of the room.

Nick returned to work, but his concentration was shot.

Eleven-thirty P.M. In the bedroom in the China Tea House Tavern where Minerva Templeton had swallowed forty Nembutal, Delilah was tossing in bed. She'd learned already that living with a writer who was facing a deadline had certain disadvantages. "I'll be there as soon as I finish this chapter" usually meant, "See you in the morning."

It must have been three whole days since they'd last made love. She laughed at herself, remembering a time when she would have thought nothing of going three weeks, three months, three years . . . but now, dammit, she was obsessed.

Tired though she was, she found it difficult to sleep without Nick beside her. The nights were long and demoralizing, for her sleep was often broken. Sometimes she wondered if this had something to do with the room. It was here that Grendam had supposedly received her visitations from the "spirits."

When they'd first moved in, Nick had lain awake expectantly. When she'd teased him about it, he'd admitted that if Helen Templeton was bleeding through from the eighteenth century, he hoped to see some evidence of it. "Think of the coup it would be for me as a biographer if my subject told me a little about her life."

But it wasn't the threat of ghostly visitors that was keeping Delilah awake tonight. She rolled over again and punched the pillow, but that did nothing to alleviate the ache in her lower body. She should have done it, gone down on her knees the way he'd wanted . . . It wouldn't have been one-sided; Nick never allowed a lovemaking session to come to an end without making certain she was satisfied.

Images of the last interlude they'd shared in the library came back to her. They'd made love on the oriental rug, then on the rocking chair in the corner, then on a low, square ottoman, where he'd pulled her down on his lap and made her ride him. She'd come like that, and then again when he'd turned her over so her upper body was resting on the ottoman, her head between her arms, her knees on the rug spread wide and her bottom there for him, and she was excited, but also a little scared.

Have you tried—

No, never.

I want to possess you utterly.

Yes. Do it. But—

I'll stop if it hurts. Tell me.

It's okay, it's—oh.

Christ.

Don't stop, keep it going, touch me in front . . . like that, yes, yes, yes.

Now she thought, lying alone in bed, I had a happy, fulfilling marriage, but sex has never been like this for me. Never an addiction, never a constant ache. And he was so good at it. Dory had proved right—Nick was the most imaginative, most exciting lover Delilah had ever known. He had no inhibitions; he'd do anything. He'd act any part, play any role. She'd told him once about her favorite pirate fantasy, and he'd surprised her two nights later by coming home in high leather boots and a blousy shirt. He dragged her into the bedroom, ripped off her clothes, and proceeded to "ravish" her into a frenzy.

God! She changed position again, wide awake now. Think of something else, she ordered herself. Think of Travis and the discovery you made last week in the packaging plant. He had proffered his resignation as she'd stipulated, but there had been something in his eyes, something that had made her wonder if Nick was right about his being dangerous. If he could smuggle drugs, who could tell what else he might be capable of?

Travis had told her he was going to spend some time in Europe, trying to decide what he wanted to do for the rest of his life. He'd sounded so hearty about it that Delilah's suspicions had been further aroused. His manner was that of a man who is confident of having the last laugh.

It had worked—remembering the conflict with Travis had driven all thoughts of lovemaking from her mind. Still vaguely troubled, she closed her eyes and fell asleep.

Midnight. Travis drove his rented car slowly past the China Tea House Tavern, noting that the lights in the master bedroom were out. *Put out the light, and then put out the light.* Othello's thoughts about Desdemona just before killing her.

He'd gone over his plan again and again. It had first insinuated itself into his mind on leaving the lawyer's office after the reading of the will. He'd rejected it immediately, of course. But when he'd examined the terms of the will more closely a few days later, the idea had come slinking back, and gradually—more and more during the last several weeks—he'd indulged his fantasy.

It had begun as a provocative what-if. What if Delilah—this woman he could never have, this woman who obsessed him, this woman who had stolen his heritage—what if she were dead? What if that lush red mouth, those sexy legs, that black mantle of bouncing hair were no longer around to taunt him? As long as she was alive he would never be free of her. If she were gone, maybe at last he would find peace.

But peace of mind wasn't his only incentive. By the terms of Minerva Templeton's will, the tea company would pass to Delilah's children. If she died childless, it would revert to him.

It was a long leap, he knew, from fantasy to reality, thought to action. But his plan had grown more practical, more coherent, every day. Even so, he'd never thought he would actually go ahead with it until last week when Delilah had told him she was going to marry Nick.

He'd known, of course, that they were sleeping together. He'd seen the intimate glances, the satisfied looks. But he'd pushed the knowledge away. If it had been some other man, he could have tolerated it, perhaps, but not Nick, never Nick.

He was going to do them both.

Travis parked the car several blocks from the Tavern. He had dressed nondescriptly in jeans, a dark blue nylon jacket, and running shoes. Before getting out of the car, he transferred the gun—stolen from his brother's collection—from the glove compartment to the pocket of his jacket. It was already loaded. He put some extra shells in one pocket of his jeans and a pair of police handcuffs—also lifted from Nick's weird collection—into the other pocket.

He was ready. Here I come.

Twelve-fifteen A.M. Nick was finally nearing the end of the chapter; his eyes were starting to cross as he stared at the amber letters on the screen. He heard a footstep behind him and said, "What's the matter, can't you sleep? If you try me again, I think I'm seduceable now."

Instead of Delilah's lips against his scalp, he felt the cylindrical coldness of a gun.

That night in front of Delilah's apartment building Nick had been prepared for a fight. This time he wasn't. When Travis slugged him with the pistol butt, he crumpled. Next thing he knew, he'd been dragged six feet away from his desk to the sliding wooden ladder that moved along a metal track in the floor. It was there to make the high bookshelves in the library accessible. Travis jerked him to his feet, slammed him against the ladder, and stretched his limp arms over his head.

Only half conscious, his head throbbing where he'd been struck, Nick tried to struggle as Travis tightened something around his right wrist, under the top rung of the ladder, and around the other wrist. Handcuffs. "Keep still," said his brother as Nick writhed. To make his point even clearer, he hit Nick again, this time with his fist.

Travis drew the draperies in the library after removing the still-burning jack-o'-lantern from the window. On some whim that convinced Nick his brother was really over the edge, Travis brought the pumpkin over and perched it on the bookshelf above Nick's head, then stood back as if to admire the sight of his brother handcuffed to a ladder beneath a glowing, grimacing death-head.

"Why are you doing this?" Nick was aware that his voice sounded frantic . . . that he was sweating profusely . . . that Travis must be able to tell he was afraid. Delilah, Delilah. Where was she? Had Travis come to rape her while he hung here, helpless to prevent it? Or . . . No, he thought. Don't even think of the other possibilities.

"According to the will," said Travis, "if she dies without issue, I get control of Templeton Tea."

Oh Jesus. "You can't be serious."

"Oh, but I am. She's going to die," Travis said flatly.

Nick's brain began screaming telepathic warnings. Wake up, Delilah! Call the cops! Run! Aloud he said, "Murderers don't get to claim their inheritance. It's not only in mystery novels that the person with the most to gain is the first person the police suspect."

"I'll never get away with it, in other words? Well, it's possible, of course, that I won't. That's the risk I'm taking. But I'll have an alibi—a lady who will testify I spent the entire night in her bed. And the real beauty of my plan is that I'm not the number one suspect. You are."

"What the hell do you—"

"My dear bestselling mystery writer—figure it out. All that interesting stuff you told me about the family curse. The tragedies that have taken place right here in this house. The psychic who predicted a repetition. Everyone knows that Charles Templeton committed murder here in the early eighteenth century. But it was your cleverness, Nick, that solved the mystery of why he did it. We know now that the wife he murdered was really his sister.

"You're going to repeat the crime, Nick. You're going to kill your lover for the same reason. You've just found out, it seems, that Delilah is your sister. You can't live with that knowledge any more than Charles Templeton could."

Nick knew he wasn't thinking clearly. His head hurt. So did his arms, which Travis had stretched painfully. He tried to concentrate, but the point eluded him. He couldn't figure out why anybody would think he was Delilah's brother when it was Travis who suffered that distinction.

Travis removed a yellowing sheet from one of his pockets.

"This is the letter given to me by Gran in 1970. It's our mother's confession of her affair with David Scofield and her subsequent pregnancy. It's significant for two reasons: it gives no dates, and it's addressed to 'To My Son.' The unfortunate son's name is never specified. If you found this letter among Minerva Templeton's private papers—which is where it was for years before she gave it to me—you would very likely conclude that it was written to you, Nick. I'm blond with blue eyes. You're dark like David Scofield. Your eyes are green, like Delilah's. You look alike—you could easily be brother and sister."

"That's ridiculous!"

Travis ignored him. "The biggest advantage to well-kept secrets is that so few people know the truth. Except for our father—your father, I should say—all the principals in this matter are dead, and as we all know, Jonathan is difficult to reach. Eventually he'll come home and explain the facts, I suppose, and everyone will shake their heads over your tragic mistake."

Jesus Christ, thought Nick. He couldn't see any holes in Travis's plan. Maybe you're going to find out a lot sooner than you expected whether or not there is an afterlife.

"I'm probably the last person who would ever commit murder," he tried. "I'm just not the type."

"On the contrary, you're the perfect type. You write scenes of appalling violence in your books. You collect guns and belong to a shooting club. You've been obsessed recently with the very incident in our family history that this act will imitate. And best of all, you've got a record of depression that has required psychiatric treatment. The police will buy it, all right.

"The gun and ammunition are from your collection, Nick. I'm going to shoot Delilah first, then you. I'm going to be real careful about the angle of the shot so no one can say it was impossible for you to have shot yourself in that precise manner. Then I'm going to leave the gun in your hand.

"I'll also leave our mother's letter, which will serve as the explanation for your crime. You see, it's going to be very clear-cut. Another tragedy in a family that's known for violence and suicide. I doubt if Boston's finest will even consider any other suspects."

He glanced at his watch. "I think I've answered enough questions. Delilah ought to be sound asleep by now. I'm going to kill her, then come back for you."

Nick's creative brain was churning, trying to think of a way out of this. But all he seemed to be able to come up with was, "Travis, for God's sake. You can't *do* this. I'm your brother. You love Delilah. I can't believe you would—"

Something flashed in Travis's face. "Yeah, I love her, all right; she's a poison I drank years ago that's still burning in my blood." He came close, his face contorted. "And she's mine, runt. She's going to know it, one last time."

He turned and left the room, gun in hand.

43

Twelve-thirty A.M. Delilah was dreaming. Grendam was leaning over her bed, shaking her, saying, "I should have told you, I should have warned you, you mustn't stay in this house." Grendam . . . or was it the auburn-haired shadow she'd seen in her dreams before?

She woke to the sensation of a hand touching her face. Not Nick's hand; he didn't touch her like that. So fleeting. So cold.

She opened her eyes. The room was dark, but enough light was coming in from the hall for her to be able to see. There *was* a hand. And in the hand there was a gun.

"Don't move," said Travis. "Don't make a sound."

She threw a glance at Nick's side of the bed, but he wasn't there. She was clad only in a flimsy nightgown that sleep had dragged up and twisted around her hips.

"What are you—"

"I said, shut up." He sat down on the bed beside her and crossed her breasts with an iron arm as she tried to sit up. Rape, she thought at once. They say it's very common. They say it's often someone you know. A former lover, perhaps, was the most likely assailant of all.

"Where's Nick?" she asked.

"He's down the hall in the library, tied up."

"Tied up?" She tried to tell herself that this was Travis, Travis, and whatever he was doing here, he couldn't really mean her any harm . . . could he? But Nick . . . he hated Nick. He'd always hated Nick, even when they were children.

"If you've hurt him . . ." Her voice trailed off when she saw him smile. She thought, he's going to shoot me. She tried to dismiss the idea. It was absurd. "Why do you have that gun?"

He didn't answer. But she knew, she knew. This is the city, she thought. There are other people less than a hundred yards away. And so she opened her mouth to scream.

Travis couldn't allow that. He slapped her, backhanded her across the face, hard. Her head snapped back and cracked against the wooden bedpost, and for a few moments she was dazed. She let out a gasp as he straddled her body and clamped his palm over her mouth. She struggled until he pinched her nostrils shut. Her eyes went wide and he saw fear come into them.

"It's not a pleasant death, asphyxiation. I'd planned to kill you more humanely. Gently, even. A gunshot is instantaneous, Delilah. You'll feel no pain."

She went limp and he could feel her body lightly trembling. He took his fingers away from her nose, and her body arched up under his as she sucked in air. Somewhere deep inside he felt sick, disgusted. *You shit, you shit, you shit.*

He had a fleeting memory of being given a text to read in German class in college, Kafka's *The Metamorphosis.* He had struggled over his translation of the first line of the story, which states that Gregor Samsa awoke one morning to find that he had turned into a large insect. Travis had checked and rechecked the glossary, sure he had the wrong translation. How could a man turn into a bug?

Eventually understanding had come, both of the phrase and of what Kafka was doing. He'd developed a passion for Kafka. *The Hunger Artist* had given him a perverse understanding of his mother. But the story that had stayed in his memory the longest was *The Harrow,* that brutal account of an execution in which the condemned man's unknown crime is carved deeper and deeper into his body by a horrific machine until he finally comprehends his sin, and dies.

I should have killed myself when our grandmother told me my crime. I should have put out my eyes. If I were dead, I couldn't hurt her. If I were blind, I couldn't look upon her body with this fever of desire.

Aloud he said, "No screaming."

She nodded. He took his palm away from her mouth. After a moment he forced himself to climb off the bed, to back away from her. He ordered himself to remember hair and fiber tests, sperm counts, blood typing, and the rest of the arsenal the forensics guys had at their fingertips. It would be stupid to screw up a good plan because he couldn't keep his hands off her.

Delilah was fighting to control herself. It seemed she was really going to die. She couldn't believe it . . . this wasn't some hoodlum, some maniac . . . it was Travis, *Travis.*

"Why?" she managed.

So he told her what he had already told Nick. And while he explained she kept thinking, he sounds so cold, so calm, so sure of what he's going to do. Travis, my old lover, my half brother. *Cain.*

She argued as Nick had done, and she could see he was impatient. She wondered why he was bothering to say anything at all. Did he want her to think him clever? Did he need to justify himself in his own eyes? Or did he simply wish to put off the moment when he must take his homicidal fantasy and make it real?

While he answered her objections, she was casting about for a plan. A way to distract him. To disarm him. To seduce him if nothing else would work.

"Are you going to rape me?" she asked, not because she feared it, but because she knew her body still held power over his. If she could get him to put down the gun . . .

"No," he said. But he leaned over and caressed the side of her face. Delilah shuddered. He touched one of her breasts through the nightgown. Looking at his hands, she saw what she'd been too scared to notice when he'd clapped his palm over her mouth: he was wearing thin surgical gloves. Which could only mean that he intended to go through with it after all.

She was going to die. She was staring down the barrel of a loaded gun. She was looking into eternity, and she wasn't ready to go. She had held everything she'd ever wanted in the palm of her hand—her man, her heritage, perhaps even her longed-for child, but in one split second it would all cease to exist. Life is so fragile. All we strive for, all we think we possess . . . just the faintest squeeze of a trigger and it's gone.

He lowered his head and kissed her mouth. All it was was a fleeting brush of his lips, oddly pleasant. Then he backed away from the bed and raised his arm. He aimed carefully at her head. "I'm a good shot. You won't feel anything. I'm sorry, Delilah."

Down the hall in the library Nick was frantically trying to free himself. He expected with each second to hear the gunshot that would mean Delilah was dead. If that happened, he wouldn't fight anymore. He'd go passively when Travis returned for him. Without Delilah he didn't want to live.

He thought miserably of Kelsey. But his daughter would make it without him—for all you could say that was uncomplimentary about Janet, she took good care of their daughter, and Kelsey would be okay.

Tears were coming now, for his lover, for his daughter, for the children he and Delilah would never have.

You sniveling asshole. Is that the best you can do—cry? There's Drake, trapped in one of his usual fuck-ups, the girl he's been screwing about to be blown away, himself about to be tortured for his old CIA information, and what does good old Drake do? He bursts into tears. That'll go down real well with your agent, your editor, your fans. You might even get a nod from the reviewers this time for verisimilitude.

Drake would find a clever way to save the day. He'd Houdini himself out of his bonds, rush to the bedroom, rescue the girl, and cool the bad guy. Drake got himself out of worse trouble than this at least once in every book, and sometimes his solutions were pretty damn ingenious.

Drake didn't get himself out. *You* got him out. Your cleverness. Your ingenuity. You've got a good brain in there. *Use* it.

Nick worked his wrists against the handcuffs, but all that did was make them tighter. He twisted his head to look at the ladder to which he was fastened. It was made of solid oak, and each of the rungs was more than an inch thick.

The ladder was against the bookshelves. If he kicked back with his leg, he could knock free some of the books from the bottom shelf. So what? On his left was his wastebasket, filled with old manuscript pages. It was overflowing, as usual, and there were balled-up pieces of paper running in a ragged line from his wastebasket to his desk. The new Drake manuscript was there along with the Helen Templeton manuscript. His eyes searched among the stuff, seeking, he didn't know what—a knife, a hammer, a chisel, a buzz saw, a stick of dynamite . . . Jesus! There was nothing that would help him, nothing.

He looked in the other direction. The window where he'd set the jack-o'-lantern was about three feet away. But it was curtained now, and no one could see in or recognize his plight. He craned his neck to look up. The jack-o'-lantern was perched on the shelf just above his head, still glowing. The sweet, sickly smell of burning pumpkin reminded him of childhood, trick-or-treating with Travis, happier days. The pumpkin grin seemed to mock him, laughing at his fears, his impotence.

Nick's gaze scanned the walls. It passed over the red dot that was blinking impassively on the ceiling over his desk, then returned to it. The smoke alarm was connected directly both to the alarm company and the city fire department. The China Tea House Tavern was a national treasure. Most of the other woodframe buildings of similar vintage had burned to the ground in Boston long ago.

The fire department would respond instantly if the alarm went off. They'd come racing the hell out here, and if Travis hadn't already shot Delilah, he wouldn't risk it then, would he? If he did, he'd never get away in time.

The fire alarm. The jack-o'-lantern. The balled up papers on the floor.

Nick thought briefly about what would happen before the fire engines arrived. The fire wouldn't be content with rejected manuscript pages. The new Drake book would go. All the work he'd done on the Helen Templeton biography would go. Her journal, at least, was safe—he'd Xeroxed the old papers and them locked up with certain other valuable items of the Templeton Trust, but all his notes were here and would be destroyed. Not to mention all the wonderful books on the shelves. Great fire fodder. And the house, possibly, depending on how long it took the fire department to respond. The China Tea House Tavern, nearly three hundred years old. There was no guarantee that Delilah would get out in time.

He himself wouldn't have a chance. Chained here to the wooden ladder, he'd go out like a martyr at the stake. A horribly painful death, too. The best he could hope for would be that the smoke would overcome him before the flames reached his body.

His life. His work. The house. For Delilah. Was it worth it?

Yes.

"Travis," Delilah said.

"Don't beg. You're brave, and I've always loved that about you."

"I'm not begging." Indeed, she was strangely calm. There was a wind rushing through her, and there were voices on the wind. She had felt it once before, on a beach in California. A strangeness—elation and grief intertwined. And a presence. Grendam? The auburn-haired woman?

The voices—her own subconscious or something else—told her what to say. "I believe you. You will shoot me. I will die. Now I challenge you: die with me."

Had she said almost anything else, Travis would have pulled the trigger. Out of kindness, if such were possible. It was cruel to tease her, to give her hope, to make her wait.

But the words *die with me* were irresistible. She had touched upon something that had eluded him until now: once she was dead, he would not be able to live. The image of himself as the undisputed head of Templeton Tea had been an illusion. This had nothing to do with Templeton Tea. This was about himself and her and Nick.

"We were warned there was to be a repetition of what happened with Charles Templeton and his wife, Lucy. You thought to make use of that tonight, and your plan was ingenious. But it wouldn't be a *real* repetition. What is meant to happen is a real repetition, Travis."

"What do you mean?"

"Nick isn't my brother. You are. You are guilty of incest, and the curse is upon you." Her voice rose in pitch and intensity. It didn't sound like her own voice; it had an almost hypnotic quality. "We are both guilty. Incest is the abomination for which we must die."

Travis said, "You'll do anything, say anything, to save Nick."

"Nick has nothing to do with this. This is between us. You and me. Forever and ever and ever." She paused. "You've gone this far. Now go all the way. You are Charles and I am Lucy—your sister, your wife. We'll go together into the night."

He stared at her. There was absolute silence in the room.

"There are crimes and crimes. There are sins and sins. There are laws you can break or ignore. But the incest taboo is too strong. You can't live and knowingly break it—that's been true since ancient times." She paused. "But you can break it and die."

Oh, you temptress. Slowly he lowered the gun.

Travis had made one mistake—he'd indulged a sadistic whim to make Nick uncomfortable by stretching his arms high over his head. If he'd bound him in a more conventional position, arms linked in the small of his back, Nick wouldn't have had a chance of reaching the jack-o'-lantern. Even now it was going to be tough.

He went up on tiptoe, forced the cuffs past his wrists and up his forearms until they wouldn't go any farther. He could just touch the edge of the shelf where the jack-o'-lantern rested. The pumpkin had a bumpy bottom, and Travis hadn't taken the time to balance it very well. If he could jostle it, it might roll.

He stretched. Nothing. Sweating, he did it again. Even if he succeeded in knocking the pumpkin to the floor, the candle inside had to continue burning long enough to ingite the paper there. The odds were against it, he knew.

Fuck the odds.

He kept trying.

"Did you know, Travis, that Charles Templeton and his wife were found naked in their bed? They had been making love. There was no sign of a struggle. It wasn't murder-suicide at all, but a suicide pact, you see. When they found her, she had a smile on her face."

Travis's voice was both husky and disbelieving as he asked, "You want me to make love to you?"

Delilah didn't hesitate. "Yes. Once more. As an act of defiance. A noble moral action like something from the sixties. A shaking of one's fist at authority, saying, *I know you're going to punish me, but I'm doing it anyway because this is right and this is just and this is what I believe in.* Do you understand?"

He smiled, that lighthearted, charming smile she hadn't seen since the night their grandmother had died. "I understand, all right, Delilah. I think you're lying. Oh, you'll go through with it, I'm sure. Maybe you'll even enjoy it, because despite Nick, that chemistry's still there between us. But sometime while we're doing it, sometime while I'm fucking my brains out, I'm betting you'll try for the gun."

"No, Travis." She forced firmness, reassurance into her voice. "I want what you want—an end to this torment. Life's been dark for me ever since Max died. I almost killed myself then. I made a suicide attempt that was very nearly successful."

"I think you're lying," he went on as if she hadn't spoken, "but even so, your suggestion appeals to me." Travis stuck the gun back into the pocket of his jacket. He took off the jacket. He draped it over the bedpost at the foot of the bed, then turned back to grab her and throw her down just as she sat up to make a break for the door.

He overpowered her easily. He pressed her down on her back and trapped her there. He was heavier than Nick.

"Don't fight me. Let's do it exactly the way you said. An act of defiance. Shaking our fists at the powers that be. Then I'll get the gun and we'll die together, I promise. Nick will be safe."

She thought, I'm better off than I was a few seconds ago. I'm still alive. The gun is out of sight. He's promised me Nick's life, and there's no such thing as a fate worse than death, not even when the man on top of you is your own brother.

So it made no sense at all that when he dragged her nightgown up and unfastened his jeans, she screamed.

In the library, the metal handcuffs were cutting into Nick's arms; he could feel the wetness of his own blood. He was sweating profusely. He knew that any second he was going to hear the report of the gun.

Instead he heard Delilah scream. He echoed her with an anguished cry of his own. He jerked again, ferociously. This time the pumpkin tottered and rolled.

The jack-o'-lantern sailed through the air and hit the rim of the wastebasket, then bounced off and struck the floor about six feet away from him. It shattered. The wastepaper basket toppled over —an unexpected bonus—spilling paper all over the place. The candle dropped on its side in the wreckage, and hot wax splashed everywhere. For a moment he thought the puddle of wax was simply going to douse the candle, but freed from the stifling environment of the pumpkin, the flame reveled in the rush of oxygen produced by the fall. It flared, caught the edge of a piece of notepaper, flashed. Jesus. More paper caught. His plan was working.

Nick kicked at the bookshelves in back of him and knocked several books onto the floor. With his feet he shoved them toward the blaze. It made him sick to his stomach to burn books—that was something no writer could countenance under ordinary conditions. One of the volumes that went into the pile was *Unholy Alliance,* by Nicholas Templeton. At least his publisher had more copies of that. There were no other copies of the latest Drake epic, nor of his precious Helen Templeton biography, which, if the fire continued to burn, would be the next to go.

The smoke was getting heavy now. Tongues of flame climbed the wooden legs of his desk. They began to devour the table, the chair. Thick black smoke billowed up toward the smoke detector.

Nick started coughing. Drake would have saved himself while he was at it. But art only imitates life. It doesn't reproduce it.

He was going to die, but even so, he figured Drake would have been proud of him.

Travis had his hand over Delilah's mouth again, but this time he did nothing to restrict her breathing. He was trying not to hurt her, despite the way she was thrashing around. He was trying to be tender. He wanted her to enjoy this, her last time. He had been her first; now he was going to be her final lover. He wanted to give her a moment of supreme pleasure—an orgasm to end all orgasms—and then kill her quickly before she had time to feel afraid again. Before she had time to love him any less.

Then he would kill himself. If he was quick, she'd still be around; they'd cross over together.

Now she was crying. Tears were pouring down her cheeks. He tried to remember if he had ever seen Delilah cry. He must have, but he couldn't recall it now.

He pressed her legs apart. She wasn't fighting so much now. She was weeping, and there was a kind of acceptance in those soft, anguished cries.

As he tried to press into her he became aware that something was wrong with him. He was flaccid. He didn't believe it for a few seconds. He'd never had this particular problem. He'd thought he was ready . . . he'd *felt* ready. But, no, dammit, no, it wasn't working.

"Travis?"

She is your sister. Your sister. You can't make love to your own sister. The gods don't allow it. If you want to give her pleasure, you'll have to find some other way.

He felt her hands, lightly, in his hair. "Travis," she whispered.

Something broke inside him. What are you good for? You can't shoot her, you can't screw her. What the hell are you good for, anyway?

And suddenly he was crying, too. They were holding each other, crying together.

Delilah said, "You told me you were falling. That you couldn't stop. That's a lie. You can stop anytime. You can say, all right, that's enough, it's gone too far."

He heard her but he didn't listen. The wheel was still turning; he was still going down. "No." He rolled toward the end of the bed. Toward his jacket, and the gun.

Delilah sat up. "Listen. There's supposed to be a way to free ourselves of the Templeton curse. Travis, stop. If you kill me, or yourself for that matter, the curse will continue. You love me. And it doesn't matter that we were brother and sister because when we loved each other, our love was pure. Love doesn't go away. There is no limit to love."

He had the gun now. He turned it over and over in his hands. Okay, he wouldn't kill her. Okay. But *he* had to die. His grandmother was dead because of him. If Delilah knew that, she'd shoot him herself.

He said, "When I found out about our incest, it all went to hell. I couldn't be the good man I'd decided to be for you. So I said what the fuck and became the sleaze I am now."

"No, no." She was excited because things suddenly made sense to her that had never made sense before. "When Charles Templeton found out he was Lucy Broadhurst's brother, he killed her and himself. That was an act of violence, and it was wrong. But you, when you found out, you protected me. You made a sacrifice for me. You took all the blame on yourself in order to spare me. That was an act of love, Travis, and an act of love goes on reverberating forever." She paused. "So does a gunshot. Charles Templeton's gunshot is echoing in this room even now."

"Repetition," said Travis.

"No. Don't you see—there doesn't *have* to be a repetition. I think you came in here tonight believing this was something you had to do, something that had already been decided. But in fact you had a choice. You could shoot. Or you could spare me as you spared me once before. An act of violence or an act of love. Travis, give me the gun. You've already decided. You've chosen love. You're not as degenerate as you think you are."

Travis's breath whistled out of him slowly. "You're really something, you know that?"

"Give it to me."

He put the gun into her outstretched hand just as the fire alarm went off.

44

The drug brought both vision and darkness, freely intermingling. She was in darkness now, heavy as the night. Although her eyes were open, she couldn't see anything but a pinpoint of reddish light, one small spark in the firmament.

She could not see, but she could smell. The burning, the burning. This was not the fire of magic, of power, of God. This was the world's fire, and a threat to the very people she hoped to save.

Helen had an intense fear of the flames. Rebecca had divined that she'd died at the stake for her beliefs in one of her earlier lives. They burned witches in the Old World. Here in the New, they were hanged.

Charles had tried to burn down the Tavern. To cleanse it, and the bodies within, of the abomination that had been committed within its walls. Charles had failed. Who was this dark-haired martyr who was trying to destroy what had been saved?

Matthew. Matthew, who would have died for her, had she permitted it. Matthew who had begged her to allow him to confess his sin and take the punishment he felt he deserved.

As Matthew had loved her, so this man loved the witchy-haired woman.

Helen entered the room where the fire raged. 'Tis in another time, and cannot touch me, she told herself to ease her shaking heart. She approached the figure slumped against the ladder, choking, barely conscious, blasted by the heat. The flames had not reached him yet, but the smoke was killing him. Helen raised a finger toward the window and pushed. The glass shattered. Cool, fresh air gushed into the room. The man breathed. The fire danced higher, delighting in the draft.

She joined the man on the ladder. He could not feel her, but perhaps he sensed her presence. She enfolded him in her arms. (He is like Matthew, she thought . . . Perhaps he is Matthew . . . a future Matthew . . . Perhaps his lover is a future me.) Then, using the last remnants of her power, she threw up the faerie ring. Golden, powerful, fraught with the oldest of magic, it surrounded them, turning back the smoke, the flames. It would hold for as long as her strength held. But her strength, which was still somehow linked to the old body she had abandoned in the eighteenth century, could not last much longer.

Now, she said to the witch-haired woman. I have helped you. Help me.

With Travis at her back, Delilah ran down the hall to the library. She could see smoke creeping out from underneath the door. Oh God, oh God. Don't touch a hot door, they said, but she didn't care. She threw it open and was into the room even as Travis was trying to grab her, to pull her back.

"Nick? Nick!" She couldn't see him. The fire alarm was whooping and the smoke was so thick. One side of the room, the area where his desk and his computer were located, was engulfed in flames. The heat was brutal and the smell of burning paper and plastic was sickening. Her stomach heaved and she started to cough. "Nick!"

"He's on the ladder," Travis muttered, pushing past her. "I'll get him; you get out of here."

He must be dead, she thought dully. Cold air was rushing in through an open window, but it wasn't enough; how could he breathe? Nick, Nick. Don't be dead. Please, please.

She reeled toward the bookshelves. She could see the ladder stabbing upward, like a stake. And a tall figure, drooping, bound to it by his wrists, which were stretched to the heavens, as if he were pleading with God. This is a game, we played it as children, they tied me to a tree and Travis set a fire . . . He didn't mean to, it was an accident . . . Jesus, he almost killed me then, and I never knew, I never realized just how dangerous he could be.

"Nick?" She flung herself against his body, terrified that he would be cold like her grandmother, like Max. That he was dead and there would be no breath.

But he was warm, and he was moving. He strained against her and whispered, "You fool, get out of here."

She could breathe, she realized. The intense heat she'd stumbled through to reach him was no longer searing her. It made no sense. As she looked back for Travis, all she could see was a circle of flame around the ladder. How could the fire have surrounded them so quickly? We're both going to die, she thought, even though the circle radiated no heat.

"Travis!" she screamed.

As Travis burst through to them, the golden ring around them vanished. Goosebumps rose on Delilah's skin as she sensed someone—or something—withdraw. Nick, obviously delirious, said, "It's Helen Templeton. She was here. She was talking to me. Now she's going. She's dying, Delilah. She used the last of her strength to help me."

The smoke enveloped them . . . and the heat. "The key, Travis," Delilah sobbed, tearing at Nick's cuffed wrists. "Give me the key!"

She felt his big hands there beside hers, and then she saw her brother's face. For a second, as those blue eyes pierced hers, he seemed to hesitate. Oh God! What if he won't unlock the handcuffs? What if it's still upon him—that madness, that jealousy, that lust for blood. He and Nick, never liking each other, never understanding each other, never getting along. Two males, battling for dominance as males have done since the beginning of time. Both of them wanting her, both of them bound to her, neither of them willing to step aside.

"Travis." She clutched at him. Tears—from the smoke, from her terror—were sliding down her cheeks. "Travis, please!"

His eyes flickered closed for a second. Then they opened, clear now, and he reached up with the key.

Nick's legs wouldn't hold him as he came off the ladder. His brother grabbed him around the waist to keep him from falling. Delilah pushed them both toward the hallway. The exposed wooden beams in the ceiling were starting to catch now as the flames rushed up at them.

The door to the hall seemed the length of a football field away, but in reality it was only a few feet. Travis was on Nick's left now, nearest the fire. Delilah was on his right; together they were supporting him, forcing him to walk.

Smoke billowed. Flames raged. All three of them were choking as they tried not to breathe the poisonous fumes. Delilah's head was spinning, her lungs burning. We're going to drop, she thought. All three of us are going to drop right here and die of smoke inhalation while the China Tea House Tavern explodes around us.

As they reached the doorway, Travis screamed. A flaming chunk of the ceiling had fallen on his shoulders. He stumbled, and Delilah had to heave them both—first Nick, then Travis—through the library doorway into the hall, which was also filled with smoke.

"The stairs, the stairs," she muttered. They still had to get down the steep staircase and out of the house. She could hear the wailing of a siren—thank God the fire trucks were closing in. But they still might be too late . . .

Nick was walking better now. He was holding the banister that ran along the stop of the staircase as they inched toward the stairs, which they couldn't yet see through the thick, black smoke. But Travis, where was Travis? Delilah panicked, thinking they'd lost him. "Travis!"

He reeled past her, his gold hair shining weirdly. For an instant she didn't know why; then she understood that his shirt was on fire and he was out of his head with pain.

"Get down! Don't run, Travis, roll, for God's sake, hit the floor!" She was ripping off her nightgown to throw it over his back when he started to fall as she'd ordered him. She was jumping at him when Nick yelled, "NO!" and seized her by the hair. She shrieked in pain and shock as her lover hauled her backward from the abyss that was suddenly looming before her. Travis toppled over the edge of the stairway and crashed down, down, all the way down, his body cracking and thumping with the most dreadful sounds Delilah had ever heard.

"The stairs," Nick said softly, partly in explanation for grabbing her before she could go over, too, and partly in awe at his sudden recollection of something that had remained buried in the unconscious mind of a four-year-old boy for thirty-three years.

This was how his great-grandfather, Harrison Templeton, had

died. He had been awake in the dark; he had seen it. It was the cause—very likely—of his lifelong terrors; that traumatic event in his childhood that he'd never been able to unearth.

His grandmother. Harrison Templeton. Travis had seen it, too, seen more and undoubtedly remembered more than his younger brother. Travis must have known that Gran had pushed Templeton, killed him . . . Nick's mind leapt. He suddenly understood his grandmother's suicide, and what part his brother must have played.

His strength returned to him—a burst of adrenaline that had a purpose for once. He gathered the naked, shuddering Delilah in his arms and guided her down those same death-dealing stairs until they reached the bottom, where the air was mercifully cooler and clearer. He ripped open the front door, letting fresh air and moonlight into the house.

Travis lay there on his back, his head twisted at an odd angle, the fire on his shirt, like the fire in his blue eyes, extinguished forever. There was an amused yet accepting smile on his lips.

Repetition. Travis had come here tonight to imitate a family tragedy. He had succeeded far better than he could ever have imagined.

"Travis?" Delilah whispered. She fell to her knees beside him and touched his face, the face she had loved. "No, no. It's not right. We were safe, all three of us. We were accepting each other, forgiving each other. We'd foiled the curse. This isn't fair!" Her fingers clawed into her brother's shoulders and she shook him. "Travis!"

Nick pulled her off him. "It's fairer than you know. Come, love. Let's get out of here."

She was weeping now. "We can't just leave him. I won't leave him, Nick!"

"He's gone. There's nothing we can do for him now. We're alive, Delilah, but we won't be for long if we continue breathing this smoke." He tugged gently on her shoulders. "My darling, it's over. Gran is gone, Travis is gone, Helen Templeton is gone, and the curse is broken. You and I are being given another chance. Now, *come on.*"

Delilah touched that golden hair and looked into those blue-blue eyes one last time, then she kissed Travis's cooling lips and left her tears upon his upturned face. He was so handsome, even now. "I loved you," she told him. "Good-bye."

She lurched to her feet and turned to Nick. She went into his arms, and together they left through the open door. As they stumbled down the walk, the fire engines pulled up, and booted, helmeted men poured out, running, yelling. Nick and Delilah watched from the street as the fire fighters stormed the Tavern. They were quick and efficient. In less than an hour, they had the blaze under control.

The China Tea House Tavern survived. The only structural damage was to the library and the rooms above and below it, which were not part of the original eighteenth-century construction. They saved the Tavern, but there was nothing anyone could do for Travis. As the ambulance bore his body away, Nick remembered sadly that the building had always outlived its occupants.

He decided to take Delilah home to Concord, where once before the combination of love and peaceful surroundings had revived her anguished spirit. As they left together, she looked back at the China Tea House Tavern, which seemed to have a brooding, self-protective quality about it. Defiant almost. What happens behind these walls has happened many times before, the house whispered. Life and death, which to you are so dramatic, are nothing more to me than the usual vicissitudes of time.

She said, "I can't believe it. It's only us now, Nick. You and me. Just us."

"We'll be enough," said Nick.

*Before she left her body forever, Helen Templeton looked once again into the probable future. This time she saw the Tavern in spring, the roses climbing a trellis outside its walls. She saw a young child playing in the garden, and another, a babe, nursing at her mother's breast. She saw a man and a woman laughing in the upstairs bedroom, the same man writing a biography (*mine, *Helen realized, delighted) at his new computer, the same woman proudly scanning the business indicators that showed the increasing profits of Templeton Tea. She saw a new faerie ring in the library floor, a circle every bit as strange as the one in the master bedroom. No one knew what to make of it. According to the fire inspector, the flames had never even reached that part of the room.*

The house was peaceful. No shadows lingered there. Helen Templeton smiled, well satisfied. The curse had been lifted at last.

It was time to leave. Down there in that wretched old body of hers—the body that had served her well this night, this May Day Eve—all breath had stopped. Her overstrained heart was silent. Her face, once so beautiful and beguiling, was frozen in its mask of death. Only a mask. Only an illusion, for she was still alive.

A blinding light surrounded her, poured through her. Willingly, she gave herself over to it.

As she crossed the gulf, she heard a much longed for, beloved voice. Turning quickly, she loosed the smile that had entranced a city and bewitched a man. "Matt?"

Her spirit, always so full of love and joy and laughter, grew fuller still, for her lover, whom she had not seen since his death forty years before, was urging her to soar with him again, high over Boston, the wild Atlantic Ocean, the blue-wrapped Earth. "Matt," she whispered, and took his hand.

ACKNOWLEDGMENTS

There are a number of people who have helped me in various ways during the three years that have elapsed since I began this novel. I must first thank Bert Schafer, my research assistant, who spent weeks ransacking the stacks of various libraries in Boston and Cambridge in order to give me what amounted to a graduate seminar in the colonial history of Massachusetts. I am also indebted to the reference staffs of the Boston Public Library, the Widener Library at Harvard University, the Acton Memorial Library in Acton, Mass., and the Concord Free Library in Concord, Mass., all of whom have helped with the countless details that come up in researching a novel that deals with so many subjects and such a long expanse of time.

For their help on researching the tea industry I wish to express my gratitude to Sam Twining, Director of R. Twining & Co., Ltd. for meeting with with me and answering all my questions, and to Joan Magnuson of the public relations firm of Grossich and Partners, Inc. I also want to thank John G. Edwards, President of Brooke Bond Foods, Inc., Ralph T. Starr, President of John Wagner & Sons, Inc., and Lucia W. Woodlan, Director of Marketing of First Colony Coffee & Tea, Company, Inc. for their helpful and informative correspondence. For his fascinating tour of an actual tea garden, processing factory, and blending and packaging plant, I must thank Selahattin Bakir of the Turkish Tea Council in Rize, Turkey. I might also add that although there are many excellent books and articles on tea, it would be difficult to write on the subject without having at one's fingertips William H. Uker's astonishing two-volume study *All About Tea,* a truly comprehensive guide.

My thanks also to Mark Roegner for his information about Southern California and to Kenneth, Margaret, John, and Carolyn Spengler for showing me through the American Meteorological Society headquarters at 45 Beacon Street, Boston, which served as the inspiration for Templeton House. My appreciation also to Tina Seal and Rebecca Fawcett, who gave me a private tour of the Monroe Tavern in Lexington, Mass. Incidentally, the China Tea House Tavern does not exist except in my imagination; nor are there any wood-frame buildings on Beacon Hill from quite so early a period. For this and other slight deviations from the facts that I have used for the sake of creating my fictional world, I beg my readers' indulgence.

I would like to thank my fine editor, Carolyn Blakemore, for her excellent suggestions, and her assistant, Howard Kaplan, for all his help. Thanks also to my agent, Larry Moulter, and my colleagues, Carla Neggers and Nancy Martin, for their critiques of early versions of the novel, and particularly to Susan Elizabeth Phillips, whose sensitive reading of the almost completed manuscript helped me enormously as I was preparing the final draft.

Special thanks to my parents, Bob and Babs Barlow, whose first-hand accounts of life in India were invaluable for that section of the book and whose love and encouragement have always been inspirational to me.

Thanks also to Merwynna and Seth.

And of course, my love and gratitude to my husband, Halûk Özkaynak, and our daughter, Dilek, my anchors to the real world.

About the Author

Formerly a lecturer in English at Boston College and Middle East Technical University in Ankara, Turkey, LINDA BARLOW holds a B.A., an M.A., and is currently completing studies for her Ph.D. in English literature. A free-lance writer and editor of nonfiction articles for a number of years, Linda received the *Romantic Times* award in 1986 as outstanding new historical novelist of the year. She lives with her husband and eight-year-old daughter in a suburb of Boston.